WHATEVER IT TAKES

by

Lynda Page

Magna Large Print Books
Long Preston, North Yorkshire,
BD23 4ND, England.

British Library Cataloguing in Publication Data.

Page, Lynda
    Whatever it takes.

    A catalogue record of this book is
    available from the British Library

    ISBN   0-7505-2414-6

First published in Great Britain 2005 by Headline Book Publishing

Copyright © 2005 Lynda Page

Cover illustration © Superstock/Powerstock by arrangement with Headline Book Publishing Ltd.

Published in Large Print 2005 by arrangement with
Headline Book Publishing Ltd.

Magna Large Print is an imprint of Library Magna Books Ltd.

Printed and bound in Great Britain by
T.J. (International) Ltd., Cornwall, PL28 8RW

WHATEVER IT TAKES

Kay Clifton has waited five lonely years for her husband Bob to come home from the war. Their whirlwind romance prior to his departure makes her feel she hardly knows him, but her hopes for the start of their blissfully happy marriage are dashed by the presence of Bob's fellow soldier Tony. Bob is indebted to Tony for saving his life and seems hellbent on repaying that debt, but as Tony starts acting more and more strangely Kay worries that something else happened in the war that Bob is keeping secret...

WHATEVER IT TAKES

For Liza and John Kozlowski
(my Lizzie and John)

It's not true that you cannot choose your family.
I am so proud and delighted you have become
such a large part of mine and vice versa.
This book is for you both
with all my love.

CHAPTER ONE

'Good Lord, our Kay, I bet Hitler looked happier than you when he shot himself! Cheer up, gel, this is one of the best days of yer life. You've prayed for it to dawn long enough yet yer've a face on yer like ... well ... like yer about to face a firing squad.'

Herbert Stafford took his threadbare jacket off the back of a dining chair and pulled it on, his lived-in face softening as he looked across at his daughter. She was standing on the other side of the well-used but cared for oak table, clutching the back of a chair as if for support. 'It's yer husband yer meeting, gel, not the devil.'

Lost in her own thoughts, Kay Clifton hadn't even realised her beloved father had entered the room. She jumped at his words, flashing him a wan smile that lightened her pretty but strained face. Her father was right, this day was going to be the best ever for her and there had been countless times over the last five years as the war had raged on seemingly endlessly when she had been terrified it would never dawn. Now, miraculously, it had. Shortly she'd be reunited with the love of her life, hopefully never to be parted from him again. But now the hour was almost upon her, she couldn't help feeling nervous. After five long years of separation during the war, with only the chaotic forces' postal system keeping them in

11

contact, it suddenly hit her like a thunderbolt that the love of her life had become a virtual stranger to her.

Mabel Stafford came into the room then, wiping her big wet hands on a kitchen towel. A no-nonsense woman, she was thick-set and large-featured, her square face framed by a thatch of wiry grey hair cut into a chin-length bob, parted down the middle and held in place next to her ears by kirby grips. Her brown work skirt and drab ecru-coloured blouse were covered by a faded blue wraparound apron. She flashed her daughter a look of surprise.

'I didn't expect to see you today. Thought yer'd have enough on yer plate without paying yer folks a visit.' She cast a critical glance over Kay's attire of a short-sleeved navy and white spotted knee-length dress over which she wore her five years old but nevertheless best dark navy woollen coat. Her pretty oval face was framed by rich auburn hair styled becomingly in a roll. Her mother nodded approvingly. 'You'll do. So, all set then, are yer?'

Kay looked at her. How she wished she could talk to her mother about how jittery she was feeling, but she knew Mabel would merely shake her head at her and in her usual brusque way tell her to stop acting like a juvenile, that she was a twenty-six-year-old married woman with respon-sibilities and should get on with it. But Kay did know someone else who'd offer her a sympathetic ear and good advice and if she made a hurried escape she still had time to pay a visit – hopefully her aunt would be in. 'Yes, I'm all set, Mam,' Kay fibbed. 'Just thought I'd pop in on my way and see how our Trevor is today.'

Folding her arms under her matronly bosom, her mother pursed her lips.

'Not the best of patients, your brother. It's the devil's own job trying to get through to him that his leg won't heal completely unless he does what the doctor instructed and rests it. He's harping on endlessly about going to the local dance a week on Friday night, can you believe? And him hardly able to use his crutches as far as the privy without the help of either me or his dad, let alone jigging about on the dance floor. I'll be reduced to using a ball and chain if he doesn't get it through his head soon what *resting* means.' Mabel turned to her husband then. 'Hadn't you better get a move on, Herbie? I want that veg at its peak for tomorrow's dinner.' She picked up a tin box from the table and held it out towards him. 'Bit of slab cake for yer break later on.'

Herbie would have liked a little more time with his daughter on this special day but fresh vegetables for the family dinner tomorrow were important to his wife and it was his duty to provide them. 'Yes, I'd best be off and see what damage the slugs have done after all that rain yesterday.' He stepped over to his wife of thirty years, taking the tin from her and pecking her affectionately on her cheek. 'Tarra, me old duck. See yer later,' he said, putting the tin into a small haversack that also held a Thermos flask of black tea which he would have much preferred sweet and milky. Despite the end of the war, however, life was harder now in 1946 than it had been

13

formerly and basic commodities were still heavily rationed. Whatever they had was being kept aside by his wife for the dinner she was preparing in honour of their son-in-law Bob the next day.

Pulling his bag on to his shoulder, Herbert made his way around the table to face his daughter, placing a hand on her arm tenderly. 'Give my best to Bob and tell him I'm looking forward to seeing him tomorrow.'

Despite a renewed flutter of anxiousness dancing in the pit of her stomach, Kay managed a brief smile. 'Thanks, Dad.'

Just then a thudding sound reverberated from behind the door at the back of the room which hid the stairs. Hands on her wide hips, Mabel tutted disdainfully. 'And where does that little so and so think he's going now?'

A grinning face appeared around the door. 'Hello, Sis, I thought I heard your voice.'

'And what do you think you're doing?' demanded Mabel.

Twenty-four-year-old Trevor, a stocky, pleasant-faced young man dressed in a pair of wrinkled green pyjamas and a rumpled Fair Isle slipover, flashed an innocent smile at his mother. 'I just came down to wish our Kay the best.'

'And if you'd just had patience she would have come up to see you herself. Now get back to bed,' Mabel ordered. 'Herbie, give him a hand.'

'Give over, our Mam, I'm bored up there,' he moaned. 'I don't know why the doc won't let me get up now and stop using these crutches 'cos I don't need 'em anymore. I can stand on me leg without falling over, and it doesn't hurt. Well, not much it don't...'

His mother's face was stricken. 'You've been standing on yer bad leg?'

'Yeah,' Trevor said proudly. 'I've been practising walking up and down the bedroom when you've been out shopping, and since Thursday I ain't fell over once.'

'What!' she cried. 'You stupid boy! I can't believe you're telling me this after all the doctor said to you.'

'It's my leg, Mam, not the doc's.'

'And the doctor's got brains – something you obviously haven't! He was very clear in his orders: bed rest until you're told otherwise. And that's what you'll do. If yer don't promise me yer'll do as yer told, next time I go shopping I'll get Old Mother Bates to come and sit with yer and drive yer batty with her senseless chatter *and* I won't let you down for Bob's welcome home dinner, special occasion or not.'

Mabel took a deep breath and clasped her hands in front of her.

'Look, son, yer not long out of hospital after being in there for months with yer leg smashed so badly the powers that be never thought yer'd walk again. Even they're amazed how well yer've come on, and if all you end up with is a limp then you are one lucky young man. Yer don't want to undo all the good they've done you and land back in hospital just 'cos of yer own stupidity, do yer?'

Trevor solemnly shook his head. 'No, 'course I don't, but can't I sit down here with it propped up?'

'No, you can't.' Her homely face softened. 'Look, when the doctor pays you his check up visit next Monday, I'll ask him about it.'

'Ah, would yer, Mam? That'd be great.'

'Yeah, well, maybe next time you'll think of the consequences before you try any more heroics, though God forbid there ever is a next time.'

Trevor's face clouded over. 'Yer don't think of the consequences when yer mates' lives are at stake.'

His mother took a deep breath, lowering her voice. 'No, I expect not. I am proud of what you did, son, we all are.'

He grinned. Others might perceive what he had done as reckless but Trevor hadn't hesitated for a second when he had driven a bullet-riddled scout vehicle holding four injured colleagues away from enemy fire at breakneck speed. They had been ambushed on the edge of a French town just weeks before the end of the war. Unfortunately for Trevor, only yards from his unit's position, a stray enemy bullet had found his leg and the impact had caused him to crash into the side of a building, breaking his already injured leg in several places as well as both his arms. Thankfully, though, the crash caused little more damage to his colleagues than they had already suffered. As far as Trevor was concerned he was glad he was alive, but more importantly glad his mates were as well.

'You're looking at the man who single-handedly won the war, Mam.'

Mabel raised her eyebrows at him. 'And I expect every son has told his mam that.' She looked across at her husband. 'Herbie, will you help yer boy back upstairs or do I have to do everything around here meself?'

As his father joined him on the stairs, Trevor said to his sister, 'Tell Bob I'm looking forward to finally meeting the man who made an honest woman of yer.'

She had forgotten her brother had yet to meet Bob. At the time of the wedding Trevor had been unable to get leave from his training camp, having just joined up.

'Yes, I will. And, Trevor, do as Mam says. None of us wants you landing back in hospital again.'

He pulled a face. 'Mothers and sisters nag worse than sergeant majors.' He gave her a cheeky grin as his father hooked his arm through his and both of them disappeared from view as they awkwardly ascended the stairs.

Mabel picked up a brown tea pot from the table.

'Cuppa, Kay? Bob's train isn't due until four, which as we all know more than likely means it won't pull in 'til six. It's only half-one now, so even if by a miracle it is on time, you've still hours.'

'Oh, er ... no, I'll pass, thanks, Mam. The train just might be early.'

'I don't think that's very likely but then, on the outside chance it is, you're right, it wouldn't look good if you weren't there to meet it. You won't be late tomorrow, will yer?'

Kay smiled. 'No, Mam. We'll be here on the dot of twelve-thirty. Are you sure there's nothing you want me to do towards it all?'

17

'You've enough to contend with settling yer husband back home, and I've everything under control here, thank you. You did air and iron those sheets I freshened up for you before you made up the bed for his return?'

Kay inwardly groaned. As much as she loved her mother, she could be so annoying sometimes. Why did she have to keep checking that her daughter had done everything to Mabel's own exacting standards? Kay had much appreciated her mother's insistence that she should freshen all the linen and towels Kay had collected over the last five years for her bottom drawer in readiness for Bob's return, she had had so much else to do getting the rest of the house in order, but nevertheless her mother must be aware that Kay was no slouch herself when it came to housework. After all, hadn't Mabel taught her how to tackle every household job perfectly?

'Yes, Mam, I did. And all the spare bedding and towels are folded up and put away.' Pre-empting her mother's next question, she added, '*And* I made the bed with hospital corners.'

Mabel looked at her sharply. Kay could see she was deciding whether the response had held a hint of sarcasm or not –which it hadn't – but just then her father arrived back.

'Well, that's him back in bed, though for how long remains to be seen.' He paused and looked at his wife. 'Poor lad is being driven doo-lally up there all by himself, Mother. I don't see what difference it'd make if he was down here tucked up on the sofa.'

Mabel's face set. 'Herbert, you heard as clear as

18

I did the hospital's conditions for allowing Trevor home. The doctor said *bed* rest, not *sofa* rest. Now I'm making an exception tomorrow because of the importance of the occasion but that's as far as I'm prepared to go. We'll see what Doctor Robinson says on Monday when he pays his next visit. Until then Trevor stays where he is, is that clear?'

Herbie looked at her resignedly. 'Yes, Mother. Oh, Trevor's asking if you'll take him a cuppa up and those magazines his mate dropped in on his way to work this morning?' He looked at his daughter. 'You stopping or going, our Kay?'

'I'm going, Dad.'

'Then I'll walk with yer to the end of the street.'

At the end of the row of back-to-back red-brick terraced houses, Herbie pulled his pushbike to a halt before straddling it.

'Right, I'll love yer and leave yer. Nobby Stibbs has found a source for some 'oss manure, and I said in exchange for a load I'd help him barrow it across – which is going to be good fun 'cos I've a hole in me barrow. But, boy, will the hard work be worth it when we taste those spuds next year.'

A pile of manure was worth more to her father than a bag of gold, Kay knew.

'What would you do without your allotment, Dad?'

He flashed her a look of absolute horror. 'Oh, me ducky, that thought don't bear thinking about! It sends me cold, the thought of not having me crops to tend. You can't deny we'd have bin hard pushed to feed ourselves with fresh produce without what the allotment provided

19

these last five years.'

That was true. And deserving cases too had benefited from her parents' generosity when a healthy yield had produced more than they could use themselves. But besides that the allotment was the one place where her father was solely in charge, the one place of sanctuary away from family strife, where he was king of all he presided over. His opinion was that the house was Mabel's domain, the allotment his. This afternoon, after a couple of hours' hard labour, Herbie and his gardening cronies from the adjoining allotments would sit for half an hour or so in old deckchairs, drinking tea from flasks, putting the world to rights as they saw it.

Kay leaned over and pecked his cheek. 'You'd best be off.' She added before she had time to check herself, 'Or you'll be late for the Old Timers' Weed and Wheelbarrow Club.'

He looked at her, startled, then laughed. 'Yer cheeky bugger, our Kay! So that's what yer call us, is it? Wait 'til I tell the lads, considering two of them are only in their thirties! But I tell yer summat for n'ote. If Churchill had sat in on a few of our discussions and used our tactics, the war woulda been over a whole lot quicker. And if the manager of Leicester City had used the players we'd chosen instead of the hairy-fairy ones he did, who I'm sure don't know what a football is intended for let alone the idea of the game is to get the ball between the goal posts, then we'd definitely have won the league last year. Not to mention our thoughts on running the country are far better than what this Labour lot we've just

20

voted in have planned.' His eyes twinkled at her in amusement. 'Yer might think yer dad's an old duffer but I'm not past it yet. I'll see yer tomorrow for dinner, looking forward to it,' he said, licking his lips.

'Don't take umbrage, our Kay, but besides finally getting to know the man you married as well as I should do, I know your mother's doing a roast, and yer mam certainly knows how to do justice to a good piece of meat.' He smiled proudly and added, 'When the butcher heard yer mam was after summat special, and why, he pulled out all the stops. And then when he turned up after dark at our back door with a leg of lamb hidden under his coat, well, even she was struck speechless. She handed over the money and a week's worth of coupons, that shocked she forgot even to thank him.' He looked at his daughter wistfully then. 'Seems strange you not living at home anymore, though. It's kinda quiet.'

It felt strange to Kay too, having her own home to take care of and doing for herself after having her mother fuss over and chide her for all but the last three weeks of her life. On confirmation of Bob's demob date two weeks previously, life for Kay had become a whirl of activity. With the help of her family she had laboured hard to find what she thought was a suitable home for them both at a reasonable rent – bearing in mind the fact that she had no idea until Bob secured himself a job what his weekly wage would be. Using the money she had carefully saved over the last five years from Bob's Army married allotment and savings from her own job as a post sorter in the main

21

Royal Mail depot in Leicester, she'd set about making it as homely as she could with what little was available from friends and acquaintances and second-hand shops. Anything on offer still dated from the early thirties or before. Despite being technically married for over five years, Kay thankfully managed to satisfy the government ruling that only newly weds setting up their first home together qualified to purchase pieces of utility furniture. It was plain but functional but this meant that at least their dining table, chairs, wardrobe and bed frame were new even if the mattress wasn't.

Just two streets away from where her parents lived, Kay's new house was a small two-up, two-down, with outhouse and privy in the tiny back yard. It had been built in the middle of the last century, part of a back-to-back terrace. Electricity was still several years away from being installed in it, she knew. In fact the majority of the working-class population of Leicester lived with light supplied courtesy of smelly, dirty gas mantles, and hot water heated by a gas geyser on the kitchen wall. But the landlord had at least replaced the antiquated range with a gas cooker and all fireplaces in the house were tiled, early-1930s style.

The house badly needed decorating, which was unfortunately out of the question as materials were not available even if you could afford them, but miraculously showed only traces of damp. The dingy walls were devoid of any pictures, the only ornaments being two plaster candlesticks placed to either end of the fireplace in the room at the back. Like most people she planned to use this as the main living area, leaving the small room at the front with its door opening on to the street unused for the time being, to keep down heating bills. Coal was strictly rationed and in shorter supply now than it had been during the war. Despite its drabness, Kay felt lucky that this house had become vacant when it had and just hoped Bob approved when he viewed it. But remembering how easygoing he was, she felt sure he would.

She laughed at her father's doleful expression. 'I don't see how you've had time to miss me, Dad, especially this last week. Every spare minute you've had has been spent helping me get my house straight and running after our Trevor now he's home.'

Her father pulled a face. 'Yes, he's running me and yer mam both ragged. But then, I wouldn't have it any other way when yer consider what could have been the case. Even so, it doesn't mean ter say I don't miss having you around, our Kay. This last twenty-six years, I've kinda got used to yer.'

After waving him off, Kay waited until he had pedalled out of sight before turning in the opposite direction. After weaving her way through several identical streets of flat-fronted, back-to-back houses, she made her way down the entry of one in particular, opened the back gate and walked up the path to the back door. She tapped on it and immediately let herself in to a tiny disorderly kitchen.

'Aunty Viv?' she called, shutting the door behind her.

'It's that you, our Kay?' a female voice called. 'What a lovely surprise! I never expected you, today of all days. Come on in, gel.'

Kay made her way into the back room where she found her mother's younger sister putting on her make-up at a cluttered gate-legged table.

A voluptuous, extremely attractive woman of thirty-five, dressed in a flattering silver-sheened button-through dress, the hemline of which ended a couple of inches below her knees, Vivian Green held a mascara brush poised in mid-air, turning to look at Kay as she entered. 'Well, ain't you a sight for sore eyes?' she exclaimed, glancing over her niece's attire. Her eyes sparked humorously and she asked, tongue in cheek, as she resumed peering in the mottled hand mirror to put on her mascara, 'Going anywhere special?'

'You know very well where I'm going, Aunty Viv, but I've time for a quick visit with you before I head off to the station. I'm not hindering you, am I?'

'Not at all, me darlin'. I'm expecting Frank to pop in sometime this afternoon to drop me crystal wireless set back. He offered to fix it for me as it wasn't working. Handy to have around is Frank. Very good with his hands. Apart from him calling in, I'm all yours.'

'Frank?' Kay queried.

Viv grinned. 'He's what yer mam would call me latest conquest but in truth he's just a friend. The poor man returned from the war to find his wife had left him for someone else and even had a baby by him, can yer believe? Frank never knew a thing about it until he walked in the door after

24

being demobbed, expecting to be welcomed home by his loving wife, and instead found the place empty and a letter from her informing him she wanted a divorce propped up on the table. It fair knocked the stuffing from him. He thought his life was over 'til he met up with me and the gels in the Salmon one Saturday night and we persuaded him to come dancing with us down the Trocadero. Between us we've shown him that there is life after death, if yer get me meaning. I shouldn't mention him fixing me wireless to yer mam, though, our Kay, 'cos she'll never believe there's nothing else going on between us and that he's just done it as a favour.'

Viv ruefully shook her head. 'Mabel can't seem to get her head around the fact that a woman can have male friends that's she's not ... well, I'm sure yer know what I mean. I can't make her understand that I loved my Archie like I could never love anyone else. Me soul mate he was, and it broke my heart when he got killed at the start of the war. It would have to be a very special man indeed to get me into his bed – after he's put a ring on me finger, that is. Me dolling meself up and going out for a bit of fun a couple of times a week ain't being disloyal to Archie's memory, it's my way of getting on with things and trying to make a life for meself.

'To Mabel, mourning means dressing yerself from head to toe in black and sitting in the house all alone until yer die yerself. That's not mourning, it's festering! It's about time my sister modernised her ideas a bit ... well, a lot, if yer want my opinion.'

Kay felt Viv grossly exaggerated her mother's ideas on mourning but nevertheless she did agree that her mother's attitudes were very Victorian. She would be hard put to convince Mam that the fixing of the wireless was just a favour done by a man for a woman, without there being more behind it than that.

'Mam just wants what she thinks is best for you, that's all, Aunty Viv.'

'Huh! Well, what she thinks is best for me, and what I think, are two different things. Passing comments all the time 'cos I don't dress in keeping with her view of what a widow woman should look like. Drinking too much ... though how she sees a couple of halves of bitter as indulging is beyond me. And, of course, I'd never keep this house clean enough for her liking if I scrubbed and polished it every day.'

Kay felt her beloved aunt always dressed very becomingly for her age. She did secretly wonder if her mother's criticism of her sister's clothes was perhaps not entirely down to the fact that she felt Viv shamelessly flaunted her shapely figure, but more to envy because Mabel's own solid shape would not allow her to wear such styles.

'There's more to life than housework, Kay,' Viv continued. 'Dust was around before I was born and it'll still be around long after I've popped me clogs. It's about time yer mam learned that. Don't get me wrong, she's a good woman, Kay, salt of the earth, and despite the fact we're like chalk and cheese, I do love me sister. But she's so bloody set in her ways! Yer'd have thought the war would have shown her how short life is and she'd have stopped worrying whether the cushions are straight, but it doesn't seem to have. I sometimes wonder how yer dad has put up with her pernickety ways for all these years. But then, I'm being a bit unfair there 'cos it's obvious to anyone Herbie dotes on her and he'd be lost without her.'

Viv gave a shrug.

'Still, I suppose it ain't all Mabel's fault she's like what she is. Our mother, God rest her soul, brought us up quite differently. She shaped Mabel to mirror herself, like her own mother had done with her, and was very strict. Poor Mabel couldn't go to the privy unless she'd got Mam's permission first. Mam was over forty when I came along and I think she was so shocked she was far more liberal in raising me.

'I have to say I did abuse that sometimes, and I did cause her more than a few headaches during me teenage years. Nothing serious, just not coming in at exactly the time she said I should, that kinda thing. It didn't go down well with our Mabel 'cos she used to get a clip around her ear should she dare be a minute late, whereas I just got a shake of the head and a warning not to do it again, which of course I did.

'I do feel sorry for Mabel sometimes for the way she took after me mam's side of the family: big-boned and not very blessed in the looks department. I took after the females on me dad's side – curvy and pretty, though I do say it myself. I know underneath she's jealous of that fact. Mind you, if yer want the truth, *I'm* envious of *her* too. I'd swap places with her any day. She's

27

got what I always wanted and that's a doting husband who's still alive, and more importantly kids.' Viv gave a wistful sigh. 'I don't suppose I'll ever have any now.' She gave herself a mental shake. 'Still, we can't have all we want in life and I've contented meself with being an aunty.'

She put the mascara brush back inside its container – a treasured item Viv had acquired the same way she did most of her clothing and other scarce things: on the black market. Clicking it shut, she turned around to give Kay her full attention. 'And I'm the best aunty you could ever wish for, ain't I, ducky?' she said, grinning broadly.

Kay nodded, smiling. 'You most definitely are.'

Viv frowned then, bothered. Kay might be smiling but there was a look in her eyes that concerned her aunt. She knew the girl almost as well as she knew herself, and all her instincts told her now that her niece was worried about something. Right from Kay's birth a strong bond had been forged between them. Despite knowing that her sister loved Kay and did her best to raise her right, Mabel's restricted outlook prevented her from giving her daughter what Viv felt to be a proper education in the ways of the world, so she had taken it upon herself to complete the job. It had been Viv who had unwaveringly offered advice and support over the years whenever Kay and her mother had clashed or when problems had arisen with friends; she who elaborated on Mabel's scant information to Kay about puberty; she who had taught her to dress in a flattering way to suit her developing figure and how to use make-up to enhance her pretty face; she who had helped calm the then sixteen-year-old Kay's nerves on her first serious date with a boy, on an outing to the pictures. It had been to Viv that Kay had first turned when she decided to marry the man she loved before he went off to fight for his country and needed advice on how to approach her parents.

Mabel had been well aware all along of her sister's input in her daughter's 'education' but had no choice but to turn a blind eye to the relationship because she did not want to risk alienating her daughter. And deep down, although she would never admit it, she knew that her sister was filling a need for Kay that her mother could not meet herself. Out of deep respect for her, neither Viv nor Kay flaunted their closeness to Mabel.

'Move that pile of ironing off the chair and take the weight off yer legs,' Viv said, indicating the shabby-looking chair to the side of her. When Kay had done so Viv said, 'So come on, tell aunty what's ailing yer, gel?'

'Ailing me? Nothing. I'm very well, Aunty Viv, thanks.'

'Don't play the smart arse with me, Kay Clifton. What's bothering you then? Summat is. I've got a built-in radar for that kinda thing, especially where me beloved niece is concerned.'

Putting her handbag down on the floor beside her, Kay clasped her hands. She took a glance around the room – one which, like the rest of this house, was filled with an assortment of odd shabby furniture and had a lived-in look about it as well as a week's worth of dust. It was a stark contrast to the neat and tidy home her own mother kept, but nevertheless a house in which Kay had always felt welcome and comfortable. This was somewhere she didn't have to watch her Ps and Qs, where she could be her true self, not feeling as if she was constantly being judged or frowned upon if she acted even marginally outside the parameters of upright living. Bringing her eyes back to rest on her aunt, her face took on a deeply worried expression as she said, 'I'm frightened, Aunty Viv.'

Viv frowned, perplexed. 'Frightened! What on earth of?'

Kay gave a helpless shrug. 'I'm not quite sure. This feeling of fear came over me when I was giving myself a last check in the mirror before I left home. You know how excited I've been over getting Bob back safely, unlike so many others who'll never see their loved ones again. Now we can finally begin a proper married life together and I'm so looking forward to that, I can't tell you how much. But ... well...'

'Well, what?' her aunt urged.

Kay took a deep breath. 'What if Bob doesn't like the house, Aunty Viv? What if he doesn't like living in Leicester? While we were courting it wasn't possible for me to journey to Northampton where he comes from so I don't know what it's like there. As you know, after his father died leaving him with no other family Bob lived in lodgings there, but even so it was still his home. He had friends there which he hasn't in Leicester so it will be like starting all over again for him. And what if ... oh, Aunty Viv!' Tears pricked Kay's eyes. She gnawed her bottom lip anxiously and blurted out, 'It's over five years since we've seen each other so what if he doesn't like ... love me any more?'

Viv leaned forward and grabbed her hands, gripping them tightly.

'Oh, me duck, you *have* got yerself into a right old tizzy, ain't yer? Now you listen to yer aunty, and listen good. Bob loved you enough to marry you. Yes, we could say it was all done in haste 'cos he was going away and no one then had any idea for how long, but give the man some credit for wanting to make you his wife, wanting you to be waiting for him when he returned. I know I only met Bob twice and briefly at that, but I consider meself a decent judge of character and I thought him a good sort. He seemed honest, and I liked his outgoing personality, and any idiot could tell how much he loved you.'

Viv took a deep breath. 'I'm not going to flannel yer, Kay, by saying that at the station you'll fall into each other's arms and everything will be hunky-dory. Yes, it does happen but mostly in books or on films.' She took another deep breath and eyed her niece meaningfully. 'I'm going to warn you that this war is bound to have changed Bob. He's five years older for a start and even the hardest of men will return affected by the fighting in some way or other. I mean, we don't know what he's been through really, do we? It's one thing seeing what's been happening on the Pathé News at the pictures or listening to reports on the wireless; entirely another being involved in it daily. I dread to think what he's witnessed and suffered, I really do.'

31

Viv's eyes glazed and a grim expression settled on her face. 'Bob was one of the lucky ones out in Burma, not to have bin taken prisoner and sent to work on that dreadful railway. Thousands died there, many, many thousands, and from what we've learned about it all since, it was a blessed release for those who did. It was a living hell for the rest of them. The Japs showed no mercy to their prisoners. Little bastards,' she hissed.

She gave herself a mental shake and Kay a wan smile. 'But he's not the only one who's more than likely changed while yer've been parted. You definitely have, Kay. You've blossomed from a carefree young girl into a mature woman who's had a lot back here at home to deal with. It ain't bin easy for any of us, far from it.' She paused and gazed lovingly at her niece. 'But I do know without a shadow of a doubt Bob is gonna be delighted with the woman he finds meeting him at the station. Any man 'ud be a fool not to be. And that's not yer aunty speaking but a woman with eyes in her head and the grace to compliment another woman when she deserves it.'

Kay stared thoughtfully at her aunt as her words sank in. 'I felt overwhelmed this morning by the feeling that I was meeting a man I hardly know.'

Viv nodded. 'Perfectly natural you feeling like that, Kay, 'cos in some respects you are, the same as thousands of other women welcoming their men back home after being parted for so long. Look, me darlin', you never get to know someone intimately until you live with them on a daily basis and get used to all their little habits, which believe me can be bloody annoying sometimes! But then, if yer love someone enough, them little habits can be overlooked.'

Kay looked at her in surprise.

'Did Uncle Archie have habits then?'

Viv laughed. 'Despite your thinking your uncle was perfect, I can assure you he did. A couple of bad ones too, but I don't want ter put you off married life altogether by going into them.' She paused and looked at her niece earnestly. 'Yer don't regret marrying Bob, do yer? Wish yer'd have waited like yer mam and dad wanted yer to until the blasted war had finished so yer could do things properly?'

'Oh, no, Aunty Viv,' said Kay with conviction. 'It was pure fate the way I met Bob. He was on a weekend pass while training at a camp in North- ampton, and a mate persuaded him to come up to Leicester with him to visit a sick relative. Then they both came into the Turkey Café while me and my pal Eunice just happened to be in there having a cup of coffee, and there was no room on any of the other tables so they asked us if they could sit at ours...'

Kay's eyes turned dreamy as she pictured the four of them falling so easily into conversation, and how quickly she seemed to forget about the presence of the other two as she and Bob chatted away like they had known each other for years.

'From the minute he sat down next to me everything inside me told me he was the one for me. Later he said he'd felt just the same about me. I've no regrets at all about marrying him, Aunty Viv. The only regret I have is that we've been denied these last five years together.' She paused and lowered her voice to a worried whisper. 'When Bob first went away he wrote to me several times a week. As the war progressed I'd usually receive the letters altogether, then I wouldn't hear from him for a while, then another lot would arrive, and that's how it went on. But this last six months I never received anything from him at all and you know how worried I was every time the door knocker went, thinking it'd be someone from the Ministry telling me the same thing as they told you over Uncle Archie. Then out of the blue a fortnight ago a letter arrived from Bob telling me he was back in England and giving me his demob date.'

'And you should think yourself lucky you got what letters you did, Kay, especially from the Far East where Bob was. Some post never got through at all, and some blokes never even bothered to write to their wives.' Viv's voice was lower and there was a note of emotion in it when she added, 'Some blokes couldn't write at all 'cos they were dead and now their loved ones have to live with that loss forever, somehow learn to get on with their life alone.'

Kay looked at her, mortified. 'Oh, I don't mean to sound ungrateful, Aunty Viv. I am grateful for every word Bob wrote to me. It's just that after not hearing from him for so long, his last letter was so short. It barely told me more than his demob date...'

'Were you expecting him to write a book?' Viv

cut in. 'Bob needn't have bothered with a letter at all. He could just have turned up on yer doorstep.'

Kay looked horrified at the thought.

'Oh, I'm glad he never! We'd have had to stay with me mam and dad then until we found a house for ourselves and got it ready to move into.'

'Seems to me that Bob can't win.' Viv smiled at her ruefully and leaned over to pat her knee affectionately. 'Yer know what I think, ducky?'

'What do you think, Aunty Viv?'

'That you've waited for this day to come for that long that now it finally has, you can't quite believe it and you've got an attack of the heebie-jeebies, that's all.'

'Oh, do you think so?'

'I'm positive. Just remember when yer pacing that station platform waiting for Bob's train to pull in that more than likely he's as keyed up as you are for the reunion. Just take each day as it comes, don't expect too much, and you'll be fine.' Viv's eyes twinkled wickedly. 'Got yerself something alluring to wear for bed tonight?'

Kay turned the colour of a tomato.

'Oh, Aunty Viv, you are a caution. No wonder Mam's always hinting you're a bad influence on me. But, yes, I have,' she replied coyly. 'The flimsy one you bought me for my wedding night, the one I daren't show Mam in case she thought I was a hussy so I let her think I was wearing my best cotton one.'

Viv laughed, 'I bet it won't stay on long!' She laughed again, a bellowing guffaw this time. 'Oh, do you remember yer mam's response when you broke the news to her that you were getting married the next morning on a special licence? I mean, her and yer dad only met Bob twice and those were fleeting visits when he called to collect you for an evening out.'

Kay shuddered.

'Please don't remind me, Aunty Viv. I thought she was going to have a seizure. If it hadn't been for Dad taking our side and making her see reason, then I think she would have. I can see her point, though, and I know she only acted that way because she had my best interests at heart.'

Viv looked at her meaningfully.

'You can never take that away from her, Kay, when all's said and done she's only ever wanted to take care of you and Trevor. She loves you both. Talking of my nephew, how is the returning hero today?'

'Up to his usual tricks, Aunty Viv. Mam's still having the devil's own job keeping him in bed like the doctor ordered.'

'And you can bet your life our Mabel will stick to the doc's instructions to the letter. Poor blighter must be going mad of boredom stuck upstairs all on his own. I know his mates pop in when they can but I bet yer mam restricts the time they spend with him. I still can't see why a makeshift bed can't be rigged up for him downstairs?'

'That's what Dad said, but Mam wouldn't hear of it until the doctor gave the nod.'

'Well, she wants Trevor as better as he can be so I can't really say as I blame her for being such a stickler in this instance. Mabel is going to let him down for a bit tomorrow for Bob's welcome home dinner, though, ain't she?'

Kay nodded. 'She's making that concession, but she's not happy about it.'

Viv smacked her lips.

'I'm looking forward to it! Our Mabel cooks just the best Sunday roast. Lamb, eh? I can't remember the last time I had lamb except for tough mutton chops that've got more fat on 'em than meat, and that's if yer lucky enough to get 'em after queuing for hours.' Her eyes sparkled mischievously. 'I did offer to do a trifle and it was no mean feat getting hold of that tin of fruit and some custard powder. I only managed *that* because a girlfriend of mine is dating an American soldier. I expect you ain't surprised to hear Mabel turned me down, though, made no bones about the fact my effort wouldn't be up to her standards, but she still had the nerve to take the custard powder off me as my contribution!'

'If it makes you feel any better, Aunty Viv, I offered my help too and she fobbed me off with the excuse that I've enough to occupy me, getting Bob settled back in.'

'Well, she's right there, you have.'

Just then there was a tap on the back door and a tall, well-built man in his late-thirties walked in, carrying a dilapidated-looking cardboard box which must contain Viv's crystal wireless set. His eyes lit up on spotting her.

'I'm popping this back as promised. It's working fine now, just a couple of loose wires that needed soldering.' Then he noticed Kay. 'Oh, I beg yer pardon, yer've visitors.'

Viv laughed, 'This is no visitor, Frank. This is me niece Kay, and my house is her second home.'

Frank cleared a space on the littered table, putting the box down on it. After glancing Kay up and down he held out his hand in greeting.

'Frank Ambleside. Pleased ter meet you. Viv's always talking about you and it's nice to put a name to a face.'

Kay accepted his hand and shook it.

'Good to meet you too.'

She secretly appraised Frank. He seemed nice enough, giving Kay the impression of an upright sort of man, and he wasn't bad-looking either in a middle-aged way. She felt mortally sorry for the callous way his wife had treated him while he was away fighting for her liberty. What struck Kay glaringly was the fact that though her aunt might say she viewed Frank Ambleside as just a friend, she had dressed herself nicely and put on make-up for his visit, and Kay had noticed the distinct gleam in Frank's eyes when he looked at Viv. Kay suspected that her aunt liked Frank rather more than she was willing to let on, and Frank definitely liked her more than he did a mere friend. But then, what man in his right mind wouldn't find her aunt appealing? It was hardly surprising.

Picking up her handbag, Kay rose.

'I'd best get off to the station, Aunty Viv, so I'll leave you to it.'

'Oh, but yer've bags of time yet, our Kay. Enough for a cuppa at least. You'll have one, won't yer, Frank? Least I can do by way of repayment for fixing me radio. I ain't half missed me programmes, especially *Family Favourites* on Sunday morning. Oh, and *Round the Horne* ... that does make me laugh.'

Frank smiled at her warmly.

'I'd love a cuppa, ta, Viv,' he replied as he sat down in the chair Kay had just risen from.

She knew it wasn't just her imagination that Frank seemed pleased she was going so he could have Viv all to himself.

'I'll pass if you don't mind, Aunty Viv. I'd hate to think of the train arriving early and me not there to meet Bob.'

'I understand, lovey.'

At the door Kay gave Viv a hug.

'Thanks for listening to me. I feel much better now.'

'Just doing me job as yer aunty. Now remember, no marriage is without its ups and downs.' She ran her hand tenderly down the side of Kay's face. 'You and Bob are gonna be fine, I feel it in me water.'

These were just the reassuring words that Kay needed. She beamed brightly. 'Thanks, Aunty Viv. I'll see you tomorrow.'

'And I'm looking forward to it.' Viv looked at her thoughtfully for a moment, then her eyes glinted with mischief again. 'I've an idea for a way I can get back at my sister for not accepting my kind contribution to the meal.'

'Oh, Aunty Viv, what are you up to now?'

She laughed, 'You wait and see, me darlin'! Now off yer go.'

CHAPTER TWO

In the event the train was an hour late. Immediately it drew to a squealing, hissing stop, sending a huge cloud of dense white smoke billowing in all directions, carriage doors were flung wide open and the station came to life. Alighting passengers and waiting greeters rushed around seeking each other. In the middle of this mayhem, with her heart thumping painfully in anticipation, Kay searched the crowd for her beloved husband. She vehemently wished she had accepted her best friend Eunice's offer to accompany her, to have her here beside her now for support and to help calm her nerves. But even Eunice, who knew and liked Bob of old, had accepted that two was company for this homecoming greeting. Oh, if only she could see Bob. Scores of men milled around in both uniform and civilian dress, and from even a short distance away many of them could have been Bob until closer inspection told her otherwise. As the seconds ticked past and the station began to empty she could still see no sign of her husband and a terrible dread began to fill her. Had Bob not caught this train for some reason? The thought tormented her. She had waited five long years for this day and any delay to their reunion, whatever the reason, seemed absolutely unthinkable now.

Eyes still darting, she began to push her way

through the dispersing crowds and accidentally stumbled over the foot of a passer by. Hurriedly regaining her balance she looked at the person, aiming to apologise for her clumsiness, and when her eyes settled on his face her heart soared and her face was lit by pure delight. 'Bob!' she joyfully cried. Then immediately realised her error and, muttering an apology, she made to continue her search. But the man's response froze her rigid.

'Don't you recognise your own husband, Kay?' She spun back round to face him.

'Bob?'

He nodded.

'It's me, Kay, honest it is.'

Was this man really her beloved husband? The man she had tearfully waved off on this very platform just over five years ago? Her aunt had tried to warn her, but Kay had not expected him to have lost so much weight. His once rounded face now verged on gauntness; the leanness of his body against his once stocky girth made him appear taller than her memory served her. Neither was his thick thatch of hair quite so flaxen as she remembered, and it was receding. His tone of voice sounded lower. He was deeply tanned, his once youthfully smooth skin now having the weathered leathery texture of someone who had spent too much time under a relentless sun. She had only ever seen Bob dressed in his uniform and now he was wearing a smart, though rather ill-fitting, navy demob suit under a dark brown overcoat. Only the colour of his captivating eyes, which had always reminded her of the sea bathed by the sun on a hot day, seemed unfaded by the

41

ravages of war.

Then it struck her that Bob's face held an anxious look and he was fidgeting on his feet. He was just as nervous over their reunion as she was. Kay's mind was racing urgently, searching for something to say to ease the awkwardness between them, when unexpectedly he leaned forward and gave her a gentle kiss on the cheek.

'It's good to be home, Kay,' he said hesitantly, then after clearing his throat, added, 'I've missed you so much.'

The Bob Kay had said goodbye to had kissed her fiercely until she had cried for mercy, then clung on to her as if afraid to let her go. Now five years later the same man didn't seem as though he had it in him to do anything so demonstrative. Again she was frantically searching for something to say to ease the tension between them when, much to her surprise, a man appeared at Bob's side, slapping him on the shoulder.

'Ah, there you are, Bob. We got parted in this crowd and I couldn't find you. Beginning to think you'd gone off without me.'

Wondering who this man was, Kay flashed an enquiring look at Bob as he said, 'I was just trying to find my wife.'

The other man turned his attention to her then, glancing her over admiringly.

'So this is the little woman then? Your photograph doesn't do you justice. Far prettier in the flesh. My time away would've passed so much more easily if I'd had someone like you waiting for me back home.' He held out his hand to Kay. 'Tony Cheadle. Me and your husband served together in the same outfit.'

He was an extremely attractive man, probably in his early thirties, a shade taller than Bob at six foot and like him deeply tanned. He had a firm, lithe body, a shock of dark hair, and deep brown eyes fringed with thick dark lashes. He had an air of arrogance about him, too.

His physical attributes were lost on Kay, though. She'd taken extreme offence at the way he was leering at her, but out of respect for the fact that he was a friend of her husband, she accepted his greeting.

'Pleased to meet you,' she said, not really meaning it.

He held on to her hand just a little too long for Kay's liking. 'You too,' he said, fixing her eyes with his suggestively. 'Bob talked about you so much on all those long lonely nights out in the jungle, I feel I know you as well as he does.'

Pulling her hand out of his grasp, she flashed him a brief smile, wishing he would take his leave so she and Bob could be alone together.

But just as she was about to suggest to Bob that they go home, Tony said, 'Right, shall we be off then? I don't know about Bob but I'm famished. Long time since I've had a proper home-cooked meal. I can't wait!'

Kay froze. She hoped she was wrong but from what Tony had just said she got the distinct impression he was expecting to come home and have a meal with them. She was open to entertaining Bob's friends, like she expected he would hers in return, but not tonight of all nights. This night was surely just for them? She looked at

43

Bob enquiringly.

He stared back at her awkwardly before taking her aside and in a hushed whisper announcing, 'I asked Tony to have a meal with us.' Then he took a deep breath and said, 'In fact, I've invited him to stay with us, Kay. I hope you don't mind?'

This news shook her rigid. Her mouth dropped open. Mind? Of course she minded, very much so.

'Stay with us! Oh, but you've just come home, Bob, and...'

He cut her short, saying tersely, 'I owe Tony, Kay.'

'Owe him?' Her face screwed up in bewilderment. 'I don't understand, Bob. Owe him what?'

'My life. Look, he's got nowhere to go. He's like me, his family's all gone. Only unlike me, he's no wife waiting to welcome him home. So I have to do this for him, Kay. It won't be for long, just until he gets himself sorted. A couple of nights at the most. Please?'

If Bob owed Tony his life then that meant he must have rescued him from some terrible situation which she was desperate to know the details of though right now was neither the time nor the place. If he'd saved Bob's life then she herself owed Tony too. Without his show of bravery she wouldn't be looking forward to her new life with Bob but instead wearing widow's weeds to mourn him. Regardless, Kay couldn't help but feel a certain amount of resentment towards the man Bob had brought back with him. She and her husband needed time to themselves to rekindle their relationship. It was going to prove very difficult in

44

their small house with Tony hanging around too. She had no idea how she was going to accommodate him. A spare bed had not been high on her list of priorities when she had hastily put their new home together. Feeding him tonight was another problem as she'd only bought food for Bob and herself for over the weekend until she went shopping again after work on Monday.

Then Kay's better nature took over. After what he had done for her husband, the least she could do was show Tony her gratitude by agreeing to Bob's request.

'Of course he's welcome,' she said with a smile for her husband.

A couple of hours later Tony pushed his plate away and with a finger nail teased a piece of meat from between his almost perfect set of front teeth. Then, leaning back in his chair, he gave his stomach a satisfied pat.

'Well, a man could get used to that. Best pork chop I've ever tasted. Worth going through five years of hell for, that dinner was.' He looked at Kay expectantly. 'What's for pudding then?'

Her eyebrows rose at his lack of manners. The journey home had proved a trial to Kay as she had trotted between the two men, racing to keep up with them as they marched down the back streets to the new house, the silence between them all broken only when she issued directions. On arriving at the house she had hardly had time to shut the back door behind them when Tony had abandoned his kit bag on the kitchen floor and made his own way into the back room where he shed his overcoat, throwing it on the back of a dining chair, then settled himself in an armchair by the fireplace. He kicked off his shoes to rest his feet on the hearth then asked her if she'd got today's newspaper, how long the meal would be, and commented that a glass of beer wouldn't go amiss while she was cooking it!

Kay had wanted to show Bob around the house, hear his approval of her achievements on their behalf and reassurances that they'd both be happy living here. She'd also hoped to grab a few minutes in private for him at least to kiss her, something denied her up to now due to the constant presence of Tony. It didn't appear to have crossed his mind that he might make himself scarce so they could have a few precious minutes alone. Instead, much to her own annoyance, Kay found herself apologising for the fact that she hadn't a newspaper, nor any beer, but asking if a cup of tea would do instead and saying that the meal would be about half an hour. Then, leaving Bob to entertain his friend, she hurried off into the kitchen to get it ready.

As she put the pan of already peeled potatoes on the stove to boil she sensed Bob's presence and turned to find him looking at her from just inside the kitchen doorway. She wondered how long he had been standing there, watching her without a word.

He looked a little awkward then.

'I ... er ... need to use the privy.'

'It's in the yard, you can't miss it.'

She looked after him worriedly as he left the kitchen. Bob still seemed very on edge, nervy, like he was expecting a bomb to go off behind him – which she supposed was understandable considering what he had just returned from.

When he came back into the kitchen she smiled at him encouragingly and said, 'Dinner won't be long.'

'It smells good,' he said, looking across at the pans on the stove.

She was about to tell him what they were having when suddenly it hit Kay full force what her aunt had been trying to prepare her for. They'd been so wrapped up in their love for each other before, their brief times together never long enough for them to hold deep, meaningful conversations, it meant they'd hardly scratched the surface of each other's normal everyday life. Sure of their love, they'd married in a rush, neither foreseeing the fact that Bob would be whisked off to the other side of the world, not to return until after Japan had surrendered in August 1945.

'I hope pork chop and mashed potatoes will be all right for you?' Kay asked worriedly, praying it would as otherwise she only had egg and chips or cheese sandwiches to offer him until she went shopping on Monday. Having got compassionate leave from her shift in the sorting office that morning due to her circumstances, she had nevertheless been up early and waiting outside the butcher's shop half an hour before he opened so she could have first choice of what little he had on offer. She'd felt herself very lucky to get the chops.

'Pork chop? I can't remember the last time I had one. Sounds like a banquet to me.' Bob gave

47

a nervous laugh. 'I expect there's nothing worse than someone getting in your way while you're trying to cook a meal? I'll ... er ... leave you to it then.'

He made to leave the kitchen. His awkwardness was causing her concern and she needed to do something to put him at ease.

'Bob...'

He turned back to face her.

'Yes?'

Conscious that their guest could hear this conversation in the other room, Kay walked over to the kitchen door and shut it.

'This is your home, Bob,' she told her husband. 'Your name is on the rent book, all the furniture and bits and pieces were bought using money from your Army married allowance together with what I managed to save from my wages. I know it's going to take you time to adjust back to life outside the Army, but I'm here to help you.' She went over to him then, tilted her head and kissed his cheek. 'Oh, it's just so good to have you back! I'm having trouble believing it myself.'

He smiled at her.

'Yes, me too.'

She hugged him briefly then realised she'd better concentrate on her cooking.

'Now while I finish the dinner, why don't you make yourself at home? I bought you a pair of slippers. They're at the side of the fireplace.' She smiled at him. 'Size nine. That's right, isn't it?'

'Oh ... well, actually, I take tens.'

'Tens? I could have sworn when you accident-ally trod on my foot once while we were dancing you laughed about not being able to control your size nines.'

Kay's heart sank. The slippers were not exactly an exciting gift to welcome her husband back home with but they had been difficult to track down, such items being virtually nonexistent since all manufacturing had been turned over to producing items essential for the war effort. Nevertheless they had been bought with love, using money that could have been spent on more practical things, and it upset her to realise that after all her trouble she had got the wrong size. What else did she not know about the man she had married in such haste because he was going away?

'Oh, well, the music was rather loud at the time,' she said in the hope of justifying her own mistake. 'Never mind, I'll take them back to the shop on Monday and if nothing else get my money back.' She eyed him hesitantly. 'You do like the house, don't you, Bob? I've done my best to make it homely for you.'

'Oh, yes,' he replied with conviction. 'I think you've done a grand job. I shall like living here very much.'

'I'm glad. Why don't you take your bag upstairs, then after dinner I'll unpack it for you. Your box of stuff is at the side of the wardrobe for you to sort through when you're ready.'

Taking a tin from out of his pocket, he extracted a roll-up cigarette from it and lit it with a Blue Bell match, drawing in smoke deeply. 'I'll do it later. I expect I've forgotten all about most of the stuff in it.'

'It'll be a nice visit down Memory Lane for you when you do go through it. I'd like to go through it with you and then you can fill me in on lots of things about your past I don't know about. You've started smoking, I see?'

'Eh? Oh.' He flashed a look at his cigarette then back to her. 'You don't mind, do you?'

'No, not at all. My brother smokes and so does Aunty Viv. I'm just surprised you've taken it up because you said you never would after your father dying of lung cancer. I'll find you something to use as an ash tray.'

He looked at her, bothered by something.

'Er ... I'm sorry to burden you with this now, Kay, but what about Tony's sleeping arrangements?'

Thoughtfully, she rubbed her chin. 'It's either the floor in the back bedroom or the sofa down here.'

'I'm sure either will be fine. He's used to camping in the jungle.'

'It must have been terrible for you both?'

Bob's face clouded over. 'It was.' For a moment he stood transfixed, a faraway look in his eyes, and Kay could see his mind was back there, facing God knew what atrocities. His life must have been hell, she thought, for the most part living rough in the harsh environment of the Burmese jungle, constantly alert for the enemy, never knowing if the next bullet had his name on it, not knowing if he'd see his homeland or her ever again. Life had been hard enough for them here but that could hardly compare with everything Bob had had to deal with. 'I never want to go through anything

50

like that again, ever,' he said with conviction. 'A man faces things in war he never dreams of. You find yourself doing things...' His voice trailed off and he looked at her strangely. Just as suddenly the moment passed and he gave a little smile. 'Anyway, those times are behind us, thank God. I want to forget all about them.'

'Yes,' she agreed firmly. 'You're home now with me. Just let any other mindless dictator start any trouble and he'll have *me* to deal with because I'm never letting you out of my sight again, I promise you that, Bob Clifton.'

Just then the pan of potatoes spluttered as the boiling water hit the gas jets below.

'I'd better leave you to it,' he said, and left the kitchen.

Kay arranged potatoes and cabbage courtesy of her father's allotment on her own plate in such a way neither of the men seemed to notice it was devoid of any meat, just as she had intended. She did not want to embarrass Bob with the fact that his friend was eating her share. As she joined them at the table she looked at her husband apprehensively, hoping he was enjoying the first meal she had cooked for him. She was relieved to see that he was tucking in with relish, as was Tony.

'So, Tony, my husband tells me I owe you a debt of gratitude for what you did for him?'

He looked across at her, smiling disarmingly. 'And you're both repaying me very graciously by inviting me into your home.'

'Well ... it's the least we can do. So what exactly happened?' Kay asked keenly.

51

Tony flashed a glance at Bob before replying, 'The whole incident was sickening for us all, but especially for Bob. We made an agreement not to talk about it. That right, Bob?'

'That's right,' he answered, staring down at his plate. 'Just want to forget all about it.' He lifted his head and looked at her. 'You do understand, I hope, Kay?'

She was most disappointed, desperately wanting to hear the circumstances in which her precious husband's life had been saved by Tony's bravery, but she supposed she had no choice but to hope that sometime in the future Bob would change his mind and tell her about it.

'Of course I understand,' she said diplomatically. 'I won't mention it again unless you do. So, Tony, are you from Northamptonshire the same as Bob? I presume you must be as you both served in the same regiment.'

'The same area but not the same town. I doubt you'll have heard of the place I hail from, it's just a backwater,' he said, shoving a forkful of food into his mouth.

She might have and it annoyed her that he'd doubt her intelligence. Before she could stop herself, she replied, 'I did do geography at school.' Then she regretted her sharp response and quickly asked, 'What did you work as?'

His face lit up proudly.

'Door to door salesman. But not your average sort – I'm good at it. Hardly a door I've knocked on hasn't led to a sale. I could sell sand to the Arabs! Got what you'd call natural talent. The war's done me a favour really, I was ready for a change of scene. Small town, small pickings, no room for expansion. From what I've seen of Leicester it looks all right, the sorta place a man could make a better living for himself. Any good pubs locally?'

'Oh, as far as I know the locals seem to like the pub on the corner. It always sounds like it's got a good crowd inside whenever I've passed by.'

'Sounds good to me.' He grinned, looking at Bob. 'Looks like you've got it made to me, mate, and I wouldn't say no to swapping places with you any day. A nice house, grand little woman running after you, *and* a decent local.' Pushing away his empty plate then, he asked what was for pudding.

This man might have saved her husband's life and be a saviour in Bob's eyes but Kay felt he really could do with lessons on how to conduct himself while a guest in someone else's home. Thankfully his stay was not to be for long as despite possessing a very tolerant nature Kay doubted even she could put up with his attitude for much longer without saying something to him about it.

'Sago,' was all she replied evenly, before hurrying off into the kitchen to fetch it.

As soon as both men had eaten their last spoonful, Tony said to Bob, 'Well, after a good meal like that a pint is called for. While your little lady clears up, shall we go and investigate the pub?'

Bob looked at him uncertainly.

'Oh ... er ... do you think that's a good idea?'

Tony flashed back a look of derision.

53

'I wouldn't have suggested it if it wasn't.'

Bob beamed eagerly then.

'Oh, well, I could certainly do with a pint.'

Kay looked at them both quizzically. It was obvious that Tony was very much the dominant personality. Within less than a minute they had left. Kay would have appreciated being asked by Bob if she minded his leaving her on their first night together. She did mind in fact, very much so, not that she begrudged his going out with his friend for a drink, but she had just done without him for five years and every second spent with him was precious to her at the moment. Still, she supposed it got the men from under her feet while she tidied up. She guessed they'd be away for about an hour. If she hurried she could get the dishes cleared away, the spare bedding sorted out for Tony and unpack Bob's belongings before they returned. Hopefully Tony would show some consideration for their situation by staying behind at the pub, leaving Bob and her alone together for what was left of the evening before they went to bed.

Bed!

Every night since his departure Kay had lain alone in her bed, yearning to lie beside Bob again, wrapped in his arms. She was longing to experience the passionate lovemaking she'd known on the two nights they had spent together on honeymoon. Now the time was almost upon her when her wish would be granted and her need of him was never greater. Yet how could they feel easy and relaxed in their lovemaking with a third presence in the house? It was unthinkable, yet so

54

was getting into bed with Bob on his first night home and just turning over and going to sleep.

A dilemma to which she could see no apparent answer.

Would Bob have one? Kay devoutly hoped so.

Having tidied up after their meal, she went upstairs to put Tony's bag in the back bedroom and then to unpack Bob's belongings in their own room. He didn't seem to have much by the way of clothes. A spare set of underwear, two pairs of thick woollen socks and two shirts, all MOD demob issue in exchange for his uniform. As soon as money permitted she would rig him out with more decent attire. Before rolling up the kit bag to store it away on top of the wardrobe, she checked the pockets. Inside one were three photographs she had sent him of their wedding and a bundle of all the letters she had written to him, tied up in a piece of grubby-looking string. They appeared to have been well read. A warm glow filled her as she visualised Bob reading them over and over, like she had done with those she had received from him and which she had kept safely too. Those letters had been their lifeline, the only things keeping them connected during their time apart. Bob obviously treasured her letters as she treasured his. Then she looked at the photographs. Like the letters, these all showed signs of the number of times they had been looked at. Maybe he had spoken to her image on long lonely nights, like she had done to his, pretending he was physically with her. Well, neither of them need do that any longer now they were back together. She placed the bundle of letters and the photographs on top of Bob's box of possessions at the side of the wardrobe, ready for him to sort through and put away when he was ready.

Chores done, she switched on the battery-powered wireless, tuning it to a station playing soothing background music. Picking up a magazine, one of several she had been passed by her aunt after they had already gone around several of her friends, Kay settled in an armchair to await her husband's return which had to be imminent. But by the time she heard a pounding on the front door it was approaching a quarter to eleven! Kay had gone from feeling upset that Bob could leave her alone on their first night together to worrying that something had happened to him and then to feeling angry with Tony who she blamed for keeping Bob away from her just to satisfy his own need for a drinking companion. Purely out of respect for her husband, she fought to hide her annoyance as she opened the door to them.

They were clinging on to each other, wearing silly grins.

Before she could say anything Tony slurred to Bob, 'Man should have a key to his own house, mate. Bloody embarrassing, having ter knock on yer own door.'

Not wanting an altercation on her doorstep Kay replied evenly as she stood aside to allow them entry, 'Bob does have a key only I hadn't a chance to give it to him before you whisked him off to the pub. I can see you both enjoyed your-selves.'

'We did that,' Tony answered, his inebriated words barely audible. 'Nice little pub, friendly lot, especially the women – though not the sort I'd touch with a bargepole. Insisted on buying us drinks when they realised we'd just been demobbed after five years in the Far East. Local heroes we are.'

'Well, I'm glad you made some friends.'

Kay tried to sound sincere despite wishing they'd chosen another night to make themselves known in the area. Her appraisal of the inebriated state which her husband was in told her that any hope she'd harboured of a passionate reunion that night was out of the question. Bob was too drunk even to speak to her. But then she wondered if she was being selfish for being annoyed at him for having a few too many pints. In all honesty, lovemaking wasn't on the agenda until their guest had departed, hopefully on Monday. Then she would have Bob all to herself, and every night thereafter could be spent in unbridled passion should the mood take them. Kay had controlled her need for him for five years, another two days seemed nothing in comparison.

Shutting the door, she followed them as they stumbled through the front room and into the back one via the connecting door. They both flopped down in the armchairs and before she could say anything were snoring. Going across to her husband, Kay shook him. 'Bob, wake up so I can help you to bed.' But he was out cold. So was Tony. Sighing heavily, she fetched the spare blankets and put one across Tony. Before she covered Bob, she gently removed his jacket and shoes.

After dousing the gas mantles she made her way upstairs where, alone in the bed she should have been sharing with her husband, she sobbed herself to sleep.

CHAPTER THREE

Kay was used to waking alone so the next morning after a restless night that situation didn't seem at all unusual to her – until she eased herself upright to rub her gritty eyes and the previous day's events all flooded back to her. She had got her beloved husband back where he belonged, true, but last night should have been her and Bob's second honeymoon, a making up for five lost years, rediscovering each other and finding joy and fulfillment before falling asleep exhausted in each other's arms. Instead they had slept apart. Her resentment against her husband's friend deepened although she couldn't lay the full blame on Tony for the state of intoxication Bob had returned in from the pub. He was his own man and responsible for his own actions. Regardless, if Tony hadn't suggested going there in the first place, Bob and she, although possibly having to temper their passion until their guest had departed, would at least have spent the night together.

Kay rose. She washed herself down using cold water from the jug and bowl on a wash stand in the chimney recess, then dressed in a sage green

A-line skirt and pretty lacy short-sleeved beige jumper, knitted with wool painstakingly unravelled from an old cardigan of her mother's. She decided not to make an issue of her husband's drunken state the previous night, feeling they had enough already to contend with in getting their relationship back to the comfortable closeness they'd shared before he went away.

She arrived downstairs to find both men sitting slumped in the armchairs, looking very hung over, cradling their heads in their hands.

'Good morning,' she said breezily.

Bob dropped his hands to look across at her sheepishly.

'Good morning. Er ... I'm sorry, Kay. One thing led to another and...'

'It's all right, Bob,' she cut in, smiling at him. 'After what you've been through, it's a poor thing if you can't let your hair down for one night with your friend. I don't begrudge you.'

'See, I told you your dear little wife would be all right about it,' piped up Tony. When Kay flashed a look of derision in his direction, he smiled back at her winningly. 'Bob really wanted to come home to you but then he'd have upset all those generous people who insisted on paying tribute to us. I know you wouldn't have wanted that, would you? Any chance of a cuppa? And a glass of Epsom salts wouldn't go amiss while you're getting the breakfast.'

A 'please' or 'thank you' would have been appreciated, too. Kay quashed the urge to remind him that this was not a hotel and herself a waitress. She looked at Bob, expecting him to

59

warn his friend to show respect for her position as his wife, and was surprised to see that as on the previous evening when Tony had several times been flippant towards her, Bob appeared not to notice. This state of affairs certainly would not have happened before he went away. He had always been very quick to jump to her defence should he witness anyone showing the slightest lack of respect towards her. It had been one of the chief qualities in him that caused Kay to fall in love with him. Maybe, though, she was being hard on her husband. After all, yesterday had been a momentous occasion for them both and this morning he was suffering from a hangover.

She looked at Tony blandly. 'I've no Epsom Salts.' Then she turned her attention to her husband. 'Cuppa for you, Bob?'

He nodded. 'No breakfast, though, I couldn't eat anything just now. My stomach is churning.'

'A piece of toast might help settle it. I'm not doing much of a breakfast today anyway as we've a big dinner in store for us. My mother and father are having a family get together in your honour. I meant to tell you last night but, well, I never got chance to. You will have recovered by then, I hope?'

Kay was most surprised to see a look of sheer terror flash into Bob's eyes at her announcement of the dinner in his honour. But why would he be frightened of meeting her parents again? After all, he hadn't showed an iota of fear when he'd confronted them both to ask for her hand in marriage. She was about to ask him when Tony piped up again.

'A roast Sunday dinner, eh? Just the tonic a man needs after a heavy session the night before. What time are we expected?'

She looked at him in disbelief. Apart from being annoyed at his automatic assumption that he was included, she knew her mother had gone to extraordinary lengths to secure the food for Bob's welcome home dinner. Since they had learned of his return Mabel had cut back on her own use of already severely rationed basics, traded carefully with friends and neighbours, and Kay doubted she'd allowed any extra to feed an unexpected guest. If there had been enough food to include other guests, then she wouldn't have had to turn down Eunice gently after she had automatically assumed that, as Kay's best friend, she and George would be invited to such a special occasion. But then, how could Bob and she go off for dinner and not ask Tony to join them? It just wouldn't be right. Despite her increasing dislike of this man, it was something her conscience wouldn't allow her to do. She just hoped her mother understood the predicament she had found herself in.

'One o'clock,' she replied faintly.

Tony laughed.

'Should have known better than to ask! The Great British Sunday dinner is always dished up at one o'clock on the dot and not a second later – something Hitler obviously wasn't aware of or he would have invaded England one Sunday at that precise time and no one would have raised a finger to stop him 'cos they'd all have been having their dinner. Hooray for British tradition,

61

eh?' He laughed sardonically. 'No such luxury for us out in Burma, eh, Bob? We were hardly aware what day it was out there. Anyway, if this dinner's a special one in Bob's honour, I'd better look my best. I'll need a shirt ironing,' he said directly to Kay, getting up from his seat and looking around him. 'Where's my bag? I'll get it for you.'

She would have appreciated his asking her to iron his shirt instead of automatically assuming she would. Her tone was tart as she replied, 'I put it upstairs in the back bedroom yesterday evening. I wasn't sure where you'd decide you'd be most comfortable, the floor in the back bedroom or the sofa, but whichever, I thought you'd want some privacy to dress.'

'Thanks,' he said, disappearing up the stairs.

Well, at least he'd expressed gratitude for something she had done for him. She supposed it was a start.

Mabel was not happy, and her displeasure had nothing to do with having an extra mouth to feed dropped on her unexpectedly. She was a patriotic woman, saw it as her duty to welcome an ex-soldier into her home, feeling it was little enough repayment for what he'd been doing to protect his country and its people. She was more than willing to stretch the food out to accommodate Tony, and especially so after finding out that her son-in-law owed him his life, though Kay had warned them all Bob didn't want it mentioning. The cause of Mabel's annoyance was the non-arrival of her sister with only minutes to go before she dished up.

'Trust yer aunt to be late,' she fumed to Kay as she bent down to check the roast potatoes sizzling in the stove, alongside Yorkshire pudding, parsnips and the leg of lamb. 'I know her game,' she said, shutting the stove door then righting herself to give the pan of gravy a stir. 'Wants to make an entrance. Well, this is Bob's day and he's the centre of attention today, not her.'

'I'm sure there's a good reason why Aunty Viv isn't here yet,' Kay said diplomatically.

Mabel tutted disdainfully. 'My sister can do no wrong in your eyes, can she? Well, I know the truth of the matter is she wants everyone ready and waiting so all eyes are focused on her when she arrives.'

Kay knew this wasn't true as her aunt didn't need to do anything to get anyone to notice her, she attracted attention wherever she went. She was a striking woman with an attractive personality, but Kay knew it wasn't envy for these qualities that was causing Mabel to complain so much as the pressure of the occasion. It was clearly getting to her, and expressing her grievances against her sister was allowing her to let off a little steam. Kay only wished her mother would unbend sometimes and allow others to lend her a hand instead of always making out she was coping with it all herself when it was readily apparent she wasn't.

Just then the back door was pushed open and a breathless Viv came hurrying in. 'Don't start, our Mabel,' she blurted out. 'It's not me that's late, it's Frank. Got the time I told him to collect me mixed up.'

'Frank?' queried Mabel.

Kay held her breath, wondering what her aunt was up to now.

'Yes, Frank. Come on in, Frank, and meet the family,' said Viv, turning around to address the man hovering on the doorstep.

The man to whom Kay had been introduced the previous day entered the kitchen, politely taking off his trilby and holding out a hand in Mabel's direction. 'Pleased to meet you. It's very good of you to invite me for dinner, Mrs Stafford.'

Mabel's eyes bulged but before she had time to say anything, Viv said, 'Go through, Frank, and introduce yerself to the rest of the family. I'll be with yer in a minute.' She turned to Kay then, threw her arms around her and gave her the usual hug and a kiss on her cheek. 'Hello, me darlin', you're looking lovely as usual.' She then turned to her sister, kissed her on her cheek too and smiled at her winningly. 'Anything I can do, Mabel, or have you everything under control as usual?'

Mabel was looking back at her furiously. 'How could you, our Viv?' she fumed.

Viv said innocently, 'How could I what? Oh, you mean bring a friend for dinner. Well, yer didn't say I couldn't.'

Mabel looked back at her knowingly.

'You've done this on purpose because I declined your offer to make a trifle. It's your way of getting back at me, isn't it?'

'Maybe it is,' said Viv, smiling. 'Mind you, I should never have offered in the first place because I know whatever I produced it wouldn't be good enough, would it?' Her eyes twinkled then. 'And that's true, Mabel, 'cos you're such a good cook I couldn't surpass you if the great Mrs Beeton herself had personally taught me. It all smells wonderful, by the way.

'Anyway, I honestly didn't think you'd mind me bringing Frank. You're always reminding me that it's up to us women to do what we can to support the war effort, and even more so now it's over to help get this country back on its feet. Well, by bringing Frank to eat his dinner here, that's exactly what I'm doing.'

Mabel looked at her, confused.

'I don't see how?'

'Well, by sharing our meal he's saving the country a bit of fuel in not cooking his own, and the food he didn't buy means there's a little more on the shelves for someone else. Besides, Frank did four years out in Europe and then the poor sod came home to find his wife had scarpered with another bloke. I thought it might cheer him up a little, sharing a family meal instead of eating all by himself. You're always telling me I should show more charity to others instead of thinking of meself all the time. I'm only following your advice. Frank and me are just friends, by the way, nothing more – as if you'll believe that.'

Mabel scowled at her.

'I'm not interested in your latest conquest at this moment, Vivian. My main worry is how to feed two extra mouths.'

Viv looked puzzled.

'Two?'

'I brought along a friend of Bob's, Aunty Viv,' Kay spoke up.

'Oh, I see.' Her face clouded over in remorse. 'Oh, Mabel, I'd never have brought Frank along if I'd have known that. Yer right, I was sore at you for turning down me offer to make the trifle and bringing someone along unexpectedly was my way of paying yer back. I am sorry, Mabel.'

'Too late now for regrets, we can't exactly ask him to leave. Besides after his doing his bit on our behalf, I've no objections to finding him a seat at our table. But it's a leg of lamb I managed to get, not a whole sheep, so your share of the meat will go to your guest. Mind you,' said Mabel, looking apologetically at her daughter, 'we've Bob's friend to cater for too, so all us women will have to make a sacrifice.'

Kay smiled reassuringly at her. 'That's all right with me, Mam,' she said, hiding her dismay. The roasting lamb smelled absolutely delicious, as had the pork chops the previous night, but it seemed twice in twenty-four hours the smell of meat was the nearest she was going to get to it. With rationing biting deeper now than it had during the war, there was no telling when decent cuts like this would be on her menu again.

Viv leaned over and whispered in Kay's ear so Mabel couldn't hear her, 'Well, that'll teach me for trying to get one over me sister, won't it? Shot meself in the foot, ain't I, and I was so looking forward to a thick juicy slice of that lamb.

'Now there's lots of questions I'm desperate to ask you about how yesterday went, but they'll have to wait for a minute 'cos I just have to go and say hello to the returning hero.' Then she raised her voice and addressed her sister. 'Be back in a minute to give you a hand.'

In the room beyond all the men were gathered around the fireplace, except for Trevor who was sitting in the armchair with his leg resting comfortably on a low stool. They all turned to look at Viv as she entered.

'Beginning to think you weren't coming, our Viv,' Herbie said, beaming across at his sister-in-law affectionately.

'I'd have to be on me deathbed to miss one of our Mabel's dinners,' she chuckled back at him. Her eyes settled on the man to one side of her brother-in-law and her jaw dropped in surprise. 'It's never Bob!' She glanced him over. 'Good Lord, if anyone's in need of a few of our Mabel's stodge puddings, it's you! Well, I know what to do if ever I'm in need of losing a couple of stone – sweat it off in the jungle.' Then she laughed. 'Don't look so petrified, Bob, I ain't gonna bite yer.' She threw her arms around him and gave him a bear hug. 'Welcome home! It's good to have yer back on English soil safe and sound.' Releasing him, her eyes danced merrily. 'Apart from having our work cut out in feeding you back up to what yer was before, which ain't gonna be easy with all this rationing, I see the tide's going out too?'

'Oh, Viv, leave the lad alone,' scolded Herbie playfully. 'He can't help it if he's losing his hair.'

'Sign of virility, so they say,' laughed Viv, her eyes twinkling wickedly.

'More a sign of getting old,' said Herbie mournfully, rubbing his hand over his own sparse offering.

67

Viv moved along to look down at Trevor. 'So how's my favourite nephew? Doing as yer mam sez, I hope?'

He pulled a face. 'As if I have any choice. She's watching me like a hawk. She's tougher than me sergeant was, and should I do 'ote wrong the punishment's worse.'

Viv looked at him meaningfully.

'She wants you to recover fully, Trevor, and is doing her best to make sure you do. Lots of men would give their eye teeth to have a caring mam like you've got, so you be grateful.'

'Just hark at you, Aunty Viv. You and me mam are always bickering about something or another.'

'Eh, just 'cos me and me sister don't see eye to eye on most things, doesn't mean to say we ain't got a great deal of respect for each other. You'd better follow her rules to the letter or you'll have me ter deal with too. Oh, now, about that social do yer've set yer heart on going to a week on Friday night with yer pals ... well, as long as I can sweettalk yer mam into letting yer go, I might be able to borrow a wheelchair for the night.'

Trevor gawped in horror.

'A wheelchair! Thanks for yer trouble, Aunty Viv, but I ain't being seen dead in no wheelchair.'

'Well, yer don't go then. Ain't that right, Herbie?'

He held up his hands in mock surrender. 'Oh, I'm keeping out of this. This sorta thing is Mabel's domain and it's more than my life's worth to interfere.'

Viv shook her head at him. 'Not scared of our

Mabel, are yer, Herbie?'

In honour of the occasion he'd dressed smartly in his one and only suit which held a faint odour of mothballs. Now he puffed out his chest. 'I'm the man of me own household, Viv, as you well know, but I'm sensible enough to realise when to keep me mouth shut and when to open it. That way peace reigns.'

Viv laughed. 'Yer not as daft as yer look, dear brother-in-law, are yer?' She turned back at Trevor then. 'Think about the wheelchair and let me know, and don't leave it too long 'cos I need to organise borrowing it from the old gent down the road as well as coming up with a way to persuade yer mam that a night out would do you good.' She turned to Tony last of all. 'Now, who's going to introduce me to this handsome young man?'

He smiled at her charmingly. 'Tony Cheadle,' he introduced himself, holding his hand out towards her. 'I'm a friend of Bob's.'

Viv shook his hand. 'Pleased to meet you.' She wasn't averse to a man showing his appreciation of her but certainly didn't like the suggestive way this man was looking at her. Pulling her hand from his grasp, she abruptly turned away from him to address them all. 'Now you've all met Frank, I trust, so that's all the introductions done. Who's going to offer me a drink? Have we got anything to drink, Herbie, and I don't mean tea?'

'I managed to get hold of a few bottles of beer to toast Bob's return but that's it, I'm afraid.'

'You did well to get them. If you've some pop I'll have a shandy, Herbie, thank you.'

'I've brought along a bottle of Scotch.'

They all looked at Frank, gawking as he pulled the bottle from his inside jacket pocket. 'Scotch!' they exclaimed in unison.

'How in God's name did you get hold of a bottle of Scotch, Frank?' asked Viv.

'Well ... as yer know, I work as a driver for Carter Patterson, the haulage firm, mostly doing local runs in and around the Midlands. About once a month, though, I get asked to do a long-distance run to a depot storing goods from Scotland and Wales before delivery to the docks. It's all luxury goods for export.'

'And the odd bottle of whisky lands in the driver's lap, so to speak,' piped up Herbie.

'Well, yes, that's about the size of it. It's more a matter of who yer know than what yer know, isn't it?'

'Well, here's to who yer know,' beamed Herbie, taking the bottle from Frank. 'Only don't let on to our Mabel how yer came across it 'cos she doesn't hold with anything that ain't strictly above board. Unlike me who's willing to turn a blind eye in certain circumstances, and this is definitely one of them. Mabel's bound to ask how yer came by it so tell her...' he gave a helpless shrug '... I dunno.'

'He won it in a raffle?' offered Trevor.

'Don't be stupid, Trevor,' snapped his father. 'Yer mam's not daft. She knows as well as the rest of us that all luxury items produced in this country, including bottles of spirits, are for export only, to help pay for clearing up the mess Hitler made.'

'Tell her your boss donated it to you from his private cellar when he heard you'd been invited to a special dinner in honour of a returning soldier from Burma,' suggested Tony.

Viv looked at him, impressed. 'Well, that's a more plausible excuse than even I could come up with.'

He ran his eyes over her then leaned over and whispered seductively in her ear, 'I'm a man of many surprises, Mrs Green. Should you fancy sampling one or two, give me the wink.'

Viv's face darkened at this insulting suggestion. Fixing him with her eyes, in hushed meaningful tones she said, 'My dear young man, you're obviously still wet behind the ears or you'd know that it takes more than the promise of a surprise to seduce a real woman like me. Try the local youth club, your charms might prove more successful with the young girls there.'

His eyes flashed darkly. 'Your loss,' he growled.

Viv smiled sweetly at him. 'I doubt it.' She turned from him then and addressed her brother-in-law. 'Get the glasses, Herbie.'

Mabel soon bustled through carrying a meat plate with the leg of lamb in pride of place on it. She set it down at the head of the table, laying a bone-handled carving knife, a wedding present from her late parents, next to it. 'Right, Herbie, you start carving. The rest of you sit down and me and Kay will bring through your plates. Trevor, stay where you are,' she said to him when she saw her incapacitated son about to struggle up. 'I've a tray set for you.'

'But, Mam...' His mouth clamped shut when

71

he saw the warning look his mother gave him. 'Thanks, Mam,' he mumbled resignedly, settling himself back.

'Yer've surpassed yerself, Mother,' Herbie said to his wife, down at the opposite end of the table, as he tucked in with relish. 'Wouldn't get a better meal at a fancy restaurant, cooked by one of them posh chefs and costing more than a week's wage.'

'Your husband's right, Mrs Stafford,' said Frank approvingly. 'The meal is delicious.'

As they all expressed their appreciation of Mabel's efforts, she puffed out her chest proudly. Eking the food out to include two extra guests had not been easy but she had managed and much to her relief the leg of lamb had gone further than she had hoped, largely down to Herbie's expert carving. All the women had a small portion on their plate. 'I'm glad yer enjoying it.'

Conversation around the table flowed congenially, the family, out of respect for Bob, making sure any topic discussed was well away from his time in Burma. Kay was pleased to note that Bob seemed a little more at ease than he had been when they had first arrived, obviously relieved the reintroductions were over. It must have been somewhat daunting for him, meeting all her family together again when he'd barely got to know them five years before. Trevor he hadn't met at all.

What most concerned her, though, was that the Bob she had tearfully waved off five years ago had been a very sociable sort, possessing a ready wit. He'd been the first to start a conversation, never afraid to offer a knowledgeable opinion on a variety of topical matters. The Bob she had welcomed home seemed to have left those qualities back in the jungle. During all the time he'd been in her parents' house he'd hardly spoken unless asked a direct question and then his answers had been short, seemingly reluctantly given. But it must be overwhelming for him, being the centre of attention at a social gathering like this, the sort of occasion Bob had not experienced for such a long time. It wasn't as though any of her family was the shy retiring sort either. At the moment her father and Aunty Viv were having a rapid exchange of opinions, each adamant on getting their own point of view across, the original subject matter completely lost track of. It was difficult for anyone else to get a word in, let alone Bob.

As Mabel rose to clear the plates to make way for the pudding, Herbie asked Bob, 'So, what are yer plans?'

He looked across at his father-in-law blankly. 'Plans, Mr Stafford?'

'Job wise, son. Yer told me and Mother when yer came to ask for our Kay's hand that yer aim was to use yer trade as a cabinet maker to start yer own business. Your skills will be in great demand now, with all this rebuilding needed. If yer not of a mind to start up on yer own just yet, yer'll be able to pick and choose who yer work for, with your credentials.'

'Oh, give the lad a break, Herbie,' said Viv, her mouth watering at the sight of the scrumptious-looking apple pie that Mabel had brought through, and far from being a greedy person nevertheless trying to work out if there'd be enough for second helpings. 'He's not long landed back on British soil and his years away weren't exactly a holiday, were they?'

'That may be so but he's a living to provide for our Kay. He promised to look after her and as her father I'm holding him to that promise.'

'And I intend to do my best for her, Mr Stafford. It's just that...' Bob gave a shrug, flashed a quick look at Kay, then back at his father-in-law. 'I don't know if my old trade is for me anymore. Don't know if I'm up to it, in fact.'

'Oh, Bob, of course you are,' Kay said with conviction.

He pulled a face. 'Five years is a long time to be out of it.'

Herbie tutted. 'Be like riding a bike for someone like you. You'd pick it up again just like that,' he said, clicking his fingers.

Bob gave a deep sigh. 'If you want the truth, Mr Stafford, I fancy a change.'

'But that's just the way you're feeling now. You'll change yer mind later.'

'Dad's right,' said Kay. 'You've hardly unpacked yet.'

'Mmm ... maybe. But for the time being I thought I'd just have a look around and see what's going that takes my fancy.'

Kay was surprised to hear him talking like this after the way he'd always enthused so much about his dream of working for himself at a trade he loved. But as his wife it was up to her to show

74

him her support in whatever he chose to do. 'As long as you're happy in what you do, I'm happy too, Bob.'

'My firm's looking for lorry drivers but it means you're away from home some nights while on long-distance runs,' piped up Frank.

'I quite like the sound of a driving job but unfortunately I don't drive,' said Bob.

'I could enquire at the factory where I work,' offered Viv. 'They might need someone in the stores or something.'

'Bob's a skilled tradesman and worthy of more than a labouring job,' said Herbie scornfully. 'You could retrain for another trade, I suppose, but I can't see the point when you've got a perfectly good one already.'

''Til Bob fancies going back to his tools again, what about on the Mail with us, Dad?' Trevor called over. 'As long as it ain't my job he gets. I want that for meself as soon as I'm fit enough to return to work.'

'Then you'd better do as yer mam sez or you'll never be up to it,' his father warned. He turned his attention back to Bob. 'I could put in a good word for you if you want me to? Can't promise what you'd get offered, though.'

Bob nodded. 'I'd thank you for doing what you can for me, Mr Stafford.'

'I'll have a word tomorrow.'

'If anyone can get you a job at the Mail, it's my dad,' said Kay. 'He got me in when the men all went off to war.' She felt positive this job would only be interim because she felt once Bob had accustomed himself to life back home he'd soon

75

feel the desire to pick up the tools of his trade again.

'I might as well tell yer about my surprise now, Bob,' said Herbie, looking pleased with himself.

Bob looked warily at him. 'Surprise, Mr Stafford?'

'Don't look so worried, lad, you'll like what I'm going to tell you, I know yer will. After you showing such an interest in my allotment when you came to ask for our Kay's hand, I thought it'd be a nice homecoming present if I got you one. I had it confirmed last week that one had come vacant not far from me own plot, and a few strings were pulled because of my standing on the Allotment Committee. So, I'm pleased to tell yer, lad, it's yours.'

Bob looked taken aback. 'Oh, well ... that's very good of yer, Mr Stafford. Not that I know much about gardening. If anything, in fact.'

'Let me tell you, son, a man's life ain't complete without his having a garden. Nothing more satisfying to a man than seeing his own hard work served up on his plate by his dear wife. Yer'll soon pick it up. Anything yer want to know, I can teach you. And don't worry yer head about gardening tools either. I've got a spare spade and fork already waiting in my shed for yer.'

'I appreciate all the trouble you've obviously gone to, Mr Stafford...'

'Think nothing of it. Yer family now, lad, and families help each other. When yer fancy going down, Kay will point you in the right direction and just ask anyone who's there for Harry Gilbert's old plot. I suggest you give it a good winter dig over soon as possible before the frosts really set in, and I've already had a supply of good 'oss muck delivered for yer, so give that a good spread over and come spring the soil will be just right for yer to start yer planting. I'll do me best to keep you and our Kay supplied with fresh veg until yer can support yerselves.'

Herbie then turned his attention to Tony. 'So what about yerself, lad?' he asked. 'Will you be looking for work in these parts or are yer thinking of going back to yer own home town?'

'I wasn't sure what I'd be doing when Bob kindly suggested I should stop with him and your lovely daughter for a while, but I have to say this town is growing on me. I think I might stick around for a while.'

This was not good news for Kay. She appreciated that Bob needed friends but was privately sure that the likes of Tony was not the best sort to have. If he was staying around, she hoped that top of his list was finding somewhere else to stay.

It seemed as though her aunt read her mind when she said, 'You'll need lodgings if yer staying. I know a woman who takes in boarders and she's clean and reasonable.'

'I'll bear that in mind,' he replied, smiling at her winningly.

Herbie was looking at Kay thoughtfully. 'I hope you've got used to the idea that yer days at the Mail are numbered, lovey? You've been luckier than most women and clung on to your job, but not for much longer, I fear. It's only right when the men need their jobs back.'

Yes, it was only right that she should relinquish

77

her job to the man whose place she'd filled while he'd been away fighting in the war, but that didn't mean to say Kay was happy about it. 'I should really start looking for something else, shouldn't I?' she mused.

'I should think not,' said Mabel, slicing the pie and putting portions into dishes. 'Your job in future is to stay at home looking after your husband.'

Although Kay was looking forward to her wifely duties she wondered how she would take to staying at home all day without the camaraderie of her work colleagues.

'Maybe Kay doesn't want to stay at home and just be a housewife,' put in Viv.

Mabel turned on her. 'Now don't you start putting no more high-faluting ideas into my daughter's head, our Viv! Her place is at home looking after her husband. When is she going to have time to go out to work with all she'll have to do? More than a full-time job it is, looking after a family. Now who's for apple pie?'

After the meal was over Viv was desperate to speak to her niece in private, to catch up on how yesterday had gone. She suggested they both do the dishes while Mabel took a well-earned rest. 'Go on, I won't break yer best pots,' she hissed at her sister. 'Fer God's sake, can't yer trust me to do anything? I'm thirty-five not a silly kid.'

Mabel looked at her accusingly.

'You broke me milk jug that time...'

'That was over ten years ago and it was chipped and cracked already when I caught it on the tap.

It was an accident, for God's sake, and I replaced it.'

'Not with the same one, though.'

'No, 'cos they'd stopped making that sort during the Napoleonic Wars. Oh, Mabel, take a well-earned rest and have a chat with the fellas. Let me and Kay clear up, it's the least we can do after the wonderful meal you cooked for us.'

Mabel knew that she wasn't going to beat her sister on this one. She was feeling fatigued after her long morning of slaving over a hot stove and the worry of gathering together all the food which had been no easy accomplishment. A sit down sounded most welcome. 'You will take care, 'cos that dinner service was a wedding present?'

Kay took hold of her mother's arm and steered her towards the back room where all the men were gathered. 'As soon as we've done the dishes, I'll bring you a nice cuppa through.'

Mabel sighed resignedly. 'All right.'

'Your mother is the limit sometimes,' moaned Viv as she poured scalding water from the kettle into the pot sink – the Staffords' aluminium washing up bowl having been given towards the war effort several years previously – and then added some cold courtesy of the huge brass tap before she rubbed Sunlight washing soap into it by way of detergent. Refilling the kettle, she put it back on the stove to boil for the next lot of washing water. 'She just doesn't believe anyone does anything as well as she does on the domestic front.' She placed a dripping plate on the wooden draining board for Kay to dry. 'Anyway, enough of our Mabel's expert housekeeping abilities ... I want to know what it feels like for you having Bob home again?

'I have to say I got a shock when I first clapped eyes on him, as I expect you did. He can hardly be compared to some poor sod unlucky enough to have landed in Belsen, but he's lost a fair bit of weight. Anyway it's as I told him, that's n'ote that can't be put right with a few good meals down him.' She paused and looked at her niece expectantly. 'So, happy now yer've got him back, are yer?'

Kay smiled as she put the dried plate down and picked up another wet one. 'Oh, yes, Aunty Viv, that goes without saying. But...' Her voice trailed off and she gave a sigh.

Viv looked at her in concern. 'But what?'

'Well, up to now we've had no time to ourselves due to a certain lack of thought on our *guest*'s behalf.'

Viv pulled a face. 'Oh, yes, him. I couldn't believe it when I found out he was stopping with you. Two's company, three's a crowd, ain't it? When's he going?'

'Hopefully tomorrow. I've no idea where, and I don't really care as long as he goes. I should be grateful for what he did in saving Bob's life, I know, but I can't say as I've taken to him. The way he acts, you'd think he was head of the house, not Bob.'

'Mmm, that man does rather think he's God's gift, I can't say as I took to him meself, but as you say, out of respect for Bob it's a case of put up and shut up. But only until tomorrow then he'll be out of your hair.' Viv screwed her face up thoughtfully. 'I wonder what did happen out in Burma?'

'I'd dearly like to know myself, feel rather hurt in fact that Bob can't open up to me, his own wife, about it, but it must have been something dreadful.'

'Yes, it must have, and I'm sure he'll tell yer when he's ready to. I only had the privilege of meeting him fleetingly a couple of times before he went away but even I can see how it's all affected him. He was always so chatty, eager to get on with things like young chaps are. Now ... well, he's certainly quietened down a lot but that's not a bad thing in a man, Kay. War or no war, Bob had to mature sometime. It's just that instead of your seeing a gradual change in him as it happens, you're seeing it all together after it's happened, if you get me drift? Anyway, how was last night?' she asked, winking knowingly at her niece.

Kay felt the red flush of embarrassment creeping up her neck. Her aunt was never backwards in asking questions others would feel strictly taboo. Her mother would never dream of doing such a thing. Kay felt she could talk to her aunt about anything but just couldn't bring herself to divulge that last night had not exactly been the romantic re-enactment of her honeymoon she had hoped for. 'It was fine,' she said breezily.

Viv knew instinctively that Kay was not being truthful. 'That good, eh?' she said sardonically.

Kay sighed. 'Nothing gets past you, does it, Aunty Viv? Oh, all right, I might as well tell you because you won't give up until I do. As soon as

81

dinner was over Tony suggested a drink at the pub and they didn't come back until closing time. Both of them were as drunk as lords and passed out in the armchairs.'

Viv tutted disdainfully. 'Oh, typical blokes that. Couple of pints and all sense and reason leave them. If that had happened to me after not seeing my old man for five years, I would certainly have been spitting feathers. Still, look on the bright side, you've still got tonight to look forward to. Well, of course, that's providing they only sample that bottle of whisky Frank brought along and not demolish it.' She mused thoughtfully, 'That was generous of him, wasn't it, considering he could have sold it on for a princely sum?'

Kay looked at her keenly.

'Developing a fancy for Mr Ambleside, Aunty Viv?'

She looked at Kay full on, cocking one eyebrow, a secret smile twitching her lips.

'I might be. The more I see of Frank, the more apparent it is that he does have some good qualities. He's asked me a couple of times to go for a drink with him without the rest of the crowd and I've always fobbed him off, but I just might accept the next time he does.'

Just then Mabel appeared and Viv eyed her scathingly. 'Come to check if I've broken anything, sister dear? Well, hard luck, 'cos I ain't.' Then she added, a spark of amusement twitching her lips, 'Not yet anyway but there's still time.'

Mabel looked at her askance. 'I never know whether you're being serious or not. All I can say is that there seems to be a lot of chatting and not much washing up going on in this kitchen. I could have been finished and made a dozen cakes by now, the amount of time it's taking you two to wash a few pots.' She picked up a drying cloth. 'I'd better give you a hand or you'll both be at it until next Sunday week. Besides, Herbie is on his soap box about the state of the country and his views on putting it all right and I've listened to it all before so this is my chance of escape. That Tony seems a fine chap, Kay, very charming I must say. It's nice for Bob to have a friend in Leicester. Tony and Frank seem to be getting on well too, I noticed they were having a chat together as I left to come and see what you two were up to.

'I'm not convinced there's nothing going on between you and Frank, our Viv. I caught the way he looks at yer. You could do a lot worse in my opinion. He's presentable, got a good job ... a very generous boss anyway. Wasn't that nice of him, giving that bottle of Scotch to us in honour of Bob's return to the family? Everyone who wanted one has had a shot from it and I've told Herbie to put the bottle away for the next special occasion. Well, if I left it to him the whole lot would be demolished and there's no telling when we'd ever see the likes of that again. And don't look at me like that, our Viv, I'm not being mean, I'm being practical.'

Viv shook her head disdainfully. 'We could all be dead tomorrow, our Mabel.'

She glared at her sister. 'And we could be wanting to toast the news there's a baby on the way and nothing to do it with,' she snapped, flashing a meaningful glance in Kay's direction.

Viv tutted. 'Oh, give 'em chance, Mabel, fer Christ's sake. Bob's only been back a day.'

'Nature doesn't take such things into account. Careful with that glass, Viv, it's one of a set Herbie bought me for our first anniversary. You're handling it like it's made of lead, not glass.'

'I *was* being careful. Oh, finish the dishes off yerself,' Viv snapped, throwing the dishcloth into the sink and splashing dirty water over the three of them. 'I'm off to be in company where I'm more appreciated.'

After hurriedly drying her hands on the roller towel on the back of the pantry door, she stormed off to join the others.

Mabel calmly took over her sister's abandoned task.

'Right, let's get these dishes finished up properly then you can make that cuppa you promised me, our Kay.'

The family get together broke up just after seven. As soon as the Cliftons arrived back home their guest looked at his watch and said to Bob, 'Sunday night, eh? The most boring of the week. There's nothing to do, not even a pub open to get a drink.' He looked at Kay, pulling a disgruntled face. 'We could have had a bit of a party if your mother hadn't been so mean over that bottle of whisky.' He gave a fed-up sigh. 'I think I'll take a walk around the area and get my bearings. See if there's anything worth seeing.' He looked at Bob meaningfully. 'I expect you two are in for an early night as you've five years of lost time to make up for,' he said, winking at his pal suggestively. 'I'll need your key to let meself in as more than likely I won't get back until after yer've gone to bed.'

Kay picked up the key she'd had cut for Bob from off the top of the sideboard and handed it to him. Despite smarting from his embarrassing comment she was delighted that at long last it seemed she and Bob were going to get some time on their own. 'I'm out at work early in the morning for my shift in the sorting office. If you sleep on the sofa I'll try not to disturb you. I trust you can see to breakfast for yourself unless you're up before I go,' she said to Tony.

Tony looked at her in surprise. 'I don't see the point in getting up early unnecessarily. I had a bellyful of hardly any sleep during my years in the Army. I do need to sort out my sleeping arrangements, though, which I'm going to do tomorrow. You don't mind, do you?'

Mind? She was jubilant Tony was going to find himself somewhere else to stay 'No, of course not,' she said, hoping she did not sound too enthusiastic at the prospect of his leaving. 'A floor or sofa is all right as a stopgap but a man needs a proper bed to sleep in.'

He smiled at her winningly. 'My sentiments exactly, Mrs Clifton. Right, I'll leave you two lovebirds to it.'

It seemed strange to Kay finally to be alone with Bob for the first time in a proper married couple's situation. Unlike yesterday, he now seemed to be making himself very much at home. She watched as he switched on the wireless set then settled himself comfortably in the armchair by the fire, pulling off his shoes which reminded her she needed to see if she could exchange the slippers she had bought him for a larger size if possible. She noticed he had left his coat on the back of a dining chair and his discarded shoes by the side of his armchair and automatically picked them up to put away. She had banked the fire up before they had gone out and it had burned low. It struck her that Bob appeared either not to notice it needed replenishing or else to be waiting for her to do it. This fact rather took her aback. She vehemently hoped that Bob had not turned into the lazy sort as although she took her wifely duties very seriously, she wasn't going to turn into a drudge. But then, she reasoned with herself, he'd only been home a day and she shouldn't be too quick to judge him.

'Can I get you anything?' she asked him, smiling warmly.

'I could do with a cuppa. Maybe a sandwich later. At the moment I'm still full from your mother's dinner.'

'Did you enjoy today? Meeting all my family properly?'

'Yes, but it's nice to get home though. Nothing like your own fireside, is there?'

She felt so happy to hear him say that. 'No, there isn't.'

Bob was fiddling with the turning knob on the wireless. 'Where is that damned station?' he grumbled. 'I'm looking forward to listening to the *Arthur Askey Show*, he doesn't half make me laugh! I've missed listening to the wireless so much while I was in foreign parts. We sometimes managed to get the news on the Home Service but that wasn't very often.'

Kay was slightly surprised by his choice of listening as she had been looking forward to listening with him to the Sunday evening play, which she had regularly done with her mother and father, all enjoying discussing its merits afterwards as they had drunk their cocoa before going to bed. All that time Kay had been desperate for the day it would be she and Bob airing their views together. But her husband was master in his own house and if he wanted to be entertained by Arthur Askey and his cronies tonight then she was happy to go along with that.

For the rest of the evening, like any other typical married couple, they sat opposite each other in the armchairs by the fire, Bob engrossed in the wireless, she listening along too but also knitting a winter jumper for him with wool unravelled from aged garments given to her by an old lady whose husband had died. On hearing that Kay's own husband was on his way home, the old girl had thought she could make good use of them. Every now and again Kay would take her eyes off her knitting to glance at her husband from under her lashes and a warm glow filled her at the sight of the contented expression on his face. She would do her best to make sure that look stayed there until the day death parted them.

The tin clock on the mantelpiece showed the time to be ten o'clock when Bob leaned over and switched off the wireless then gave a yawn and stretched himself. 'Well, it's been a long day, I'm off up to bed.'

Kay's heart lurched. A whirl of excitement began in her stomach. This was the time she had dreamed of for so long. It was upon her at last and miraculously their guest had not returned. He'd obviously found something or someone to occupy him, or maybe out of respect for them both, which she found a little surprising if indeed it was true, he had purposely stayed out so they had the house to themselves – whatever, she was grateful for his absence. She ran a mental checklist. She'd set the table for breakfast; her clothes were hanging ready to put on for work in the morning; shoes were polished; the rubbish had been put out in the dustbin, milk bottle on the doorstep and the bedding for Tony neatly piled by the stair door for him to make up his bed on either the sofa or in the back bedroom. She smiled over at Bob as she rolled the excess wool back on to the ball and stuck her needles through it before putting it away in her knitting bag at the side of her chair. 'Well, I'm ready if you are. If you check the house is secure, I'll go up and make myself ready.'

In the dimly lit bedroom, a shadowy light cast by the flickering gas mantle, she found she was trembling in excited anticipation as she fumbled to undo the buttons on her blouse. She heard the door open behind her, Bob's footsteps enter the room and the door click shut as he closed it behind him. She turned and looked at him as he walked past her round to the other side of the bed and turned the mantle to its lowest. With his back to her, he began to undress. Still fumbling with her own clothes, Kay remembered their wedding night when as soon as they had entered the hotel room, paid for as a wedding present by her Aunt Vivian, they had embraced passionately and in their urgency to consummate their union almost ripped each other's clothes off, neither of them concerned in the slightest that the room was still brightly lit.

She watched as, now dressed in his pyjamas, Bob slipped into bed, still with his back to her, and laid his head on the pillow, pulling the covers up around him. After putting on her flimsy nightdress, Kay doused the light completely and slipped under the covers. She lay for several minutes staring up at the ceiling, wondering if Bob had gone to sleep. Then she realised he must be as keyed up as she was over their first time together after such a long gap. Turning towards him, she laid a reassuring hand on his arm, hoping it would let him know she understood how he felt. Her heart began to pound as he turned to face her.

The next thing she knew he had pushed her flat and was on top of her, one hand groping beneath her nightdress, wrenching it upwards to expose her nakedness. Then his hand clamped her breast, kneading it hard. Then he was kissing her. It was a rough kiss, urgent, his breath coming fast. In seconds he had spread her legs and was entering her, pumping hard. He gave a loud groan and a shudder, then lay still for a moment on top of her, panting, before he rolled off to turn over and almost immediately start to snore.

Kay lay frozen in shock at what had just happened. It had been so quick, not at all mirroring their wedding night. Then Bob had been passionate yet very considerate, making it clear he wanted her to feel as fulfilled by their lovemaking as he did. Tonight he had shown no consideration for her whatsoever, just satisfied his own needs, leaving her feeling empty. But worse than that, neither his kiss nor his touch had evoked any emotion in her.

What was wrong with her? Why hadn't she felt even a stirring of any kind when he had touched her?

But then, Kay reasoned with herself, it had all happened so quickly she'd hardly had chance to catch her breath, let alone allow his advances to rouse passion within her. Bob had been her one and only love and as a result she was no expert in the ways of men's sexual behaviour but even she realised that after five years of living a monk-like existence his need of her in that way must have been so great that he had become consumed by it and didn't realise how selfishly he was acting towards her. Despite still feeling robbed of her own fulfilment, she felt sure that the next time he would return to his loving, caring self. Rearranging her nightdress, Kay turned over to snuggle up against his back, closed her eyes and before long was sound asleep.

CHAPTER FOUR

Eunice Smith, a pretty woman of Kay's age, looking very much the harassed young mother she was, having risen early to get her husband's breakfast before he set off to work then attended to her eighteen-month-old toddler before hastily dressing herself, waved in delight when she spotted Kay coming down the road towards her.

'Oi, Kay,' Eunice called out as she hurried up to her. 'I've been thinking about you all weekend. I wanted to pop around and see you both, welcome Bob home at least, but George wouldn't let me. Said you needed some time to yourselves and there were plenty of chances in the future for all that kind of thing once he'd had time to settle. So how did it all go then? Bob arrived back safely, did he? What's it feel like to have him home again? Come on then, spill the beans,' she urged.

Kay was delighted to bump into the woman who had been her closest friend since they had met at the age of fourteen, both on their way home after starting work that same day, Kay as a junior in a shoe shop, Eunice as a waitress in the British Home Stores cafeteria. They had sat down together on the crowded bus and as a conversation was struck up it became apparent to them both that there was an affinity between them. They quickly discovered they had much in common such as a mutual liking for music and recreational pursuits like visits to the cinema and nights at the local youth club. They soon became inseparable friends, supporting each other through the trials and tribulations of their lives ever since.

Kay laughed, 'I will if you give me chance to get a word in! Yes, Bob is back safe and sound and it's good to have him here, as if you needed to ask.' She frowned at her friend. 'What are you doing out at this time in the morning?'

'Oh, me mam heard that Home and Colonial have had a delivery of tins and I've left Joanie with her so I can get in the queue.'

'Tins of what?' Kay asked interestedly.

Eunice shrugged. 'Dunno. I've got to the stage when I ain't fussy, Kay. Fruit, tomatoes, Spam, pilchards ... I don't care, I want some, and if it means being up before the crack of dawn then so be it.'

'Shame I've to go to work or I'd have joined you. I doubt there'll be any left by the time my shift finishes.' A helping of tinned tomatoes to accompany the cheese and potato pie she planned to make tonight for dinner would have helped to perk up its blandness. It suddenly hit Kay that despite the wartime rationing she had always appreciated the appetising meals her mother had put before her, but hadn't fully appreciated the effort it had taken her to do so. In all fairness to her mother, Mabel had tried to warn Kay that she was going to find it extremely difficult to work while also being responsible for looking after her husband and house, but since she'd learned of Bob's return she had been too wrapped up in the excitement of having him back and getting a house together to think any further than that. Her mother had said yesterday that being a housewife was a full-time job and Kay was just realising that her mother was right. But regardless, until Bob started work, which she hoped he would shortly, her wage was all they had coming in so she would somehow have to cope.

'I'd get you some tins if I could,' said Eunice. 'That's if the rumour is true and they have had a delivery. But yer know what sticklers they are for the rules: one tin of each item per person, and first come, first served.'

Kay smiled appreciatively at her friend. 'I know you would, Eunice. More than likely I will be wasting my time but I'll go straight after my shift. You never know, I might be lucky.'

'Oh, well, now Bob's back you'll be giving up yer job to look after him, then yer can be first in any queue should yer want to. Does he still plan to set up on his own as a joiner like you told me he dreamed of doing?'

'That is his aim but at the moment he just wants to get himself settled. Dad's going to have a word at the Mail and see if he can get Bob something there for the meantime. And knowing what kind of man Bob is, I expect he'll be out looking to see what he can get for himself.'

'Well, I'm sure the likes of your Bob will be snapped up, but even if he doesn't get set on for a few weeks you'll be all right 'cos you can live off his gratuity payment. Luckily my George's old job was still there for him so we used most of his payment when it came through to get a couple of pieces of utility furniture for our house, some clothes for us and some stuff for the baby.'

Kay was looking at her, puzzled. 'Gratuity payment?'

'Yes, the money the government is giving all men leaving the services on top of their pay. I think it's a pittance really after risking their lives like they did, but I suppose it's better than a kick up the arse. The amount depends on the rank of the soldier. My George and your Bob were corporals so they get seventy-five quid.' Eunice pulled a face. 'Lots of wives, I expect, will never get to find out about this payment and those men will have a high old time getting rid of it over the counter of the pub or doing whatever else takes their fancy. Thank God we ain't got that sort, eh? Anyway ours came through a couple of weeks ago.' She paused and looked at her friend eagerly. 'Have you had yours yet, and if so what do you plan to spend it on?'

Kay knew nothing about a government gratuity payment being awarded to all demobbed service men, Bob had never mentioned a word to her about it, but then in fairness the subject of money had not been raised between them yet. He would tell her when the subject was discussed.

'Oh, I don't know what we're going to spend ours on yet, we haven't decided.'

'Well, if yer want, someone to come and help you when you do decide, let me know. So everything went all right on Saturday then?'

'Bob's train was late and...' Kay momentarily paused, not really wanting to go into the saga of their guest at this moment in time, knowing that although Eunice would have accepted her husband's friend in her home out of respect for him, she would not have stood for that friend treating her with the disrespect Tony was showing Kay. Eunice was the sort instantly to stand up for herself whereas Kay preferred to do all she could to keep the peace first and only made a stand when there was no other option left open to her. Maybe this was cowardly but it was her nature and she couldn't change that. Besides, there was no point in telling Eunice about Tony as thankfully he'd be settled in his new place by the time she went home tonight. 'Yes, it all went well, thank you.' She looked at her friend thoughtfully. 'Eunice, er ... how was it for you when George first came back?'

Eunice frowned at her quizzically.

'Wadda yer mean exactly?'

Kay gave a shrug.

'Well ... did you just pick up from where you left off before he went away?'

Eunice shrugged. 'Like an idiot, I expected everything to fall straight back into place but I soon realised that wasn't going to happen and George was going to take time to settle. If I'm honest, it was quite a hard time really, the first few weeks anyway.'

Kay looked at her, aghast.

'You never said anything to me, Eunice. You seemed so happy whenever I visited.'

'I was happy ... well, for the most part I was. I'd got George back and that was everything to me. Look, I never said anything to you 'cos you'd enough on yer plate wondering about Bob, and your Trevor had been badly injured, and you was so worried about him my problems seemed trivial in comparison. But being's you've asked now, I'll tell yer.

'When he first came back George was ever so restless, couldn't sit still for two minutes, was up and down like a yoyo, and every time there was the slightest noise, like a car backfiring in the street or summat was dropped on the floor, he'd leap out of his skin and make a grab for his rifle – which of course weren't there – and then he'd go into a mad panic and I had a hell of a job to calm him. He still does that sometimes but it ain't nearly so bad as it was when he first came home. It took him ages to sleep comfortably in our bed again after sleeping on the ground for so long. Getting him to change his underwear regular was another matter. He'd go days sometimes or even weeks without being able to wash those he had on when he was on the front line, or himself for that matter. Apparently all the blokes stank to high heaven but they were just used to it. He washes regular now, let me tell yer.

'I was upset too because he couldn't remember the date of my birthday or our anniversary. But it wasn't just his memory that played him tricks 'cos mine did too. I could've sworn blind on me mother's life liver was his favourite and cooked it for him as his homecoming meal, then he told me he hated it and ended up with bread and chips. He actually accused me of having another man keeping me company while he was away and said that's how come I'd made the mistake. Stupid man! I had hell of a job convincing him otherwise.

'I have ter say that in all honesty when he first came back it was very hard to get used to having him around again. I'd got into me own routine and then I had him to consider. As for my poor George, well, he came home to a child and hadn't a clue how to be a father to her. He quickly had to learn. He also had to adjust back to working normal hours. He never said anything to me ... yer know what men are like, don't like to show they ain't coping in case we think they ain't masculine enough ... but I think he found difficulty settling back into the routine. Yeah, it was hard to start with, but we're okay now.' She looked at Kay in concern. 'You and Bob are all right, ain't yer?'

Her friend's response had made Kay feel better about things. 'Yes, we're fine, thank you,' she said, smiling warmly.

Eunice winked at her knowingly. 'Yer never know, Kay, yer might have a little one to look after soon like I do, then yer'll have yer hands full, believe me.'

Kay tutted. 'Oh, you sound just like my mother. She's hinting about babies already. I'd like at least two little miniatures of myself and Bob to run after, but I'd like some time with him first, to do the things we never seemed to have time to do before. When he was on a pass it always seemed to us that no sooner had he got to Leicester than it was time for him to catch his transport back to camp. I'm so looking forward just to going to the pictures and seeing the whole film through or else a concert at the De Montfort Hall. And maybe a trip, a week even, to the seaside and not having to part afterwards but actually going home together.'

Eunice smiled at her in understanding. 'I was luckier with my George. We never got much courting time either but at least he was based in Leicester, not Northampton like Bob, and I was luckier with his posting to Europe – if yer can say any posting was lucky, that is. But at least George got home on leave a couple of times, and that's how I fell for my Joan.' She gave a sigh. 'I sometimes wonder how we got through it, Kay, living with all the worry of whether we'd ever see our men again, all the time missing 'em like hell, but it's over now, thank God. I couldn't live through that ever again.' Eunice smiled. 'George is looking forward to meeting Bob, by the way. I've told him that it's the rule that him and my best friend's husband get on. Mind you, my George gets on with anyone.' She paused for a moment, looking thoughtful. 'I wonder what happened to Bob's mate Mike, the chap who was with him in the café when you first met him?'

'Mike Newcome? Oh, I don't know, I'll have to ask,' mused Kay. 'Bob did mention in one of his letters that on reaching India their unit was split and sent off to different garrisons, but that's all I know. He was a nice chap was Mike. I hope he came out of it all right.'

'I liked him too – shame he didn't fancy me as much as I did him. As yer know, I was quite upset about that at the time but I soon got over him when I met my George. I'd still like to know what happened to Mike, though. What about Saturday, Kay? You and Bob come round then and the men can get to know each other. I'll do a bit of supper. Hopefully I'll get some tins today. One might be Spam, or if we're very lucky corned beef, and I can make some sandwiches.'

Kay smiled. 'Sounds good to me. I'll ask Bob and let you know but I'm sure he'll be delighted to accept. How's my little god-daughter, by the way?'

Eunice pulled a face. 'A bloody handful! She's just about walking and I can't turn my back for a second as she's into everything. I bet my mother's got her work cut out with her this morning 'cos she was right grizzly when I left her. Cutting her back teeth, I think. Mind you, they seem to behave better for their grannies than they do their mothers as me mam sez Joanie's never any trouble when she's got her.' Eunice gave a tender smile. 'I wouldn't be without her, though. We're trying for another. George would like a boy but neither of us is bothered as long as it's healthy.'

'Oh, I'll keep my fingers crossed for you,' Kay said sincerely. She suddenly realised that time was wearing on. 'I'd better get off or I'll be late. I'll pop over one night later in the week to arrange about Saturday, I'm really looking forward to it.'

A while later, her face screwed up, Kay was trying to decipher the address on a letter, one of a pile she was sorting, putting them into their various street-labelled pigeon holes to bundle together later for the postmen to deliver. During her time in the job Kay had prided herself on

99

honing her ability to read the worst scrawl but this one was so bad it was eluding even her. She turned to the colleague beside her. 'Harry, what street do you think that says?'

Peering at it through his pebble-lensed glasses, Harry Dinsman shook his head and said, 'Your guess is as good as mine, me duck. Looks like it's in foreign to me. Stick it in the Double Dutch tray along with the others for us to try and work out later. I dunno,' he grumbled as he resumed his own task, to any onlooker seeming like he was dealing a pack of cards as he expertly scanned addresses and tossed envelope into the right slot, 'people complain bitterly about late deliveries, but if they took the trouble to write legibly in the first place we could have got it out on time instead of us having to hold on to it to work out the address.'

Just then Hubert Goodman, the foreman of the sorting department, joined them. He was a middle-aged and portly man, kindly in nature and well respected by those under his charge. He was known to them affectionately as Goody. 'Morning, Kay ducky,' he addressed her, puffing on a cigarette. 'Saturday went all right, I trust, and yer husband's back in the fold safe and sound?'

'Yes, he is, thank you, Mr Goodman. And I want to thank you again very much for arranging my compassionate leave.'

'Oh, ducky, that's the least the Royal Mail could do in the circumstances. You've been a credit to this department all the time you've been here and you've done your job as well as any man

100

could. You Staffords have served the mail service admirably, what with your contribution and yer dad having over thirty years' service and, may I add, putting in extra duty as a volunteer fireman during the war as well as making sure his post round didn't suffer. And yer brother's to follow in his father's footsteps. I trust young Trevor is making a good recovery and will be back with us shortly?'

'He will as long as he does what my mother tells him. He's very restless, Mr Goodman, not making a good patient. I know he can't wait to get back to work.'

'That's good to hear.' He shuffled uncomfortably on his feet then, took a last drag from the butt end of his cigarette and dropped it to the floor, grinding it out with his foot before bringing his eyes back to rest on Kay. 'This is not easy for me, ducky, but, well ... maybe now yer husband's back, the timing is right.'

Kay instinctively knew what was coming and was torn between being glad that she could now concentrate on being a full-time housewife and sad because she would miss her job and the friends she had made during her time at the Royal Mail. 'The man I replaced is coming back to work, I take it, Mr Goodman?'

'That's exactly it. Fred Nuttall didn't have an easy war, spent most of it in a prison camp. To be honest, he's lost that much weight I hardly recognised him and his hair's all white – the man's only thirty-five! But apparently the doctors have signed him off now as fit enough to work, though whether he is or not remains to be seen.

I doubt anyone ever recovers completely from what that man's been through. Still, he ain't on his own, there's thousands like him and it's up to us that stayed at home to help them adjust back as best we can. Fred's just left after having an interview with Mr Craven, the Sorting Office Manager. They've arranged he'll start back tomorrow. I know it's short notice, Kay, but then you always knew your job here was temporary. Come and see me before you clock off.'

She gave him a wan smile. 'I will, Mr Goodman.'

Harry looked at her sadly as Hubert departed. 'I'll miss yer, Kay lovey. Fred Nuttall's a good bloke but he ain't so pretty to look at as you.'

She smiled at him. 'Thanks, Harry. I shall miss working with you too. I suppose I've been lucky, I'm one of the last women to leave the Royal Mail.' Now Eunice had told her of the gratuity payment she wasn't so concerned about the immediate need for Bob to find work. Besides, he had never come across as the kind to rest on his laurels and she guessed he would be out today in search of work and hopefully have some good news to tell her when she got home. There was also the fact that her father was making enquiries here at the Mail and that might bear fruit also. That would mean the lump sum Bob received from the government could be put towards his starting his own business when the time came.

The rest of the day was marred for Kay. She was having difficulty accepting that this was the last time she would stand in her spot in this very busy department, doing a job she had been proud to do, helping to keep the postal service running smoothly during difficult times. But it seemed her job now was to care for her husband and their home. At clocking off time, having said emotional goodbyes and received well wishes from her colleagues, she made her way to Hubert Goodman's office.

Smiling warmly, he rose from his battered chair behind a cluttered desk as she knocked and entered. 'Ah, I'm glad yer remembered to call by.' As he walked around his desk to approach her, he picked up a small wrapped parcel which he handed to her. 'Just a little token from yer friends here, to wish you well. All the department chipped in. I can't say as much for some of the women we employed, but you will be one of those we miss.'

Kay was most taken aback to receive a gift as none of the other women leaving had done to her knowledge. She was also very aware that times were hard for everyone and most touched by her workmates' generosity. Tears of gratitude pricking her eyes, she mumbled, 'I don't know what to say except thank you, Mr Goodman.'

He patted her shoulder, smiling warmly at her. 'Well, God forbid there ever is another war, but if we need to draft in women to help keep things running again, I won't hesitate to suggest you. Now you go and take care of that husband of yours. Oh, yer due wages and cards,' he said, turning to pick up a brown envelope from his desk then handing it to her.

Accepting the envelope, Kay thanked him and, after clocking off for the last time, made her way out.

CHAPTER FIVE

Her mind fully occupied by events at work, Kay entirely forgot about her planned trip to the Home and Colonial shop and automatically went straight home. She found Bob sitting at the utility dining table, so deep in concentration putting together what looked to her like a model of an early bi-plane he hadn't heard her come in. The air was thick with smoke, the saucer he'd been using as a makeshift ashtray piled with cigarette butts. His coat was slung carelessly over the back of one of the dining chairs.

He jumped when he realised she was standing beside him. 'Oh, never heard you come in.'

Kay expected him to get up to greet her with a hug and kiss after she'd been away from him for over ten hours, especially as he'd still been asleep when she had left at seven that morning. She was to be greatly disappointed though because he didn't, just returned to his task. As well as the piled ashtray, the table was cluttered with the remains of breakfast and a plate containing crumbs from the sandwich he had obviously made himself for lunch. She felt annoyance rise within her that he hadn't even attempted to clear up before she came home. She was glad, though, to see no sign of Tony.

'Had a good day?' she asked, taking off her coat and retrieving his to hang up with her own.

Holding the main body of the wooden plane, Bob picked up one of the wings and looked at it assessingly. 'Yes, I have. After breakfast I went out to have a look around the area, get a feel for the place.. I found a second-hand shop and, with not much else to do, went in to have a rummage. I couldn't believe it when I found this tucked on the back of one of the shelves.' Laying down the wing, he picked up the lid of a box from the seat of a chair next to him. His face bathed in a rapturous expression, he showed it to her. 'A Frog scale model construction kit! It's even got little tins of paint so I can paint it when I've finished putting it together. The old dear in the shop told me it had been a kid's Christmas present before the war but the family got hard up and had to sell it. It'd been hidden behind a pile of other stuff, that's why it hadn't been sold before. Thick with dust it was when I found it. I dreamed of having one of these when I was a kid but was never lucky enough to have one.'

She looked at him sadly. When Bob had explained his orphan status to her while they had been strolling together by the canal bank one evening not long after they had first met, he had spoken of his parents in very loving terms. Although apparently his mother had died when he had been very young, he remembered her as a good woman who'd loved him dearly. After she'd died his father, a factory worker, had done his best to raise the child but money had been tight, leaving little over for such things as model kits. Choked with emotion, Bob had explained how his father had spotted his potential as a carpenter

105

at an early age while spending time with him whittling wooden toys from old pieces of wood, and had encouraged that talent on his leaving school. At great financial sacrifice to himself, Bob had told her, his father had secured him an apprenticeship with a reputable firm, but just as Bob had completed his apprenticeship and before he could begin to ease his father's financial burden by contributing properly himself, his father had taken ill, been diagnosed as being in the advanced stages of lung cancer and died only weeks later. Bob hadn't had to tell her how painful that time had been for him and how hard he had taken his father's death.

'It must have been terrible for you,' Kay said softly now.

Bob turned his head and looked at her, puzzled. 'Eh?'

'Losing your parents, 'specially your mother so young. I don't know what I'd do if anything happened to mine.'

He looked at her for a moment before saying dismissively, 'You just get on with your life. It's the future that's important, not the past.'

After all the death and destruction he must have witnessed and the atrocities of war, she could appreciate his feelings at the moment. Hopefully they both had a wonderful future together. Kay would do her best to make sure it was. She smiled at him tenderly. 'Any luck today?'

He looked back at her quizzically. 'Luck?'

'In getting a job?'

Returning his attention to the plane, he said, 'Well, I didn't bother today as your father's putting in a word for me at the Mail. Thought I'd wait and see what happened there first.'

'Oh, I see. Well, I suppose I can see your point. I got took on myself because of my dad speaking up for me.' She looked at him, a bit bothered. 'But maybe it might not be a good idea, you pinning all your hopes on something coming up there, Bob. After all, the Mail might not need anyone else with so many men looking for work and snapping up anything that's offered them.'

She was just about to tell him she had received her notice when he spun round to face her, his face dark with anger. 'Oh, for Christ's sake, can't you women ever just leave a man to do things in his own time without nagging? Never let up, do you? I thought I'd got away from all that when...' He suddenly stopped abruptly, to swallow hard, a horrified expression clouding his face. 'I'm sorry,' he blurted out. 'It was just ... just ... just that I was always being told what to do in the Army and I thought I'd left all that behind.'

She had never seen Bob lose his temper before, and his losing it so quickly and, she felt, so unwarrantedly, shocked her to the core. 'I wasn't trying to tell you what to do, Bob. If you thought that then it's me that's sorry. I just asked how you got on with looking for work today because, you see, I was given my notice. They actually finished me today so the wage they gave me is my last one. We'll be all right for money for a bit, though, won't we, as we can use some of your gratuity payment to live on until you get work?'

'Oh, that ... well, I was going to surprise you with it when I got it. It takes a while to come through. I have to keep checking at the Post Office. It could take weeks.'

'Oh, I see. Well, we'll just have to manage as best we can until you're earning then. Hopefully my dad's enquiries will come up trumps, but regardless, Bob, I know you'll be snapped up. No employer in their right mind would pass up the opportunity of having you working for them,' Kay said encouragingly. 'I'll make a start on dinner then.' She'd made to walk into the kitchen when a thought struck her and she turned back to face her husband. 'Oh, as he's not here, I trust Tony got sorted with suitable...'

Just then they both heard the front door opening and Tony's voice, sounding as though he was issuing instructions to someone. Kay flashed an enquiring look at Bob, dropped the coats on the arm of the sofa then rushed off to investigate what was happening. The sight that greeted her made her jaw drop. Tony and another man were trying to manoeuvre a single oak wardrobe through the front door.

'What's going on?' she demanded.

Still struggling with the wardrobe, Tony turned his head to look at her, his eyes holding a contemptuous expression. 'Obvious, ain't it? Tell Bob to come and lend a hand with getting the rest of my stuff in.'

Kay's mouth gaped even wider. 'Rest of the stuff?'

Returning his attention to his task, Tony laughed at her. 'Well, I can't sleep in a wardrobe, can I? I've a bed and a tallboy and a few other bits and pieces outside on the cart. You said yourself that a sofa or floor is only all right as a make do.' He slapped his hand against the wardrobe. 'All second-hand and I haggled a good price. It'll do me for now, but it's the very best stuff I'm having when I've made me fortune.' He gave a secret smile. 'A way to make that has presented itself very nicely and, I must say, far quicker than I ever thought it would. All I've got to do now is set things in motion.'

He turned his attention back to the delivery man. 'Left a bit, mate, that's it. Right, to me, and that should do it.'

Kay watched dumbstruck as they positioned the wardrobe in the recess by the front room's fireplace. Tony took a look around the room, inspecting it. 'This is bigger than the back bedroom,' he mused. 'In fact,' he said, bringing his eyes to rest on Kay, 'this room would suit me far better. I could use the front door to come and go as I please, without disturbing you in the back.'

'We gonna get the rest of it in, squire? Me wife 'as me dinner on the table prompt at six and I need to get the 'oss back to the stable and the cart stored for the night before I head off home,' urged the delivery man.

'I'm looking forward to me own dinner,' Tony agreed, looking at Kay. 'Ten minutes should see us clear here, then I'll be ready to sit down. You can make up my bed after. I'm off out tonight, have to see a man about a bit of business, so your time's your own for doing that. Right, come on then, mate, let's get this over with,' he said, slapping the other man on his shoulder as they headed back out of the front door.

Kay couldn't believe the cheek of the man! A

couple of days was all she'd understood he would be staying with them for. Buying furniture to make himself more comfortable meant he was moving in. She also wondered what he had meant by his announcement that his plan for making money was looking very promising? It sounded shady to her. Or maybe Tony had wanted her to think that he was some big shot making a deal when in truth he was probably negotiating to buy a pile of towels or dusters to sell around the doors at a shilling a time, which she felt was more than likely the case.

Spinning on her heel, she dashed through the connecting door into the back room to tackle her husband, still sitting at the table constructing his model plane. 'Bob, Tony is taking up residence in our front room. He's bought himself some furniture.'

Without lifting his head from his task, he said, 'Oh, he got what he wanted then, did he?'

She stared at him in shock.

'You knew what he planned to do?'

Bob shrugged.

'He mentioned it this morning when we were having breakfast. You can't expect the man to sleep on the floor or the sofa for long, can you, Kay?'

'I certainly didn't expect him to buy bedroom furniture. I was under the impression he was going to find himself proper lodgings. You said two days at the most, Bob. Just how long is he planning to stay with us?'

Bob shrugged again.

'I don't know. Until he gets enough money

behind him to set himself up, I suppose.'

'The money he used to buy that furniture could have paid for two or three months in lodgings, Bob, by my reckoning at least. There's hardly room in this house for us as it is without having Tony as well. I planned to make the front room into a dining room when we could afford the furniture, somewhere nice for family and friends to sit when they come round for a meal. Besides, we've just started our married life together, we need to be on our own. I want you to ask him to go, Bob.'

He looked at her, clearly shocked.

'You want me to ask Tony to leave? But I can't do that. I can't go back on my word. I promised him a roof over his head until he gets himself sorted. I owe him after what he did for me.'

'I respect that, Bob, and I'm grateful for whatever it was he did for you, but how long do you propose to stay indebted to him?'

'As long as it takes,' he snapped, and looked at her closely then. 'I didn't think you'd turn out to be like this, Kay.'

'What do you mean? Turn out to be like what?'

He gave a deep sigh. 'I thought you'd be the sort to let her husband be master in his own home.'

'But of course you're the master of our house.'

'No, I'm not, Kay, or you wouldn't be telling me to ask Tony to leave after all he did for me. Just because he's bought himself some furniture to make himself comfortable while he stays here. I mean, it saves us from forking out.'

'Well ... it's just come as a shock after I thought

111

he was leaving us today. Is he at least going to pay his way while he's with us?'

Bob looked aghast.

'I can't ask him to do that!'

'But you have to, Bob, we can't afford to keep him.'

To her surprise he jumped up from his chair and started heading out of the room.

'Where are you going?' Kay asked, looking at him in bewilderment.

'I need the privy.'

She felt tears prick her eyes. She had not envisaged starting married life accompanied by a lodger, especially a smart-alick type like Tony, who her husband seemed hell-bent on accommodating to his own detriment. All she could hope was that Tony would tire of this situation and leave soon. She glanced around the room, at the debris Bob had created with help from their lodger and left for her to clear up. She hoped this was not a taste of things to come, then reasoned with herself that her husband was still adjusting back to civilian life. He had got carried away with excitement after finding the prized model kit. She realised time was wearing on. If she didn't get the dinner started it would not be cooked before seven o'clock. She ought to put that on first before she started tidying up.

As she made her way towards the kitchen, Tony came in, flopping down into an armchair. 'Dinner about ready?' he called over to her.

Before she would stop herself, Kay spun to face him and replied sharply: 'No, dinner is not ready. It'll be about an hour.'

He looked at his wristwatch. 'I hope it's no longer than that, I've arranged to meet someone at seven-thirty.'

Kay took a deep breath and said evenly, 'I'll do my best to make sure it's not. Oh, as it seems you're staying with us for a while, I'll need your ration books.'

He smiled at her sweetly.

'Okay, I'll give them to you. Where's Bob?'

'He's gone to the toilet.'

'Huh! I bet he scarpered soon as yer told him I wanted help in shifting me furniture. In the Army he was always the last to volunteer for anything.'

Anger rose in her at his attack on her husband and before she could check herself, Kay blurted, 'How dare you speak about Bob like that? He told me he was one of the first to volunteer to join up in Northampton when war was looming, and I know from his letters despite the fact he couldn't tell me any details that he put himself forward for several dangerous missions.'

A smile of mockery twitched at Tony's lips and he looked at her for several moments before saying, 'Any chance of some hot water for a wash?' He grinned at the look that flashed over her face. 'Don't worry, I shan't embarrass you with the sight of my half-naked body in the kitchen while you're cooking the dinner – don't want you to worry about what you're missing! I've bought meself a jug and bowl so I can take care of me ablutions in privacy. The front room looks quite good now I've arranged all the furniture. It could do with some homely touches, though,' he added, looking at her expectantly.

113

She was still smarting from his unjust accusations against her husband, a man who was supposed to be his friend and who had offered him a place to stay. Most people would be grateful for that, it never entering their heads to have the bare-faced cheek to hint their benefactors might make their room more homely. As for his suggestion she would find his physique far more appealing than Bob's, that was unforgivable of him. Her dislike of this man was growing rapidly. She wished so much she was more like Eunice, the type to put Tony in his place, but she wasn't and out of respect for Bob she had no choice but to put up with his friend's obnoxious ways until he left, which couldn't come too soon for Kay. She looked at Tony coldly. 'I'll check the kettle for you,' she said, spinning on her heel and heading off into the kitchen.

Bob still hadn't returned from his visit to the toilet during all the time it had taken her to make the cheese and potato pie which was now baking in the oven and it upset Kay to think he was keeping out of her way after them having words. She headed for the back room to tidy it up before she set the table for their evening meal. Tony was in his own room still getting ready. She was pleased about that, and also glad he was going out that evening. As far as she was concerned, the less she came into contact with him the better. She'd hardly made a start when she heard the back door open and her father call out to her.

'In here, Dad,' she called back, smiling a greeting when he appeared.

Herbie walked across to her and gave her a

peck on her cheek. 'Hello, lovey. Yer mother's with me too.'

Kay inwardly groaned. As delighted as she always was to see her parents, she wished they had picked a better time for a visit. She knew the state of this room was not going to go unnoticed by her mother.

Mabel came in then and smiled warmly at her daughter as she took off her coat.

'I was just introducing meself to yer neighbour over the garden wall. Seems a nice old duck. She was telling me she lost her son and daughter-in-law when the bomb dropped on the Freeman, Hardy and Willis factory, and as she was already a widow that left her with no one. It seems she didn't get on very well with the old gent that lived here before you moved in, said he was the cantankerous sort, so having you as a neighbour now will be like a breath of fresh air for her. I told her if she needs any shopping or any other help just to ask and you'll gladly oblige.'

'Yes, of course I will. I'll go and introduce myself to her as soon as I get time. Let me take your coat for you, Mam,' Kay said, walking across to take it from her.

'We're not stopping long,' said Mabel, handing it to her. 'Yer father has a bit of news for Bob so I said I'd accompany him. We should have left it a bit later until you'd had yer dinner but these nights are drawing in and my ageing bones like to be by the fire of an evening.' She looked at the mess on the table and pulled a disapproving face. 'You're really going to have to sort yourself out, Kay. This won't do, will it? What must Bob be

115

thinking of you, allowing a mess like this to gather?'

'Now, Mother, leave the gel alone,' warned Herbie.

'I've not raised my daughter to shirk her responsibilities, Herbert. A decent man like Bob expects his home keeping proper.'

Herbie knew better than to pursue this any further and pretended to take great interest in the workmanship of the grouting between the tiles on the fireplace.

'I was just in the process of clearing it up when you came in,' said Kay in her own defence. 'I haven't long got home from work.'

'Well, that just proves my point, going out to work and being a housewife don't mix,' said Mabel. She pulled up the sleeves of her cardigan. 'I'll give you a hand.'

'It's all right, Mam, I can do it. Sit down and I'll make you a cuppa.'

'Yer mother means well,' Herbie whispered to her.

Kay smiled at him. 'Yes, I know she does.'

'Something smells good,' said Mabel, reluctantly sitting down in an armchair.

'Cheese and potato pie,' Kay told her, hurriedly gathering dirty plates from off the table.

'Plenty of salt and pepper to make it tasty?'

'Yes, Mam.'

'And you've kept some cheese back to grate on the top and brown under the grill as a finishing touch?'

Kay nodded and Mabel smiled approvingly.

'Where's Bob?' asked her father, standing with

his back to the fire, his arms folded behind him.

'He's ... er ... in the toilet. He shouldn't be long.'

'Has he had any luck today finding work?' Herbie asked her.

Having rushed into the kitchen to stack the plates in the sink, Kay had arrived back in the room and was now boxing away the bi-plane construction kit, careful not to break anything or lose any pieces. 'Er ... no. No, he hasn't.'

'Then he might be glad to hear what I have to tell him,' her father said, smiling and looking pleased with himself.

Mabel rose to her feet.

'I can't sit here when so much needs doing, I'll mash the tea.'

Before Kay could stop her she had gone off into the kitchen. A few minutes later she set a tray of tea down on the now cleared table, poured it out and told them both to sit down.

Taking a sip of his, Herbie looked at his daughter knowingly.

'I heard yer got yer notice today, Kay?'

The fact he knew didn't surprise her as gossip travelled around the Royal Mail quicker than Reuters got their information.

'The timing's perfect,' said Mabel, looking pleased.

After the mess she had arrived home to today, and remembering that missed chance to get in the queue for some tins of whatever Home and Colonial had had delivered, Kay reluctantly agreed with her mother. 'Yes, now Bob's home I need to be at home full-time. That doesn't mean to say I won't miss working, though. Oh, I've just remembered, my work mates clubbed together and bought me a present and I haven't opened it yet.' She went across to fetch it from her handbag, which she had put by the side of the armchair when tidying up, then returned to the table, ripping off the paper covering. The parcel contained a silver-plated photograph frame. 'Oh, isn't it pretty?' she gasped. 'How nice of them to buy me this as a memento. My wedding photograph will look so much nicer in this than the wooden one it's in now.'

'Shows how much they all thought of yer, lovey. That's not something that's done very often,' said her proud father.

'The Royal Mail have much to thank the Staffords for,' Mabel declared, 'and it's about time due appreciation was shown.' She took a glance around her. 'This room is nice when it's tidy. Needs a rug by the fireplace and a few other little touches, but you'll get those come time.

'Oh, that reminds me, Kay – Mrs Rowbottom is going to live with her daughter. Well, she's finding it difficult to manage on her own and she ain't been the same since her husband passed on. Upshot is that she's having to get rid of her furniture as her daughter's no room for it. Most of it's not up to much but she's a nice table and chairs and has promised me first refusal. I know yer plan to turn yer front room into a proper dining room for entertaining, so if yer'd like them me and yer dad will get them for yer as you and Bob's Christmas present.'

Kay looked at her mother gratefully.

'Oh, Mam, that's lovely of you and I would have jumped at your offer but ... well...' She paused, hoping her voice did not betray her true feelings on the matter. 'Tony's going to be staying with us for a while and as a matter of convenience the front room's been turned into a bedroom for him. It's just until he sorts himself out. He's in there now, getting ready to go out this evening after we've had dinner.'

A look of approval filled Mabel's face and she leaned over and patted her daughter's hand.

'Well, I have to say, I'm proud of you and Bob, offering a place in your home to an ex-soldier, especially after whatever it was he did for Bob out in Burma. It's up to us to help those men all we can after what they've done for us. The lodging money will come in handy too now you're not working.'

Yes, providing she got some, Kay thought.

Just then they heard the kitchen door open and shut and moments later Bob walked in.

'Ah, just the man I came to see,' said Herbie, smiling a greeting.

On spotting his in-laws as he entered the room, Bob stopped short and looked at them warily.

'Er ... nothing wrong, is there?'

Herbie laughed, 'Not as far as I know – unless there's summat you ain't telling us? Yer not averse to yer in-laws paying you an unexpected visit now and again, are yer, son?'

Bob looked awkwardly at his father-in-law.

'No, of course not. I'm sorry I wasn't here when you arrived.'

'That's all right, can't expect yer to greet us

119

ceremonially every time we pop round. Kay's told me you've had no luck in finding work today, which I can't understand meself. I'd 'a' thought someone like you would be snapped up. Anyway, I had a few words with my boss and he made some enquiries, and with me being one of their most valued employees and you coming highly recommended by meself, they want to see you at ten tomorrow morning. I'll keep my fingers crossed they offer you something.'

'Oh, that's wonderful,' cried Kay. 'Isn't it, Bob?'

He nodded. 'Thanks, Mr Stafford.'

'Glad to be of help. When you arrive, tell the receptionist you've an interview with Mr Askew.' Herbert rose from his chair. 'Right, come on then, Mother, let's leave these young things to it.'

Kay saw them to the door and, having kissed them both on the cheek, looked at her father gratefully. 'Thanks again, Dad.'

'No need ter keep thanking me, lovey. Families look out for each other, in these hard times especially.'

At the mention of the word 'families', Kay gasped, mortified, 'Oh, goodness, I forgot to ask how our Trevor is?'

'That's understandable, lovey, yer've lots of other things to occupy yer,' said Mabel. 'He's much happier in himself now. The doctor came for his visit this morning and said that the injury is healing nicely. If it carries on like this, in about a month's time Trevor should be all right to start putting some weight on his leg. The doctor agreed that we could make a bed up for him downstairs which we did when yer dad finished work this

120

afternoon, before he went to the allotment.' She pulled a face. 'Yer Aunt Viv's bin on at me to let her take Trevor in a wheelchair to that dance a week on Friday night, and of course our Trevor's never let up about it, but I ain't sure.'

'Won't do the lad any harm, Mabel,' said Herbie. 'He's been cooped up too long, he needs to be out with his mates, and our Viv will look after him.'

'Come on, Mam,' Kay urged. 'It'll do our Trevor good. Aunty Viv won't let any harm come to him.'

'I know my sister means well, and I know she wouldn't intentionally hurt a hair on my son's head, but all the same she can be what I'd call a bit of a flibbertigibbet sometimes...

'Look, I won't stand here all night arguing the toss. I can't turn my back on Trevor for one minute without him trying something daft. I wouldn't put it past him to have seized the opportunity of us being out to hobble round to one of his friends on crutches now he's not got the stairs to negotiate first. Come on, Herbie, let's be off.'

He winked at his daughter and, tongue in cheek, said, 'Best do as I'm told or I'll be getting sent to bed without me cocoa. I'll drop yer some veggies in, Kay, on my way home from the allotment tomorrow afternoon.' He pulled a face. 'Stuff's really starting to go over now the cold weather's setting in but I've Brussels, cabbages, turnips, parsnips and spuds. I need to lift the last of the spuds to store for winter then string up the onions, that's me job for the weekend.'

121

'Kay ain't got time to listen to you rambling on about yer allotment, Herbie, she's got a husband to look after,' Mabel chided him. 'Now hurry back inside and get Bob his dinner. Poor lad must be famished,' she instructed her daughter. 'And yer've a lodger to see to,' she added, looking at her meaningfully.

Shutting the door after her parents, Kay picked up the cutlery and took it through with her to the back room. She found Bob waiting for her and by the look on his face she could tell he was upset.

'Where's my model kit?'

'I packed it away, we need the table for dinner.'

He looked downcast.

'Oh, now I'll have to sort all the bits out again.'

Just then the connecting door opened and a smartly dressed Tony came in from the front room, shutting the door behind him. 'Dinner must be ready by now,' he said, sitting down at the table.

'I was just about to dish it up,' Kay snapped at him as she turned and headed off into the kitchen.

She couldn't help but notice a look that meant 'Is this all we're getting?' on his face when she put a plate of cheese and potato pie before him, and was most put out after placing a bowl of rice pudding on the table for afters when Tony stated that he'd give it a miss as milk pudding twice in as many days was more than he could stomach. Then, without even so much as a thank you for what he had eaten, he left the table, announcing he was going straight out.

Her fond illusion that she and Bob would

spend their leisure time chatting congenially while listening to interesting radio programmes and discussing their merits afterwards were shattered again. Not offering to give her a hand with any of the domestic chores, and seeming to forget she was even present, Bob spent the rest of the evening at the table finishing off the construction of his model plane, the wireless tuned into a light entertainment station and turned up rather too loud for Kay's liking. She sat in her armchair by the fire, occupied with her knitting. Several times she made to speak to him but thought better of it, worried she would shatter his concentration. The last thing she wanted to do was incur his displeasure again today.

Just before ten he glued the last piece into place and gave a triumphant exclamation: 'Done it!' Cradling the model gently in his hand, he swivelled around in his seat, holding it out for her to see. 'Isn't it a beaut? Be even better when I've painted it. I'm really pleased with what I've done. I'm going to scour the second-hand shops and see what other models I can find after I've finished this one off tomorrow.'

Model construction kits were aimed at young boys. Bob was a highly skilled carpenter and she couldn't quite understand his obvious pride in successfully putting it together. 'You have an interview to attend tomorrow,' Kay gently reminded him.

He gave a shrug.

'That isn't going to take all day. Just a formality, according to your father. I expect I'll be starting next Monday so I want to make the most of my last few days of rest.'

'What about us going out on Saturday night to celebrate you getting a job? For a meal or something?' Then a memory suddenly struck her. 'Oh, we can't this Saturday, we've been invited to Eunice and George's for a bit of a get together.'

He stared at her, non-plussed.

'Eunice and George?'

She raised her eyebrows at him in surprise.

'Eunice was with me the night I met you, remember? She's my best friend and George is her husband.'

'Oh, yes, of course, how stupid of me. It'd slipped my mind, that's all.'

Kay smiled tenderly at him.

'Eunice said George's memory was dreadful when he came back from Europe. Said he couldn't even remember her birthday or the date of their wedding anniversary. It's understandable, isn't it, in the circumstances?'

'Half the time we didn't know what day it was, let alone if it was our birthday or someone else's. Look, about Saturday ... you haven't said we'll go, have you?'

'No, of course I haven't. Not without asking you first.'

Bob looked relieved.

'I'm not keen. I mean, I'm only just settling back, getting my bearings in Leicester, and I've enough on my plate with that and getting a job. Besides, it wouldn't look good, us swanning off out leaving Tony to fend for himself.'

Kay could appreciate his reasons but felt very disappointed. She had been looking forward to an evening spent with Eunice, and the opportunity for George and Bob to get to know each other. As for Tony, he was quite capable of fending for himself. She looked at Bob for a moment, fighting with her conscience as to whether or not to tell him of the derogatory comments Tony had made about him earlier. She thought better of it. Best Bob found out his friend's true colours for himself. Sooner rather than later, hopefully, and then they could get rid of him.

He gently laid the model on the table and gave a loud yawn, stretching himself. 'I'm bushed, better be off to bed,' he said, rising and heading towards the door leading to the stairs.

Kay stared after him, dumbstruck. He had left the table cluttered with debris which meant she had to clear it before she could set it for breakfast, and he'd not offered to help her secure the house for the night or fill the coal bucket ready for lighting the fire in the morning. Did Bob feel that all household jobs were entirely her responsibility? Did it not occur to him that she needed help with the heavy ones? Once again she reasoned with herself that he was adjusting to his new life and she needed to give him time. Then she remembered she hadn't yet enquired about his friend Mike and made a mental note to do that tomorrow. Like Eunice, she too was intrigued to know what had happened to him.

By the time she arrived in their bedroom Bob was snoring soundly. Quashing her disappointment not to have enjoyed a kiss and a cuddle before she went to sleep, Kay undressed as quietly as she could, slipped in beside him and snuggled down. She was just dozing off when the sound of the front door opening and banging shut jolted her awake. Tony had arrived back and it obviously hadn't occurred to him to move quietly so as not to disturb his hosts. Then she heard voices. He was talking to someone. High-pitched laughter followed. Annoyance reared within Kay. Not only had he the cheek to bring a visitor back to their house unannounced, that visitor was a woman! How dare he? she inwardly fumed. It was most disrespectful of him. Then she heard the squeak of bed springs and her anger mounted as it was obvious what was going on in the room below. This was too much. Having Tony as a lodger, and as things stood at the moment a nonpaying one, was one thing, but him believing he could actually use their home as somewhere to entertain women in this manner was just not on. She would have words with Bob about this. Even he would draw a line at such improper conduct, regardless of his debt of gratitude.

CHAPTER SIX

As much as she tried Kay could not sleep. It was hard enough to relax now she knew Tony was occupying the room below theirs, but with a strange woman there too and knowing what they were doing together, it was just impossible. Kay kept praying to hear the front door click shut. With the woman gone sleep might come, but she didn't. At just after six she finally gave up. Doing her best not to rouse Bob, she got up, hurriedly dressed and made her way downstairs to make herself a much-needed cup of tea.

At just after seven, the fire lit and a pan of porridge simmering on the stove, Kay was nursing her second cup of tea when a tousled-looking Bob appeared. She smiled at him lovingly. 'Good morning. Did you sleep well?' she asked as she picked up the tea pot and poured him out a cup.

Still dressed in his crumpled pyjamas, hair sticking up wildly, thick stubble covering the lower half of his face, he gave a yawn as he sat down in the chair opposite, giving his manly parts a vigorous scratch before he reached for his baccy tin. He took out a roll up, and as the smoke hit his lungs gave a loud phlegm-ridden cough.

'Like a baby. Spark out as soon as my head touched the pillow.'

Kay tried to hide her disgust at the uncouth habits he had picked up from his Army pals and hoped he'd soon lose them. She was also disappointed that he didn't greet her with a morning kiss. Their five years apart and his lack of any female contact in the meantime had obviously quashed Bob's affectionate nature. It was up to her to rekindle his displays of affection by encouraging his attentions.

In order not to upset him again about his biplane model, Kay had left it as he had the previous night, spread out on the table, and only used the remaining space to lay for breakfast. She watched as he picked up the model plane and carefully examined it, his face holding a

127

rapturous expression. She remembered the times when that look would have been for her, not a model plane.

'I can't wait to see how this looks when I've painted it,' he said. 'I'll get down to it as soon as I'm back from my interview then I'll see about getting another one to keep me occupied.'

As she passed over a cup of tea, Kay eyed him hesitantly. He was freely spending money on his hobbies but hadn't yet offered her anything towards the housekeeping. In all the excitement of coming home, all thoughts of money had probably escaped him.

In an apologetic tone she said, 'Bob, I'll be needing some money from you towards the housekeeping.'

He looked at her, startled.

'Oh! But you had your wage yesterday. What have you done with it all?'

'Well, I've put the rent aside for Friday, and by the time I've put a couple of shillings in the meter I reckon I've just about enough to cover us for food for the next couple of days. My wage wasn't that much, Bob.' She wanted to remind him that it was keeping Tony too but felt it was best she didn't for now.

His face clouded over in dismay.

'Oh! Well, I've a bit left from my Army pay. I suppose I could give you a few shillings. I'll need the rest myself for my baccy and bus fares to work and back. The clothing coupons I was given on my demob ... well, I was going to use them towards rigging myself out as all the old stuff you kept for me is far too big for me now. I've hardly anything to wear. I suppose we could sell a few of the coupons if we have to. How much do you think you'll need to tide you over?'

Kay wondered if he realised how guilty he was making her feel for asking for money. More to the point, although she knew it wouldn't have been all that much, what had he done with all his last pay from the Army? Apart from his night down the pub with Tony, when according to them the locals had supplied their drinks all night, the only money he had spent to her knowledge was on his model kit and that couldn't have been all that much.

'I'll need more than a few shillings to keep me going until you get paid.' Then a memory suddenly struck Kay. 'What about your savings? Your bank book was in that box of possessions you left with me. I know because you told me you'd left instructions with the bank to allow me to withdraw some should I need to while you were away. I haven't touched it though, Bob, because you intended to use it to start up your business. Well, now you're not going to do that for the time being it won't hurt to use some of it to tide us over for housekeeping. We could make sure we put whatever we use back once you're earning, for such a time as you feel you are ready to take up carpentry again.'

His whole face lit up.

'Oh, yes, of course, my savings. I'll dig the book out as soon as I go upstairs to get ready.'

Just then they both heard the front door open and shut.

'Tony's going out early,' Bob said, looking

129

surprised. 'Where on earth can he be going at this time in the morning, without having any breakfast?'

Kay took a deep breath.

'It's my guess it's not Tony going out but the woman he had staying with him last night.'

'A woman! Well, he certainly wasted no time, did he?'

Kay looked at him, shocked.

'You don't mind that he brought a strange woman into our home and she stayed the night?'

Bob shrugged nonchalantly.

'No, why should I? Tony's a grown man and he's entitled to his pleasure. Is that porridge I smell?'

'Pardon? Oh, er ... yes.' Kay was unable to believe that he seemed happy for Tony to use their home in any way he pleased. 'Bob, I'm not comfortable with this.' He looked at her, puzzled.

'Not comfortable with what?'

'Tony using our home in this way. It's not even as though he asked us out of respect if we minded him bringing someone back, let alone what they were obviously doing. We need to set some house rules with him.'

He looked at her as though she had asked him to jump off the edge of a cliff before sighing resignedly and saying, 'I don't see what all the fuss is about myself. But if you really want me to have a word with him, then I will as soon as I get a chance.'

After breakfast Bob stood at the sink, having a shave and strip wash. Trying to work around him, Kay was clearing away the remains of breakfast when a pyjama and dressing gown-clad Tony sauntered through, looking very much like a man who hadn't had much sleep. He leaned on the kitchen door, yawning.

'God, I'm famished, what's for breakfast?'

The saucepan containing the remains of the porridge in her hand, Kay looked at him sourly.

'I was just about to throw this away as time is wearing on. I was under the impression you were giving breakfast a miss today and having a lie in.'

Dressed in his string vest and trousers, shaving brush in hand, face half-lathered, Bob turned to face his friend.

'Morning, Tony. Sleep well, did you?'

'So, so,' he grunted, advancing further into the kitchen to look down into the saucepan Kay was holding. He pulled a disgusted face. 'I hope that's not for me? I can't stand porridge. I prefer a proper cooked breakfast. I'll have a cuppa while I'm waiting.'

'Go and sit down. Kay will see to it,' said Bob, carrying on with his shaving.

As Tony walked into the back room, Kay turned to her husband.

'I haven't got anything to give Tony for a cooked breakfast.' She wanted to add that out of respect for them both he should have been up at a reasonable time to have his breakfast. She hadn't time to waste preparing another. She had a mountain of things to do this morning before she made a start on the dinner. 'And, Bob, you did say you were going to have a word about him bringing a woman home to stay last night.'

'Now isn't the time to talk to him about that,

131

Kay. I need to do it man to man in private. I told you I'd do it when I get a chance, and I will.' He looked down into the pan, then back at her. 'You can't expect Tony to eat that. He's a guest. Besides, you heard him say he doesn't like porridge.' Bob's face clouded over. 'You must have something in the pantry you can give him?'

She'd a bantam egg, these being cheaper than hen's and more readily available, albeit a lot smaller. But she had planned to use that to make a sponge for pudding, feeling she couldn't dish up either sago, tapioca or rice so soon again after Tony's derogatory comments.

'I've an egg but...'

'Then give him egg on toast,' Bob interjected in a relieved tone. 'Now I need to get on with my shave or I'll be late for my interview.'

Kay sighed as she scraped the pan clean of its congealed contents into a brown paper bag of kitchen rubbish, putting it back on the stove to soak then washing the rest of the pots after Bob had finished using the sink.

A short time later she put the egg and two slices of toast spread with margarine in front of Tony, and in a clipped voice said, 'I hope that will suit, it's all we have.'

She hoped her hint might prompt him to offer some board money but she was to be disappointed when all he said casually was, 'It'll have to do then, I suppose.'

Just after one Kay was looking at the clock, wondering where Bob had got to. After she had freshened up his smartest shirt and his suit by giving them a press and had seen him off for his interview, she had made the beds, dusted and swept the downstairs of the house, cleaned the toilet out back, swept and washed the front step, then brushed the yard. After acquainting herself with her elderly neighbour to enquire if she needed anything fetching she had then rushed down to the local Worthington's grocery shop to buy that day's food and returned home to prepare their dinner of corned beef hash followed by steamed sponge – having had to buy another egg to replace the one Tony had had for breakfast – which was now keeping hot on the stove and would spoil if Bob didn't return soon. In an effort to make herself look nice for her husband she had discarded her wraparound apron, brushed her hair and applied a light coat of lipstick.

His interview couldn't have lasted more than half an hour so where he had got to, she couldn't fathom. Where Tony was either she had no idea, not that she cared. He had gone out earlier, without even informing her first – not that she was bothered but she never had chance to ask if he expected any dinner or to tell him what time she was putting it on the table. After her sleepless night and heavy morning Kay was feeling ready to drop.

At a tap on the door she spun around, expecting Bob to walk in, though why he should knock on his own door did not occur to her. She was disappointed at first when her Aunt Vivian entered, her face in a wide grin. She took off her coat and hung it on a peg on the back of the door. Despite wearing an unflattering work overall over an everyday calf-length brown skirt and worn-looking

133

cream blouse, her hair wrapped casually in a scarf turban-style, she still looked extremely attractive.

'Hello, me ducky. Rather than sit in the canteen having my lunch listening to all the Moaning Minnies around me, I decided to come and have it with you and see how you're getting on.' She suddenly paused and looked at Kay in concern. 'You look washed out.'

'Just ready for a sit down. I haven't stopped all morning. I'm quickly realising that being a housewife is far harder than going out to work. I feel better already for a visit from you.'

Viv gave her a broad knowing grin.

'And, of course, you and Bob have a lot of catching up to do so I expect yer not getting much sleep at the moment.' Seeming oblivious to the fact that she had made Kay blush by her remark, Viv commented, 'Summat smells good.'

'Corned beef hash. Would you like some, Aunty Viv?'

She would have loved to accept Kay's offer, especially knowing it would have been made using one of Mabel's delicious recipes, but she was conscious that Kay would only have catered for themselves, and knowing her niece as well as she did it would be her share Viv would be eating if she said yes.

'I've got me own dinner sorted for when I get home tonight and I've sandwiches with me. Waste not, want not, as yer mam's fond of saying. Thanks for the offer, though. But don't let me stop you from inviting me around for dinner one night. I will have a cuppa, ta. Where's Bob?'

Kay moved aside the pan keeping the sponge

hot, replacing it with the kettle. 'He's not back from his interview at the Mail yet. Dad arranged it for him.' She handed Viv a plate for her sandwiches from the wooden rack hung on the wall to one side of the sink. 'I hope he's back before his dinner ruins.'

'Oh, I'm sure he will be. These things sometimes take longer than you think they will,' said Viv, putting the plate on the draining board and taking a brown paper bag out of her handbag. She untwisted the top, removed two fish paste sandwiches and put them on the plate. 'After snapping Bob up on hearing his credentials, they're probably just showing him around and outlining the job to him, or maybe fitting him for his uniform if they've offered him an outside job. Whatever he's set on as, it'll not be for long 'cos he'll be clamouring to set up his own carpentry business soon. You married well there, our Kay. A man with Bob's abilities will never be out of work.'

The tea made, they went through to the back room to sit at the table. Accepting the cup of tea Kay passed her, Viv asked as she picked up a sandwich, 'I know it's only bin a couple of days but how are you settling down to married life together? Is having Tony stopping here making yer life difficult? I popped in to see yer mam and dad last night to have another go about taking Trevor to that dance and she mentioned Tony was staying with you for the time being. I must admit I was a bit shocked to hear it. Well, I mean, the last thing you and Bob need right now, in my opinion, is a lodger. 'Course, yer mam sees it

135

differently from me. She's so proud of you for doing yer patriotic duty for an ex-soldier and says his lodging money will help you out, but yer can hardly be yer natural selves with a lodger around, can yer?'

Especially one who uses the house as he feels fit and treats me like a servant. And the board money everyone thinks will be so useful is up to now non-existent, Kay thought. But she couldn't tell her aunt any of this, knowing that it would anger Viv so much she'd not be able to stop herself from saying something to Tony about it, and that would only cause more trouble between Kay and Bob. She planted a smile on her face.

'I admit Tony's being here is not ideal, but we're managing fine. He's bought himself some furniture and is using our front room.' She made herself sound as though she was pleased he had done as much.

Viv bit into her sandwich, munching on it for a moment before she said, 'Yes, yer mam did tell me that. I suppose he couldn't sleep on your settee for long, and him buying the furniture stops you feeling obliged to find money you haven't got for a bed for him. Where is he now, out touting for work?'

Kay gave a small shrug.

'I presume so.'

Viv gave a sudden laugh.

'You and Bob starting yer proper married life together got me to remembering when me and yer Uncle Archie were newly weds. Oh, God, did I make a hash of things! Burned yer uncle's dinner more times than I care to remember;

shredded the sheets in the mangle, and them a wedding present from yer mam and dad so *she* weren't best pleased; used far too much starch on Archie's shirts until he got an itchy rash so bad he almost scratched himself red raw. I could go on … you name it, I done it. 'Course, if I hadn't bin so high and mighty and had listened to some of yer mam's advice I wouldn't have sabotaged half what I did. Good job yer uncle loved me enough to turn a blind eye and had a sense of humour. He had his mates in stitches with my antics.

'Mind you, how I'd have coped with a lodger as well doesn't bear thinking about. Poor chap would probably have done a moonlight flit as far away from our house as could possibly be to escape me as his landlady. Tony must think himself a lucky man, landing himself with one like you, but don't make him too comfortable, Kay, me darlin', else he'll never go.' Viv laughed loudly. 'And then yer could have all and sundry knocking on yer door 'cos Tony will have spread the word about what great lodgings you provide.' She leaned over and affectionately patted Kay's hand. 'The main thing is you've got Bob home.'

She shook her head then, her face clouding over.

'The more stories that are coming out about what went on over there, the more amazed I am that any of our chaps came home at all. This might sound a terrible thing for me ter say but I'd sooner yer Uncle Archie had died quickly like he did than got captured and suffered the awful things our soldiers did in them prison camps,

German or Jap, they were both as bad. Our men were forced to live no better than animals. They'd monsters as their captors with no regard for human life. It's not surprising the men that were lucky enough to come out of them alive have the problems they do, physical and mental.'

Kay realised then that although Bob had temporarily seemed to have lost his outgoing personality and had picked up some not very savoury habits from his Army pals, she should at least be grateful that her husband was otherwise perfectly fine.

'More tea, Aunty Viv?' she asked.

Viv glanced at the clock on the mantel. 'Oh, go on then,' she said, passing across her cup and saucer. 'I've time for a quick one before I have to get back.' She suddenly noticed the model plane. 'Been babysitting for one of the neighbours?'

Pouring out the tea, Kay stopped what she was doing and looked at her aunt quizzically. 'Pardon?'

'The model plane. Kids left it behind after you babysat them, have they?'

'Oh, no, it's Bob's,' she said, resuming her task. 'He found the kit in an old junk shop and he's really enjoyed putting it together.'

Viv looked surprised.

'Wouldn't have thought something as simple as that would interest Bob, a man with his carpentry skills. Still, it's good he's got a hobby. Better him sitting at the table doing that of an evening than being like lots of other men who abandon their wives for the pub.'

Kay hadn't thought of it like that. Despite the

fact Bob engrossed himself in his hobby, seeming to forget she was there, at least he was at home with her.

'You said you'd spoken to Mam and Dad about taking Trevor to the dance a week on Friday. Is Mam still digging in her heels?' she asked, changing the subject.

'Well, that's the surprising thing. I was convinced she'd never agree but I can only say we must have all worn her down because she's given us the green light. Mind you, not without we agree to her rules first. I've to get Trevor back no later than ten o'clock. 'Course yer brother voiced his feelings on the matter, saying he wasn't a kid to have to be home so early, but it's as yer mam said and I have to agree with her here: Trevor's lucky to be alive, and after being in bed for so long his stamina is low. If we tire him out too much it could set his progress back. Ten o'clock home it is. I'm looking forward to it, it'll be a laugh. I shall play the protective aunt fighting all the women off my handsome nephew.' Viv paused and added casually, 'Frank's kindly volunteered to help me push him there and back, and make sure his mates don't get carried away and decide to have high jinks with Trevor in his wheelchair. They're a good lot really but men lose all sense and reason when drink is flowing.'

'That's nice of Frank to offer,' Kay said, looking at her aunt intently, having a feeling there was more to this than just a friendly gesture.

'Yes, it was, wasn't it?' Viv replied dismissively. Then she gave a bellow of laughter. 'Oh, I might as well tell yer but this is to go no further at the moment, I don't want yer mam getting wind 'til I'm more sure.' Her face took on a serious expression. 'I know my Archie's been gone for over four years now but yer mam might not agree as I've spent enough time mourning him yet. The last thing I want just now is her being all disapproving with me and our relationship having a setback now she's relented enough to trust me with Trevor. But me and Frank ... well, we've started seeing each other.'

'Oh, Aunty Viv, I am pleased!' Kay cried in genuine delight. 'Mam doesn't expect you to mourn Uncle Archie forever. I'm sure she's just worried that in your grief over him you could take up with someone ... well, that she didn't think was right for you. But she liked Frank, told me he was a very nice man, in her opinion. I think you make a lovely couple. I'm so pleased for you, Aunty Viv. You above anyone deserve another chance of happiness.'

Viv looked at her sharply. 'Eh, don't get carried away, our Kay. We're not a couple, just two friends having a night out together. Well, two, to be truthful. Three after this Friday as he's taking me to the pictures to see *Gone With The Wind*. You should get Bob to take you to see that, I've heard it's ever such a good film.' She gave a deep sigh. 'Despite everyone thinking I'm a woman of the world, it wasn't easy for me, agreeing to go out with a man on me own, even though I'm well acquainted with him. I wasn't sure if I was ready to direct me feelings to another man. But then, decent men like Frank don't come along very often and I'd be stupid not to give him a chance.

140

He might get fed up with waiting for me to make my mind up and someone else could catch his eye. When I'd got over me schoolgirl's nerves I really enjoyed meself. He is a nice man, Kay, ever so attentive, and wouldn't let me get me purse out. It's early days but I'm optimistic for what the future could hold for us. 'Til I'm ready to go public, this is between you and me, though, okay?'

'You can trust me with your secret, you know that, Aunty Viv.'

She looked across at the clock. 'Goodness, I really must be off,' she said, ramming the last of her sandwich in her mouth, hurriedly chewing it down and gulping back the dregs of her tea. Putting the cup back in its saucer on the table, she picked up her handbag then stepped across to Kay, who had now stood up to see her aunt out, held her to her and gave her a smacking kiss on her cheek. 'Tarra, me old duck. Stop fretting yerself about Bob. He'll be home soon and, I'm positive, with good news.'

CHAPTER SEVEN

It was well past five and the late October night was beginning to close in by the time Kay heard the back gate squeaking open. Worried sick now over where Bob had got to, praying it was him, she dashed to the back door. Yanking it open, she couldn't believe her eyes when she saw her husband wheeling a dilapidated-looking motorbike through the yard gate.

As she rushed down the path to join him, his face split into a broad grin of delight. He propped the bike against the adjoining garden wall and stood back to look at it admiringly. Before Kay could tell him she'd been worried sick about his whereabouts and was relieved to see him home, Bob said in an excited tone: 'What do you think then? I've always wanted a motorbike. It was such a bargain! I can't wait to take it for a spin.'

Momentarily speechless, Kay cast her eyes over the bike. She was no expert on motor vehicles of any sort, but despite her naivety this one looked unroadworthy to her. It was very rusty in parts and both tyres were bald and flat. But more to the point, she couldn't believe, no matter how much of a bargain it was, that Bob had parted with his hard-earned savings to pay for it. That money was meant to be used to start his business with.

'Does it go?' she asked. To her it didn't look like it possibly could.

'Er ... well ... not exactly at the moment, but it will like a dream once I've finished with it.'

So as well as being a skilled carpenter Bob possessed mechanical skills too? Kay smiled at him proudly. 'I'm sure it will.' Suddenly a thought struck and her face lit up excitedly. 'Bob, you buying the bike ... does this mean you got a job?'

He was still gazing at the bike, preoccupied. 'Oh, that, yes. I told you it was just a formality.'

Kay waited for him to tell her all about his new position and when he didn't she urged, 'Please tell me all about the job, Bob? What will you be doing? Are you on the sorting like I was? If so I can give you some hints.'

'Eh? Oh, no, I'm on the collecting.' He dragged his eyes away from the bike and looked at her. 'Going around emptying the post boxes. I'm on the early shift, five till one. I'm not that struck on the five o'clock start as it means I'll have to be up at four, but the boxes have to be emptied and the post brought back so the sorters can deal with the local stuff before the postmen start going out with the first delivery.' Kay already knew what a collector's job entailed but politely let him continue. 'Then I have to go out again to empty them of that morning's post and make collections from post offices. Then the next shift take over.

'I'm in training for a couple of weeks, have to go out with an experienced man, then I get me own permanent round. The pay's better than what yer'd get labouring in a factory so I'm happy with it. The good thing is that the early shift means I've the afternoons free to do what I like, such as fixing up my bike.'

'Whose is that pile of junk?'

They both jerked their heads around to see Tony sauntering down the cinder path towards them. He was looking at the motorbike with a smirk of amusement.

Bob looked at him, hurt. 'It's no pile of junk. I admit it looks neglected...'

'Given to you as a joke, was it?' he interjected before Bob could finish.

'Don't be like that, Tony. I paid good money for it. I did get a bargain, though.'

143

'It was the owner who got the bargain, Bob. Whatever you paid for it was far too much. It's falling to bits. It'll cost you a princely sum to get it fixed up.'

'I'm going to do it myself,' Bob said proudly.

Tony looked at him speculatively.

'Oh, a mechanic now, I see, as well as all yer other skills. Is there no end to your talents, mate? If I'd known you'd money to waste then I could have advised you of a much better deal with a definite profit. More, I suspect, than that bike will ever make you.'

Kay looked at Bob, expecting him to counteract Tony's critical comments, and was most surprised when he responded with, 'When I've fixed it up, I'll be able to give you a lift on it.'

Tony laughed. 'You've got to be joking! I wouldn't be seen dead on the back of that old thing, spruced up or not. Right, I'd best get cracking. I've a date tonight and don't want to keep the lady waiting, do I?' He looked at Kay. 'I'll help myself to hot water for my wash from the kettle. Tomorrow night I'll have a bath. About seven will suit me.' He turned to leave them, then stopped and turned back. 'Oh, if dinner is that dried-up looking stuff on the stove then I'll opt for eating out tonight.'

He then marched off, leaving a speechless Kay staring after him. She turned to face her husband. 'Why do you let him speak to us like that, Bob? He ridicules you and treats me like a servant.'

He flapped a hand dismissively. 'You're making too much of it, it's just his way. I've told you before, he doesn't mean anything by it.' He looked at her uncomfortably. 'I ... er ... have to say that you're not exactly pleasant to him yourself so is it any wonder he's like he is with you?'

Kay gawked at him, stunned. Was it possible that due to her resentment Tony was staying with them she was taking all he said out of context, making more of it than was meant and using it as an excuse to get Bob to ask him to go? If she was doing that then she wasn't being fair to the man who had saved her husband's life. Was Bob right? Did Tony act towards her like he did because he sensed her own antipathy towards him? Maybe he wouldn't treat her with such disrespect if he knew his presence in their house was more welcome – something she hadn't really gone out of her way to make him feel, if she was honest. She still didn't like the man but, regardless, if she made more of an effort to be pleasant towards him then he in turn might treat her more acceptably.

She took a deep breath. 'You're right, Bob, I haven't exactly made Tony feel at home, have I? After what he did for you, it's unforgivable of me. I will try harder for the rest of his stay.'

He smiled at her, mortally relieved. Moving to the back of the bike, he lifted up the lid of a box strapped to the back, pulling out a brown paper parcel. 'I got another two kits today from the toy shop on the High Street. One's the *Queen Mary* and the other is an airship. I can't wait to see how it's put together – looking at the box it seems quite complicated.'

Judging from the instructions on the back of

the box Bob was now studying, it didn't appear any more of a task to construct than the bi-plane had, it just had a few more pieces. But if it kept Bob content that was all she cared about. As her aunt had pointed out, it was better he was at home with Kay than propping up the bar in a pub like lots of men did.

'I can do these in the evening when it's too dark to work on my bike,' he continued, and looked at her expectantly. 'Right, well, if dinner's ready I could certainly eat it.'

A thought suddenly struck Kay then and she gnawed her bottom lip anxiously. If he'd bought the kits from a toy shop then these were new and far more expensive than the one he had found covered in dust in the second-hand shop. He was spending his savings very freely. If he carried on there would be nothing left to start his business with when the time came. She guessed his savings couldn't be huge considering he hadn't been earning a proper wage after finishing his apprenticeship for long before he volunteered to join the Army, and out of that wage had first to pay for his lodgings and other living expenses, surely not leaving that much each week to put by? There was so much they needed for the house and a new coat, even a second-hand one, for herself wouldn't go amiss as the one she had was at least five years old and starting to show the wear. After her marriage Kay had made do as much as she could with her existing clothing so that any spare money could be put away towards setting up home on Bob's return.

Then a thought suddenly struck her. For the

last five years, while serving first in India then in Burma, Bob had more than likely had hardly any opportunity to go into a shop. Now he was free to go into one whenever he wanted, and after all had used his own money that he'd saved before their marriage to buy the bike and the model kits. What right had she to spoil the enjoyment he must have experienced today, by reminding him of his commitments? There were years ahead for them to be sensible in, and after the last five years of hell Bob surely deserved a little frivolity. He hadn't as yet mentioned giving her any money for the housekeeping but she assumed that in the excitement of making his purchases it had temporarily slipped his mind.

Kay hooked her arm through his, reached up to peck his cheek and then smiled at him lovingly.

'Come on, let's get you fed.'

As soon as she began to clear the table of the dinner dishes, Bob sat down and prepared to start painting the bi-plane.

'Bob, I thought we should go round and tell my parents the good news about your job tonight.'

He didn't appear keen.

'Oh, they won't want us calling in at this time,' he said, using the end of a teaspoon to lever open the lid of the grey paint.

'But it's not seven yet. I think it's only fair we tell my father after all the trouble he went to to help you.'

'He more than likely knows already through gossip at the Mail. Look, by the time you've cleared up and I've had a wash and change, time will be wearing on. I really don't think it'd be fair of us, disturbing their evening.'

Kay smiled tenderly at him for this show of thoughtfulness.

'I appreciate your concern but my parents would be glad to see us whatever time of night it was.'

He gave a heavy sigh. 'Kay, I'm really tired after my hectic day. All I want to do is stay by my own fireside. You go if you want to, but I don't see why you can't pop around tomorrow afternoon after your father gets home from work. Have you got a bit of old rag I can use to catch any drips?' He smiled at her. 'Don't want you nagging me for getting paint on the table.'

She fetched him several cut from an old vest of her father's which her mother had given her to use as dishcloths. She stood looking at him hesitantly for a moment before taking a deep breath and asking, 'Bob, I'm sorry to remind you, but you were going to give me some money towards the housekeeping.'

'Oh, yes. Er ... how much do you want?'

'Well, it'll be two and a half weeks until you get your first pay as you have to work a week in hand. Before then we'll need to pay the rent twice again, which is two pounds ten shillings a week, and we'll want another bag of coal at least, and I'll have other bills to settle as well as buying food. So well, eight or nine pounds should just about cover it.'

He seemed surprised by the amount. 'Oh, that much? I'll get it for you later.'

'Thanks, Bob. When I've finished the dishes I'll pop round and tell my parents about your job.

They'll be so pleased and they won't understand if we leave it until tomorrow.'

But he was completely engrossed in his task. 'Mmm ... all right.'

After hurriedly completing her chores, Kay tidied herself. Before she left she went over to Bob to say her goodbyes. 'Right, I'll be off then,' she said, leaning over to kiss his cheek. 'I won't be long.' She was hoping he had changed his mind and would accompany her after all, but to her disappointment he didn't appear to have done so. As she turned to leave her eyes fell on the near-empty coal bucket to one side of the fireplace which normally she would have refilled before she sat down for the evening. It had slipped her mind to do it. Now it would mean her getting all dirty and having to tidy herself again. Surely Bob wouldn't mind doing it for her? 'Bob, I've forgotten to fill the coal bucket. There's just about enough in it to keep the fire going tonight along with the wood, and there's also a parcel of kitchen rubbish, but it means there won't be any left for me to light the fire with in the morning. Would you fill it for me, please?'

'Eh? Oh, yes. I'll do it in a minute.'

Her family were delighted to see her. 'Bob not with you?' her mother asked as she laid down her knitting and got up from her armchair to put on the kettle.

'He sends his apologies but he's had a long day of it in one way or another so I left him at home. He got offered a job with the Mail, Dad, as a collector. Starts on Monday.'

149

Herbie, relaxing in the armchair opposite his wife's, folded up the newspaper he was reading and beamed with delight.

'It'll suit him grand. Actually, I did know. Sid Askew came to see me before I clocked off. He told me that because Bob was my son-in-law, and as I'd already told Sid his background and credentials in the hope it would persuade him at least to see Bob, Sid never bothered with the usual interview but just offered him the job. Don't tell Bob, I wouldn't want to demean the man. Best let him think he got the job off his own back.'

'I won't, Dad, but thanks so much for your help.'

Kay smiled at her brother then as she stepped across to perch herself on the edge of his makeshift bed which was arranged across the far wall, the rest of the furniture huddled together to make room. 'How's it going?'

Trevor gave her a fed up look. 'How d'yer think, Sis? I'm slowly going mad. I know how caged chickens feel now.'

She laughed. 'Oh, Trevor, hardly! You've got Mam running after you, your mates popping in and out ... you're even going to the dance next Friday.'

He sighed, 'If I hadn't got that to look forward to, I really would be going doo-lally. Mam's put a curfew on me of ten o'clock, can you believe?'

'Aunty Viv told me, but at least she's allowing you to go so stop moaning.'

'Did you bring me any magazines?' he asked hopefully.

She shook her head. 'The only ones I have are women's types from Aunty Viv which I pass on to Mam and Eunice. I wouldn't have thought women's fashions or tips on stretching rations out was your type of reading matter.'

'Huh! I'm getting to the stage when the label on a packet of tea is interesting to me.'

Kay did feel sorry for her brother then. A lively, inquisitive child once, always full of mischief, he had grow into a popular young man, never short of friends, boys or girls, and liked the usual pursuits of most single men of his age. He was a dear brother to her and a good son to his parents, always readily volunteering a hand when he could, especially to his father down on the allotment. Kay knew that being incapacitated, unable to do anything for himself, stuck inside the house week after week with as yet no definite end in sight, was Trevor's idea of a living nightmare. A thought suddenly struck her. 'Would you like a model construction kit to help keep you occupied?' she asked.

'Eh?' Trevor gave her an 'Are you serious?' look. 'What, yer mean those kids' toys?'

'Grown ups do them too,' she said defensively.

He sniggered. 'Yeah, soft-headed ones who consider trainspotting an exciting hobby! Thanks for yer offer, Sis, but I'd have one of those put together in less than ten minutes, and if any of me mates caught me at it I'd never hear the end of it.' He looked at her queryingly. 'Has Bob got himself a motorbike?'

She gawped at him.

'How do you know about that?'

'Ronnie Smithers called in on his way back from work tonight and told me he'd seen a tall fair-headed man heading into your entry pushing an old relic of a thing. From his description it was obvious it was Bob. What was he doing with a bike?'

'He's bought it to do up.'

Trevor pursed his lips.

'I wish him luck then. Ronnie knows a bit about bikes as his dad's had one or two over the years and he said he doubts even a museum would want that one.' He looked at his sister uncomfortably. 'About Bob, our Kay...'

She eyed him, confused.

'What about him, Trevor?'

'Well, it's just...' He paused and gave a shrug. 'After everyone describing him to me, I was expecting him to be sort of...'

'What?'

'Well ... he just ain't what I was expecting, that's all. I pictured him to be more the outgoing type. But he's not, is he? Doesn't seem to have much to say for himself. I just can't imagine him having the backbone to run his own business. I can't honestly see what you saw in him.'

She stared at him aghast.

'Oh, Trev, how could you say such awful things about my husband when you've hardly got to know him?'

'I didn't mean to upset yer,' he said gruffly.

'Well, you have. For goodness' sake, he's just been through five years of hell...'

'I never exactly had a picnic of it, Sis.'

'No, but not everyone treated the war like it

152

was one big adventure.'

'Eh! I took me job seriously, joking about it is my way of coping.'

She sighed, 'Yes, I understand that. But in fairness to Bob, it's not just the effects of the war that he's coping with. He's also settling into a new town, having to make new friends, and into marriage with me. He's only been back days and already he's got a job, admittedly with Dad's help, but all the same...'

Trevor pulled a sheepish face.

'I'm sorry, Sis. I judged him purely by seeing him at Mam's dinner, and I suppose meeting us lot all together must have been worse than finding a Panzer tank bearing down on him. I didn't mean to be so nasty about his bike. If yer want the truth, I'm envious. I'd offer to give him a hand if I could. D'yer think he'll give me a ride on it when he gets it going?'

Kay smiled.

'I'm sure he will. I'm certain you'll like Bob when you get to know him properly. I know it doesn't seem like it just now but he's really interesting to talk to. He's made it his business to find out about things by reading a lot and by what he listens to on the wireless, and he's got a great sense of humour. He used to make me laugh so much with his quips and ... well, at the moment he's just lost that side to him but I know it will come back in time then you'll see exactly why I fell in love with him. He told me when we got married that he was so looking forward to meeting you. Never having had a brother of his own, he thought it was great he'd got one now.'

'It'll be good for me having a brother too, when I need an ally 'cos me sister's started nagging me.'

'You cheeky devil,' she laughed as she playfully slapped him on his arm.

Trevor hitched himself back up against his pillows in an effort to make himself more comfortable, wincing at the pain his injured leg still gave him. 'Can't say as I took much of a shine to that mate of his – Tony. I know I never got much of a chance to know him at the family get together but I know a spiv when I see one. You watch yer back with him, Sis.'

'Yes, well, I haven't exactly taken a shine to him myself. I've met the sort of man Bob usually has for his friends and they're nothing like the sort Tony is. But after what he did for Bob, the least we can do is make him welcome in our home until he gets a place of his own.'

'Yeah, I suppose. The four lads I drove to safety have all kept in touch and they want to meet up with me for a drink when I'm back on me feet, by way of thanking me.'

'Well, at least you didn't bring them home with you and expect Mam to put them up,' Kay said with a wan smile.

Trevor looked at her questioningly. 'What exactly did happen out in Burma? Has Bob told yer yet?'

'No, but I know he will once he's ready to.'

'What are you two cooking up?' their mother demanded as she came through carrying the tray of tea things.

They both looked across at her. 'Nothing, Mam,'

they said in unison.

'Kay's fibbing,' Trevor called out. 'She's helping me plan a break out.'

Mabel gawped in horror, then tutted disdainfully when she realised he was winding her up. 'Come and get your tea, Kay, before it gets cold,' she ordered.

'When you're back at work traipsing the streets in the frost and snow, delivering your letters, you'll be wishing you were back in that bed,' Kay told her brother.

'That I won't,' he vehemently insisted. 'I'd sooner be facing the Nazis than this torture.'

As Kay sat down at the table her mother held out a plate of Arrowroot biscuits. She shook her head. 'I've not long had my dinner.'

'What did you give Bob tonight?'

'Corned beef hash.'

'You used my recipe and followed it exactly?'

'I did, Mam, and it was lovely.'

She didn't think it wise to tell her mother that by the time they ate it it was all dried up. Thankfully Bob never seemed to notice. He'd scraped his plate clean and Kay suspected his mind was too preoccupied by thoughts of fixing the motorbike for him to notice what he was eating. Tony's comments were another matter. As her mother was under the impression that her husband's friend was a decent man and they were all living in the house amicably together, Kay felt it best not to let her know things were not what they seemed. Mam had enough to worry about getting Trevor back on his feet.

Mabel smiled at her proudly. 'Then I know

your Bob's had a decent meal. You're turning into a grand wife, Kay, and I'm proud of yer. Feed a man well and keep his house clean and you won't lose him. That right, Herbie? Herbie?'

Herbie lowered his paper which he had resumed reading when his wife had departed to make the tea and his daughter started talking to her brother. 'Eh? Oh, er, yes, dear.'

Mabel returned her attention to her daughter. 'I'm so pleased Bob's got fixed up with a job. Yer've no problems facing yer now, ducky. Yer've the means to pay yer bills and a lovely little house to live in. And yer lodger, doing all right, is he? Is he fixed up with work yet?'

'He seems to be doing all right for himself.'

'That's good to hear.' Mabel paused and looked at her daughter awkwardly, giving a small nervous cough. 'I'm so glad Bob's finally home and yer settled in yer own place together 'cos I know these last five years without him by yer side, worried to death about him, 'as bin really hard for yer. You know I wasn't happy about you rushing into marriage, yer dad neither, and with a man you'd hardly had time to get to know and us barely more than acquainted with him ourselves. But me and yer dad only had yer best interests at heart, Kay. We didn't want to see you live to regret acting in haste. Still ... we both know you're no fool and wouldn't have been so determined to wed Bob if yer weren't really sure about him. Yer dad and me just want yer to know that we realise we was wrong to try and make you wait until after the war was over, and now that we see yer happy with Bob, we hope you don't hold

156

it against us how we acted when yer broke the news of yer marriage to us?'

Kay felt tears prick her eyes. She knew it hadn't been easy for her mother to be so open with her. She leaned across and laid her hand on top of Mabel's, giving it a gentle squeeze.

'Of course I don't think badly of either of you. I know you both love me and want the best for me. I love you both too, couldn't have wished for better parents than you.'

Mabel cleared her throat and said stiffly, 'Well, that's out of the way. You'd better be getting off home to that husband of yours.'

Kay was hurrying in the direction of her house, eager to get home to Bob, when she suddenly remembered she really ought to inform Eunice about Saturday. She wasn't looking forward to telling her friend that they would not be coming and hoped she would understand the reasons why. To delay any longer wouldn't be fair as she knew Eunice would be planning what food to give them. With rationing and shortages as they were, the simple task of providing a meal or a few sandwiches had to be planned like a military operation.

Eunice and George lived a few streets away in an almost identical rented house to Kay's own with ageing facilities, furnished as best they could manage with what money they had scraped together, helped along a little by George's gratuity payment, and donations from their own families. Like Kay and Bob, as relative newly weds much was still needed but they'd acquire it come time. When she arrived Kay tapped on the front door lightly so as not to risk waking their daughter who she knew would be long in bed by now.

'Kay, how lovely to see you!' Eunice cried in genuine delight on opening the door to her. 'Come in, come in,' she urged, standing aside to allow her entry. 'George,' she called out loudly, 'it's Kay so fasten yer trousers up.' She gave a bellow of laughter when she saw the look on her friend's face. 'It's okay, you ain't caught us at anything. It's just that when we've no company, George likes to sprawl out comfortably in the armchair with the waistband of his trousers undone after his dinner.' She gave a tut. 'My dad would never dream of passing wind from either end or exposing the top of his underpants in front of me mother or us kids, but it's my George's opinion that behind closed doors a man should be free to do what makes him happy. I might not like it, but my George being comfortable in his own home is what's important to me.'

Kay hadn't thought of it like that. So what she had perceived as bad habits was in fact Bob showing her he was comfortable in his new sur-roundings. Eunice was right. A man should feel at liberty enough in his own home to act how he wanted. She vowed in future to be more tolerant.

George was standing up and tucking his shirt into his trousers when Eunice showed her through. 'Hello, Kay,' he said, smiling warmly in greeting. 'Sit yerself down. Cuppa?'

She smiled back at him. 'Not for me, thanks, I've just had one at my mother's.'

'I will though,' said Eunice.

Kay watched dumbstruck as George went off

into the kitchen. 'He makes you a cuppa?' she asked.

'He brings me one up in the morning before going to work and usually makes the cocoa before we go to bed. Lots of men think it's beneath them to turn their hand to anything domestic but my George thinks I deserve him mashing me a cuppa after all I do for him. Bob does the same for you, doesn't he?'

Kay couldn't bring herself to tell her best friend that since he had arrived home it hadn't seemed to have occurred to Bob to offer her a hand with any of the domestic chores. But she knew he would when he became more settled in.

Eunice gathered discarded children's clothing and several toys from off the settee and put them in a pile at the side of it. 'Sit yerself down then,' she instructed Kay.

Kay perched on the edge of the settee and after her friend had sat down beside her, clasped her hands together and said, 'About Saturday, Eunice.'

'Oh...' she interjected, looking at Kay excitedly, '...I'm looking forward to it and so is George. He's going to get a jug of beer from the pub. I'm afraid I didn't get 'ote special to make the sandwiches with in the tin line from the Home and Colonial, it was only tomatoes and pineapple chunks they'd had delivered, but as you're me best friend I'm gonna see if I can get some cooked ham from the butcher's. If he ain't got none then it's luncheon meat or Spam. George asked me if Bob liked a game of cards? I should think he does, like most men. We can have a game of whist. Only matchsticks for stakes but it'll be fun. About sevenish suit you?'

Kay gulped. 'I'm sorry, Eunice, I've come to ask if you mind if we postpone Saturday?'

Her friend's face fell in disappointment.

'Oh? Why, have you something better on?'

'No, it's not that. Bob's not ready for social get togethers with friends yet.'

'Why, what's wrong with him?'

'Nothing is wrong with Bob, Eunice, he's just got a lot on his plate, that's all. He's come back to a completely new life and needs time to adjust to it. Your George took a while to settle, so you told me.'

'Mmm, yes, he did. But I'd 'a' thought meself that a nice evening with friends would have helped him settle quicker, knowing he's fitting in like. You're not trying to fob us off with an excuse because he doesn't want to come, are yer, Kay?'

'No, not at all, Eunice,' she said, mortified that her friend could think such a thing. 'Please don't think that. I've told you the truth, honest I have. I've only asked if you mind if we postpone coming round, not cancel it altogether.'

'And I was so looking forward to it.' Eunice looked forlornly at her husband as he came through carrying two cups of tea. 'Kay's asking if we mind putting off Saturday for the time being. Seems Bob's not up to having a bit of fun yet.'

She ignored the look Kay gave her for the way she had put it to her husband.

George pulled a disappointed face. 'Oh, well, yeah. 'Course not, Kay. You let us know when he's ready and we'll look forward to it then, won't we, darlin'?'

His wife pulled a face. 'I suppose so.' Then she looked at Kay apologetically. 'I'm sorry, I'm being a right old grump over this, but I was so looking forward to it. Now we've Joanie we can't get out much together so having friends around, especially me best friend and her husband, is a right tonic to me.' She looked meaningfully at her husband. 'Well, I'm sure me and you can find something to occupy us once our daughter is in bed on Saturday night.'

'I'm sure we can.'

Eunice laughed, 'Oh, look, we've made Kay blush and 'er a married woman too.' She nudged Kay in her ribs and, leaning over, whispered in her ear, 'It's my guess you're really cancelling Saturday 'cos you and Bob are still making up for lost time together.'

If only that were true, Kay thought. He had only approached her in that way once since his return, and due to his abstinence had been clumsy in his lovemaking. Eunice had previously told her that George hadn't been able to control his passion when he had first come back and nearly wore her out in that department. Then it struck Kay that Tony's occupying the room beneath them was not only making her feel uncomfortable. Maybe it was affecting her husband too, and as he'd been the one to offer Tony their home to stay in, he couldn't bring himself to tell her. That had to be the answer. Tony was out tonight. If she rushed home, hopefully she and Bob could have some time together in bed before the lodger came back. She would even put on her special nightdress to make herself look more inviting for him.

'Well, I must be off or else Bob will think I've left him,' she quipped lightly, not wanting Eunice to have any inkling why she was in such a hurry to get home or her friend would rib her mercilessly. 'Again, I apologise about Saturday but we'll rearrange it as soon as Bob is feeling up to it.'

As Eunice saw her off at the door a memory struck her and she asked, 'Did you ask Bob what happened to Mike?'

'I haven't really had chance to but now you've reminded me, I will.'

Tingling with anticipation of what lay in store, Kay was mortally disappointed to arrive home and find Bob had already gone to bed. It was just after nine o'clock. On the edge of the dining table he had left nine pound notes which she assumed was her housekeeping money until he got paid in two and a half weeks' time. But again he hadn't attempted to tidy away any of the clutter he had made on the table. In fact, he hadn't replaced the lid on the tin of paint. It would dry up if left overnight which meant he wouldn't be able to finish the model he'd abandoned half-painted. She noticed then that neither had he replenished the coal bucket for her. Kay felt tears prick her eyes. The mess he'd left her to clear away was not what was upsetting her the most. It was the fact that he'd gone to bed without waiting to make sure she'd returned home safely first.

CHAPTER EIGHT

Just over a week later, early on Friday morning, Kay sat at the dining-room table, poring over two books her mother had given her: *Gert and Daisy's Wartime Cookery Book* and *The Kitchen Front*, hoping she would find a tasty recipe to make Bob for his dinner when he came home from work just before two o'clock. This was his fifth day at work and he seemed to like what he was doing well enough from what she could gather.

She gave a deep sigh and placed her elbow on the table, cupping her chin in her hand and staring thoughtfully into space. Bob seemed content enough with the life he had created for himself since his return, at the moment showing no signs of rekindling any of the interests she knew he had keenly followed before he went off to war. As yet he hadn't picked up so much as a newspaper to read, let alone a book of any description, and his preferred wireless listening was still light entertainment shows. It was as if he'd lost interest in the outside world apart from that small part that immediately affected him.

On his very first day of work a pattern had emerged on arriving home. He would eat his dinner, then fall asleep in the armchair for a couple of hours. On waking, after drinking a cup of tea Kay had made him, he would go outside and work on his motorbike until she called him in for his supper. Up to now he had got as far as dismantling half the bike, the parts lying in a heap and practically blocking the route to the outside privy. Since starting on the bike he'd abandoned his model kits, still hadn't finished painting the bi-plane, and fed up with hoping he'd tidy it away, Kay had done it herself. After eating his supper Bob would switch on the wireless then settle in the armchair, seemingly oblivious to anything else around him, laughing now and then when something in the show being broadcast amused him. At exactly nine-thirty he would switch off the wireless and, without offering to help her secure the house for the night, announce he was going to bed. As she had to get up with him at five in the morning to get his breakfast and see him off to work, Kay retired at that time also, but by the time she arrived upstairs he'd already be sound asleep. He never asked about her day. In fact, since his arrival home nearly two weeks ago now she hadn't really had a meaningful conversation with him. Neither had he offered to take her out anywhere.

It seemed to her that all Bob's previous enthusiasm for life had been left back in the jungle. As for their relationship, she felt that as things stood she was in fact not much more than a housekeeper to him. Kay desperately wanted the old Bob back, the one she had fallen in love with. She knew his true self had to be inside him, it was just a case of bringing it back to the surface again. The more he settled into his rut, though, the harder it would be to get him out of it. She felt a desperate urge to seek advice on what course of action she could take to help him, especially from her dear Aunty Viv who she knew would readily offer her help. So would Eunice, should she ask, but by opening up to them about her husband Kay feared she would seem disloyal to Bob, and also evasive to them since she'd covered up the truth when they asked her about him previously.

What a dilemma she was in. She sat for a while mulling over her problem then an idea struck her. Maybe there was something she could do ... if she bought him a newspaper and left it in a strategic spot, Bob might pick it up. It might just help to rekindle his interest in things outside the limited confines of his current preoccupations. She could get him a book to read from the library too, one of the novels he had told her he had read before and had thoroughly enjoyed. Reading it again might just remind him of his love of literature. Money was tight but if she was extra careful until she got more housekeeping from Bob when he received his first pay in a week's time she could just about scrape enough together for them to go to the pictures tomorrow night – something else he had previously enjoyed enormously. These few small things might be all it took to ignite his old spark, and once ignited she would do her utmost to make sure its flame was kept fanned. A surge of hope filled her. It was worth a try. It was worth trying anything to bring Bob back to his old self.

She had just readied herself to go out to shop for that evening's dinner when the door to the front room opened and Tony came out. He too was dressed ready to go out in a smart overcoat over his suit, trilby in his hand ready to put on over his slicked-back hair. Since her pledge to Bob she had been politeness itself to their guest, and although it galled her greatly to do so, she had to admit that relations between them had become more harmonious. Kay still resented his presence in their home, still felt it was responsible for the lack of activity in their bedroom and couldn't wait for the day when Tony announced he'd be leaving them. She had a sneaking suspicion also that her outwardly changed attitude towards him had not in fact pleased him. She realised he had derived much pleasure from treating her like a resentful servant, it had seemed to feed his ego. He still tried to bait her at every opportunity but now Kay did not rise to it. As far as she was concerned he could get his ego fed elsewhere because she wasn't going to do it anymore.

He smiled charmingly at her now.

'I know you'll be pleased to know you'll have my company tonight. Thought it was about time I spent an evening with my gracious hosts.'

Kay's heart sank. This news was not good so far as she was concerned. It was arduous enough spending evenings with her withdrawn husband, trying at every opportunity to draw him into some sort of conversation and getting no joy, without having to put up with Tony's sarcasm as well. She wasn't about to let him see how she truly felt about his announcement, however, although she did wonder why he had chosen this particular night to grace them with his company

166

when every other night since he'd been with them he'd been out, on many of them not coming home until the early hours of the morning. Then she'd have to go quietly about her housework the next day until he decided to rise, usually around eleven, when he'd eat the breakfast she felt obliged to cook him then immediately get ready and go out again, never volunteering any information as to where he was going or what he was doing. Not that she was interested, mind. Thankfully, though, to the best of her knowledge he hadn't brought another woman home with him. Whether he had seen the error of his ways and was showing respect for his hosts, or whether he just hadn't met a woman he wanted to bring back and spend the night with, she didn't know but suspected it was the latter. He took for granted the fact that Kay would take care of his laundry and still hadn't offered anything towards his keep. She had now given up hope of his ever doing so.

She forced a smile to her face.

'We'll look forward to it. Will you be wanting any dinner today? Providing I can get some liver from the butcher's, I'm doing that with onions and mashed potatoes. I'll be dishing up when Bob gets home from work just before two.'

Tony cocked an eyebrow at her.

'I'm rather partial to liver and onions myself. The last time you cooked it, it was almost as good as my old grandmother used to make. If I'm not back and you promise not to dry it up, keep it hot and I'll eat it when I get in.' He made to depart then stopped, locking his eyes with hers, an amused twist to his lips. 'Oh, and I expect you'll be delighted to hear that I won't be with you much longer. Never liked me living under your roof, have you, Mrs Clifton, despite your recent obvious attempts to make me believe the opposite? Well, I'm on the verge of making myself a nice tidy packet and as soon as that's in my pocket, I'll be off to London. That's where the real opportunities lie for a man like me. Yes, Leicester has certainly served its purpose but I've bigger fish to fry. This backwater might do for some but for me it has its limitations.' He smiled disarmingly at her as he put on his hat, adjusting it to sit at a jaunty angle. 'I shall look forward to our cosy evening in together.'

Just then the back door knocker sounded and Eunice charged in.

'Kay, I'm glad I've caught yer. Me mam's got our Joanie for a couple of hours while I do me shopping. I wondered if yer wanted some company while we queue for our rations? Oh!' she mouthed, eyes suddenly settling on Tony. 'I didn't realise you had company, Kay.'

He held out his hand to her in greeting. 'I'm Mrs Clifton's lodger, Tony Cheadle. Pleased to meet such an attractive lady.'

Accepting it, Eunice gulped, 'Pity I'm a married one then, ain't it?'

Still gripping her hand, Tony leaned towards her, fixing his eyes on her attentively. 'I can assure you, the regret is all mine.' He released her hand. 'You will excuse me? I'm just going out. Good day, ladies,' he called as he departed.

Eunice looked at Kay accusingly.

168

'Strewth! Yer never told me you had a lodger. And what a corker. He certainly got my knees knocking.'

'Well, I didn't think he'd be with us this long so it didn't seem worth mentioning him to you. He's a friend of Bob's from the Army. Saved Bob's life once, apparently, and in return we offered him a place to stay until he's found his feet. He's no family of his own. And he might be good-looking, Eunice, but let me tell you, as far as I'm concerned that's all he's got going for him. Tony's full of himself and sarcastic with it. I'm sure he thinks all women swoon at the sight of him. Well, not this one. Anyway, he's just made my day by telling me the most wonderful news. He's moving on shortly so Bob and I can finally have the house to ourselves!'

'Oh, yer must have taken him wrong, Kay. That man's charm itself. I wouldn't say no if I wasn't already spoken for! I tell yer summat for n'ote, I'm glad it weren't my George who brought him home. I couldn't have coped with looking at his attributes across the breakfast table each morning without drooling in me porridge, and I can't for the life of me see how the hell you have. Your Bob is good-looking enough and so is my George, but him ... well, he's got film-star looks, ain't he?'

Kay desperately wanted to get off the subject of her lodger. 'Shall we go shopping or I won't get any liver for Bob's dinner?' she said, hooking her arm through her friend's. 'And hopefully we might find a couple of spare coppers to treat ourselves to a cup of tea and an iced bun in the

169

market café.'

Tony's news had cheered Kay so much she was impervious to the biting mid-October wind that whipped through her clothing as they walked into town, the saved bus fare to be used for their treat at the café when they had finished their shopping. By the time they had patiently queued at the Maypole for their rations of cheese, sugar and tea and a few other provisions, then again at the butcher's for their meat, the baker's for bread, then fought their way through the crowds of other shopper for their vegetables off the market – Kay not having to buy as much as Eunice as her vegetable requirements were topped up courtesy of her father's allotment – they were both more than ready for a cup of tea.

'Who'd be a housewife?' Eunice moaned as she bit into her lemon iced finger bun. 'The men have it easy, don't they, going to work? D'yer reckon your Bob really has a clue what it's like to queue for ages on end for what you eat, feet killing yer, and then at the end of it yer can't buy what yer really need, just what yer ration allows – 'cos I'm sure my George doesn't. My tea's cold, is yours?'

Kay shook her head. 'Mine's fine. Have you any more shopping to do?'

'You in a rush to get home or summat?'

'Remember I have Bob coming in for his dinner just before two. George doesn't come home for his until the evening, it's too far for him to travel, so you have all afternoon to prepare yours.'

'Oh, yeah, I forgot that. Well, that way at least you don't have the bother of making a pack up each night and the worry of finding summat different and tasty to put in sandwiches each day like I do.'

'Yes, I do. I always make Bob a snack and a flask of tea for mid-morning, and I still have the worry of what to give him for his tea each night.'

'Oh, yeah, I suppose. We have the same bothers really then, don't we? Me mam certainly knows how to pull a fast one, doesn't she? In exchange for the pleasure of her having her granddaughter for a couple of hours, I have to queue to get *her* groceries as well as me own and lug them all back home. I'm not walking back today, saved pennies or not, I'm catching the bus. Oh hell, I never got me Oxydol soap power and it's a halfpenny cheaper at the Maypole than it is at Worthington's. Oh, bugger it, Worthington's it is 'cos I ain't queuing again, not today I ain't. How's Bob liking his job?'

'Oh, seems to well enough, thanks for asking.'

'So we on for arranging another get together?'

If Kay's plan worked then shortly the enthusiasm for doing such things would be kindled within Bob. 'Soon, I hope, Eunice.'

She pulled a disappointed face as she popped the last of her lemon bun into her mouth and drank down her tea. 'Well, if you've n'ote else to get, shall we be off?'

'I have actually,' Kay said as she stood up and gathered her bags. 'I want to get Bob a newspaper and a book from the local library, but I can do that when we get off the bus.'

'My George read a book once,' Eunice said as she elbowed her way out of the café.

Following closely behind her, Kay said, 'Oh, I

171

didn't know he was a bookworm.'

'I said book, not books. He said it changed his life.'

They were outside on the pavement now. 'Oh, really? What book was it?'

'*How To Survive As A Married Man.*'

Kay giggled. 'Oh, you. Come on, let's catch that bus before I drop this lot.'

Why was it, she thought as she turned the corner of her street and began to make her way laboriously to her own house, that the shopping bags she was carrying seemed to get heavier with each step she took? She would be glad to offload her burden, she felt her arms were about to drop off. After saying her goodbyes to her friend and arranging to see Eunice again soon, she called in at the local newsagent's for a *Daily Sketch* then proceeded to the library where she was delighted to find a copy of *Mr Standfast* by John Buchan, a suspense thriller of the type which she knew Bob once enjoyed. If she could get him to pick it up, she knew he would soon become engrossed in its pages. She felt sure that after this book would follow another, and so on.

As she neared her house, desperate now to be home, she suddenly stopped short. A well-dressed man was knocking at her door. She frowned, wondering who this could be as she wasn't expecting anyone, especially someone as presentable as this.

She came up to him. 'Can I help you?'

The man spun round to face her, a look of shock on his face. 'Oh, goodness, you gave me a scare. I was told the Cliftons live... Kay! It is you, isn't it?'

She frowned at him. 'Yes, it is. Do I know... Mike!' she cried. 'Mike Newcome. Well, I'll be blowed. What a sight you are for sore eyes. Eunice and I were only talking about you the other day. We wondered how you came out of it. I'm so glad to see you have safe and sound. You do remember my friend Eunice?'

He laughed. 'As if I could forget! Nice girl, not backwards in coming forwards, I seem to remember.'

Kay laughed too. 'That's Eunice.'

'How is she?'

'She's fine. Happily married with a toddler.'

'That's good to hear.'

'So what are you doing here? Not that it isn't great to see you.'

'I'm come to see Bob.'

'Yes, of course you have, how silly of me. Oh, where are my manners? Come on in. Let me get you a cuppa.'

'Let me take your bags,' he offered, relieving her of them.

'Oh, thanks,' she responded gratefully. Briefly explaining that they had a guest staying with them at the moment who was using their front room that opened directly off the street, hence the reason for her not using the front door, she led him down the entry, through the back gate, and after unlocking the back door into the kitchen.

'Put the bags on the floor. I do appreciate you carrying them in for me.' She hurriedly checked the kettle for water, lit the gas under it then turned back to face Mike. 'I can't believe you're here. Oh, it really is so good to see you. You found

173

us all right then?'

He leaned back against the sink, taking off his hat and laying it on the draining board.

'I remembered Bob telling me the street you used to live on.' He smiled at her fondly. 'As soon as he met you, he talked about you all the time. No disrespect to you, Kay, but so much so I had to tell him to shut up sometimes. It was blindingly obvious to me from the start that he was bowled over by you, and as far as he was concerned had met the woman he wanted to spend the rest of his life with.

'Anyway, I made some enquiries, eventually spoke to your mother, and she pointed me here. I knew Bob had come home safe. Made it my business to find out from Army records. I expect he told you we lost touch not long after we both arrived in India? Our unit was split and we were dispatched to different garrisons, then my unit got sent on to Singapore when it became clear the Japs were showing more than an interest. As luck would have it, I and a few of my colleagues were put on escort duty on the last ship bringing British citizens back home. I say lucky because those in the unit who stayed behind were captured, the whole garrison was, and those still alive after the battle spent the rest of the war as POWs.' Mike's voice lowered then and he added emotionally, 'And not many of them returned. The rest of my war was spent in Europe. I must be one of the few who never got a scratch. Thank God it's all over, eh? I just pray we never have to go through anything like that ever again.' He took a breath and eagerly asked, 'How is Bob? I can't wait to see him and have a good catch up.'

Kay smiled warmly at him. A visit from his friend Mike was just the tonic Bob needed. If anything was going to help bring him out of himself then this would be it. 'He's at work at the moment, gets home just before two. He'll be so thrilled to see you, I know he will. You will have dinner with us, won't you? Are you staying in Leicester long? Are you moving up here? Oh, it'd be grand if you were. Have you found a nice girl yet and settled down?'

Mike laughed and said, 'Whoah! Slow down there, old girl, let a man get a word in.'

She laughed too. 'Sorry, I was doing a Eunice, wasn't I?'

He pulled back the sleeve of his coat and looked at his watch. 'Actually, Kay, this is just a short visit. It was a long shot, trying to catch Bob at home, but I was really hoping to have a couple of hours with him before I went to see my aunt. You remember I have an aunty living in Leicester? Bob had come with me to visit her the night he met you.'

'Of course I do. How could I forget, Mike? I have a lot to thank your aunty for, haven't I? If she hadn't gone against your grandparents' wishes and moved from Northampton to Leicester as a young woman, in the hope of making a better life for herself, I might never have met Bob.'

'And she did make a better life for herself, I'm glad to say, much better than she would have had. But even without my aunt doing what she did, I think you and Bob would have met somehow. You two were meant to be together, any fool

175

could see that. Anyway, Kay, as I said it's just a short visit up to Leicester to see both Bob and my aunt. I've a train to catch to London at five then the overnight to Southampton.'

'Southampton? Have you got a job down there?'

'No, I'm catching a boat. I'm sailing for Australia tomorrow afternoon.'

She gawped at him, stunned. 'Australia?'

He nodded. 'I'm trying my luck there.'

'But why? I mean, Australia ... that's the other side of the world. What about your family?'

'I'm not like Bob, Kay, with a lovely wife waiting for me to come back from the war and every reason to build a future here. I've only my mother and sister, and the place they live isn't exactly Buckingham Palace. Getting somewhere better at the rent, we can afford to pay out between us is just impossible as things stand. My mam couldn't afford for me to do an apprenticeship like Bob, and any hope I have of bettering myself in England without a trade or any capital behind me is near non-existent, the way things are in this country just now. If all goes well for me in my new venture, I'm going to send for my family, and my mother might persuade my aunt who's a widow now to come too. Then we'll all be together over there and hopefully I can give them a better quality of life than they'll ever have here. Okay, my aunt did well for herself but she's far from rich. She hasn't said as much as she's proud is my aunt, but I know she's struggling on the money my uncle left her and lonely now he's passed on.'

Mike took a deep breath and folded his arms.

'I was demobbed six months ago. Tried to settle back into my old life. Got my old job back in the shoe factory. Every Friday night went down the pub with my old muckers. Played darts, snooker, took out a couple of girls ... all the things I used to do before and enjoy. But I found I wasn't happy anymore, Kay. It's not enough for me to hope that at the end of the week I might have enough in my pay packet to treat my mother to a stout at the local. That'll never improve unless the bosses decide to pay their workers more than the pittance they can spare from funding their own worthless existences. They live in luxury while their workers barely have enough to buy themselves new shoes without having to sacrifice something else to do so. I'm sorry to be sounding so despondent, Kay, but in fact I am. This country has made me feel that way. I'm fed up with walking down dismal streets, looking at people's hopeless faces.'

'Oh, but Mike, it won't always be like this. The politicians have promised us a better country, and once we're back on our feet after being battered by the war...'

'And you believe the politicians, Kay? The rich in this country keep the poor down. It's always been like that, and it'll take more than words from politicians' mouths to change it. Men like Bob with a real skill will prosper from this war, Kay, because their talents are needed to rebuild this country. His father worked all the hours God sent to get the money together to make sure his son stood a chance of a better future. He never lived to see his sacrifices pay off because by working like he did for Bob, he ruined his health. My mother wasn't able to do as much for me, though she wanted to, believe me. She was already a widow when it came time for me to leave school and finding the money to pay for an indenture for me was impossible. As it was she had to pawn her wedding ring to get the money to pay for a pair of secondhand trousers and boots for me to wear to my factory job.

'Kay, I hope to meet a woman one day, settle down and have a family, but I want a better life for them all than I feel will ever be offered here. I met a couple of Aussies while I was in the Army and got on really well with one of them. He told me about all the opportunities in his country for men like me. Even a labouring job on a farm pays far more there than sitting in a dreary factory bent double over a clicking machine, never seeing daylight during working hours. That's where I feel my future lies, Kay. The climate will do wonders for my mother as she suffers dreadfully in our awful winters. I shall do my best to make a go of things.'

After listening intently to what Mike had said, Kay could appreciate fully his reasons for seeking a better life for himself in Australia. She knew that what he was saying was true. Her own father had worked loyally for the Royal Mail all his life but had hardly anything to show for his labours by way of material possessions, and despite her parents' careful handling of every penny he'd earned from his wage, he had only a frugal retirement to look forward to. Because of Bob's father's sacrifices in making sure his son acquired a trade they did have the chance of a more fruitful future, once Bob relented and allowed himself to use his skills. Not many of the people she lived among had a chance like Bob and she did. They were stuck in the poverty trap because, like Mike, their parents had always been poor, desperately needing the money from their children's wage to supplement their own as soon as those children reached working age, like her own parents had needed help from herself and her brother. Unless the politicians meant what they said and forced the bosses to give the deprived of this country a chance to improve their lives with better pay and working conditions, life would forever be a vicious circle for the lower classes.

'But maybe peacetime will change things for the working man, Mike, and everyone will get opportunities to improve their lives?'

'It might, but I can't waste my life waiting around to see if it will. We can only live in hope, Kay. Barney, that's my Aussie friend, is going to put me up and help me find work. I have to say, I'm really excited about it all but I don't want to go off without seeing Bob. I don't know when I'll be back in England.' Mike looked at his watch again. 'If it's all right with you, I'll change my plans around. I'll go and see my aunt first, then come back about two-thirty and leave from here direct for the station. I've left all my belongings in the left luggage at St Pancras ready to collect before I hop on the overnight to Southampton.'

'Yes, two-thirty will be fine. I'll have something to eat ready for you.'

'That's good of you, Kay, but knowing my aunt as I do, she'll have me stuffed full before she allows me out of her house.'

She stood at the door to see him off and as he made to side-step the pile of motorbike parts in the yard, he looked down for a moment then back to Kay. 'Is this Bob's?'

'Yes, he bought it cheap to fix up.'

'It's looks a bit of a relic to me, but in Bob's hands I know it'll be like new when he's finished with it. Always was good with his hands, was Bob. Pity I won't be around to have a go on it. See you in a bit, Kay.'

CHAPTER NINE

Kay busied herself putting away the shopping. Not feeling it right that Mike should return and find them in the middle of dinner, she made Bob a sandwich, feeling sure he'd understand her reason for delaying their meal until that evening. She just hoped Tony did not return meantime and intrude on Bob's short time with his friend.

Her husband came in at ten minutes to two, stripping off his coat and hanging it on the back door along with his knapsack for Kay to empty later of its Thermos flask and the box that held his snack, ready to wash them for the next day. She was busy at the sink peeling potatoes. Before she could greet him and explain, Bob noticed there was no pan bubbling on the stove and, face puzzled, asked, 'No dinner?'

Dropping her peeling knife, she grabbed a drying towel and wiped her hands, saying excitedly, 'We're having it later. Oh, Bob, you've had a visitor! Oh, I can't wait to tell you. Your friend Mike Newcome's been. He remembered you mentioning to him the street I lived on with my parents and asked around. Eventually he spoke to my mam and she pointed him here. As you weren't expected home for a while, he's gone off to see his aunt but he'll be back any time now. He's emigrating to Australia tomorrow afternoon. Got to catch a train back to London at five. He'll tell you all about that himself, but he wanted to see you before he went. He's so looking forward to catching up with you. If you hurry to wash and change, I've a sandwich ready to keep you going until we have our dinner this evening.'

He was looking at her, stunned, then his face lit up with a broad smile. 'Mike? Oh, well, that's great. It'll be good to see him again.' He grabbed his coat from off the back of the door, heedless of the fact that he had also unhooked his knapsack along with it which fell with a clatter to the floor. 'I'll go and get a couple of bottles of beer from the off licence. Can't not offer my friend a drink, can I? I won't be a tick.'

As he shot out of the back door a warm glow filled Kay. Judging by his reaction to the news of Mike's visit Bob was just as thrilled as she'd hoped he'd be. This visit was going to do wonders for him, she knew it was.

Picking up his knapsack and rehanging it, she hurriedly cleared away the peelings, covered the potatoes with cold water ready for boiling later, set a tray ready with the tea things should Mike prefer tea instead of beer, and despite his already telling her his aunt would be feeding him, also arranged pieces of currant slab cake cut from a larger chunk she had bought that day from the Maypole, knowing her mother would have tut-tutted at her for buying cake instead of making her own. With everything ready for their visitor, she rushed upstairs to change her workaday jumper for a pretty blue short-sleeved, Peter Pan-collared blouse, and brush her hair.

Back down in the living room, Kay frowned as she looked at the clock on the mantelpiece. Bob had been gone over twenty minutes. The off licence was only a couple of streets away on the main road in the row of shops there. She couldn't for the life of her think what was taking him so long. Mike would be arriving any time now and Bob wouldn't have had time to wash or change or eat his sandwich.

At four o'clock, Kay looked at Mike helplessly and for the umpteenth time apologised to him for Bob's non-arrival. 'I'm so sorry, Mike. I just can't imagine where he's got to. He only went to the local off licence for a couple of bottles of beer so he could offer you a drink. I couldn't see any sign of him when I went out to look not long after you arrived. The woman in the off licence said she couldn't remember serving a man of Bob's description. If he didn't arrive at the off licence, where on earth did he go to? And he was so looking forward to seeing you. You should have seen the way he acted when I told him. He was overjoyed.' Then her face screwed up in worry and she wrung her hands tightly. 'He couldn't have had an accident, could he? No, if he had done the police would have called by now. I don't know what to think. I'm so sorry, Mike, really I am.'

'I'm sorry too, Kay. I really was looking forward to seeing him. Obviously something came up, that's all.'

'I can't think what would keep him from a visit from his best friend, Mike, especially as he knows you're emigrating to Australia. I told him that.' She glanced at the clock. 'You have to go now or you'll miss your train.'

'I can't go and leave you like this, so worried. I'm worried too. I can't be on that boat for six weeks not knowing what's happened to him. It was bad enough during the war, not knowing about Bob.'

'But if you don't catch the train, you'll risk missing your boat. You have to go, Mike.' Despite being worried sick, Kay tried to sound positive for his sake. 'Look, as I said, if Bob had met with an accident we would have been informed by now. Something has kept him away but I'm sure it's not that serious.' Oh, God, she dearly hoped not. 'Is there any way we can get a message to you before you sail?'

He shook his head. 'Not that I know of. Oh, yes, my aunt has a telephone. You could leave a message with her and I'll call her from a telephone box as soon as I arrive in Southampton tomorrow morning.' He pulled a piece of paper

183

out of his pocket and a pen. After writing down a telephone number, he handed it to Kay. 'That's Aunty Edna's number, and also the address I'll be staying at for the time being in Australia which I'd already written down for you. You will ask Bob to write to me, won't you?'

'Of course I will.'

He stood up and took his coat off the back of a dining chair where he had put it earlier.

Kay stood up to join him, going over to him and giving him a friendly hug. 'I know I speak for Bob too when I wish you all the luck in the world. You will take care of yourself, won't you, Mike?'

He smiled. ''Course I will. I learned how to watch my back in the Army, remember. I'm sure not all the people in Australia are descended from vagabonds and cut throats. I'll say it again, Kay, I'm so sorry not to have seen Bob before I went, but at least I know from you that he's all right. He's going to do well is Bob. He's the sort of chap you feel confident about as soon as you meet him. And he's got a wonderful woman like you behind him so I know without a doubt he's going to make a success of himself.

'I'm only sorry to hear he's no enthusiasm yet for starting his own business, like he always told me he planned to do. He said there'd be a job for me, in fact, which I might very well take him up on if things don't work out for me Down Under. But after what happened to me when I came back here, how disillusioned I felt, I can appreciate the way Bob's feeling at the moment. He just needs time to adjust, that's all. Knowing him

184

like I do, he won't be down for long. One day soon he'll come home and surprise you by telling you he's jacked in his job on the Mail and is ready to pick up where he left off before he joined up. When you've made your money, you will come out and visit me, won't you?'

Mike's visit had done wonders to make Kay appreciate a little more of what her husband was going through, and to vow to be more understanding. Bob, she had no doubt, would have benefited greatly from seeing his good friend and she felt it was a real shame that, for whatever reason, he'd been denied the chance. She smiled warmly at Mike. 'Of course we will.'

He leaned over and kissed her cheek, then picked up his hat and left. As soon as she'd closed the door after seeing him out, worry about Bob's whereabouts overwhelmed Kay. She began to pace the kitchen floor, mind whirling frantically, but couldn't come up with anything that would account for his absence. Just then she heard the back gate slam against the garden wall as it was thrust open. She raced to the kitchen door, yanking it open to see a breathless Bob racing up the path towards her.

She ran out to join him, crying, 'Oh, Bob, Bob! Thank God you're safe.' She threw her arms around him, hugging him fiercely. 'I was beginning to think... Oh, God, Bob, where have you been?' she demanded.

He was gasping for breath, beads of sweat trickling from his brow. Obviously he'd been running hard. 'Have I caught Mike, Kay? Is he still here?'

'No, you've missed him. He's not long left.'

'Oh, no,' he wailed. 'Oh, but if I run I might catch him,' he cried, spinning around to chase back down the path and out of the back gate.

He returned ten minutes later, his face miserable. 'I just missed him. The bus was pulling away as I got there. I tried to flag it down but the driver didn't see me. Oh, hell,' he groaned.

She smiled sympathetically at him. 'I'm so sorry, Bob.'

She helped him out of his coat and told him to go and sit down while she made him a cup of tea. That done and placed on the floor to the side of him, she sat down in the armchair opposite and waited patiently while he lit the roll-up he'd taken out of his baccy tin, drawing deeply from it. Unable to contain her patience any longer, Kay asked, 'What did happen to you, Bob? I left Mike here while I went out to look for you but the woman in the off licence said no man of your description had been in recently.'

He blew a cloud of smoke into the air.

'That's because I hadn't. I got as far as the corner of our street when this old dear in front of me collapsed in a heap, her shopping rolling all ways.'

'Oh, my goodness,' Kay exclaimed. 'Who was she?'

'I've no idea, I'd never seen her before. I rushed to help her and she looked ghastly. I thought she was going to die on me right there and then. Of course, there was no one else around, there never is in situations like this. Thankfully she seemed to rally after a bit and some colour came back into her cheeks but it was obvious she wasn't well.

186

'I managed to get her up and she told me where she lived but she was more concerned about her shopping than she was for herself. I sat her on a doorstep while I gathered it all up then walked her home. Once there I sat her in an armchair and made her a cup of tea. I tried to leave her then as I realised time was wearing on and you must be wondering where I'd got to but she took another funny turn again, fainted right away, and dropped the cup of tea I'd made her all down herself. I was in quite a panic, wasn't sure what to do. I rushed around several neighbours but none of them was in so I did the only thing I could and went to the nearest telephone box, asking the operator to put me through to the local doctor. I explained to his wife what had happened and she said he would come straight out, then I went back to the old dear's house to wait for the doc to visit. Well, I couldn't leave her on her own, could I?'

'No, you couldn't, Bob. Certainly not.'

'The doctor seemed to take ages to arrive but when he finally did, I explained who I was and he examined her while I waited in the kitchen. Eventually he came through and told me the old lady hadn't been looking after herself very well, not eating right and her low blood pressure was what had caused her to faint. He felt it best to get her into hospital and properly checked over and asked me if I'd wait with her while the ambulance came as he had to get back to his surgery to do the phoning. Well, what could I say but yes, of course I would? Anyway he went off and I did my best to make sure the old lady was comfortable and the ambulance arrived about half an hour later and just as it did her daughter came in. Thankfully it seems she always pops in on her mother on her way home from work. Of course I had to explain why I was there and she was ever so grateful I'd helped her mother and said this was the final straw, she was coming to live with her whether she liked it or not. Anyway, she went off in the ambulance with her mother and here I am.'

Kay brushed away tears from her eyes hearing about this poor old lady's ordeal but was so glad her husband had been on the scene to help her. 'Oh, Bob, an act of kindness caused you to miss seeing your old friend, not to mention the worry you caused me.'

He shrugged. 'Well, it's just one of those things. You do what you have to at the time. I am so sorry I missed Mike, though. I was looking forward to seeing him again and having a catch up. You saw to him all right, though, didn't you? Australia, eh? I can't see why he wants to go myself. What's wrong with good old Blighty? Still, I wish him luck. God, I'm tired after missing my afternoon sleep. Famished too.'

Kay jumped up. 'I'll get the sandwich I made you earlier. That'll keep you going while I cook the dinner. After you've eaten the sandwich, why don't you have a snooze while I nip down to the telephone box?'

He looked at her sharply. 'What do you need to go to the telephone box for?'

'I promised Mike I'd leave a message at his aunt's for him, just to let him know you're all right.'

'Oh, I see. Yes, of course, you must let him know I'm fine. And say I'm sorry I didn't get to see him, but I'm sure he'll understand in the circumstances.' Bob relaxed back into his armchair, resting his feet on the hearth. 'This fire needs a bit of a perk up.'

You could offer to help me by doing it, thought Kay, then felt guilty for thinking it. Bob must be exhausted after his traumatic experience with the old lady, and after all he'd been up since four and done a hard shift's work. She seemed to forget that she too had risen at the same time to get his breakfast and see him off to work, and it had been a long day for her too. 'I'll do it when I've fetched your sandwich.'

She brought the newspaper and library book back with her and, handing him the plate with the sandwich on, put them on the arm of his chair.

'I got you a newspaper, Bob. You always liked to keep up with the news and I thought maybe you might want to start that again. I got you a book too, hopefully the type you like. You always loved reading and now the nights are really drawing in, I thought you might like it.'

He glanced at them as he bit into his sandwich.

'Oh, right, thanks. I'll have a look at them later.'

Her heart soared. At least he'd said he'd have a look. She just knew that once he started to read he'd realise what he'd been missing. As she knelt before the fire and began to replenish it, Kay said, 'I wondered if you fancied going to the pictures tomorrow night? Aunt Viv told me about a good film she thought we might like to see. We

189

haven't been out together since you came home and it would be nice, wouldn't it?'

Bob pulled a face. 'See what we feel like tomorrow night, eh? But the next episode of *Dick Barton* is on the wireless and I don't really want to miss it.'

Her heart started to sink once more. He really had got himself into a comfortable rut and didn't seem at all willing to prise himself out of it. As for the likes of the *Dick Barton* show, the Bob she had fallen in love with would never have listened to that kind of thing, he'd far more interesting things to do with his time.

'Well, maybe the cinema another night then. Er … maybe you might fancy going for a drink down the pub later, being's it's Friday night? Most men like to go for a drink on a Friday night, don't they?'

'I might. I'll see how I feel later,' he added, yawning.

The fire replenished sufficiently, she replaced the tongs in the companion set and stood up.

'So … how was your day at work?'

'Good. I'm getting the hang of it all now. There's a lot to remember.'

'I'm pleased to hear it. You haven't forgotten about the allotment, have you, Bob? Only my dad did advise you it needs a dig over before the winter really sets in.'

'No, I haven't forgotten. I was thinking I might go down at the weekend, I'll see how I feel then.'

'And what about the motorbike? How's it coming on? Making good progress, are you?'

'Come to a standstill at the moment. I need a

manual. No point in doing any more on it until I get one,' he said with another yawn.

'Oh, didn't the man you bought it from give you the one that came with the bike?'

'No.' He stretched himself lazily. 'I'll see about getting one when I have the chance. Maybe a motorbike shop has one lying around somewhere.'

Kay frowned at him, bothered. It seemed to her that he was losing interest in the bike, too, just as he had in the models. Oh, Bob, her mind screamed, what has the war done to you? Was he, like Mike, despondent after returning to find the country on its knees, people weighed down by severe rationing and the advancing winter doing its bit to make the already dismal streets even drearier? Bob wasn't in any position to escape this country like Mike as he had a wife to consider.

She sighed heavily, feeling at a loss as to what to suggest next that might kindle within him that old spark of determination. But nothing else she could think of seemed to help. Then she remembered her pledge to herself to encourage Bob into believing she wanted him as a man. It wasn't easy for her to make such a move but, steeling herself, she took a deep breath, leaned over to kiss his cheek and, looking at him lovingly, suggested: 'If you don't fancy going out, maybe we could have an early night?'

'Eh? Oh, I'm a bit tired tonight, Kay, what with all that's happened. Maybe tomorrow night, eh?'

She felt terrible rejection sear through her. Yes, maybe tomorrow night, she thought as she turned from him and made her way into the kitchen. That

191

was Bob's answer to everything at the moment. 'I'll do it in a minute' or 'Maybe tomorrow' ... and nothing ever materialised.

Mike's aunt was relieved to hear that Bob was all right and promised to pass the good news on to him as soon as he telephoned.

A while later, the dinner just about cooked, Kay was laying the table, going quietly about her business as Bob was still snoozing, when she heard the front door open and shut. A moment later, the connecting door to the back room opened and Tony breezed in. Kay noticed he was looking pleased with himself as he plonked himself down in an armchair, stretching his legs out on the hearth. Obviously his deal to put enough money in his pocket to set himself up in London was going well. She was just desperate for its finalisation.

'I've timed that just right,' he said, holding his hands out towards the fire and giving them a rub. 'Dinner just about ready, is it? It smells good.'

This was a rare compliment, if indeed that was what it was meant to be, and she looked over at him, surprised.

Just then Bob woke up. 'Oh, hello, Tony,' he said, yawning and giving himself a stretch. 'Just come in, have you? Had a good day?'

Kay felt hurt that he was keen to know how Tony's day had gone but not how his wife's had.

'My day was great, mate,' Tony replied with a satisfied grin. 'Everything is taking shape very nicely. Very nicely indeed.' He looked enquiringly at Bob. 'And ... er ... everything all right

192

with you, is it?'

Bob nodded vigorously. 'Oh, yes, everything's fine, Tony. Thanks for your help.'

Kay looked at him quizzically. What help could he possibly be thanking Tony for? Before she could enquire from her husband, Tony piped up, 'Has your good lady told you I'm having a night in with you both tonight? I got us some bottles of beer but I wouldn't mind your company for a pint first down the pub.'

Bob looked pleased. 'Yeah, that sounds great. Be good to get out. I'll have a wash and change as soon as dinner's over.'

Kay looked at him questioningly. Her husband seemed very eager to accompany their lodger for a drink at the pub but not in doing anything with her.

She addressed them both. 'If you'd both care to sit at the table, I'm just about to dish up.'

Immediately the pudding bowls were scraped clean, both of them went off to ready themselves for their trip to the pub. Kay was washing up when they arrived into the kitchen ready for the off.

'Right, we won't be long,' said Bob, buttoning up his overcoat.

'Enjoy yourself,' she said, smiling at him though inwardly hurt. They hadn't even tried to persuade her to join them.

'I'll make sure he does,' said Tony, giving her a meaningful wink.

CHAPTER TEN

Household chores done, Kay tuned in the wireless to a station playing soothing contemporary music, sat down in her armchair by the fire and leaned over the side of it to pick up her knitting bag. She had completed the back and front of the jumper she was knitting for Bob, which just left the sleeves. She was pleased with her efforts, thought the jumper would suit him and hoped he was pleased with it, although she felt the finish on it would have been much better if she had had new wool to knit with. Then she sighed despondently, remembering she had some darning to do.

Darning wasn't one of her favourite pastimes. Despite her mother's patience in teaching her, she had never quite mastered the art of weaving a neat flat patch like Mabel always achieved. However hard Kay tried, her own somehow looked puckered. Regardless, a pair of Bob's socks were showing the signs of wear on their heels and she could hear her mother's words ringing in her ears. 'Holes in a man's socks or buttons missing off his shirts are a sign of a sloppy housewife.' All right, Mam, Kay said to herself, darning it is. She went to fetch her darning bag only to discover she had no pieces of wool matching the colour of Bob's grey socks. She could use the colour she did have, but should her mother catch sight Kay would be

194

berated severely for sending her husband out in such a state. She guessed her mother would have some grey wool.

Kay glanced at the clock. It was just coming up for a quarter to seven. She'd time to hurry over to her parents' house before Bob and Tony returned from the pub, if indeed it was only a pint they planned to have and it didn't turn into a session like it had the night they had come home. The thought of a visit to her parents pleased her. She hadn't seen them or her brother for a couple of days and that visit, like several previously, only fleeting calls on her way home from the shops before she hurried off to prepare Bob's dinner. Most times her father had still been at work so it would be nice to catch up with him. She hadn't seen her aunt either since Viv had called in nearly two weeks ago to have lunch with her. She guessed her aunt was giving her space to settle into her marriage with Bob, either that or all her spare time was now being taken up by her blossoming romance with Frank Ambleside.

She was surprised to find her mother alone when she arrived. Mabel was delighted to see her. Immediately Kay walked in she laid down her knitting and got up to mash a pot of tea.

'I can't stop too long, Mam,' she said, stripping off her coat and following her mother back into the kitchen. 'Tony's taken Bob for a pint and they said they'd not be long.'

'Oh, that's nice for Bob,' Mabel said as she lit the gas under the kettle.

'Yes, it is. He's not been out since the night he arrived back so I'm hoping it will do him good.'

195

That was said sincerely despite wishing the friend Bob had gone out with had been a more suitable one.

'You just be grateful you've got a man who doesn't go out and leave you on your own like Winnie Vine's husband next door and lots of other men I could mention,' replied Mabel, gathering together tea cups and saucers and putting them on a tray on the draining board. She stopped what she was doing and looked at her daughter questioningly. 'What do you mean by hoping this trip to the pub will do him good? Nothing wrong with Bob, is there? You are looking after him properly?'

'I'm doing my best to, Mam.' Kay smiled and added, 'I haven't poisoned him yet.'

Her quip was lost on her mother. 'Good, I'm glad to hear it. Food poisoning is a nasty business, Kay. Remember always to wash your hands before you touch food. Now, how did Bob's visit with his friend go this afternoon? That was a nice surprise for him, wasn't it, his old mate travelling so far to come and see him? And he seemed such a nice polite young man to me. I hope he followed my directions to your house and found you all right?'

Kay told her mother what had transpired.

'Oh, but what a shame Bob missing him like that, and him on his way to Australia. Still, these things happen, don't they? What Bob did for that old lady is very commendable, very commendable indeed. She was lucky he was on hand to help her.'

'Yes, she was,' Kay agreed wholeheartedly.

'Where's Dad and Trevor, Mam?'

'Yer father's down at the allotment. As soon as the light stops him and his cronies doing whatever it is they're doing, they're gathering in your father's shed as it's his turn to host the monthly Allotment Committee meeting. I was expecting him home well before now. It only usually lasts an hour or so and from what yer father told me they hadn't got that much to discuss tonight.' She paused and her face screwed up knowingly. 'Oh, I bet I know what's keeping him. Ted Chivers will have taken along a batch of his home brew to the meeting to get their opinion on it. Yer father likes a tipple now and again but he can get carried away if I'm not around to keep an eye on him. The last time he sampled Ted's brew he fell asleep in the shed and his so-called gardening pals left him there. It wasn't until I got so worried about his absence I went up there that I finally realised what had happened. What a job I had to wake him up, and getting him home was another matter. I warned him if he ever did that again I wouldn't bother fetching him but leave him to it. He's not had his tea yet neither.

'As for Trevor, well, it's the night Viv's taking him to the dance. Though when I saw that wheelchair she arrived with, I nearly put a stop to it. Talk about antique! I just hope it gets Trevor there and back in one piece, that's all I can say.'

Her mind clouded with concern for Bob, Kay had forgotten this was her brother's night out. 'They'll be fine, Mam,' she said reassuringly.

Mabel picked up a cloth to protect her hand from the kettle's handle and poured water into

197

the tea pot, saying, 'Yes, well, that remains to be seen. I'm still not sure I was right to trust Viv with yer brother's safety. I just want ten o'clock to come and to have him back here where I can keep an eye on him meself. That Frank seems a nice chap, a real gentleman. My sister must think I'm stupid not to see there's more going on between them two than just the friends she keeps telling me they are. Stupid or blind, one of the two.'

'Well, maybe Aunty Viv doesn't want to say too much until she's more sure of what's going to happen between them. She knows you worry about her, Mam, and the last thing she wants is for you to think that she's...' Kay's voice trailed off as she tried to think of a word to describe how Viv viewed the way her sister saw her.

'She's what?' her mother demanded.

'Well...' No other word to replace the ones Viv had used came to her. 'A loose woman?' Kay said tentatively.

'A loose woman! I'd never think that of my own sister, how could she think I would? I admit I feel she flaunts herself in the type of clothes she insists on dressing in, and she certainly likes to go out to places I think are ... well, I ask yer, dancing at her age! Tea dances, yes, but not throwing yerself around the floor at the Trocadero ... jiving, is that what it's called? Them Yanks have a lot to answer for, if you ask me. And besides, that sort of carry on is for the younger ones. It's about time our Viv grew up. Huh! I'll give her what for, thinking I'd class her in the same light as those women who bed a different man every night. I might feel my sister needs to dress a little more ... well, in keeping with a woman of her age, and not go to the sort of places she goes for a night out, but that's all. Oh, and she could dust her house more than once a week too. Now tea's ready so go and sit at the table,' she ordered Kay as she picked up the tray to carry it through.

'How's your neighbour?' her mother asked as she poured out the tea.

'She's fine. I pop in before I go to the shops to see if she wants anything and check every morning to make sure her curtains are open.'

'I would expect no less of you, dear. It's our duty to keep an eye on the elderly. And how is your lodger?'

'He told me today he'll be moving on soon.'

'Oh, I expect you'll miss him. Bob will certainly miss having his friend around. You'll miss his lodging money too.'

'Mmm,' Kay mouthed as she took a sip of her tea.

They chatted together in general for a while before Mabel glanced across at the clock. 'Just where has your father got to? It's well past eight. I hope he's not too sozzled on Ted's brew to remember to bring me some potatoes, I've run out. You must be about ready for some veg yourself. I'll remind yer father to drop in a winter cabbage, some Brussels and some spuds tomorrow afternoon on his way home from the allotment. Well, every little helps.'

'Yes, it does, Mam. Thanks,' she said appreciatively. 'Oh, I was hoping you'd some dark grey wool for me to darn Bob's socks with?'

'I'll get it for you.'

After searching in her mending box, Mabel handed over a twist of grey wool, a near enough match to the colour of Bob's socks, which Kay thanked her for and put in her bag. Enjoying her visit with her mother, she had stayed far longer than she'd intended and was just about to take her leave when the front door knocker sounded.

'It's just as I thought,' said Mabel, a disapproving look on her square face. 'Yer father's got himself intoxicated and his mates have brought him home. At least they *have* brought him home this time, so I suppose I should be grateful for that.'

'I'll let them in, Mam,' Kay offered, rising and heading towards the front door. She opened it fully expecting to see her father being supported between a couple of his friends. Her mouth fell open as she looked into the kindly face of Constable Pringle, the portly middle-aged policeman who'd been pounding the beat around this area for the last twenty years.

'Hello, Kay lovey. Is yer mam in?' he asked.

Her mind was whirling, wondering why the constable would be calling on her mother, especially at this hour of the evening. 'I'll call her for you. Mother,' she shouted, 'Constable Pringle wants you.'

Mabel was at the door before the words had left Kay's mouth. She smiled a greeting at him. 'Good evening, Constable. You're well, I trust?'

'Yes, thank you, Mrs Stafford.' He shifted uncomfortably on his large black-booted feet. 'Look ... there's bin an accident, I'm afraid.'

Kay gasped. 'Oh, my God!'

If this news shocked Mabel she did not show it. 'An accident, I see. How bad is my son, Constable Pringle?'

'I haven't got any details, Mrs Stafford. The station got a telephone call from the hospital asking us to inform you yer wanted down there. I was dispatched to tell you.'

'I see.' She turned to Kay. 'Could you fetch my coat and handbag for me, Kay, please?' She turned back to Constable Pringle. 'I'll go down straight away. Thank you for taking the trouble to inform us.'

'Can I be of assistance in any way?' he asked.

'No, thank you, Constable. I expect you need to be getting back to the station.'

Kay had already returned with their bags and coats.

Having put hers on, Mabel said to her, 'Before you leave, could you write a note for your father, telling him where I've gone?'

'But I'm coming with you, Mam,' she cried.

'There's no need. You've a husband to get home to.'

'Mam, I'm not letting you go on your own and Trevor is my brother,' Kay insisted. 'Oh, Mam, I just hope it's not bad. I couldn't bear it if so.'

'Now, Kay, control yourself. There is no point in wailing and crying when you have no idea what you are wailing and crying about.'

'Yes, you're right, Mam. Look, you start making your way to the hospital while I write. Dad a note. I'll catch up with you.'

As they hurried through the back streets

towards the hospital, Kay was amazed by her mother's ability to control her emotions. This news must have upset her but she wasn't showing it. As for Kay herself, her emotions were in turmoil. She worried frantically over what had befallen her brother, and despite her mother's frequent requests for her to control herself, found she couldn't.

'Oh, I hope it's not bad, Mam! Do you think he fell out of the wheelchair and redamaged his injured leg?'

'There is no point in asking me questions I can't answer, Kay. We'll find out when we get there, won't we?'

Arriving at the hospital, Mabel calmly approached a nurse who asked them to wait while she went off in search of information. Sitting beside her mother on an uncomfortable wooden bench in a long corridor, Kay's worry mounted.

'What's taking the nurse so long, Mam?'

'This is a hospital, Kay, your brother is not the only one receiving treatment here. She'll be back when she has news for us.'

'Yes, of course.' Kay looked up and down the corridor. 'I can't see any sign of Aunty Viv.'

By the look her mother gave her Kay knew exactly what was going through her mind. Mabel thought her sister was avoiding her after letting her down so badly.

A long half an hour passed before the double doors at the end of a long corridor opened and a doctor came towards them.

Mabel rose to greet him. 'Are you looking for me, Doctor?'

'Mrs Stafford?'

'I'm she. How is he, Doctor?'

The doctor's face was grave. 'Both his legs are broken and he's extensive bruising to the upper part of his body where his attacker or attackers beat him with whatever weapons they used. And, of course, he must have landed heavily when he came off his bike when he was first struck.'

Mabel was gaping at him, utterly confused.

'What's this about a bike? Surely you mean a wheelchair, Doctor?'

He looked at her, puzzled. 'No, I'm sure your husband said he was riding a bike. You must excuse me, I should get back to my patient. We shouldn't be long now in finishing plastering him up then you can see him. We're happy there are no other complications but we aren't sure if he's suffering from concussion so we'll be keeping a close eye on him. We'll need you to bring some things in for him when you come back tomorrow. Providing everything goes well, he'll be with us for about a week.'

It was bad enough for Kay thinking it was her brother who was receiving medical attention, but to find out it was actually her father... She spun round to see that her mother's face was drained grey and she was staring at the doctor.

'Mam, oh, Mam. Oh, me dad.'

Mabel glared at her. 'Compose yourself, Kay. This is a hospital. Please leave your hysterics for a more appropriate place. Now, wait here for me.'

'Why? Where are you going?'

'To arrange to take your father home. I'm full of admiration for the nurses and their abilities

203

but if the doctor is convinced your father is not suffering from concussion then I am quite capable of caring for him at home, where he belongs.'

With that Mabel headed off after the doctor. From the other end of the corridor the double doors burst open and Viv charged through them, dashing up to Kay.

'What's happened?' she demanded. 'I found your note when I took Trevor home and I didn't know what to think. I can see it's not you who's injured, so it must be your mam or dad.'

Kay told her all she knew and, just as she had finished, Mabel returned.

'Well, that's all arranged. Providing Herbie spends a comfortable night, I can collect him tomorrow.'

The nurse they had requested help from earlier then appeared by their side. 'You can come through now but only for a few minutes; we're taking Mr Stafford to the ward.'

Kay gasped in shock at the sight of her father lying in bed. He appeared to be in extreme discomfort, his exposed chest and shoulders covered in bruises, both legs encased in fresh plaster of Paris.

Viv's hands flew to her face in horror. 'Oh, Herbie,' she groaned.

Mabel, her face the colour of a freshly laundered sheet, approached his bed slowly, lowering her bulky body down on to the chair at the side of it. Leaning over, she took his hand gently in hers to stroke it. 'Oh, Herbie, what have they done ter yer?' she uttered.

The terrible pain he was suffering was very apparent but despite it he managed to smile at his wife. 'Hello, me old duck. Bit of a mess, ain't I?'

From her position at the other side of the bed, her aunt gripping on to her for support, it shocked Kay to see tears of distress well in her mother's eyes. She had never seen her mother cry in her presence even when news was received of Trevor's terrible injuries. Neither had she witnessed any close exchange between her parents except for a peck on the cheek if either was going out, leaving the other behind. If she'd ever doubted the love they felt for each other, she was in no doubt now.

Tears of distress blurring her own vision, she asked, 'What happened to you, Dad? Can you tell us?'

He slowly turned his head and looked at her wearily. 'Hello, lovey. What are you doing here? You should be with that husband of yours. And what are you doing here too, our Viv? I thought you was looking after our Trevor?'

'Don't you be worrying about your son, Herbie,' she said in a throaty voice. 'He's fine. Safe and sound at home, waiting for you. Can yer tell us what happened to land you in a state like this?'

He slowly turned his head back to face his wife. 'I was minding me own business, riding home on me bike, worried 'cos the meeting had gone on longer than it was meant to and I knew you'd have me tea ready and be cross with me for being later than I'd said. I was just riding out the entrance to

205

the allotments when I felt this whack straight across me back. It knocked me clean off me bike and next thing I knew I was being battered with … well, it felt like a tree trunk to me. On and on it went. I thought it was never going to stop. I heard a crack from one of me legs and knew it was broken. I must have blacked out for a bit then because next thing I knew Harry Walters was bending over me, telling me to keep still and an ambulance was on its way.' His looked remorsefully into his wife's eyes. 'They took the bag of veg you asked me to bring home, Mabel, I'm ever so sorry.'

'Oh, Herbie,' she tenderly scolded him. 'Don't you dare worry about that. Do yer know who did this to you?'

'Never got a chance to see. It all happened so quick. I couldn't tell yer, lovey, if it was one bloke that attacked me, two, or a herd of elephants.'

She patted his hand. 'Well, I hope that veg chokes 'em, that's all I can say.'

A porter arrived then to wheel away the bed and the nurse came over with him, smiling kindly at Mabel. 'We're going to take Mr Stafford up to the ward now.'

'Right you are, Nurse,' Mabel said stiffly. Still clutching Herbie's hand, she half rose, leaned over and pecked his cheek. 'Now you take care, you hear me? Have a good night's rest and providing there's no mishaps during the night, the doctor said I can take you home in the morning.' She straightened up and addressed the nurse. 'Thank you, Nurse. I much appreciate what yer doing for my husband.' She looked sternly at Viv and Kay. 'Come along then. Let's leave them to do their job.'

Back in the Staffords' house the three women sat round the table with cups of strong tea.

'I think a drop of that whisky left over from Bob's welcome home do is called for Mabel,' said Viv. 'You sit there, I'll get it.'

'Yer can put a ruddy great dollop in my tea as yer passing, Aunty Viv,' Trevor piped up from his makeshift bed. His face was set grimly. 'Who'd want to do that to me dad, for Christ's sake? All for a bag of veggies. Just let me catch...'

'And we'll have less of that talk, Trevor,' ordered his mother. 'Whoever it was must have been desperate, that's all I can say.'

'Snatching a bag of veggies is one thing, Mam, beating someone senseless for it is another,' he snapped gruffly. 'My dad's never hurt a fly in his life and if they were so desperate for that veg they'd only to ask Dad, he would have given it 'em.'

'Let the police deal with this, Trevor,' said Kay, wearily rubbing her aching forehead. 'What was done to Dad is bad but he'll mend, that's the main thing.'

'Listen to yer sister, Trevor. Two wrongs don't make a right. I'll have no talk of reprisals, even if you were in a position to try. Is that understood?'

He looked sheepishly at her. 'Yes, Mam.'

Over by the sideboard, looking for the bottle of whisky, Viv glanced across at her nephew and quipped, 'Look on the bright side. At least you've company now, our Trevor.'

207

Mabel twisted round in her seat and flashed her a look. 'There is a time and place for jokes, Vivian, and this isn't one of them.'

'Er ... no, sorry.'

She arrived back at the table with the bottle of whisky and poured a good measure into her sister's cup. 'Drink that down, gel, it'll do yer good.'

Mabel gave Viv another look. 'I don't drink, yer know that.'

'It's medicinal, Mam,' Kay said, leaning across to pat her hand. 'Aunty Viv's right, it will do you good. It'll help you sleep.'

'I shall sleep fine, thank you,' she said with conviction.

'I'll stay with you tonight, Mabel,' Viv offered. Having doled out the whisky to each of them she had resumed her seat at the table.

'I thank you for your offer but there's no need, Viv. I've Trevor here and enough to keep me occupied getting things ready for Herbie coming home. I shall have to organise another bed down here somehow 'cos he won't be able to get upstairs. I borrowed the Put-u-up for Trevor from Cissie Hardcastle a few doors down ... maybe she might know someone who's got another I can borrow.'

'No need, Frank's got one,' said Viv. 'He'd gladly lend you it. I know it's late but I'll pop around now. He's not an early bedder so he's more than likely still up. Probably fixing a wireless set or a clock for someone. He's good at that kinda thing is Frank. I'm sure he'll get the bed to you first thing in the morning before he starts work, if I ask him nicely.'

'How do you know he's got a Put-u-up?' Mabel asked suspiciously.

'I haven't been upstairs in his house, if that's what you think,' Viv snapped back.

Mabel puffed out her chest indignantly. 'That thought never crossed my mind. Whatever you might think I think of you, Vivian, I know you to be a woman of high moral standing. But having possession of a Put-u-up is hardly the sort of thing that comes up in general discussion, is it?'

'Oh, no, I suppose not,' said Viv, feeling guilty for jumping to the wrong conclusion. 'And it's nice for me to know you don't think quite so badly of me as I was under the impression you did.

'Anyway, Frank happened to tell me that when his wife left him he went into a decline and took to drink, spent all his money on it. Thankfully he saw the error of his ways and gave himself a good talking to, stopped drinking and got himself his driving job. Trouble was, he was behind with the rent by this time and owed a few people so he sold off his furniture to help pay his debts. He bought the Put-u-up cheap from the Army and Navy Stores until he could afford a proper bed. He never parted with it later in case it came in handy.'

'Well, I'd be grateful if he could see his way to letting me use it for a while,' Mabel said. She gave a cough and glanced awkwardly at her sister. 'I owe you an apology, Vivian.'

Viv looked at her wide-eyed. 'You owe me an apology?'

'I do. When the policeman came to the door, I immediately jumped to the conclusion that it was our Trevor he'd come about because you hadn't kept yer eye on him, like yer promised me you would.'

'Well ... that's all right, Mabel, I understand.'

'No, it's not all right. I judged yer harshly and I'm sorry.'

Viv smiled at her. 'Yer always judging me harshly, our Mabel, but yer've never apologised before.' She leaned over and patted her sister's hand. 'Apology accepted.' She stood up and picked up her handbag. 'I'd best get off and organise that bed. Do yer want me to do anything else for yer, Mabel?'

'No, yer've done enough, thank you.' Mabel looked at her daughter. 'And you drink that tea down and get yourself off home. Bob must be wondering where you've got to.'

Kay drank her tea and collected her things. 'You will be all right, Mam?'

'Of course I'll be all right. No point in me falling apart, is there? What good would I be to your father if I did?'

'Do you want me to come with you to the hospital tomorrow morning?'

'You've your husband to look after, not forgetting your lodger. Come around in the afternoon after you've seen to Bob's dinner. I'll have your father all settled by then.'

Outside on the pavement as they prepared to say their goodbyes, Viv looked at her niece in concern. 'Your father will be in the best hands at home with yer mother, Kay.'

'Yes, I know. But I can't take this all in, Aunty Viv. Who would do that to my dad?'

She shook her head sadly. 'I just can't imagine what kind of animal would. But it's yer mother I'm more worried about at the moment, Kay. She's keeping her usual stiff upper lip, but I know this has cut her up summat terrible. Once she's on her own where there's no one to see her, she'll break her heart.'

'She cried in the hospital, Aunty Viv. I've never seen Mam cry before.'

'I noticed. Mabel will try to cope with this on her own, feeling it's her duty. We'll have to help however we can. Now get off home, lovey, you look ready to drop.'

Kay flashed her aunt a wan smile. 'I never asked how it went at the dance, Aunty Viv. Did Trevor enjoy himself?'

'He did. It was a tonic for him. I enjoyed it too. It was packed, and with him not being used to crowds, having been laid up for so long, it took it out of him, just like yer mam suspected it might. All due respect to Trevor, he asked me and Frank to bring him home, we didn't have to tell him.

'I have to say, even in a wheelchair my nephew is a popular young man. The girls were swarming around him, and one in particular I noticed he had a twinkle in his eye for. It wouldn't surprise me if we saw her again.' Viv gave a heavy sigh. 'Pity we had come back to find what we did. It's fair put a damper on the night. I didn't find the note you'd left until Frank had helped me settle Trevor back in his bed and had left himself then to take the wheelchair back to the old geezer I'd

211

borrowed it from. I know he'd have offered to come to the hospital with me if he'd still been around when I found the note. The more I find out about Frank, the more I find I like him. And on that note, I'd best hurry to see him about that bed before he goes to sleep himself.'

An extremely sombre Kay arrived home and was surprised to find Bob still up, considering his usual routine of early to bed. He and Tony were sprawled in the armchairs. The fire was blazing which it annoyed her to see at this time of night as their ration of coal did not allow for such luxury, and several empty bottles of beer stood at the side of each chair along with empty plates. She noticed the library book and newspaper she had got for Bob were both lying in a heap at the other side of his chair where they had obviously fallen off the arm.

'Oh, there you are,' Bob said, looking at her tipsily. 'I was wondering where you'd got to.'

Despite her anguish for both her parents, a warm glow filled her at his show of concern. It was doused as quickly as it had flared when he added, 'We had to make ourselves a sandwich.'

She wanted to say she knew they had as she had noticed the mess they had left for her to clear up as she had walked through the kitchen. 'I'm sorry I wasn't here to do it for you. I just popped over to see my mother. Didn't intend stopping long.' Tears welled in her eyes then. Her bottom lip trembling, she said, 'My father's been hurt.'

'Hurt?' said Bob. 'What do you mean, hurt?'

Tony sat bolt upright in his armchair, twisting

212

around to look at her. 'Hurt bad?'

Kay sighed heavily. 'Bad enough. He's two broken legs, not to mention severe bruising. Looks like he's been hit by a bus. Providing he has a good night the hospital are allowing him to come home tomorrow so that my mother can take care of him there.'

'I'm sorry to hear that,' said Bob sincerely.

'What happened?' Tony asked her.

Kay was surprised at his interest in her family when he'd never shown any before and thought it nice that he was doing so now. 'Seems he was beaten for a bag of veggies off his allotment. What is the world coming to when a middle-aged man is attacked for things that'd cost pennies to buy?'

'Any idea who did it?' Tony probed.

She shook her head. 'Be a miracle if anyone is caught. My dad never saw his attacker and no one else was around to witness what happened.' She smiled wanly at them both. 'If you don't mind, I'm going to bed. You will see the fire is banked down safely, won't you, Bob? I locked the back door when I came in. I'll see you in the morning.'

'I'll be up myself in a minute,' he said, looking at the clock and giving a yawn. 'I didn't realise it was that late. I've to be up at four for my shift.'

Kay had just turned off the light and got into bed when Bob came in. After quickly undressing, he got in beside her. She fully expected him to put his arms around her to offer her comfort and realised he must think she was already asleep when he didn't but as usual settled down with his back to her. Kay turned to him, snuggling against his back. 'Oh, Bob,' she whispered, 'it's awful what's happened to my dad, isn't it?'

He gave a loud yawn. 'Yes, it is, but he'll be all right. He's your mother to look after him when he gets out of hospital.'

'As if she hadn't got enough on her plate already, looking after my brother! I'll need to do what I can for her, Bob. Well, what she'll let me do. It's going to be hard on her, having two invalids to look after.'

'Oh, yes, of course you must do what you have to. Hopefully it won't be long before your dad's back on his feet. Good night then, Kay.'

'Oh, good night, Bob.'

At his total failure to offer her any physical comfort, a wave of despair filled her. Didn't it occur to him that if she had ever needed the comfort of his arms, now was the time? In fact, since he'd come back, although she might share his bed, she felt she was more of a mother or a sister to him than a wife. Then a horrifying thought struck her and a lump of real distress welled in her throat. Could it possibly be that the real reason for his being so undemonstrative towards her was that he had come back after five years to find he didn't love her anymore, but couldn't bring himself to tell her? She had feared this could happen and had voiced that worry to her aunt who had done her best to reassure her otherwise, but what else could be making Bob act like he was?

'Bob?' she whispered.

'What now?' he snapped. 'I need to get to sleep, I've to get up at four.'

'Yes, I'm sorry, I know you do, but I just have to know... Are you ... are you sorry you married me?'

'What made you ask that? I couldn't be happier. Now I really need to get to sleep. Good night.'

Kay turned from him to pull the covers around her protectively, although they did not give her the comfort she would have derived from her husband's arms. She had been mortally relieved to hear him say he was happy, but regardless she still didn't feel any better about their relationship as it was at the moment.

A wave of hopelessness swept over her. She felt so useless. She had no idea what was making Bob like he was, no idea how to help him. All she could do was be a caring, loving, supportive wife to him, and hope that gradually over time Bob would revert to his old self.

CHAPTER ELEVEN

Kay heaved the small sacking bag of potatoes on to the draining board, smiling warmly at her mother who was busy at the kitchen table making up potted meat sandwiches ready for tea later on. 'There you go, Mam. There should be enough to last you a couple of days, let me know when you want more.'

Mabel lifted her head from her task and nodded gratefully. 'I appreciate what yer've done, but I could have managed. It's not as if you haven't enough to do yourself.'

Kay was at the sink now, washing her hands beneath the protruding cold tap. Under no circumstances would she ever have allowed her mother the hard task of having to fork around in the deep straw-filled pit her father had dug to store their winter supply of potatoes in. Then, having got what she needed, to have to lug them back home. It had been freezing down at the allotment, the soggy earth sticking to Kay's winter boots. The task had been hard enough for her to tackle and she was far younger than her mother. 'As if you haven't enough to do too, Mam,' she said, drying her hands on a piece of towelling. 'I'm happy to do anything for you, you know that, and don't worry. Nothing I help you with interferes with my own housework.'

'Oh, well, that's all right then as it's the last thing I'd want. How's Bob?'

'He's fine, thank you, Mam.'

'Good. I am surprised he ain't popped in though to see your father, after what happened to him.'

Kay's mind whirled frantically to come up with a plausible excuse for Bob's apparent lack of concern for his wife's parents. How could she explain her husband's behaviour when she didn't really understand it herself? 'Oh, well, he's busy getting to grips with his new job and ... well, he knows you've so many people traipsing in and out offering help he just feels another is the last thing you want under your feet.'

Mabel sighed. 'Well, he does have a point. I appreciate other people showing such concern

216

but I just wish they'd leave me alone to get on with it. I'm spending more time at the moment mashing cups of tea for visitors than I am anything else. I never got my ironing done this afternoon as your father's boss called in to see how he was progressing. While he was here, I couldn't very well stand at the table doing it.'

'I could take it back with me and do it for you?' her daughter offered.

'That's very kind of you, dear, but hopefully if no one else calls around I can tackle it this evening. You've enough ironing to do of your own without mine on top. Anyway, you tell Bob he's family and welcome any time, whether I've a houseful of other visitors or not.'

Just then Viv breezed in through the back door. 'Oh, bloody hell, it's freezing out there,' she said, rubbing her hands and stamping her feet. 'Oh, hello, Kay, lovey, glad I've caught you. Since Herbie's trouble we ain't had time to call in on each other, have we? It's got to be the night Herbie was taken to hospital since I last saw yer. How are yer then, gel?'

'I'm fine thanks, Aunty Viv. And yourself?'

'Never bin better, ta, ducky.' She gave Kay a secretive wink, as though to say, And you know why: because things between me and Frank are coming along very nicely.

Kay gave her aunt a look back to acknowledge she understood this and was pleased for her.

'Lodger still with yer?' Viv asked.

Kay nodded.

'Mmm,' mouthed Viv, pulling a face at Kay as if to say, Well, I think it's about time he moved on and gave you two yer house back to yourselves. 'Right, Mabel,' she said, stripping off her coat. 'Reporting for duty.'

Mabel inhaled sharply. 'I keep telling you that there really is no need for you to call in every night. After all, you work in the day and have yer own house to look after. I've everything under control.'

'As if I expected anything else,' Viv said, flashing Kay a look that said, What did I tell you? My sister wouldn't accept help if she was on her knees with exhaustion. 'Oh, I'm sure there's summat you need doing. These the spuds?' she said, opening the sack that Kay had deposited on the draining board. 'I can peel some ready for tomorrow's dinner.'

'There's no need, really, Viv.'

But her sister took no notice of her. Taking potatoes out of the sack, she put several in the sink and turned on the cold tap. 'Pass me a saucepan to put the peeled spuds in, would yer, please, Kay? Mabel, you tell me how many you want doing.'

Passing her aunt the saucepan, Kay decided to leave the women to it. Time was wearing on and she'd informed Bob when she had left him to have his afternoon snooze that she was going around to her parents', to see if there was anything she could help with. But she'd said she'd be back at six to put his tea on the table, and she liked to keep her word. 'It's about time I got off, Mam. I'll just pop in and say my goodbyes to Dad and Trevor first.'

'Tell them both I won't be long bringing

through their tea.'

'I will, Mam.'

Kay perched herself at the side of her father's makeshift bed. The bruises on the visible parts of his body not covered by his pyjamas were not so angry and swollen-looking now, although she knew he was still in a great deal of discomfort from his broken legs and for a proud man such as Herbie was it must be difficult for him to cope with the fact that there wasn't much he could do for himself.

'I'm off now, Dad. I'll pop back in the morning to see if Mam needs any shopping fetching while I'm getting my own.'

He smiled at her affectionately and patted her hand. 'Yer a good gel, our Kay. Do me a favour and don't take no for an answer from her. She's running herself ragged looking after us two while still trying to fit in everything else she has to do. She's hardly sat down for a rest since this happened to me. I'm worried she'll wear herself out.'

'I'll do me best, Dad, but you know what's she's like. Aunty Viv's in the kitchen with her at the moment, and as much as Mam tried to stop her, she's peeling potatoes for tomorrow's dinner so Mam doesn't have to do it.'

'Viv's a good gel too. You're both a blessing.' He paused, and lowering his voice, asked, 'Er ... you and yer Aunt Viv being close, I just wondered what's going on?'

'Going on, Dad?'

'You know, with her and that Frank chap she brought here for Bob's welcome home dinner a couple of weeks ago. Is she seeing him?'

'What makes you think that, Dad?' Kay asked cagily. Her aunt had taken her into her confidence over her relationship with Frank. Now, despite its being her father who was questioning her, the last thing she wanted was to betray her aunt's trust in her.

He gave her a knowing look 'Oh, not much, Kay. Just the fact that whenever she's here his name always seems to crop up in some way or other. Frank this ... Frank that. She speaks of him like she thinks the sun shines out of his backside! I've never heard our Viv mention a man's name with such praise since yer Uncle Archie died. I've a high regard for my sister-in-law. I'd like to think she could be happy again.'

She could appreciate her father's concern and, choosing her words carefully, hoping she wasn't betraying her aunt's trust in her, Kay replied, 'Well, I don't know much myself but if it puts your mind at rest, I think things seem to be going well between them, Dad. I hope so anyway.'

'So do I. I must say, he seemed a decent enough chap to me even though I never got that much of a chance to speak to him when we were introduced. It's about time our Viv had some luck. I hope it works out for her.' He paused again and looked at Kay in concern. 'Is ... er ... your Bob enjoying his job all right, our Kay?'

'Oh, yes, he seems to be. Why?'

'Oh, nothing,' her father said awkwardly.

'But something made you ask that, Dad?'

He swallowed hard. 'Well, it's just that me boss called in to see me this afternoon, to see how I was, and just happened to mention that he was

220

talking to Sid Askew this morning in the tea queue at break time. During the conversation he asked how my son-in-law was getting on, and Sid told him he was a bit bothered by Bob's attitude towards his work.'

Kay frowned. 'What do you mean, Dad?'

'Well, just that he seems to be making silly mistakes and acting like he's not concerned, apparently. I feel a bit responsible, especially after me going on about how capable Bob was. He doesn't seem to be making any effort to get on with his workmates either. Sid did say the man Bob's working with has noticed he keeps his eyes peeled on the clock for finishing time and downs tools, so to speak, the second it's clocking off time for their shift. It's like he's not putting himself out to keep this job, Kay. I mean, I know it ain't exactly up to the standard a man of his calibre could expect, but all the same until he's ready to pick up his carpentry tools, this job's better than a lot he could be doing.'

Kay was dismayed to hear this and knew her father would not have spoken to her about it if he wasn't deeply concerned. 'Well, it's early days, Dad. Bob's only been in the job a week today so I think Mr Askew is being a bit unfair. He doesn't seem to be making allowances for the fact Bob's just returned from serving his country for five years. Apart from coping with what he went through out there, he needs more time to settle back into life back home.'

'Yes, yes, I agree with yer, and I told my boss as much which I know he'll pass on to Sid. I'm surprised he's not showing Bob a bit more tolerance

221

after serving in the Great War himself. He's first-hand knowledge of what it's like adjusting afterwards.' Herbie gave a heavy sigh, his face looking aggrieved. 'The war we've just been through was bad enough but the First was one long bloody battle. I don't think anyone who fought in it believed they'd ever see British shores again.

'Your mam and I weren't long married when I was called up but, as yer know, thankfully I wasn't dispatched to fight. Because of my experience on the post I was sent to help at the camp that handled all the forces' mail. I never had a problem settling back when I got home, and yer mam never had the same worries about me that lots of other women did over their men. Anyway, that's by the by. I'm sure Bob will be fine, Kay. Like you say, he just needs time to settle down to his new life. But I felt I ought to mention it to you.'

She leaned over and pecked his cheek. 'Mam told me to tell you she'll be bringing your tea through shortly.'

He smiled. 'Good, 'cos I'm famished. Lying here with not much to do means the little pleasures of life are so much more important than they normally are.' He flashed a look across at Trevor in his makeshift bed on the other side of the room. 'There's only so much a father and son can find to talk about, and these last six days we've just about exhausted it.'

Rising, Kay went across to her brother, perching herself on the low stool to the side of his makeshift bed. He was engrossed in the pages of a Biggles Annual.

'Glad to see you've found something to occupy you,' she said, a hint of amusement in her voice.

'Eh! Oh, hello, Sis. Yeah, I'd forgotten how good these stories were until Mam got so fed up with me moaning I'd nothing to do that she went and dug out a couple from the bottom of my wardrobe.' Trevor beamed excitedly at her. 'Did she tell you me good news?'

'No, she's too busy trying to convince me and Aunty Viv she doesn't need our help, that she's everything under control as usual. What good news?' Kay asked eagerly.

'The doc called in this morning and he's so pleased with me progress, he says that from Monday I can start using me crutches and begin putting some weight on me leg at long last! Oh, God, Kay, it's just the best news, ain't it?'

'Yes, it is. Don't dare think of running before you can walk though, our Trev.'

He pulled a face at his sister's attempt at a joke. 'Oh, very funny. Don't worry, Mam's already laid down the law to me. She reckons if she catches me doing 'ote stupid, she'll burn me crutches.'

Kay laughed. 'She will, you know, so you'd better do exactly what the doc says you can and no more until he's checked on your progress again and gives you the full go ahead.' She stood up. 'Right, I'd better be off. Oh, just a thought, Trevor. That mate you have whose father tinkers around with motorbikes?'

'What about him?'

'Would he happen to know where Bob could get a manual from for the bike he's bought? Only he can't go on with it any further until he gets

223

hold of a copy as the man who sold him the bike didn't have it. Well, he never passed it on anyway.'

'He might know. I'll ask him when he next comes in.'

As Kay arrived back in the kitchen, her mother asked, 'Where did you put the cabbage and Brussels tops I asked you to bring back from the allotment when you insisted on going?'

Kay looked at her blankly. 'They're in with the bag of spuds, aren't they?'

'Well, I can't find 'em.'

Then a memory struck. 'Oh, no, Mam! I did cut a cabbage and some tops but I put them down when Ted Chivers came over to talk to me. He was leaving the allotment for the night but wanted to enquire how Dad was and to say he'd be in to see him soon. I forgot to give Dad his message so will you, please, Mam? I'll just run back to the allotment now and get the veg for you.'

'No, you won't. Those allotments will be deserted by now, not to mention dark, and you never know who might be lurking, especially after what happened to yer dad. I'll go up myself in the morning.'

'It's my fault, Mam, so I'll go up in the morning.'

Mabel pursed her lips. 'I haven't time to stand here arguing the toss with you. I'll leave it to you then, if you insist. Right, I need to take the tea through to yer dad and brother before it spoils. Now yer've done enough for me for one day so get yerself off home, there's a good gel. And you too, our Viv, when yer've finished those spuds. And ... er ... I appreciate what you've done.'

224

Picking up the tray of tea things, Mabel disappeared.

'Right, that's them done,' Viv said as she put the pan of peeled potatoes on top of the stove for the next day. 'Now I'll just clear these peelings away then, as my dear sister has made it very clear she's n'ote else she wants me to do, I'll go in and have a quick chat with the boys before I take myself off.' Hurriedly, she scooped up the peelings from the sink and put them on newspaper on the draining board, to dry out for putting on the fire later. She looked at Kay and whispered, 'I'm hoping Frank gets back from his long-haul trip at a decent time tonight then maybe he'll pop in and see me. I haven't seen him since Monday night and ... well ... I've kinda missed him.'

Kay went up to her aunt, kissed her on her cheek and gave her a hug. 'I hope he does then,' she said sincerely. 'I'll see you tomorrow, same time, same place, eh?'

'More than likely. My sister ain't getting rid of me until I feel she really doesn't need my help and isn't just saying she don't. I'm worried about her, Kay. She looks fit to drop, but I know Mabel. She'll soldier on until her legs give way under her. Tarra, lovey. Take care of yerself, and not forgetting that husband of yours.'

Just before seven that evening Kay sat down in the armchair opposite Bob. After her long day she was tired and in truth would be glad when it was time to retire to bed. As she picked up her knitting from the tapestry bag at the side of the chair she hoped Tony wouldn't breeze in, expecting her to get up immediately and make

225

him something to eat. She was already annoyed that she'd had to throw away the dinner she had made for him earlier. In an effort to keep it hot she'd put it inside the oven on a low setting instead of her normal practice of putting it on a pan of hot water on top of the stove, because she'd been out herself most of that afternoon, getting the vegetables for her mother, and wouldn't be around to make sure the pan did not boil dry. She had returned to find Tony had not been in to eat it meantime and the dinner so dried up she couldn't really expect him to.

Kay noticed the library book and newspaper, which was by now days out of date, still lying untouched at the side of her husband's chair. Also Bob had not made any attempt yet to empty and put away his box of belongings, apart from unearthing his bank book the other day.

Beginning her knitting, she casually asked him, 'The library book any good, Bob?'

'Eh? Oh, I haven't had time to have a look at it yet.'

'The newspaper neither, I see. Shall I get you another when I'm out tomorrow?'

'Eh? Oh, I shouldn't bother unless you read it yourself. I get depressed enough hearing the blokes at work harping on about things, without reading about them too.'

'Oh, but it's not all doom and gloom in the newspaper, Bob. There's lighter things too. I'll start getting you a copy daily just in case you change your mind. And any luck in getting a manual for your motorbike? And ... er ... maybe you should think about covering up the parts you've already removed, Bob. I did notice they're getting rustier, lying exposed in this damp weather we've been having.'

'Eh? Oh, yes, I'll do it tomorrow. And no, I haven't got around to looking for a manual yet. By the time I finish work, I just want to get home and put my feet up. This five o'clock start is no joke.'

She knew it wasn't as she was up with him at four herself. Admittedly some mornings she went back to bed for an hour after seeing him off to work, but it wasn't the same as sleeping through and she never had the luxury of a snooze in the afternoon like Bob did. She eyed him cautiously. 'You ... er ... do like your job, don't you, Bob?'

'It's all right. Why?'

'Oh, I just wondered.'

He gave a sigh. 'Can I listen to my programme now or is there something else you want to ask me?' he said, leaning over to turn up the volume.

Kay had been going to ask if he'd thought any more about going down to the allotment as the weather was really turning wintery and if he didn't make a start soon the ground would be far too hard for digging. Instead she looked at him remorsefully, realising Bob could start viewing her as a nagging wife which was the last thing she wanted. 'Oh, I'm sorry, I didn't mean to disturb you.'

Just then there was a knock at the back door and almost immediately it was heard to open and Eunice called out loudly, 'Cooee, it's only me.'

Kay threw down her knitting and shot out of her chair, rushing into the kitchen and closing the door behind her just as her friend was unknotting the scarf covering her head. 'Oh, Eunice,' she declared, 'what brings you here?'

Stopping what she was doing, her friend looked at her sharply.

'I didn't realise I needed an excuse to visit me best friend? But as it happens I do have one. George's mate called in to see him and they're talking about football and God knows what ... all the other boring things men talk about, so I've left 'em to it and come to have a proper conversation with you. I wanted to check how yer dad's getting on too. Rum do that, weren't it? Real rum do. George said if you ever find out who's responsible, he'll knock them to kingdom come for yer. Of all people, your dad getting knocked about like that just for a bag of veggies ... I still can't credit it. And I wanted to say hello to Bob as I ain't seen him since he got back. Yer could look more pleased to see me,' she snapped.

'Oh, I am, of course I am, only...'

'Only what?'

'Oh ... er ... well...' How could she explain to Eunice that as things were with Bob at the moment the reception she would get from him would be distinctly low-key? She didn't want her best friend to see Bob until he was more like his normal self. Kay needed a way to stall her, but how? Thankfully, an idea struck her.

Quick as a flash, she stepped around Eunice and grabbed her coat off the back of the door. She smiled and said, 'You've just caught me on my way out. You can come with me,' she added, dashing to the door to the back room and opening it just far enough to pop her head through. 'Bob, it's Eunice. I'm popping out with her for a minute.'

She thought he seemed pleased by her announcement.

Shutting the door she rushed back to Eunice, hooking her arm through hers while simultaneously opening the back door and propelling her friend through it.

Halfway down the short cinder path to the back gate, Eunice snapped, 'Where we going?'

'To the allotment.'

'What? But it's bleddy freezing, Kay. Anyway, what do you want down the allotment at this time of night? Eh up, gel, I don't mind doing anything for your dad, but I draw the line at digging in the dark.'

Kay giggled. 'Don't worry, my dad has some candles in his shed.' As she shut the back gate after them she saw the look of absolute horror on her friend's face and laughed aloud. 'Don't be silly, Eunice, I'm only kidding. I left some veggies behind when I was down there earlier, though.'

'Get them tomorrow.'

'I haven't really time. Mam needs them for the dinner, and anyway we're on our way now.'

They chatted the whole twenty minutes it took to reach the allotments. It was mostly Eunice doing the talking as she regaled Kay with stories of the day-to-day trials and tribulations of being a wife, mother and daughter.

The metal railings that had once cordoned off the allotment area had long since been removed for the war effort and as yet the council had not got around to replacing them. The allotments were situated on a large piece of land edging a section of the Grand Union canal that ran through Leicester. According to Ted Chivers when he'd spoken to Kay earlier that day as she'd been picking Brussels there was a rumour that the council were planning to use this land for new housing. Knowing how passionate Herbie was about his allotment, Kay had asked Ted not to mention this to her father when he visited but to wait until the rest of the Committee had confirmed it to be true. She knew this news would outrage her father and didn't want him to become upset while he was still ill.

A full moon shone down brightly from an almost cloudless sky as the women, arms linked together, entered the deserted gardens. Bare winter-dug ground glistened as frost was beginning to form on it; rows of winter vegetables that hadn't yet been harvested stood stiffly to attention; bare branches swayed lazily in the night wind; patched, dilapidated sheds cast long eerie shadows.

As they made their way down the central mud path splitting the allotments before they took a narrower one leading to Kay's father's plot, Eunice shivered and pressed herself closer to her friend's side.

'It's bleddy creepy in here at night, ain't it?' she whispered. 'I've only ever been here in the day. It wouldn't surprise me now if the ghost of a long-dead gardener didn't suddenly appear, brandishing his fork threateningly at us...'

'Oh, stop it,' Kay whisperingly scolded her, wishing she had never thought of coming up here by way of an excuse of getting Eunice out of the house. 'You'll give me the heebie-jeebies talking like that.'

Eunice stumbled and only managed to stop herself from falling by the fact that she was clutching Kay's arm.

'Should have worn your boots instead of those heeled shoes,' Kay observed.

'Huh! If I'd had any inkling what I was in for when I decided to pay you a visit, I woulda kept me slippers on and stayed where I was!' she whispered back. 'I might have bin bored to death listening to George and his mate droning on, but at least I'd have bin warm and not risking me neck.' She suddenly pulled Kay to a halt. 'If I remember right, ain't that your dad's allotment over there?' she said in a low voice, pointing across to a garden three plots away from the one they were just passing.

Kay squinted in the direction she was pointing. 'Yes, it is. Why?'

'Well, I could have sworn I just saw a man coming out of your dad's shed.'

'Stop trying to scare me with your stupid ghost stories,' snapped Kay.

'No, I ain't. Seriously, Kay... Oh, I was right, there's another man just come out. Look, he's heading off in the same direction. Oh!' she mouthed, clutching Kay's arm tighter. 'They must be robbing yer dad's shed.' Then she pulled a puzzled face. 'Although I never saw either of them carrying anything, but then it is dark, they mighta bin.'

'Well, they won't have got away with much,'

231

said Kay. 'Dad never locks up the shed 'cos all he's got in there is gardening equipment he's had for donkey's years. Oh, and a couple of frayed old deckchairs. He says if anyone is that hard up they're welcome to it all as it'd cost him less to replace the stuff he's got than to get a new door for the shed after they'd smashed it to get in. Oh, I hope he hasn't been robbed, not on top of what's just happened to him!'

'Well, they've gone now. Shall we go and check to see if 'ote is missing?' Eunice suggested.

Kay sighed. 'If there is, I'm not telling my dad until he's better.'

They made to resume making their way across when suddenly they both froze rigid as they saw the two men returning. This time they were each carrying two heavy boxes and labouring under their weight. They watched in stunned silence, hearts beating painfully, as the two shadowy silhouettes disappeared inside the shed, then moments later came out minus their loads to disappear again.

Kay and Eunice looked at each other, baffled.

'What d'yer reckon they're up to?' Eunice whispered.

'Looks to me like they're storing those boxes in my dad's shed, and they must be coming back again as they've left the door open. Probably got a van parked somewhere. They looked to be heavy boxes. I wonder what's in them? But that's by the by,' said Kay, grabbing Eunice's arm and shaking it urgently. 'How dare they use my father's shed for whatever it is they are? We ought to fetch the police because they're up to no good, those men, it's obvious. You stay here and keep your eyes peeled. I'll go and find a telephone box and call the police.'

'Eh, you ain't leaving me here on me own?'

'Well, you go then and I'll stay here.'

'Not on your nelly! I'm not walking back through those dark allotments on me tod.'

Kay threw up her hands. 'Well, what do you suggest then?' she hissed.

'Er ... let's see if we can get a closer look at the men so at least we can give the bobbies a description of them when we go and call them together.' Eunice grabbed Kay's arm. 'Come on, we can creep along and squat down behind yer dad's rows of Brussels. We'll have a better view from there.'

Kay blew out her cheeks. 'If we get spotted...'

'Oh, just come on, and let's hurry before they come back.'

Bending over as low as they could, they crept their way past the next two allotments and on over to the six deep rows of Brussels plants laden with sprouts, standing tall and proud in Herbie's garden.

Squatting down behind them, Eunice said, 'We can't see anything from here. The Brussels are too thickly packed together for us to see through. We'll have to get closer.'

'We can't, there's nothing else to hide behind.' Eunice rose up just enough so she could see over the Brussels tops, her eyes darting around. 'Look, there's a bush just over there. It's nearer to the shed than these Brussels are too.'

Kay rose to look also. 'What, that blackcurrant

bush? That won't hide us, it's lost all its leaves.'

'It will, trust me, and we can see better through it. Those men ain't looking for anyone spying on them, are they? As long as we don't make a sound, they won't know we're there. Quick, before they come back!'

Eunice made a dash for the bush and Kay had no choice but to follow her.

They had just secreted themselves behind it, both making sure they had a good view across to the shed door, when the men appeared around the corner of the shed, labouring again under the weight of the boxes they were carrying.

The bush Kay and Eunice were hiding behind was only a couple of yards away from the shed and almost in line with the door. As they watched Kay held her breath, the sound of her own heart pounding in her ears, terrified the men would sense they were being watched.

Thankfully they seemed to be concentrating too hard on their task to notice anything else. The men went inside the shed then moments later came out, minus their loads. This time the taller of the two shut the door behind him. Reaching into his pocket, he took out something and appeared to be fiddling with the door. Kay realised he was padlocking it. The two men faced each other. The taller one took what looked like a thick envelope out of his inside coat pocket and, slapping the other on his shoulder with one hand, thrust the envelope at him with the other. Very clearly the women then heard him say, 'There you go, mate. It's all there as I promised. Pleasure doing business with you.'

The other man grabbed the envelope and shoved it into his coat pocket. Shoulders hunched, he hurried off, disappearing down the path at the side of the shed.

The taller man stood still for a moment, a look of satisfaction on his face, before squaring his shoulders, thrusting his hands deep into his pockets and sauntering off in the direction Kay and Eunice had arrived from. As he passed by the bush they were crouching behind, they both froze rigid, scared witless he would spot them. Luckily for them his mind was obviously fully occupied by other things and he didn't.

Moments later in the distance they both heard an engine start up and the sound of a vehicle driving away.

They waited for an age before they both dared breathe a sigh of relief.

It was Eunice who spoke first. Her face was grave and so was her voice. 'I recognised that tall man. It was your lodger, wasn't it?'

Her face ashen, Kay nodded.

'What about the other one? I didn't get a clear look at him so I've no idea who he was. Do you?'

Kay had seen him and recognised him, but she couldn't tell Eunice who it was. 'Never seen him before,' she lied. 'Oh, dear God,' she agonised. 'What am I going to do?'

Eunice looked at her askance. 'What do yer mean, what yer gonna do? Go to the police, that's what. You were right about your lodger, Kay. He's a bad 'un, ain't he? Obviously stolen stuff in those boxes or why else would he be hiding them in your dad's shed? Shame, though, 'cos he ain't half good-looking. Right, we off to telephone the rozzers?' she said, rising.

Kay grabbed her arm and pulled her back down again to a squatting position. 'Oh, but we can't!' she cried.

'Can't? Why?'

'Because if that is stolen stuff then my dad's shed is being used to hide it in. The police might think he and my lodger are in this together. Oh, this is just awful! I thought Tony was bragging when he said he'd a nice deal taking shape that was going to make him a lot of money, I'd no idea he meant this kind of deal or that his plan involved people...' Her voice trailed off as she realised she was about to blurt out information she didn't wish Eunice to know. 'The police could also think me and Bob are involved in this because Tony lives with us. We can't get them involved, Eunice, we just can't,' Kay insisted. 'My mam and dad have never had a stain on their characters. Even just being involved in all this in any way would shame them so much they'd never be able to hold their heads up again, innocent as they are.'

Eunice looked at her for several long moments. 'No, yer right, we can't get the bobbies involved. Neither can we just walk away and leave those boxes. What if PC Plod does happen to have a nosey around for any reason and finds them there before yer lodger shifts them?'

'So what do you think we should do?' Kay asked, her own brain whirling frantically.

'Well, we could take them out of the shed and leave 'em somewhere well away from here then

236

call the police anonymously and let them "find" the stuff where we leave it. Even if they do manage to trace the stuff back to Tony, then they can't accuse you and Bob of being involved just 'cos he lodges with yer, can they?'

'No, they can't, but they can trace those boxes back to where they originally came from.'

Eunice looked at her, bemused. 'Why should that matter? The chap who sold the stuff on to Tony is as much of a crook as he is.'

Panic was mounting in Kay. She feared that at any moment someone could come along and question why they were there. 'Look, we just can't call the police, Eunice, and that's that. And we can't leave those boxes in my dad's shed neither. We need to get rid of them where no one will find them,' she said urgently.

'Why are you so worried about those boxes being traced back to the chap who sold them to Tony?'

'Please, Eunice, stop questioning me and think how we can get rid of them once and for all. Come on, think!'

She shrugged. 'Me brain's gone dead. I wonder what's in those boxes?'

'Malt whisky for export,' Kay said distractedly as she tried to think what best to do.

'How do you know that?'

'Eh? Oh, I'm just guessing. Could be anything for all I know. The canal...'

'What?'

'We throw them all in the canal! Could be years before anyone dredges them up and by that time I doubt anyone could piece together the puzzle of how they got there.'

'But how the hell are we going to carry them all the way over when your lodger and that other man were struggling? Lugging heavy shopping is one thing, Kay, but those boxes looked like they weighed a ton each to me.'

'We'll wheelbarrow them. Dad's got a barrow and there's bound to be another on an allotment close by. Go and have a look around while I see how we can get the shed open now it's been padlocked.'

'Oh, that's easy,' Eunice said knowledgeably. 'We just need to find something to jemmy it open with. Like a crow bar or something. Shouldn't take much doing. The door on yer dad's shed's rotten in places, I can tell that from here.'

Kay looked at her sharply. 'Have you done this kind of thing before?'

'No, but I've locked meself out me house and had to get in, and paying for the back door to be fixed were no joke, believe me.'

Kay shook her head. 'You never cease to amaze me, Eunice. Right, we need another barrow and a jemmy of some sort. Let's have a scout around and see what we can find.'

'Together?' said Eunice, looking around fearfully.

Kay tutted. 'All right, together.'

Fumbling their way across to the adjoining allotment, they thankfully discovered a wheelbarrow tipped up against the shed wall and a spade next to it. Between them they righted the wheelbarrow, and Kay wheeled it back across to her father's allotment while Eunice carried the spade. Together they wedged the flat end of the spade firmly in between the hinged edge of the door and the wall of the shed. Then, both pushing on the wooden handle of the spade, they heaved until the sound of splitting wood was heard. They did this several times until the door sprang off its hinges, and then together they heaved their own body weight against it until it finally broke free with a loud crack.

Clinging on to each other they stepped tentatively inside the gloomy shed and, aided by the moonlight shining through the grimy windows, stood and stared at what they found.

'You were right, Kay,' whispered Eunice in a shocked voice. 'It *is* malt whisky. At least two dozen cases of it. How many bottles would that be altogether?'

'Twelve bottles to each case. Two hundred and eighty-eight, by my reckoning.'

'Bleddy hell, Kay. This lot'd fetch a small fortune on the black market.'

'That's what Tony planned. Come on, we've no time for idling.'

It took them just over an hour to load the wheelbarrows with three boxes to each barrow, then to push them slowly over the hard rutted ground the two hundred or so yards to the sweeping bend in the canal edging the allotments. Each time they arrived at the canal, they scanned the tow path up and down to be as sure as they could that no one was around before they heaved each box between them into the canal's depths.

Their task finally complete, and pushing the shed door back into place as best they could, despite its being bitterly cold, they squatted down on the shed step to catch their breaths, both sweating profusely.

'Remind me not to take you up on your offer of a walk next time I visit you at night,' Eunice said to Kay.

She looked at her friend pleadingly. 'You must promise me, Eunice, that you won't mention this to anyone? You do promise, don't you?' she asked earnestly.

'No one'd believe me if I did. No one in their right minds'd do what we just have. We've just thrown a fortune in the canal, Kay! And I can't believe I agreed to help you do it.'

'You did it because you're my best friend and were helping me save my family's good name.'

'Well, when yer put it like that... Oh, and Kay, yer must promise me faithfully you'll never breathe a word of what we've been up to tonight, 'cos my George would go mad if he found out I'd put meself in such danger even if it was all in aid of me best friend.'

'I promise you, Eunice, and you know I'll never let you down.'

'Oh, I know that much for nothing. Right, can we go home now?'

They got up together and linked arms, ready for the potentially hazardous journey back across the dark allotments. As Kay pressed her body close to Eunice's she felt something hard dig her in the side. She looked at her friend sharply. 'What's that in your pocket?' she snapped accusingly, as if she didn't already know.

Eunice looked back sheepishly. 'Only two

240

bottles, Kay. You can't begrudge me them, after what I've just done for you? George will be over the moon when I give them to him. Don't worry, I shall say I found 'em lying in the gutter when I was on my way home from your house.'

'And you think he'll believe you?'

'He's got no choice 'cos that's me story and I'm sticking to it. Are we going home then or what?'

As they set off Eunice asked Kay, 'So what you going to do about lodger boy, then?'

'Get him out of my house, once and for all, that's what,' she replied with conviction.

CHAPTER TWELVE

After saying her goodbyes to Eunice at the corner of her street, giving her a fierce hug and thanking her profusely for what she had helped to do, Kay hurried home, desperate to be there to sort out this terrible matter with Bob. As far as she was concerned she had a criminal living under her roof, one who had blatantly involved her family in his scam to feather his own nest, and she wanted him out of her house as soon as possible.

Leaving her boots outside the back door to be scraped clean of mud later, she hurriedly stripped off her coat, hanging it up on the back of the door, and rushed into the back room where she found Bob slumped comfortably in his armchair, still engrossed in listening to the wireless. Rushing across to it, she switched off the wireless and

241

immediately Bob sat bolt upright.

'What did you go and do that for? I was listening to it,' he complained.

She hurried back around his chair to perch on the edge of the one opposite, clasping her hands in her lap. 'I'm sorry for interrupting your programme, Bob, but we need to talk. Has Tony come back in?'

'Eh? Not as far as I know, he hasn't. Why?'

Hopefully he was down the pub celebrating his success, mentally counting his gains when he'd sold all those bottles on at a hefty profit. It was going to take more than a few minutes to tell Bob what she'd uncovered about his so-called friend. Her news was, going to shock him deeply.

'Because...' Kay took a deep breath and gave him a detailed account of what had transpired that night. She finished off by saying, 'I'd only gone to get the bag of veggies for my mother that I'd forgotten to bring back with me this afternoon, but thank goodness I did or we'd never have known what Tony was up to. Oh, damn, I forgot about them again! Oh, never mind, I'll have to go back and fetch them tomorrow.' She looked at him remorsefully. 'Bob, I'm so sorry to be shattering your illusions about your friend, but now you know: he's a common criminal with no qualms at all about using my family just to line his own pockets. I dread to think what could have happened if it had been the police who'd discovered those boxes in my dad's shed and wouldn't believe he wasn't involved in Tony's scam.' She took a deep breath, looking at her husband expectantly. 'So what are you going to do?'

He was looking at her, panic-stricken. 'Tony doesn't have a clue what you've done? Are you positive?'

She nodded. 'Absolutely positive.'

He sighed, mortally relieved. 'Oh, why didn't you leave well alone, Kay?'

She was shocked by his response. 'But I couldn't. I've explained my reasons for doing what I did. I had no choice.'

He jumped up from his chair and began pacing the room. 'What Tony does is his own business, Kay. Nothing to do with us.'

Bewildered, she cried, 'Of course it is when he's put my family in jeopardy with one of his dodgy deals!'

Bob stopped his pacing and looked hard at her. 'But you don't know that what he was doing wasn't above board.'

'Oh, Bob, it was obvious. Why else was the deal done at night and in a deserted place, explain that to me?'

He gave a shrug as he began his pacing again. 'But there could be any number of reasons for that. Not all business is done in daylight.'

Kay gawped at him, shocked.

'Why are you making excuses for him, Bob?'

He stopped his pacing again.

'I'm not,' he snapped. 'I'm just trying to make you see that you could have got this all wrong. Tony's my friend, after all. Someone has to stick up for him. You've never liked him, have you? How do I know you're not making this up as an excuse to ask him to leave?'

She gasped, 'Are you saying you don't believe

me, Bob?'

'No, just that you might be making more of this than it really is. So you saw Tony load some boxes into your father's shed and hand a man an envelope? You don't know what was in that envelope, do you? Not for certain you don't unless you saw what was inside it. And how do you know Tony wasn't working for someone else and just taking delivery of the boxes? And anyway, what if he has done a deal with that man for some boxes of whisky? You don't know for sure it was an underhand one. He could have thought he was buying them honestly, for all you know.'

Kay opened her mouth to tell him she knew for a fact that the whisky was not bought legitimately by Tony and he must have known it, but that would mean telling Bob she knew the identity of the man he had bought it from, and knew without a doubt how *he* had acquired it. But by revealing the identity of the other man all this might get back to someone she loved very dearly and cause that person a lot of hurt. She couldn't risk that. She also wanted to tell him that Eunice had been with her and had witnessed all she had and come to the same conclusions, but she had promised her friend she would not mention a word of her involvement and would never break her promise.

Lips pressed tight, Kay gave a deep sigh.

'All right, Bob, say Tony did buy the whisky honestly, that still doesn't excuse his using my father's shed to store it in without his permission. I want you to ask him to leave.'

He looked horrified at the thought. 'I can't do

that! What excuse would I give him? Using your father's shed without permission is a trivial thing, not reason enough to ask him to leave. It's not like your father is using it at the moment. Tony more than likely took advantage of the fact but that doesn't mean he's a thief. I can't brand him one just because you're telling me he is, Kay, not without any proof. I promised the man he could stay until he got himself sorted and I can't believe you're asking me to break my word to him. Aren't you forgetting I owe him my life?' His face clouded over. 'Tony's going to be furious when he discovers those boxes missing, and who can blame him?'

He wrung his hands tightly and Kay thought she must be mistaken when she saw a look of fear in his eyes. 'You should have left well alone, Kay, you really should. All this is going to achieve is the one thing you didn't want and that's to delay Tony leaving this house. I'm going to bed.'

He turned towards the door leading to the stairs. As he reached it, he looked back at her. 'Just be thankful Tony has no idea what you've done to him. Best thing you can do is forget this all ever happened, like I'm going to do.'

As he disappeared up the stairs, Kay sat staring after him, stunned. She couldn't believe his reaction to what she had told him. All he'd done was stick up for Tony and insinuate she had elaborated a simple money-making scheme of Tony's into a major theft just so she had an excuse to ask Bob to make him leave their house. Despite all the excuses her husband had given her, though, she knew that she was right about

Tony and what he'd been up to. A terrible hurt filled her then, a hurt so deep it cut her to the quick. Bob had sided with his friend over her, his wife. Taken his side, not hers. Tears of distress pricked Kay's eyes. Why couldn't Bob open his eyes and see Tony for what he really was? Was he so blinded by gratitude that the other man could do no wrong as far as Bob was concerned?

A wave of despair filled her. She had thought she had discovered a way to be rid of Tony but all she seemed to have done was delayed his departure indefinitely and made herself look terrible in her husband's eyes. Oh, why did she have the stupid idea of going up to the allotments tonight? But she had, and had acted as she had, and could not turn back the clock.

But she couldn't think about this now. She had another pressing matter she had to deal with which couldn't wait, despite the lateness of the hour, or else she risked someone she loved very much suffering more pain than was necessary.

CHAPTER THIRTEEN

Frank Ambleside was most taken aback to see who his visitor was when he opened the door at just before ten o'clock.

'Mrs Clifton, what a pleasure,' he said, smiling. Then his face clouded. 'There's n'ote wrong with yer aunt, is there?'

'My aunt's fine, thank you,' Kay replied stiltedly.

'I apologise for calling on you at this time in the evening but I'd like a word with you.'

'Why, yes, 'course,' he said, standing aside. 'Please excuse the mess,' he said apologetically as he led her through to his living room. 'I've not long got back from a four-day long-haul trip and I've not had time to unpack me stuff yet. I did find the time to call on yer aunt, though. Couldn't wait to see her, in fact.'

You'll not be seeing much more of her after what I have to say to you, thought Kay.

As she arrived in the back room of the small terraced house, despite her mind being fully occupied with what she was about to say, she did note that apart from a shabby-looking holdall containing his still unpacked clothes on the floor, the sparsely furnished room was clean and tidy otherwise.

He was puzzled by her manner towards him. 'Er ... you said you wanted a word with me? You did say it's nothing to do with Viv, didn't you? Oh, where are me manners. Why don't you take your coat off and have a seat? Can I get you a cuppa?'

'No, thank you. I am not proposing to stay long and this is not a social visit. As I said, my aunt is fine, Mr Ambleside. She likes you very much. In fact, I'd say she more than just likes you from what she's told me.'

He smiled, pleased. 'I like your aunt very much meself. She's a wonderful woman.'

'Yes, I couldn't agree more. I'd go so far as to say that she's under the illusion that you're a wonderful man, Mr Ambleside. Honest, trust-

247

worthy, just the sort of man to deserve my aunt's affection.'

He was looking at her non-plussed, clearly wondering where this conversation was heading.

She reared back her head and took a deep breath, clasping her hands in front of her. 'You're not honest and trustworthy, though, are you, Mr Ambleside? I know my aunt isn't exactly averse to getting her hands on something she needs without asking too many questions. We're only human after all and most of us turn a blind eye now and again, don't we, Mr Ambleside? Especially with all the shortages and rationing we're having to cope with. Like, for instance, the bottle of whisky you brought along with you to my husband's welcome home dinner.

'I wonder, though, how my aunt would react if she knew you'd stolen several boxes of it from your employer? A couple of dozen, to be exact. And for all I know, that's just the tip of the iceberg. Not quite in the same league as acquiring the odd bottle now and again, wouldn't you agree, Mr Ambleside? That's what I call major theft. I wonder how my aunt would feel about you if she knew what your pastime was? And what else, I wonder, doesn't she have a clue about that you've kept hidden from her?'

Frank was looking at her, stricken.

'You're wondering how I know about your little sideline,' Kay continued. 'I was down at the allotments tonight, just happened to be there, unfortunately for you, and I saw what took place between you and my lodger. He's another matter. At the moment it's your relationship with my

Aunty Viv that most concerns me. It would devastate her if she should ever find out the truth – that she was falling in love with someone no better than a common criminal, someone fleecing his employer to line his own pockets.

'Has it crossed your mind, Mr Ambleside, what it would do to Viv if she found out what you're up to? She'd never trust another man again. She was broken-hearted when my Uncle Archie was killed, never thought she'd meet another man who came up to his standards. It took her a lot of soul-searching to give you a chance. My aunt deserves better than you and the trouble you're going to bring her. I think far too much of her to stand by and let her risk the shame of visiting you in jail, because you'll be caught eventually. It's not many criminals who escape justice.

'So I want you to let her down gently, make her think it's just not working out for you. That way she'll be none the wiser and won't be soured against the attentions of another man who'll bring her more happiness than ever you will.' Looking at him in a way that left him in no doubt she meant every word, she said, 'If you don't agree to do what I ask then, though it grieves me, I'll have no choice but to tell her myself. I can't risk her getting more deeply involved with you and consequently hurt even worse. Now, I hope you think enough of my aunt to do as I ask?'

Frank was looking at her, wild-eyed. 'Oh, Mrs Clifton, you have me all wrong...'

'I don't think so. I told you what I saw.'

'Yes, but it's not like you think. Please listen to me,' he begged. 'I would never hurt your aunt

249

intentionally, believe me I wouldn't. I am an honest man. It's just that at the time I felt I had no choice but to do as I did. It was a one off, believe me it was. I didn't enjoy a minute of it. I was worried witless I'd get caught. I'd never put meself through that again, never! Not for all the money in the world I wouldn't. It's not worth it.' He raked his hands through his hair. 'Tony Cheadle knocked on me door the night after I'd been introduced to him at yer husband's welcome home dinner. He said he'd a proposition for me. Stupidly thinking it was something to do with supplying me with stuff to fix up, which of course I'd be interested in as it's a way I make meself a bit extra, I let him in. I'd no idea then how he found out where I lived, but now I realise he's the sort of man who'd find out anything he'd a mind to. Maybe I told him meself when we were chatting before we sat down to dinner.

'Anyway, he came straight to the point. Said I was his golden opportunity of making himself a decent amount of money at one go instead of messing about acquiring it through piddling little deals over a long period of time. He'd got big plans for himself, he said, and the only thing stopping him was having the money to show the big boys he meant business. He wanted to buy himself into their inner circle and get the chance to make himself some proper money.

'I couldn't see where I fitted into his big scheme of things, told him so an' all. He laughed at me, said was I thicker than I looked. I had a way to acquire the sort of goods for which he'd get a buyer, no problem. People were clamouring to get their hands on the type of stuff I transported to the docks for export and would pay handsomely for it. Then I twigged what he was after. I told him I wasn't open to that kinda thing, made no bones about it. "Suit yourself," he said, "that's if you don't mind losing the woman I know you're keen on." He'd seen for himself, of course, at your mother's house, how much I think of yer aunt. He said he only had to click his fingers and Viv would come running to him. Well, let's face it, Mrs Clifton, stand me and Tony Cheadle side by side and I can't hold a candle to him, can I? Apart from his looks, he's a good ten years younger than me.'

'You should have given Viv more credit than to fall for a man like Tony Cheadle just because he's good-looking,' Kay snapped at him.

Frank looked at her, shame-faced. 'Yes, knowing Viv as I do now, I should have. But I wasn't thinking straight at the time. I just saw a man who meant what he said, and the thought of losing Viv for any reason ripped me apart. I was devastated after finding out what me wife had being doing behind me back. I promised meself I'd never fall for a woman's charms and get meself into such a position again. That was, until I realised my feelings for Viv. They kinda crept up on me before I realised what were happening to me, and by that time it was too late, I was well and truly smitten by her. Meeting up with Viv and her mates that night down the pub when I was drowning me sorrows was really my salvation. But mostly it was down to Viv. She befriended me. It was her that made me see that there was life after death, if you get my drift, and not all women were cheaters like me wife was. I got a job, straightened meself out.

'I knew that what Cheadle was asking me to do was wrong, but I said if he'd give me his word that this was a one off and afterwards he'd leave me and Viv alone, I would do what he asked. Mind you, who knows what a promise is worth coming from the mouth of a man like him? But it was either trust him to keep his word or risk him carrying out his threat to take Viv from me.

'I ain't stupid, Mrs Clifton, I don't go around with me eyes shut and I know exactly what kind of underhand business goes on in my line of work. By this time I'd twigged how Cheadle expected me to get hold of the goods he wanted. Some of the loaders at the warehouses and the off loaders at the docks I visit are open to receiving a backhander for loading more on a lorry than the quantity on the loading docket instructs them to, or else saying they've off loaded twenty boxes when the real total is fifteen. How can a boss ever dispute that when the short-ages are discovered unless they're personally standing at the back of a loader or off loader and counting the goods themselves while the lorry is being dealt with? So that's how I got the two dozen boxes of whisky. I delivered them to the allotment tonight as arranged with Cheadle before I checked back in to my firm after my return from my trip.

'Believe me, I couldn't wait to get rid of the stuff. I'm not proud of what I did. I know it's not the point neither, but the money he gave me for my trouble ... well, after I'd took out what it cost me in backhanders, I was left with twenty quid. I meant to add it to what I'd already saved to buy Viv something nice, a bit of jewellery, a brooch or something, to show her how much she meant to me and that I was serious about her.' His face took on a pained expression. 'Me wage ain't too bad and I do get extra for covering the long-haul loads and from the bits and pieces when people ask me to have a go at mending stuff for 'em, but it still takes a while to get a few quid together to buy something decent, the type of thing I wanted to get for Viv. I felt nothing less would do for a lovely lady like her.' He gave a deep sad sigh. 'I suppose it's all bin futile now, though.'

Kay thought long and hard. Finally she said, 'You could use the money towards an engagement ring when the time's right, Mr Ambleside. I can't say as I approve of the way you got some of the money, but what's done is done. You might as well put it to good use now you've got it.'

He looked at her, stunned, then hope lit up his face. 'Does this mean you believe me, Mrs Clifton?'

Kay swallowed hard. 'Yes, I do. You've convinced me you only did this because of how you feel for my aunt. But in future, Mr Ambleside, don't underestimate Viv. She has far more integrity than people give her credit for. She would never have given a good man like you up for a fling with Tony Cheadle.'

'I realise that. I think I knew deep down even when I agreed to what I did, but as I said, at the time I wasn't thinking straight.'

Kay smiled at him warmly. 'I owe you an apology, Mr Ambleside. I just hope you can forgive me?'

'Oh, please call me Frank. Why do you owe me an apology?'

She took a deep breath. 'Because I jumped to conclusions about you when I saw what took place between you and Tony Cheadle. I should have realised that if you had been as crooked as I accused you of being, my aunt would have realised it a long time ago. Please call me Kay. It seems to me that we'll become family in the not too distant future.'

'I do hope so,' he enthused. 'I only pray Viv will accept me when I pluck up enough courage to ask her.'

'I've a feeling she will.'

'That means a lot to me, coming from you. And as for me forgiving you, if I'd been in your position and witnessed what you did then I guess I'd have jumped to the same conclusions meself. So ... er ... you're not going to mention any of this to Viv then?'

'No. This will remain between you and me.'

'And what of Tony Cheadle now you know what you do about him? I mean, he lodges with you, doesn't he?'

She sighed. 'Mr Cheadle is another matter. I'm not sure what's going to happen on that front. I really don't want to say any more on the subject.'

'But surely you can't allow him to live under your roof, not now you know what sort of man he is?'

'With all due respect, Frank, this is for my husband to sort out. Tony Cheadle isn't just a lodger, he saved my husband's life and Bob is a loyal man. He finds it very hard to break his word when he's given it, regardless of the circumstances. Mr Cheadle, I have no doubt, will be dealt with by my husband in his own time and in his own way.'

'Oh, yes, I see.'

'I just ask of you not to let my aunt in on Mr Cheadle's true character as I don't...'

'No need to say any more, Kay,' he interjected, a knowing expression on his face. 'Look, can we forget tonight ever happened?'

'That's fine by me.'

'Would you like me to get you a cuppa?'

'No, thank you, I really must be getting home.'

Frank smiled at her warmly.

'Your aunt sings your praises, you know. I have to say, everything she's told me about you is true.'

CHAPTER FOURTEEN

Kay had no idea what the time was. It had been just after eleven-thirty when she'd arrived home after her visit to Frank and since then she had been sitting curled up in her armchair, her coat draped around her, the only other warmth in the room from the dying embers of the fire, the only light a dim flicker from the gas mantles turned to their lowest, her only company her own thoughts.

She hadn't bothered going to bed, knowing

there was no point as she wouldn't sleep and didn't want to risk disturbing Bob as she tossed and turned. She had upset him enough tonight with her accusations against Tony. Despite Bob's reasoning and desperate excuses for his friend's behaviour, she herself still had no doubt that Tony was a crook and was deeply worried that this man's illicit activities could bring trouble on them while he was residing under their roof.

But that was not the only thing causing her restlessness.

Since she'd been out late, she had no idea if Tony had returned and was already in bed, dreaming of the good life he'd gain from the sale of his illicit goods which he clearly planned to do imminently. Or was he still out, trying to find a buyer now he had the goods? Or maybe he had returned to the shed with a buyer only to discover his plunder missing and was now trying to find out who had dared cross him and was out for their blood.

Bob had told her it was best to forget what had transpired tonight, but she didn't know whether she could. After all, she didn't just dislike Tony for his attitude towards her, bad as it was. Now she knew without a doubt his true nature, and despite feeling she was right to do what she had by way of getting rid of his ill-gotten gains, when all was said and done, she was guilty of ruining Tony's opportunity to make himself quite a sum of money. For all these reasons she wasn't sure how she could look him in the face again without his suspecting all was not right with her and asking her awkward questions.

Suddenly the sound of the front door opening and banging shut and footsteps stumbling across the linoleum reached her ears. Kay froze. Tony had returned and it sounded to her like he was very much the worse for drink. She heard the connecting door open and he came lurching into the back room.

She hardly dared to breathe, fearing what had brought about a need in him for so much alcohol. Was it to celebrate or to drown his sorrows?

Just about to throw himself down in the chair Bob usually sat in, Tony suddenly realised he wasn't alone. For a while he swayed on his feet, fighting to focus his eyes so he could recognise whose company he was in. 'Oh, it's you,' he finally slurred. 'What a' you still doing up at this time in the morning?'

She managed to find her voice. 'Oh ... er ... I didn't realise it was so late. Just couldn't sleep. You get those nights sometimes, don't you?'

He collapsed in the armchair, lounging drunkenly back in it, and Kay saw he was brandishing a bottle of what appeared to be colourless liquid.

He noticed she had spotted it and thrust it out towards her. 'Cheap gin. Want a swig?'

She shook her head. 'No, thank you.'

He laughed. 'No, don't suppose you would. Cheap gin not your sort of tipple, I take it? What is your tipple, Mrs Clifton? Or are you one of them tee-totaller types?'

She swallowed hard, feeling mortally uncomfortable and not just because he was in such a state of high intoxication. She was unsure yet why he was so drunk and felt it best to humour him. 'I'm not averse to a drink, Mr Cheadle. I like a sherry now and again, and I don't mind a glass of beer.'

He sniggered as he shifted around in his seat to throw one leg over the arm. 'A right woman's drink is sherry! Wouldn't be seen dead drinking that myself unless I was desperate. So I can't tempt you with a drop of this then? Can't offer you anything better at the moment 'cos this is all I can afford now.' His eyes suddenly blazed darkly. 'Thought I'd be drinking champagne tonight.'

The murderous glint in his eyes then confirmed her fear that he knew of the disappearance of the whisky, and her heart raced as she feared he would somehow discover her involvement. She felt a need to escape, and made to rise.

'Oi, where yer going, Mrs Clifton? Stay where you are and keep me company. Not often you and me have a chat, is it?'

She felt she had no choice but to remain for fear of arousing Tony's suspicions.

With great difficulty he lifted his leg off the arm of the chair and dropped it back on the floor. Then he leaned over and thrust his face in her direction. 'Do you want a laugh, Mrs Clifton? I know this will make you laugh. Well, I'll tell you, whether it does or it doesn't.' He lifted the bottle to his lips and took a large gulp, then gave a loud belch which he made no attempt to apologise for. 'I made a deal ... best fucking deal I've ever dreamed of making. It dropped in my lap when I was in the last place I ever thought I'd meet such a source. So I grabbed it. Only a fool wouldn't have. It went along like clockwork. I lined up the goods, got myself a buyer willing to pay more than I expected, goods arrived as promised which cost me practically every penny I had to my name … but what the hell? Considering the profit I was going to make. Then I returned to my storage place with my buyer and his transport, ready to do the final deal, and – hey presto! No goods. Some fucker had swiped 'em while I'd been gone. The whole lot, every last bottle of the finest Scottish malt money could buy.

'You'd have thought whoever it was would've been kind enough to leave just one bottle behind as a token of generosity, wouldn't you, eh, Mrs Clifton? Instead of me having to drown my sorrows in this gut rot. I looked a right fucking idiot in front of my buyer and he's promised he'll spread the word around the sort who matter that I'm not to be trusted,' Tony snarled furiously, eyes black as thunder now. 'Well, no one makes a fool of me, let me tell you. No one!' he spat.

Kay gulped several times in an effort to moisten her dry throat. 'Oh, I'm so sorry, Mr Cheadle.' She hoped she sounded sincere enough and also that in his drunken state he could not see the red tide of guilt creeping up her neck.

'Oh, and I know why you're sorry, Mrs Clifton! 'Cos you realise this means you won't be getting rid of me so quick. No telling how long I'll have to stay put here now. I tell you who else will be sorry, Mrs Clifton, the bastards who helped themselves to my stuff. 'Cos if I ever catch up with them, they're dead.'

She gulped again. 'Do … er … you have any idea

who it might be who did this to you?'

'No,' he spat, then glared across at her, his bloodshot eyes boring into hers. 'Why, do you?'

She had a terrible feeling he suspected she knew something and a surge of sheer terror filled her. 'No,' she blurted. 'I had no idea about any of this so how could I?'

His head was wobbling from side to side. It was very apparent he had no control over it. 'Huh! Someone did, though. Someone must have been watching mc or how else did they know what was in that ... well, where I'd stored the goods. They'd just better hope I never find out their identity, that's all I can say.' He thrust the bottle in her direction again. 'Sure you don't want a drink?'

'No, thank you. Look, don't you think you've had enough? Why don't you go to bed?' Kay suggested in an attempt to get out of this situation.

'Hey, I can judge for myself when I've had enough,' Tony hissed, taking another draught from the bottle which by now was nearly empty.

She saw his eyes droop then and his hand slacken on the bottle. Getting up from her chair, she grabbed the bottle and gently eased it out of his hand before putting it on the hearth. Then she put one arm around his back and coaxed him to stand up.

'Let me help you to bed.'

Thankfully he was now in no fit state to protest and together they stumbled their way into his room where he immediately collapsed on his bed and passed out.

Looking down at him, Kay ran her hands down the sides of her face, took a deep breath and slowly exhaled.

Her lodger seemed to have no inkling of her involvement in the sabotage of his money-making scheme, and she dearly hoped it stayed like that.

CHAPTER FIFTEEN

At eleven the next morning Kay was standing at the sink, staring blindly out of the window, so lost in her thoughts she hadn't seen her friend run up the path. She jumped almost out of her skin in shock when Eunice charged through the back door.

'Oh, I couldn't wait to find out what happened when yer told Bob about last night! I got me mother to have our Joanie for an hour – well, I bribed her with getting her shopping for her. Didn't want us to be disturbed while you told me all. Oh, when I gave my George those two bottles of whisky yer should have seen his face! He was so gobsmacked he never questioned my story of how I got 'em. Just said, "Well, I'll be blowed, miracles do happen."

'Eh, I had a thought last night after we'd parted to go home,' said Eunice, stripping off her coat and hanging it on the back of the door. 'Yer don't think that Tony had anything to do with yer father's bashing up, do yer? Well, it makes sense. He needed to be got out of the way so Tony could have free use of the shed to store his dodgy goods in until he sold them on.' She laughed. 'Fat chance of that now though, eh, after where we chucked 'em?'

'Keep your voice down,' Kay hissed to her, putting a finger to her lips.

'Why, Bob in bed, is he? Did this upset him that much he had to miss a day's work? Well, I suppose he did think that Tony was his mate, and yer never think mates will do the dirty on yer, do yer? Must have been shattering for him, hearing what you had to tell him.'

Ignoring her for a moment, Kay went into the living room and returned with two chairs which she placed to either side of the small pine table she used to prepare food on which stood against the wall opposite the kitchen window. Then she went across to the stove and lit the gas beneath the kettle. Back with Eunice she said, 'I expect you want a cuppa?'

'Don't be daft, when have you ever known me to refuse? But I also want to know what happened when you told Bob last night. Chuck that Tony straight out, did he?' she said, making herself comfortable on one of the chairs Kay had brought through. 'What are we sitting in here for?'

'So we can't be overheard.'

Eunice pulled a face. 'Bob'd have to have hearing like a bat's to hear what we're saying down here from the bedroom, 'specially if he's asleep.' Then she noticed the state of her friend. 'Good God, gel, you look like death warmed up! You didn't sleep a wink last night, did you? Well, I expect that's understandable. Or is it that you

262

ain't been to bed, as if I ain't mistaken them's the same clothes you were wearing when I came in last night before you marched me off to the allotments.'

'Eunice, please keep your voice down,' Kay urged her again. 'Bob is at work, it's Tony I'm worried about. Though hopefully he'll stay in bed for a long time yet, considering how drunk he was.'

Eunice's mouth fell open wide enough to fit a bus through.

'Tony! No ... he can't still be here?'

Kay sighed deeply as she sank down on the chair opposite her friend. 'Yes, he is.'

'But... but how come? Wouldn't he go, was that it? Got a fight on yer hands to get him out?'

Kay wiped a hand wearily over her forehead.

'Bob never asked him to go.'

Eunice stared at her, taken aback.

'What d'yer mean? No man in their right mind would allow a criminal to continue living under his roof, not knowingly, whether they felt obliged for a good turn or not. Mate or no mate, my George would have stuck his boot up that bloke's arse and kicked him all the way down the street after finding out what he'd been up to, especially when he'd blatantly put his own wife's father at risk of a jail sentence.' She looked at Kay hard. 'There's summat going on here. What ain't you telling me?'

'Nothing.'

'Pull the other one! Listen, gel, me and you have been friends a long time and I know when you're holding back on me. What's going on,

Kay? You'd better spill the beans 'cos I ain't moving from this spot 'til you do,' she said, leaning back in her chair and crossing her arms defiantly.

Kay knew she meant business and suddenly had a desperate need to unburden herself, feeling she couldn't shoulder her problems alone any more. She sighed miserably. 'Where to start, Eunice?'

'At the beginning is usually the best place.'

Kay took a deep breath. 'Well, it's really all to do with, Bob. I'm so worried about him...'

'Why? He's not ill, is he?'

'I'm beginning to think he could be.'

'In what way?'

'He's just not himself, Eunice, not at all. Hasn't been since he got home, in fact. I know I told you otherwise but I thought he was just finding everything strange after being away from normal life for so long, needed time to adjust. And of course we hadn't really lived together, had we, not as a married couple, so that was all new to him too and so is Leicester...'

'What d'yer mean, he's not himself?'

'It's hard to explain.'

'Well, try.'

Kay folded her arms and leaned on the table, a disturbed expression on her face.

'Before Bob went away he was so ... well ... full of life. Now...' She paused, gnawed her bottom lip anxiously.

'Now what?' Eunice urged.

'Well, it's like he's lost interest in everything he used to love doing, has no enthusiasm at all, even

264

... even for that side of things,' she said, looking at Eunice meaningfully. She wanted to tell her friend how disappointed she had been the one time Bob had made love to her, but she couldn't as that subject was far too private for her to discuss with anyone, even her best friend. 'Just after he came home he bought a few model-making kits to do as a hobby but the one he started is still half-finished and gathering dust, the others still unopened in their boxes. He bought an old motorbike to do up, then half dismantled it and now says he can't go any further as he needs a manual. But he's made no attempt that I know of to get one and the bike is rusting worse than it already was when he bought it, out in our yard. You must have seen it, you have to sidestep it as you come up the path. And he hardly talks to me, Eunice, I mean, proper conversations.

'He's no interest in going out anywhere himself or with me, just with Tony a couple of times for a drink. And he goes to work, of course, but then he has to earn a living so he's no choice. He doesn't offer to do anything in the house. Even when I ask him for his help he says he will then never does. George at least appreciates what you do for him and makes you a cup of tea from time to time. Bob seems to take everything I do for him for granted. All he seems to look forward to is his meals and then sitting in an armchair by the fire, listening to the wireless.'

She gave a despondent sigh. 'I got to the stage when I'd convinced myself he didn't love me anymore and that was why he was acting like he was, because I made him unhappy and he couldn't bring himself to tell me. So I asked him if he regretted marrying me. He seemed surprised. Said he was very happy. When Mike turned up to visit him the other day, I really thought that seeing a friend would do him good.'

'Mike? Mike Newcome came to visit?' Eunice butted in. 'Oh, how is he?'

'He looked really well. He asked about you and I told him you were married with a baby and really happy. It was only a fleeting visit. He tried to settle back home after being demobbed but he just couldn't, said he wanted a better life for himself than he could ever get here, so he's trying his luck out in Australia. He'd travelled up to see Bob and his aunt 'specially before he went as he doesn't know when or if he'll be back again. He'll be well on the way by now.'

Eunice looked impressed. 'Australia, eh? Oh, I wish him luck. I bet Bob was pleased to see his old friend again?'

'Well, that's just it. As luck would have it, Bob never got to see him and so my high hopes of them reminiscing over old times, reminding Bob of all the things he used to love doing and rousing his interest again, were wasted.' Kay sighed again. 'I feel I don't know Bob at the moment, Eunice. He's not one bit like the man I fell in love with. I know we didn't have that long a courtship, not years like some people, and only two days of being married before he was shipped out, but I'd enough time with him to know without doubt that he was the man for me. I want that Bob back, Eunice, but I don't know what to do to get

266

him back when he doesn't seem to want to help himself. I don't know whether he even realises what he's like at the moment. That's why we ended up at the allotments last night because I didn't want you to see him like this. Am I making sense to you?'

Eunice blew out her cheeks. 'Phew! Er ... no, not really.' The kettle starting whistling then and she held out a warning hand to her friend. 'You stay where you are, I'll mash the tea. I don't know about you, but I more than need one after hearing what you've told me. I thought you and Bob were so happy together. It's really upset me, hearing things aren't going so well as I thought.'

A few minutes later Eunice sat back down at the table and poured them both some tea, pushing Kay's cup across to her. 'Have you spoken to anyone else about this?'

She looked appalled at the very thought. 'Oh, no, Eunice, I can't. Like you did until I just told you, all my family think Bob and I are so happy, I can't let them know we're not. Well, that I'm not. He seems to be quite happy with the way things are. They've all enough on their own plates as it is without me adding to their worries. Besides, it was hard enough explaining all this to you ... I don't mean that as it sounds, but it's not easy to put in plain words something like this, is it? Not when you're not exactly sure what's going on yourself.'

Eunice looked at her knowingly. 'I'm no expert but it seems to me that you're making too much of this. You've got to give Bob more time, Kay. He's not been back home that long, has he? A

267

month ... not even that. As yer said yerself, he's settling into marriage with you, getting to grips with his new job, *and* living in a different town. It's all new to him. As fer starting something then losing interest, my George is always doing that. I have to nag him summat rotten until he finally gets around to finishing off what he started. That's men for yer, Kay, and Bob is a man after all.

'I've told yer what it was like for me when my George first came back. What I went through getting him settled sounds nothing compared to what you're facing with Bob, but when yer consider that lots of men have come back and landed up in the nut house 'cos they've been so badly affected, it makes how Bob's behaving not so bad, doesn't it? And come on, Kay, after not having any home comforts for five years, living rough with just other men for company, Bob's finding it strange being a husband to you. And wouldn't you want to put yer feet up by a fire whenever yer got the opportunity after five years of not having a comfy chair to sit in or a fire to sit by, let alone a nice meal waiting for you?

'Seems to me yer just expecting too much of yer husband, too soon, gel. You're not the only one who's made the mistake of thinking there'd be a fairy-tale reunion and then you'd be able to pick up from where you left off, 'cos I did too. Time will tell, gel, you'll see.'

Kay sighed. Her Aunty Viv had tried to warn her the day Bob came home that it could take him a while to settle down and not to expect too much of him too soon. Now Eunice was telling her exactly the same. Trouble was, despite her sympathy for what he'd been through and the difficulties he faced adjusting to life back home, it was hard to live with Bob when he was behaving like he did. It was not the way she'd ever expected a husband to behave. But then she reminded herself that she was his wife and, regardless of how hard it was for her, she needed to support him, not give up until she'd got him through this difficult time.

Kay gave her friend a happy smile, leaned over and placed one hand affectionately on hers, giving it a squeeze. 'Yes, time will tell, won't it? And I'll do whatever it takes to help Bob through this time. Thanks, Eunice, you've made me feel so much better.'

'I just wish you'd spoken to me before instead of coping with this all by yerself. Mark my words, Bob will be back to his old self soon enough and driving you crackers, like my George is me. So just what was his reaction when you told him about Tony?'

'He thought I was elaborating on what I saw just to get Tony to leave.'

Eunice looked aghast. 'He what? You're saying he didn't believe you?'

'Not exactly. He said that what we saw Tony doing might not have been as bad as we thought and he couldn't brand him a thief and turf him out of the house with no proof.'

Eunice looked at her, worried.

'He could have a point, Kay. I know what we saw looked very suspicious but maybe Tony had bought that whisky honestly? Oh, dear, say that

269

he had?'

Kay shook her head.

'No, Eunice, I know he was up to no good. You know it too. And he was wrong to use my dad's shed and put him at risk. It wouldn't even surprise me to find out he was behind my dad's injuries like you suggested, but I can't prove it, can I? Tony just can't seem to do any wrong in Bob's eyes. That's why he refused to believe what I'd told him and made excuses.'

'Well, you do stick up for your friends, so you can't really blame Bob. If someone tried to tell me you were a thief, I'd smack them in the mouth for daring to say such a thing about you. I'd only believe them if I saw you doing something myself. And after all, Tony did save his life and Bob must feel grateful to him.'

'Oh, I just wish he'd open his eyes and see Tony for what he really is! But I can't seem to get through to him about this. I wish too that we'd never gone to the allotments last night. Oh, Eunice, you don't know how much I wish we hadn't! It was bad enough having Tony under my roof and putting up with his bad manners but now ... well, now I know the truth about how he makes his money, I'm going to be worried sick every time the door knocker goes that Constable Pringle is on the other side to arrest him and could think we were knowingly harbouring a criminal.'

'Constable Pringle knows yer better than that, so I shouldn't worry on that score. But all the same, after what we found out last night about Tony, if he'd been George's friend and living with us, I'd have had his bags packed as soon as I got home. And if George hadn't liked it, I'd have told him to sling his hook too.'

'I'm not like you though, Eunice. Sometimes I wish I was. I can't bring myself to go against Bob's wishes and take matters into my own hands.'

'Well, I hate to say it, but more fool you. You'll just have to get on with it then. So what about Tony? Have you come face to face with him since last night?'

'Yes, I have, and it was awful, Eunice. I couldn't sleep last night and didn't want to disturb Bob so I sat in a chair just … well, thinking about things. Tony came in about two-ish, I think, and roaring drunk. I was petrified he knew what I'd done to ruin his scheme and that he'd turn violent. He made me sit and listen to his ramblings. Apparently he went back to the allotments with his buyer after we'd left and discovered what we'd done. He's furious, Eunice, and threatening all sorts should he ever find out who did it. Thankfully he appears to have no idea who it was, not an inkling I've anything to do with it, and I just hope to God it stays that way.'

'Me an' all,' Eunice said worriedly. 'I was there too, remember?'

'I made a promise to you and I'll never break it. Upshot is, though, that awful man is with us indefinitely now because he put his last penny into that scam. If I had the money to replace what I put a stop to Tony making, I'd give it to him gladly to be shot of him. I'm worried what he's going to get up to next, but it's not like I can

271

ask him, is it? If I start probing him with questions about where he's going and what he's doing in future, when I haven't shown any interest before then, he could realise I know he's up to no good and might just start putting two and two together. If he realises I had anything to do with last night, I shudder to think how he'll wreak his revenge on me.

'Oh, Eunice, why did it have to be the likes of Tony who saved Bob's life, and not a decent sort of man who wouldn't have dreamed of taking advantage of the situation like he most certainly has?'

'That's just the way it goes, lovey, it's called sod's law.' Eunice pulled a rueful face. 'Just glad I ain't in your shoes.' Rising, she picked up her handbag from the floor by her feet. 'I'm sorry, ducky, I've got to go and collect Joanie from me mam's. I still haven't done me shopping yet.'

'No, neither have I, or made a start on my other chores. I've no idea what to give Bob for his dinner, haven't given it a thought yet.'

'Well, that's understandable, yer've had other things on yer mind, ain't yer? Give him egg and chips, that's what I'm giving my George tonight. If yer want to talk again, Kay, I'm always here for yer, you know that. Day or night.'

Kay rose to kiss her affectionately on the cheek.

'Thanks for listening to me ramble on today, I much appreciate it. You've really helped, I feel so much better.'

At just before one o'clock Kay had finished cutting peeled potatoes into chunks for chips to go with the egg for Bob's dinner when she sensed a presence behind her and spun around to see Tony entering the kitchen. Since Eunice's departure a couple of hours before, shoving her own fatigue aside, she had been functioning on automatic pilot as she hurried to catch up on her daily chores, constantly on edge for the moment she would come face to face with her lodger again. Fear that he could still somehow guess her own involvement in his failed business venture caused a permanent sickening swirling sensation in her stomach.

Tony looked dreadful. His skin had the greyness of a grubby sheet. His eyes were lifeless and puffy, movements slow and lumbering. He was still wearing his suit from last night which was concertina-crumpled. He made no attempt to acknowledge Kay.

Forcing a smile to her face, she said, 'Good morning.'

He looked at her as though she was stupid. 'Is it?' he grunted.

'Well, it's afternoon really. Er ... can I get you a cup of tea?' she asked tentatively, wondering if he had any memory at all of their conversation in the early hours of the morning or that she had helped him to bed.

'Need a cup for some water,' he demanded, arriving beside her at the sink.

She hurriedly unhooked one of six hanging off the bottom of the plate rack. As she handed it to him, she asked, 'Are you ... er... all right?'

He ignored her for a moment while he filled the cup with water to drink it straight back and

273

immediately poured himself another. 'Why shouldn't I be?' he snarled.

'Oh, well, I just asked because you look like you might have had a lot to drink last night.'

He shot a sneering glance in her direction. 'So what if I did? Might be that I had good reason to drink myself into oblivion.' His lip curled sardonically. 'Nice to see my landlady showing such concern for her lodger,' he said, gulping down the water and pouring himself some more. Gulping that down, he dropped the cup on the wooden draining board none too gently, announcing, 'I'm going back to bed.' Just before disappearing out of the door, he stopped and looked back at her. 'Oh, and it seems I won't be leaving you so soon after all. Thought that news might please you.'

After he had gone and she'd heard his door slam shut, Kay sagged back against the sink, cradling her head in her hands. Thank goodness he seemed totally oblivious to the prime role she had played in his loss, but his continued presence in her home was an intolerable situation for her and she just prayed she could cope with it.

Before he'd even shut the door on arriving home from work, Bob asked, 'Have you seen Tony today?'

The chips were sizzling away in the pan. Having seen Bob coming through the back gate, Kay was just about to crack an egg in with them when she stopped and looked across at him apprehensively.

'Yes, I have.'

'And?' he demanded.

'I saw him briefly when he came through about one to have some water. He found out last night that his stuff was gone but he doesn't have a clue how. Well, doesn't seem to yet. He can't know I'd anything to do with it.'

Bob sighed, looking mortally relieved. 'Thank God for that. So where is he now?'

'Still in bed. I think he had rather a lot to drink last night and he's suffering today.' Kay swallowed hard, a remorseful expression on her face. 'Bob ... I'm sorry if you thought it was my intention to blacken Tony in your eyes. Maybe you're right and what I saw last night wasn't as bad as I thought and I ... well, acted in haste.'

'Well, it's as I said then, best forget this ever happened, especially as far as Tony's concerned. I mean, he's bound to be angry and we can't afford to replace the money he's lost which he'd demand we do if he found out you were responsible. In future, Kay, leave well alone.'

She was in no doubt this was a warning her husband was giving her.

He looked at her expectantly as he stripped off his coat. 'So what's for dinner then? I'm famished.'

A while later Bob was tucking into his meal with relish. Kay, though, found she'd no appetite for her own and was merely pushing her food around the plate with her fork. Despite her apology to him, she still felt there was an atmosphere between them which she desperately wanted to resolve. She smiled across at her husband, asking brightly, 'How was your day, Bob?'

After taking a bite from some bread scraped

275

sparingly with margarine, he responded, 'Much better now I'm on my own. I was getting really sick of being watched like a hawk by the bloke they'd put me with while I got the hang of things. It felt like being back at school.'

She remembered the conversation with her father and her fear he could lose his job. Before she could check herself, she'd blurted, 'Oh, so they did bear with you then? I'm so pleased.'

He lifted his head and looked at her quizzically. 'What do you mean by that?'

Kay shifted uncomfortably in her chair.

'Oh, well, probably what I was trying to say was that people who didn't join up for whatever their reason don't appreciate what the men coming back from the war have been through and make allowances for them, just expect them to get on with things like nothing ever happened. That's all I meant. I'm so pleased to hear you're getting on all right in your job. You are enjoying what you do, aren't you?'

Bob shrugged.

'I suppose so. At least for the most part I'm out in the van on my own and that's what I really like about it. People can be a nuisance, accosting me when I'm emptying a box and asking stupid questions about the letters they're posting, expecting me to know the answer. Well, how can I tell them the minute it will be delivered, I ask you? And the post office staff, especially the women, get on my nerves, offering me cups of tea as soon as I go in to make my collections.'

'Oh, that's nice of them, being so friendly.'

'No, they're not, Kay. They just want to find out

all my business so they can gossip about me amongst themselves. Well, I think they're getting the message now that my business is my own.'

'Oh, maybe that could be the intention of one or two of them but I'm sure the others are just making a friendly gesture. You'll see that once you get to know them better, after you've been doing the job a bit longer. How are you getting on with the other men at the main depot?'

About to place a forkful of food in his mouth, Bob paused and said, 'I don't come into contact with them that much. Why?'

'Oh I was just thinking it would be nice if you hit it off with one or two in particular. You were never short of friends before you joined up and I know you must be missing your mates from the Army, especially Mike. Apart from Tony...' She broke off because as far as she was concerned Tony was no friend to Bob. 'I'm just trying to say, what with you being new to Leicester and not knowing many people, it would be nice to make a friend to go for a drink with now and again, or maybe invite with his wife over here for a meal and then we could all become friends.'

'Well, I haven't come across anyone in particular that I want to become friendly with, but then I haven't worked there long, have I? Any more bread?'

'Oh, yes, I'll fetch you some.' She made to rise then stopped to sit back down again. 'Bob, while you have your nap I'm going to go over to see if there's anything I can do for my mother. I never managed to get there this morning because ... well ... anyway, if Mam is being as stubborn as she usually is and there's not much she'll let me help her with, I'll only be an hour or so. I was wondering if you wanted me to come down to the allotment with you afterwards – if you were planning on going that is? I could keep you company.'

She smiled as a memory struck her.

'When I was a little girl I used to go down to the allotment every Sunday morning after Sunday School with my father and our Trevor while Mam cooked the dinner. Dad had sectioned off a small patch each for us and me and Trevor used to have competitions to see who could grow the biggest sunflower. He got really mardy one year as mine was at least a foot taller than his, so he snuck up the allotments one evening with Billy Hames, his best mate at the time, and chopped the head off. Oh, I was so upset! Cried buckets over that, I did. Of course Trevor swore blind he knew nothing about it but then had no choice but to admit what he'd done as he was seen by one of the chaps on the other allotments. As a punishment Dad made him hand over his sunflower to me and for the rest of the summer, every Sunday instead of coming to play down the allotments, he had to stay behind and do a list of jobs Dad had set him. Anyway, if there's a spare spade knocking around, I could help you start to dig over the patch.' She thought her suggestion might encourage Bob to make a start. She was to be disappointed when he replied.

'I wasn't planning on going. We had a hard frost last night and the ground will be like iron. I was thinking it might be best to leave it until spring now.'

'Oh, I see. Well, if that's what you think best. How about we go and see if we can find a motorbike shop and buy a manual for your bike?'

He pulled a face. 'We could, I suppose. I am tired, though. See how I feel after I've had a snooze.'

Kay flashed him a wan smile.

'I'll fetch your bread.'

CHAPTER SIXTEEN

A while later Kay found Mabel sitting at her kitchen table kneading dough for a loaf of milk bread. Despite its name it was actually more of a scone that was shaped into a low flat round, and after being baked was sliced up and eaten spread with margarine and a topping such as jam or cheese. It was very cheap to make and filling.

Despite her mother's usual smile of greeting when she entered, Kay did note a look of strain on her face and instantly worried that this nursing of Dad as well as Trevor, along with her usual full complement of household chores, was getting too much for Mabel. Determination rose within her. She was going to insist her mother allow her to do more to help ease the burden.

'Hello, dear,' Mabel said. 'Bob having his nap, is he?'

Kay nodded.

'Mmm,' mouthed her mother with a hint of disapproval. 'Yer father's never took to that practice after a shift, he always has too much to do to spare the time. Anyway, each to their own, I suppose.' She looked at her daughter enquiringly. 'You look tired.'

'I'm fine,' she said lightly, despite feeling ready to drop. 'I must say, you look tired yourself, Mam.'

'Don't you start fussing, Kay. I've enough with yer father doing that. I'm just making a loaf of milk bread for tea as they both like that spread with my home-made jam. Mind you, this year's batch isn't up to me usual standard as I never managed to get the quality of sugar I needed. I'm really disappointed with the runny set of it and it's a little tart-tasting.'

'It tastes fine to me, Mam, and Bob seems to think so. We've already got through two of the jars you gave me, of gooseberry and apple, and rhubarb.'

Mabel smiled, looking pleased. 'Well, that's nice to know, but I for one won't be sorry to see the end of rationing. You can't do anything properly without the right ingredients. Your father's favourite is lemon curd but you need lots of best butter and eggs to make that how it should be so I haven't been able to for a couple of years now. Still, never mind, things could be worse.'

Could they? thought Kay, not thinking of the nightmares of rationing. 'I'm sorry I never got here this morning only … well, I had so much to do at home. What can I do for you now?' she asked, taking off her coat.

'Everything is under control, lovey, thank you. I keep telling you, you've really no need to come

280

haring over here every day on my behalf, although I know yer father and brother look forward to seeing you. You could make yourself useful by mashing a cuppa as I expect both the chaps are ready for one by now as well as the young lady that's visiting our Trevor.'

Kay looked at her, surprised. 'Young lady?'

Mabel floured the table and turned over the dough.

'Seems my son has an admirer from the night of the dance. She's been in a couple of times since to see him. Thankfully something nice seems to have come out of that dreadful night. She is a nice girl, the friendly sort, although I fear she needs taking in hand if things progress between her and Trevor as, by the way she's spoken of a couple of things, I don't think her mother has taught her the correct way to do things.'

As she was talking Mabel shifted position on her chair and as she did so grimaced a little with pain.

'Mam, are you all right?' Kay asked. 'Come to think of it, I've never seen you sitting down to make pastry or bread before.'

'You were making the tea, weren't you?' she said, an unaccustomed edge to her voice.

Kay frowned as she busied herself with her task. All was definitely not right with her mother, but getting her to admit it would be another matter.

The young woman perched on the stool at the side of her brother's bed smiled at Kay when she went through with the tea tray, which she put on the table. She was wearing a Corporation bus conductress's uniform.

'You must be Trevor's sister,' she said. 'He's told me all about you.'

Kay looked at her brother enquiringly. 'Oh, yes?'

He grinned back cheekily. 'Only good things, honest. This is Lena. We got chatting at the dance and she's been popping in since after finishing her shift on the buses, to see how I'm getting on with me walking. When I can venture further Lena's offered to come with me for support.'

'That's very good of you,' Kay said to her.

She blushed bright red and said coyly, 'Oh, I don't mind, really.'

'Eh up, Sis,' piped up Trevor. 'I'm getting on real well. Got as far as the gate and back today without the use of those damned crutches, and only lost me balance a couple of times.'

'Oh, that's marvellous, well done! But it's still early days, our Trevor, so no marathons yet awhile.'

He pulled a face. 'What did I tell you, Lena? Right bossy boots is my sister.'

She slapped him playfully on his arm. 'Yer want to be grateful you've got a sister that cares about you so much.' She looked at Kay then. 'He never told me you were the bossy sort at all. From the way he talks about you, I can tell he thinks the world of you.'

Kay appraised the other woman. She was very petite and, although she was sitting, Kay guessed she could hardly be more than five foot in height. She was certainly pretty with large lively blue eyes, a small turned-up nose, and a mop of unruly-looking short blonde curls framing a small oval face. Kay was not stupid, she knew there was more to Lena's interest in Trevor than merely popping in to see how he was progressing. This woman liked him, it shone from her eyes, and Kay knew she wasn't, mistaken in guessing he liked her back.

She smiled at Lena.

'Do you take milk and sugar in your tea?'

As she handed over Trevor's cup to him moments later, he said, 'Ta, Sis. Oh, I've got something for you.' He leaned over and picked up a tatty-looking booklet from off the floor by his bed, handing it to her.

'Oh, it's a manual for Bob's bike!' she said, taking it from him in delight. 'How did you get hold of it?'

'Ronnie Smithers got it from a chap called Sam Champion. He's crippled, but as far as Ronnie's dad's concerned he's the Leicester expert on everything to do with motorbikes. Runs his own repair business from his back yard off Lough-borough Road with the help of a young daughter, Frankie, who seems to know nearly as much about bikes as her dad does. Anyway, Ronnie's dad said that whenever he gets stuck on a problem with one of his bikes he turns straight to Sam Champion, and every time he's put his finger on the solution right away.

'Well, as a favour to me, Ronnie made the trip over and luckily Mr Champion happened to have this right at the bottom of a pile of dusty old manuals in the outhouse he uses as a workshop. Ronnie said he seemed surprised by the choice of bike Bob bought to do up as in his opinion they were never that reliable when they first came on the market thirty years ago.'

'I'm sure Bob knows what he's doing,' she said defensively. 'Please tell Ronnie I very much appreciate the trouble he went to. This means Bob can get cracking on it again.'

Having given the young pair their cups of tea, she went across to her father. 'Hello, Dad,' she said, putting his down on the little table by the side of him then leaning over to kiss his cheek. 'How are you today?'

Herbie gave her a mournful look. 'Let's just say I can't wait for the day when I get these casts off. Another five or six weeks at least.' He gave a disdainful tut. 'Feels like years to me. Sitting doing nothing all day is driving me mad.' He looked a bit bothered and, lowering his voice, asked, 'Is yer mam still busy in the kitchen?'

'Yes, she's making milk loaf for your tea. Why?'

'Well, it's just that I'm worried about her, Kay. She went out this morning to do her shopping and was gone a lot longer than she normally takes, and she ain't been the same since she came back. I've asked her several times if there's summat up but yer know what's she's like. Just keeps telling me not to make a fuss. I feel so useless lying here while she's having to wait on us hand and foot. I can't even get the coal in for her, can I? I wondered if you could find out if I'm just making a palaver over nothing or if there is really summat the matter with her?'

Not wanting to worry her father further by telling him she didn't just suspect but knew there was something wrong with her mother, Kay smiled at him. 'I'll have a word with her, but I'm sure you're worrying about nothing.'

Herbie knew he wasn't and the look on his face told his daughter that. He looked at her in concern then. 'You look tired yerself, gel.'

'Oh, don't start fussing about me as well, Dad. By the way, Bob told me today he's been put on his own round now and seems to be liking his job well enough, so thankfully your word to your boss to pass on to Sid Askew did the trick.'

Herbie looked relieved. 'Good, I'm glad. I still can't understand meself though why Bob's abandoned his trade like he has to do a job that ... well, to my mind is beneath a man with his skills. Maybe he'll think better of it soon and want to pick up his tools again. He could earn a damned sight more money than what he's doing now.'

The housekeeping money Bob had given her, with careful handling, just about covered their needs with a couple of coppers left over for emergencies so they were getting by on his wage from the Mail. Nevertheless the living he was earning them would always be a narrow one if he stayed where he was. That fact was not the most important thing to Kay though, her husband's happiness was, and if he was content staying put then she was happy too. 'As long as Bob is happy in his job, Dad, that's the main thing to me. And he seems to be.'

Herbie pulled a face. 'That's all well and good, Kay, but I don't want to see you having to scrape by like me and yer mam have had to do. Bob's got the ability to provide better for yer, like he led us to believe he would when he asked for yer hand. Anyway, how's the allotment coming along? Has he finished giving it a winter dig yet?'

She couldn't bring herself to tell her father that, after all the trouble he'd gone to to secure the plot, Bob hadn't made a start on it yet and it seemed he'd now decided to leave it until the spring before he did. 'We've had hard frosts this past couple of nights so it's not been exactly digging weather recently.'

'No, I suppose not. Thank goodness I managed to get all my plot dug over before this happened,' he said, tapping one of his legs. 'Go and see how yer mother is, please, ducky, and if I'm worrying over nothing or if there really is summat the matter with her.'

Her mother looked relieved to see Kay when she arrived back in the kitchen. 'Oh, pass me that baking tray, please, lovey, save me getting up. And while yer at it, yer might as well put the bread in the oven for me.'

Her mother asking her to do something for her? Now this was most unusual.

'Mother, what's wrong?'

Mabel pulled a stubborn face. 'You've already asked me and I've already told yer, n'ote. If you won't do it for me then I'll do it myself.' She placed her hands flat on the table and tried to heave herself up but as she did so a spasm of pain gripped her and she gave an agonised groan.

Kay rushed to her side, thrusting one arm around her to help ease her back onto her chair. That done, she looked at her mother. She was

286

shocked to see how pale she was and that there were tears of pain in her eyes.

'Mam, it's your back, isn't it?'

'Shush,' Mabel mouthed. 'Please keep your voice down. I don't want your father getting an inkling anything is wrong with me. I'll be all right in a minute.'

'Well, you're too late for that because Dad already knows you're hiding something from him and asked me to try and find out what it is. He's worried about you, Mam, and so am I. Any fool can see you won't be all right in a minute. You're in agony.' Her voice softened and she looked at her mother pleadingly. 'Something is wrong with your back, please don't try and tell me it isn't.'

Mabel looked at her for several long moments before sighing. She admitted, 'I'm in a bit of discomfort at the moment. Must have slept funny last night.'

'Mam, it's more than just a bit of discomfort you're suffering! Now I'm not going to let up until you tell me.' Kay could see how much of a struggle it was for her mother to admit to anyone she was not as infallible as she liked everyone to think. 'Mam, please?'

'Oh, all right, I admit it,' Mabel finally said, a worried expression on her face now. 'I've never been in such pain since I can remember. I fell over this morning while I was out and landed heavily on my side. I had such a struggle to get home... I thought it'd be all right after a couple of Aspro, but they didn't seem to do much good so I had another two and they didn't seem to do much neither. I'll be all right, though, after a good night's sleep. Now, are yer happy I've told yer?'

Kay moved around the table and sank down on the stool opposite her.

'You fell? Oh, Mam, where? How?'

'That doesn't matter,' said Mabel dismissively.

'It obviously does matter or you'd tell me how and when you did it. I want to know, Mam.'

'Well ... if yer must know it was down the allotments,' she snapped.

'The allotments? What were you doing down there, Mam? I asked you to tell me if you needed anything and said I'd go for you.'

Another spasm of pain flowed through Mabel then and she winced, gripping the edge of the table for support. 'Oh, mercy me,' she uttered, her face wreathed in torture. 'I'd just gone to fetch the veg you forgot to bring back yesterday as I needed it for dinner today. I didn't tell you because I knew you'd feel guilty for your forgetfulness. I don't like to ask people for help when I'm quite capable of managing myself.'

Her mother was right, Kay did feel extremely guilty, but she could not say that she had actually gone back to fetch the bag of veg because then she would have had to explain why she had forgotten to bring it back a second time. 'You never ask anyone to help you, Mam, we have to make you let us.'

'That's just how I am.'

'Then it's about time you realised you can't always do everything yourself, and it's not like I mind. I'd happily do anything you ask of me, you know that.'

'Yes, I do, Kay, but you've enough to do as it is. Look how tired you are yourself.'

'That's because I didn't sleep well last night. We all get nights like that, don't we? Right, I'm going to fetch the doctor.'

Mabel looked at her, appalled. 'You are not! That's just a waste of good money, and it's not like he hasn't enough to do, dealing with really sick people. I told you, I'll be all right after a good night's sleep. I can't possibly be off my feet with yer father and brother to look after.'

Kay looked at her, unconvinced.

'I'm sorry, Mam, I can see how much pain you're in, and I might not have any medical experience but I know when an ailment is not going to be cured by a good night's sleep. You need Doctor Robinson to look at you.' She jumped up from the stool and took her coat from the back of the door, pulling it on. 'I won't be long.'

Half an hour later Kay returned with the doctor. She found her mother exactly where she had left her. 'As luck would have it, Mam, Doctor Robinson was at home.'

'Hello, Mrs Stafford,' he said to her briskly. He was a tall, thin, no-nonsense but basically kind man who had ministered to the sick in the area for the last forty years. He had a wispy goatee beard on the end of his long pointed chin and his short-sighted eyes peered through round wire-framed spectacles.

It had always grieved Maurice Robinson deeply that the more affluent members of society commandeered the majority of his time, mostly over minor problems that really didn't need his skills, whereas the poorer people who desperately did could not afford his fees and often went untreated. He vehemently hoped that this situation would drastically change once the new Health Service the government was trying to set up was in place. He quickly assessed that the woman seated before him was the sort who would only call a doctor out for herself as a last resort.

'You've done me a favour actually, Mrs Stafford. My wife, God bless her, had me helping her entertain a few of her lady friends for afternoon tea, and I have enough of listening to women's ailments during surgery hours! I was grateful for a good reason to escape. I can't remember the last time you came to my surgery or ever being called out to see you, in fact.'

'That's because I've never had cause to,' Mabel responded stiffly. 'I've a good constitution and I'm no time-waster like some that fill your waiting room. There's nothing wrong with me, Doctor, that a good night's sleep won't cure. I'm very sorry my daughter took it upon herself to waste your time.'

He put his large black Gladstone bag on the table and said firmly, 'Well, while I'm here I might as well take a look at you, then I can judge for myself whether my time's been wasted or not.'

'I'll leave you to it, Doctor,' said Kay diplomatically, ignoring the look her mother was giving her.

An anxious twenty minutes was spent while the rest of the family waited for the doctor's verdict, Lena having tactfully left.

'You have a stubborn wife, Mr Stafford, but I expect after all the years you've been together you don't need me to tell you that,' Doctor Robinson finally said to Herbie when he came through to report his findings.

'What's wrong with my wife, Doctor?' he asked worriedly.

'Mrs Stafford has badly jarred her back when she fell.'

'She fell?' he gasped, mortified.

'It's my fault, Dad,' Kay uttered, deeply distressed. 'I forgot to bring the veg back from the allotment yesterday and she went to fetch it this morning and fell over while she was there.'

'Don't you go blaming yerself, if it's anyone fault it's mine. If I wasn't laid up, neither of yer would have had any need to go to the allotment in the first place.'

'I don't think apportioning blame for Mrs Stafford's accident is going to achieve anything,' said Doctor Robinson crisply. 'It's happened and we need to get on with it. Mrs Stafford needs total bed rest but I fear it's going to take a little longer than the one night she thinks.' He turned to look at Kay. 'She needs to be got up to bed immediately.' He pre-empted Herbie's response. 'Don't even think about offering to help get your wife up the stairs, Mr Stafford, unless you want to be incapacitated for longer than necessary. You neither, young man,' he said, flashing a look at Trevor. 'You're hardly able to walk unaided yourself at the moment, let alone help us get your mother up the stairs. Right, shall we get to it, Mrs Clifton?'

A good while later, Kay looked down at her mother lying in bed. The pain she had suffered on her arduous journey from kitchen to bedroom had told on her, the stairs having proved a major hurdle despite the help of Kay and Doctor Robinson. 'Now you know what the doctor said, Mam. You don't move from here until all the pain's gone or you could aggravate it and end up having to stay in bed even longer.'

Mabel pulled a face. 'Doctor Robinson doesn't know what he's talking about. After all, he's a man, isn't he? We women have to suffer bad backs all the time and soldier on regardless.'

'Not as bad as what you're putting up with. Mam, for goodness' sake, admit that what you're suffering can't be brushed aside. You need looking after.'

'All right, yes, I do,' she snapped. 'But there's yer father and brother...'

'And you're saying I'm not capable of making sure they're fed properly and have all they need for a few days? And before you say it, Bob won't suffer meantime. I've got it all worked out. I can get your shopping along with mine and prepare the meals here. I'll take Bob and Tony's around on plates. I can fit your housework in each morning and do mine in the evenings after I've made sure you're all all right. I'm sure Aunty Viv will offer a hand too.'

Mabel looked horrified at the thought. 'I'm not letting my sister loose in my house or by the time I get out of this bed it'll be in utter chaos!'

'Now stop it, Mam. Aunty Viv might not be as tidy as you or such a good cook, but then not many people are. Come on, concentrate on getting better and stop worrying about everything else. I bet this is the first time you can ever remember when you've had the luxury of spending a few days in bed. All right, so it's not in the best of circumstances, but even so.'

Mabel gave a haughty sniff.

'Did you put that bread in the oven for tea?'

'Yes, and I'd better go and check on its progress. Now, anything I can get you?'

'No, thank you,' she said off-handedly.

'How is yer mother?' Herbie demanded when Kay returned to him.

'Not happy, Dad, and especially not with me as I'm the villain of the piece and called the doctor in. Still, she can be as annoyed with me as she likes, I know I did the right thing. Right, if neither of you needs anything at the moment I'd better check on that bread for tea and see what else needs doing.'

Viv was deeply upset to hear of her sister's condition when she arrived as usual after work to see what she could do. For several moments she stared at Kay, shocked, before taking a deep breath and saying, 'Poor Mabel.' Then in the next breath she added, 'But it bleddy serves her right for being so stubborn! Pride comes before a fall, it's said, and that's certainly apt in her case. Now she's got no choice but to accept our help.' She rubbed her hands together gleefully, a glint in her eyes. 'I'm going to enjoy having our Mabel at my mercy,' she chuckled, rolling up her sleeves as she prepared to set to. 'Right, you turn the oven up to its highest setting so we burn whatever's in there and I'll make a start chipping all her pots. Well, that's what she expects me to do and who am I to disappoint her?'

'Aunty Viv, stop it,' Kay scolded. 'This is your chance to prove to Mam that she's been a little unfair to you for all these years.'

Viv gawped. 'A little?' Her face broke into a smile then. 'Oh, stop yer worrying, me darlin', this is just my fun. Mabel has a point, I am slap-dash by her standards but I think the best thing is for me to move in until she's back on her feet. I can sleep in Trevor's bed. I'll see to breakfast before I go to work then take over from you as soon as I get back at night. If you can manage the shopping, lovey, and see to dinner and whatever the invalids all need attending to while I'm not here, I can do the washing and cleaning and 'ote else that wants done.

'No buts, our Kay. You've got a husband to look after not to mention a lodger, and I ain't. A bit of dust piling up in me own house don't bother me none and I've nobody living with me to complain about it. When I can safely leave them for an hour later, I'll pop home and get my stuff together. Right, off you go then and leave me to it.' She saw her niece about to protest and raised one hand. 'There ain't no negotiation on this. It's not like you won't have yer work cut out for you with all yer'll have to put in on top of yer own daily chores. Does your Bob know what's happened yet?'

'I haven't had time to tell him.'

'Ah, well, that explains why he ain't here himself then, seeing what he can do. I bet he's wondering where you are and thinking his throat's been cut 'cos he's not had his tea. I leave for work at seven in the morning so just get here as soon as yer can after that. They'll be all right on their own for an hour or so, don't break your neck. Thankfully Trevor can get around by himself a bit, it all helps.'

Kay looked at her questioningly. 'What about Mr Ambleside, Aunty Viv?'

'Frank? What about him? You of all people I don't need to remind that family comes before anything else. If Frank ain't happy doing without me for the time being, in the circumstances, then he ain't the man for me. I happen to know, though, that once he hears about this he'll be offering his help too.

'Now you look ready to drop to me, gel. Dealing with all this has fair took it out of yer. My advice is to get home and put yer feet up as soon as yer can after seeing to Bob. We need you in full fettle for tomorrow.'

'If you're sure you can manage, I will then, Aunty Viv. I'll just go and say my goodbyes to them all.'

Bob looked relieved to see Kay when she arrived back, although he didn't attempt to get out of his armchair to greet her. 'Oh, there you are. I was wondering where you'd got to.'

'It's my mam, Bob. She's ricked her back and I had to get the doctor in. It's bed rest for her for the time being. I can't believe how unfortunate my family are! Three members of that household all bed-ridden at the moment, except Trevor can get around a bit now, thank goodness. Aunty Viv is moving in meantime but I hope you understand that I will be spending quite a bit more time around there until Mam's fully back on her feet. Aunty Viv still has to go to work so I can't leave her to do everything. But don't worry, I shan't be neglecting you. My housework might suffer a bit but I'll make sure you're still fed and looked after properly.'

He looked relieved to hear that, finally adding, 'I'm sorry to hear about your mother.'

'Maybe you could drop in and say hello to them all? I did explain to her you hadn't been before because you didn't want to get under her feet while she was running after my dad and brother. But ... well, it would be nice if you showed your face.'

He gave a deep sigh. 'I should, I suppose. Truth is, Kay, I'm not very good around sick people at the moment. I saw so many wounded and dying, dead even when I was out in the Far East, I just can't seem to face that kind of thing now. It'd bring back so many bad memories.'

She felt instantly remorseful.

'Oh, I see. I'm sorry, Bob, that was unforgivable of me. I never gave it a thought. I'll explain to my parents and I know they'll understand. I expect you're hungry now so I'll get your tea, shall I?'

His eyes lit up. 'Yes, I'm famished. I could eat a horse.'

'I'm afraid you'll have to make do with Spam sandwiches,' Kay said jokingly. Then she suddenly remembered the manual for the motorbike and pulled it out of her handbag. 'Here's something to keep you occupied while I'm busy taking care of my family. Trevor's mate Ronnie Smithers kindly fetched it for you from a man who's an expert on motorbikes over on Loughborough Road. Wasn't that good of him?'

He flashed a glance at it then leaned over to put it at the side of his chair on top of the library book and the several unread newspapers Kay had bought him during the last couple of weeks.

'I'll look at it later.'

'You can get back to fixing up your bike now, can't you, Bob?'

'Well, it's a bit cold to be working outside at the moment but I can once the weather improves.'

'But surely if you wrap up warm...'

His face suddenly darkened.

'For God's sake, stop nagging, Kay! I'll get around to the bike again when I feel like doing so.'

She flinched in shock.

'Oh! Look, I'm sorry if you thought I was nagging, Bob, it's just that I thought you were keen to get it in working order again. You said you were so looking forward to taking it for a spin.'

He looked ashamed then.

'I'm sorry for snapping, Kay. I will get it done, in my own time.'

This was the second occasion since his return that Bob had flared up at her when she had been trying to encourage him to do something. Kay didn't like this side of him that was emerging and hoped it was just a temporary development, like his apparent lapse into laziness. She was making

297

her way to the kitchen when a worrying thought occurred and she turned back to Bob.

'Have you seen Tony today?'

'Yes, he has,' a voice behind her answered.

She spun around to see Tony coming through from the back.

'I was out in the privy,' he said, plonking himself down in the armchair opposite Bob's. 'Why all this concern about me?' he asked her sullenly.

The man looked dreadful: unwashed, unshaven, his usually immaculately groomed hair sticking up wildly. His bloodshot eyes were boring into hers as he waited for her answer and Kay found she was quaking inside.

'I ... I was just wondering if you were feeling any better?'

'Why, am I supposed to be ill?'

She gulped, 'Well, it's just you weren't yourself this morning when you came through for some water and then went back to bed. You were obviously suffering from a bad hangover.'

'A man has every reason to get drunk when some mindless excuse for a human being robs him blind,' spat Tony. Then he looked at her expectantly. 'Are we getting tea?'

Kay felt a tremendous weight lift from her shoulders. Obviously he still didn't have a clue that the mindless excuse for a human being was in actual fact herself, and it was unlikely now that he would ever find out. *She* certainly wasn't going to tell him, and neither would Eunice, and she was absolutely certain that apart from themselves the allotments had been deserted last night when they had carried out their deed.

CHAPTER SEVENTEEN

'Kay, for God's sake, stop gulping down yer tea. I know yer've got to get back to see to the invalids, but surely five minutes longer won't hurt?'

It was six days since her mother had been forced to take to her bed. Eunice had worked hard to persuade Kay to have a cup of tea and a currant bun in the market café before they caught the bus home after doing their shopping. Kay's baskets were laden with having to shop for the two families. It was only eleven-thirty and she had been up since four. After seeing Bob off to work she had tackled her own housework before making her way around to her parents' at just after eight.

Eunice leaned over and patted her arm in a friendly gesture. 'If you carry on like this, you'll be joining them.'

Putting down her cup, Kay replied, 'I'm fine, Eunice, really.'

She pulled a knowing face.

'No, yer not. I should know that running one house is hard enough, let alone two *and* nursing invalids. I know you and yer Aunty Viv are doing it between yer, but even so, if you keep racing around like this you'll be meeting yourself coming the other way and disappearing up yer own back-side!'

'Oh, Eunice, you are a tonic! I've no choice but to rush around as there just doesn't seem to be enough hours in the day at the moment. As soon as I go in of a morning, Dad needs a bowl of hot water and all the other bits and pieces for his wash and shave. I leave him to do that while I go and see to Mam's wash. Thank goodness our Trevor can see to his own ablutions at the sink now he can put his weight on his injured leg. It's getting on for nine by the time I've cleared all that away, and then they're all ready for a cup of tea. I wash the breakfast pots then, and after making sure they're all comfortable for a while, it's off to do the daily shopping. Immediately I get back they're ready for another cup of tea before I have to make a start on the dinner so it's ready for one.

'After I've dished up, I leave them to eat while I rush home with the plates of dinner for Bob and Tony just as Bob's getting in from work. If there's no sign of Tony I have to put his on low in the oven and just hope to God it doesn't dry up – that's if he does bother to come in and eat it, that is, otherwise I salvage what I can from it and the rest goes on the back of the fire. Mam would be so grieved if she saw the food I've had to waste because of him, but I have no choice.

'Anyway, then it's back to Mam and Dad's to clear up after dinner and mash them all a cup of tea. That done I make a start on the housework, and after that it's time to get the tea ready for when Aunty Viv comes in at five-thirty. I rush home then and get Bob and Tony's tea, and do any other chores I haven't done that day that can't be left.

'Oh, and I haven't mentioned the bed pans! I know they're my family and I love them dearly, I'd do anything for them, but I hate that bit. Dad's all right. I give him the po and he manages to get himself on and off it, I just have to empty it. But Mam is another matter. It's a real struggle and it's so painful for her. Three times now we've had accidents when the po's tipped up while I've tried to help her off it because her bottom has stuck to it and then I've had to change the sheets and give them a wash. And that's not funny, Eunice, so stop laughing. The worst thing is, I know how embarrassing it is for them having their own daughter do this kind of thing for them.

'Still, Mam seems to be on the mend. Although she's still in a lot of pain, she actually managed to sit propped up a little this morning so that's a sign her back is getting better. It's driving her mad, being stuck in bed, and it must be awfully lonely for her even though I go up as often as I can to check on her and she's plenty of visitors popping in and out. That's another thing ... those visitors all expect cups of tea.'

'Tell 'em yer too busy to mash 'em one.'

'I can't do that, Eunice, it would be so rude of me not to offer when they've taken the trouble to visit. Anyway I did have a rest from it all on Sunday as Aunty Viv sent me packing as soon as I arrived, telling me to spend the day in my own house with my own husband. She said she could manage fine well on her own and wouldn't have any argument over it.'

'That's summat, I suppose. So did you and Bob

do anything together on Sunday?'

'Well, not really. I spent most of it catching up with the things I hadn't managed to get done in the week, and Bob seemed happy enough listening to the wireless.'

Eunice eyed her sympathetically. 'I'm glad I ain't you at the moment, Kay, in more ways than one. Hopefully it won't go on for much longer, for your sake. I don't just mean yer mam's bad back either.' She folded her arms, leaning heavily on the table and looking at Kay keenly. 'Anyway, you mentioned the other day when I saw you that Trevor had a new girlfriend. So what's she like then? Is it serious, do yer think?'

'She seems really nice. Her name's Lena. I'm not sure whether you could class her as a girlfriend yet but they do seem to like each other. She's popped in every afternoon this past week or so after finishing work to see Trevor, using the excuse she's come to help him with his walking exercises.' Kay laughed and added, 'As if we all believe that excuse! I must say Trevor seems pleased to see her. More than pleased. She always offers to lend a hand with mashing the tea, and when I was washing through some towels yesterday, before I could stop her she was pegging them out on the line for me.'

'Oh, getting her feet under the table, is she?'

'I wouldn't put it like that, Eunice. She said she came from a large family herself and has to take her share of the housework so she appreciated what I was facing. I thought it was nice of her myself. I wouldn't mind if things between her and my brother took a more serious turn. He

302

could do a lot worse than Lena in my opinion.'

'Oh, maybe we'll hear wedding bells then. As your best friend I'll expect an invitation. Love a good wedding, I do. Couldn't class either of our weddings as a good do, could yer? Ten minutes in the Register Office, and a ham sandwich and glass of beer back at our folks'. Still, at the time I couldn't have given a toss. I was marrying my George and that's all I cared about. So what about this bloke of yer aunt's? Frank, ain't it?'

Kay remembered the night she had gone to his house, all guns blazing, fully intending to put a stop to the relationship between him and her aunt after she had discovered him in league with Tony Cheadle. She was glad she had chosen to give him the benefit of the doubt after hearing his side of the matter and trust that what he had done was just an isolated incident. Seeing him with her aunt on several occasions since that night when he had turned up at her parents' house to offer his help, had left Kay in no doubt that the pair were meant for each other. It was a pure delight to see her Aunt Viv's eyes light up when she opened the door to him and the adoration that beamed back from Frank's.

'He's been a Godsend, Eunice. Work allowing, he comes over as much as he can to do the heavy work, and as he's been passing farms on his travels he's stopped and bought potatoes and whatever veg he can get to save us making trips to the allotment. He won't take any money for them. Dad looks forward to his visits, they both sit and chat about men's stuff. I think in their case there'll definitely be a wed–' She suddenly realised that Eunice was not listening to her but looking out of the window, seeming very interested in what was going on out in the market place. 'Am I boring you, Eunice?'

'I thought it was him!' she exclaimed. 'Look, it *is* your lodger,' she said, pointing out of the window. 'He's flogging stuff from a suitcase. Can you see what he's selling?'

Kay looked through the window to see Tony standing a foot or so away from a handbag stall, trying to attract the attention of several shoppers passing by. Whatever he was saying seemed to do the trick as they'd stopped and were looking down at the contents of a large suitcase by his feet.

'No, I can't, because those shoppers are in the way.'

They both watched for several moments as money and goods changed hands. Then, weaving his way through the stalls and shoppers, a policeman approached. Tony spotted him and, much to the surprise of the shoppers gathered around him, quick as a flash he grabbed unpaid-for articles out of their hands. Throwing them back inside the case, he bent down to slam it shut, grabbed it and raced off like an athlete to be swallowed up amongst the crowds of other Saturday morning shoppers.

Eyebrows raised, Eunice looked at Kay.

'Well, whatever he's selling, it's obvious it's under the table stuff or why scarper when he saw the copper? What yer gonna do, Kay?'

She sighed, 'There's not much I can do, Eunice. I can't exactly accuse Tony of selling suspect merchandise without proof, can I? He could turn nasty on me. I doubt he'd admit it anyway. And if I tell Bob what we've seen today he could think I'm still trying to cause trouble between them. To get rid of Tony I need concrete proof to show Bob that leaves him in no doubt we're harbouring a criminal. How I get that I've no idea. All I can hope at the moment, Eunice, is that whatever is in that suitcase is not being stored in my house should any policemen follow him home.'

Kay was feeling particularly tired when she arrived home that evening. All she felt like doing was curling up in an armchair though it was out of the question because she still had the tea to prepare and clear away afterwards, and a pile of ironing that she hadn't been able to do before now as it hadn't been dry enough. The approaching winter was mild for once but the dampness of the air was no help at all to the drying of her weekly wash which she had done the previous Monday morning before she went round to her parents' house. It had been hanging on the drying cradles suspended from the kitchen ceiling ever since. Besides, she couldn't curl up in her armchair even if she did have the time as it was currently occupied by Tony.

He and Bob were both deep in conversation and had clearly not heard her enter. As she made her way into the back room to announce her presence she thought she heard Tony say to Bob in an annoyed tone, 'For God's sake, if no one's twigged by now, they never will so...'

'Kay!' Bob exclaimed on spotting her, his shock

305

at seeing her standing just inside the doorway most apparent. 'Er ... we didn't hear you come in. What's for tea?'

Tony screwed his head around to look at her. 'By the time I got in my dinner was all dried up,' he complained. 'I could do with something hot, it was bloody freezing on the market today. Thought there'd be more people buying, it being so close to Christmas. Seems to me people round here don't know a bargain when they see one. Can't interest you in a top quality hot water bottle, can I? Five bob each, that's all I'm asking.'

It was a good price but she wouldn't have entertained the idea of buying anything from him that she suspected had been obtained illegally. Before Kay could stop herself she said, 'Maybe you should think about getting yourself a proper job, Mr Cheadle, one with a regular wage.'

He smirked at her. 'What, like Bob has, you mean?'

'To do Bob's job you have to be responsible and trustworthy, handling the type of things people put in the post. Some of it's quite valuable and you...' Kay realised what she was about to add and stopped abruptly before she said anything she could regret. It was then that she realised Tony was looking at her in a strange way. 'Is there something wrong, Mr Cheadle?' she asked tentatively, a possible reason for the way he was looking at her striking fear through her.

'With me? No, nothing.' He leaped up from his chair. 'Bob, can I have a word? In private,' he said, inclining his head in the direction of his room.

Kay watched them go into the front room, Tony shutting the door firmly behind them. For the next twenty minutes she was on tenterhooks as she prepared the tea, and was just putting a plate of sandwiches on the table when she heard the bedroom door open and turned around to see Bob coming out. He looked deeply concerned.

'What's wrong, Bob? You look worried. What did Tony want?' Her voice a whisper, she asked, 'Has he guessed what I did, is that it?'

Bob pulled out a chair. Sitting down on it, he took a sandwich from the plate and bit into it.

'Tony just wanted to know if he could borrow some money to go out with tonight for a drink,' he said finally. 'I had to tell him I'd none spare and I didn't like turning him down, that's all.'

It seemed to her that they were in the bedroom rather a long time for just that to have passed between them.

Just then Tony came out of his room. Gone was the harrowed expression he had worn ever since the night Kay had scuppered his money-making scheme. Now he looked very pleased with himself, not at all like a man who'd just tried to borrow money from a friend and been turned down.

As he arrived at the table and sat down she waited for his comment that she hadn't cooked him a hot meal like he had requested and was most surprised when he tucked into the sandwiches without a word.

When Tony had had his fill he scraped back his chair, announcing he was off to get ready to go out. As soon as his door was shut, Kay looked at

307

her husband quizzically.

'I thought Tony had no money. He tried to borrow some from you, you said?'

'Well, that's what he told me. Maybe he's found he did have enough for a pint or two after all.'

'But he must have some. I saw him when I was with Eunice in town getting the shopping today. He was selling stuff from out of a suitcase and had a decent crowd around him. Some of them were buying.'

Bob flashed her a look of annoyance.

'Kay, you asked me what Tony wanted me for and I told you. Just because you saw him selling stuff doesn't mean to say he made a profit, does it?'

'No, I suppose it doesn't.' She looked at him, puzzled. 'What Tony was saying when I came in, something about, "If no one's twigged by now, they never will". If no one's twigged what, Bob?'

He looked at her blankly.

'I don't remember him saying any such thing.'

'But he did, Bob, I heard him. He was speaking like he was annoyed with you.'

'Well, he *is* annoyed, and I don't have to remind you why. He came in just before you did and was ranting on about all sorts. I'd only just woken up from my sleep so I was only half-listening. Oh, is that the time?' he said hurriedly. '*ITMA*'s starting soon and I need to get the wireless tuned in.'

Kay watched him as he went over to the wireless set and sat close to it, twiddling with the tuning knob. She felt terrible for thinking it but she didn't quite believe the explanation her husband had given her. But what reason could

Bob possibly have for lying to her? Maybe she had misheard... After all, she had arrived mid-conversation so hadn't heard all that was being said. Tony could have been talking about anything.

Her eyes caught sight of the clock. If she didn't get a move on and get the dishes cleared away and her ironing done, there'd be no time left for a sit down for her tonight.

CHAPTER EIGHTEEN

A week later Kay turned up as usual at eight o'clock to tend to her family. To her surprise, as she walked into the back room to say her good mornings to her father and brother, she heard raised voices coming from above.

'What's going on, Dad?' she asked.

Herbie looked most disturbed. 'It's yer Aunt Viv and your mother. Viv took the morning off from work today, told her boss the situation with her family and got herself excused from her shift. She meant to tell you herself last night so you wouldn't come charging over here at the crack of dawn but it slipped her mind. Anyway, just seconds before you arrived she went upstairs to put some shirts of mine and Trevor's she'd ironed last night to hang in the wardrobe and ... well ... you can hear for yerself.'

'Aunt Viv ain't happy about summat,' said Trevor, who was perched awkwardly at the table, trying to accommodate his healing leg on a chair while finishing off his breakfast. 'Not often yer hear Aunty Viv raise her voice.'

'I'd better go and see what's going on,' said Kay, dashing up the stairs. As she rushed into her parents' bedroom she got a shock to find Viv bodily preventing Mabel from getting out of bed. She had her hands flat on her sister's shoulders and was pushing her back against the pillows.

'Now you listen to me, Mabel Stafford! You ain't getting out of your bed 'til yer one hundred per cent.'

'I am, I tell yer,' she cried. 'Why won't yer believe that I woke up this morning and all me pain had gone?'

'That would mean a miracle had happened, you were still in agony yesterday, and I don't believe in miracles. I know why you're insisting on getting outta bed so soon, it's 'cos yer don't trust me to look after yer family or yer house properly.' Viv suddenly realised her niece had entered the room. '*You* tell yer mother, Kay,' she demanded. 'Tell her that everything is fine downstairs. I ain't poisoned her husband or son yet with me cooking or me sloppy housekeeping.'

'Everything is fine, Mam,' Kay insisted. 'Dad and Trevor are well and the house is all ship-shape. Well, it might not be up to your standards but we've done our best, haven't we, Aunty Viv?'

'That's just it,' said Viv in knowing tones. 'Our standards aren't up to yours, are they, Mabel?'

She pursed her lips.

'Well, you in particular don't do things properly and that's a fact, no matter how many times I've

310

tried to put yer right.'

Viv let go of her sister and righted herself, looking down at her stonily.

'I came here with every good intention as soon as I knew yer needed my help. I suspected you'd find fault with everything I did, and I was right 'cos you did. You've accused me of cutting the bread too thick for the sandwiches. Me sponge cake sagged a bit in the middle 'cos according to you I hadn't beaten it for exactly ten minutes so there wasn't enough air in the mixture. I only sliced once through the bottoms of the Brussels for Sunday dinner instead of making a neat little cross, and I didn't add a teaspoon of bicarb as well as salt to the water when I was boiling 'em. Well, like all the food I've cooked since I've bin here it all got eaten and I was complimented for it so it's only been *you* that's complained I ain't prepared it right.

'You've moaned every time I sorted yer bed, too, saying I'm not doing the hospital corners exactly square. Have you ever tried to make a bed with someone in it? It's bleddy awkward, let me tell yer. Now the latest is I ain't hung Herbie's shirts just so on the hangers after ironing them. I could stand here all morning and reel off your complaints against what you see as my slip-shod attitude since I came here to help out, and besides that you're always having a go at me for something or other you don't think I do to your high standards. Now, I love you dearly and yer a good woman, Mabel, but yer've one really annoying habit which is that you're never backwards in coming forwards in telling me my faults. Now I'm going to tell you yours, whether you like it or not.

'People either do things your way or you pull a disapproving face, making them feel inferior. You think no one knows how to do anything better than you. Well, maybe that's the truth of it. Maybe no one does. But just 'cos I ain't as house proud as you, can't cook as well as you, don't dress according to your tastes, happen to like to go out for a drink with me friends down the pub for the company instead of sitting in on me own, it doesn't mean you can look down on me or say I have a sloppy attitude.

'And while we're at it, you do the same to yer daughter. If she's planning a meal for her husband, you demand she use's your recipe so according to you he's being looked after proper. And come hail or shine Monday's got to be the weekly washing day 'cos that's always been the tradition. What's wrong with doing it on Tuesday, Mabel? Or Wednesday, come to that? Or, more to the point, why can't you just leave us both to get on with things the way we want to do them, not try and ram your ideas down our throats every time we do summat that ain't your way of doing it?'

Kay was staring in astonishment at her aunt, never having seen her in such a temper before. She could not believe all that was spewing from Viv's mouth.

Mabel was staring at her sister wild-eyed, her mouth opening and closing, fish-like.

To both Kay's and Viv's shock they saw tears fill Mabel's eyes then. They trickled down her face. Bottom lip quivering, she uttered, 'I just thought

I was being a good housewife and mother and sister by trying to put you right. So you always conduct yourselves well and are seen as the good people you really are.'

'And keeping a spotless house and doing everything just so makes a person good, does it, Mabel?' Viv shook her head at her. 'That's what our mother instilled in you, I know. Oh, Mabel, she was *wrong* to be so dictatorial with you, make you believe that if you were less than perfect in everything you did then other people would see you as a failure. 'Cos that's the truth of it, ain't it? It was Mother's view that if you weren't seen to be in control of things, and yer housework wasn't absolutely perfect, and yer weren't dressed in what she felt were the proper clothes, then you were a failure.

'If that was how she chose to carry on then all well and good for her, Mabel, but it was Mother who was the failure for not letting you develop into your own person. She moulded you to be just like her, the same way her mother did with her. I wouldn't let her do it to me. I wasn't going to turn into her, not if I could help it. There's more to life than making sure not a speck of dust is visible, the covers on the backs of me chairs are perfectly straight or that I've taken just the right amount of peel off the spuds. I'm not saying she was a bad mother, Mabel, she looked after us well and I had a lot of respect for her, but she was so narrow in her views and there was no changing her, despite all the arguments I gave her.'

'Just like me, you mean,' Mabel said in a choked voice.

'Yer very set in your ways, there's no denying that, Mabel, but you're a good woman with a heart of gold. It's just you need to realise what Mother couldn't seem to, and that's that we can't all live up to the standards she set.' Viv's voice softened and she looked down at her sister tenderly. 'I know yer heart's always been in the right place. I know you feel that as my older sister and Kay's mother you should try to guide us in the only way you know how. That's why I've never really spoken out so bluntly before. But after you having a go at me for not hanging Herbie's shirts on the hangers just so when I'd stood there ironing 'em, proud of meself for doing a good job, well, I'd had enough. I'm sorry if I upset yer, Mabel, but yer bloody upset me, let me tell yer.'

Mabel sniffed back a sob and said miserably, 'No, it's me that's sorry. You're right, I do think my ways are the only proper ways to do things because that's what Mother told me. She was such a strong woman, Viv, you know she was, and so adamant about everything she believed in. I thought she really did know best. I used to think you were such a naughty girl, openly defying her like you did, but I also loved you so much, Viv, and worried you'd be looked down on by others because of your approach to life which went against Mother's teachings. I was horrified when I knew you went to public houses for a drink as Mother always said that only low women were seen in such places. And she said the type who wore clothes that flaunted their figures ... well, they were just floozies.

'You're not a low woman, Viv, or a floozy,

314

you've got morals and principles, but I worried so much that people would think you were a low type because of the way you carried on. I went on at you in the hope that you'd see the error of your ways, that's all. I was just worried for you, Viv, you've got to believe me.'

She looked at her daughter then, mortified.

'Have I made yer life a misery, Kay, by insisting you do everything the way I feel it should be done?'

Kay dropped down at the side of her bed and took her hand, squeezing it gently in her own.

'No, Mam, no,' she insisted. 'You've been a wonderful mother, I couldn't have wished for better. Although, yes, you have always insisted that I do things your way or woe betide, and it would be nice for me to be allowed to experiment with ways of my own, just now and again. The ways Grandmother taught you are so old-fashioned now, Mam, there are new ways of doing things that make housewives' lives so much easier.' Concern filled her face. 'I will be honest with you, Mam, and tell you that I haven't always done things your way even though I've told you I have when you've asked me. I hope you're not angry with me for that?'

Mabel looked at her, deeply wounded.

'I can't say hearing any of this is making me feel good. When you pride yerself that you've been a role model to yer own family, and then find out that you haven't but instead...'

'Oh, but you have, Mam,' Kay insisted. 'You've taught me all I know and given me a good grounding, I've much to thank you for. I'd not be

315

equipped to run my own house or look after Bob like I do without your lessons. I know girls whose mothers didn't bother with them when they were growing up, and they got married not even having a clue how to boil an egg. I can boil one perfectly, thanks to you, and pretty much everything else I turn my hand to.'

'That's all well and good, Kay, but some of the things I should've been able to help you with in a mother and daughter way, well, I just couldn't, could I, 'cos I'm not up on the ways of modern thinking. So you had to turn to my sister. According to my mother, you should keep yer problems to yerself and get on with it. That's how I am.' Mabel smiled wanly at her sister. 'I do have a lot to thank you for, Viv. I know I've accused you of leading my daughter astray with some of the advice you've given her over the years, but deep down I knew you were guiding her in ways I couldn't. And it's obvious it was good advice you gave her 'cos of how she's turned out, a daughter any mam would be proud of. I just wish ... well ... that things had been different inside me 'cos there's bin times I desperately wanted another view on a matter that was bothering me that I wasn't sure how to deal with, Viv, but I just couldn't bring meself to ask in case you saw me as anything other than the strong dependable type.'

'It's not too late to change yer ways, Mabel.'

'Oh, I don't know about that. I'm fifty-three years old and I've had a lifetime of being the way I am. If yer think it's easy for me lying here speaking like this, well, it's not. I can hear

316

Mother's voice ringing in me ears: "Mabel Turnbull, it's happened so get on with it like I had to do." She never tried to tell me *how* to get on with it, I had to work that out for meself the best way I could.

'I was dreading the time that Kay starting asking me probing questions about the changes in her body as she grew up, and although I resented the close bond you two shared, I was so relieved that you dealt with that for me, Viv, saved me the embarrassment. I know I would only have told her the same as my mother told me: "It's happened so get on with it." She swallowed hard and wiped her wet eyes on the edge of the sheet. 'Look, I can only tell you both that I will try in future to be more kindly disposed towards you, and try to keep reminding meself that my way isn't always best.'

'That's something, Mabel,' Viv told her. 'And the other thing yer can do is learn to accept help graciously. It's yer own bleddy fault for landing up in yer bed because you didn't.'

She pulled a face.

'Whatever else I might be, I'm not stupid. All the time I've been lying here I've been cross with meself for the way you're both running yerselves ragged doing everything for me. It wouldn't have come to this if it hadn't been so hard for me to admit I needed help. I am grateful for what yer've both done, I am really. But yer asking me to act against me nature, remember, Viv. I can't promise you I will, but I can promise I'll try.

'Now, I was telling the truth when I said me back's better and I really would like to get up and

317

see my husband and son.' A hint of amusement sparkled in her eyes when she added, 'And to see what damage you've caused while I've been indisposed, naturally.'

Viv laughed, shaking her head at her sister. 'I'd better leave now then, hadn't I, to avoid the fall out. Do yer want a hand getting up, Mabel?'

'No, I can man–' She stopped abruptly, took a deep breath and smiled. 'I really can manage to dress meself, but thank you for yer offer.' Then she looked across at Kay. 'I ... er ... wouldn't mind a cuppa if it's no trouble when I come down.'

Kay knew that the simple matter of asking her daughter to do something for her that she was quite capable of doing herself had not been an easy request for her mother to make and hoped to see more of this behaviour from her in future.

'I'd be delighted to, Mam. I really think it's wise you take things easy for a while, just to make sure you're fully recovered and don't have a relapse. I still want to help you, if you'll let me?'

'Yer daughter's right, Mabel,' Viv said sternly. 'Yer should tek things slowly for a day or so at least. I'm quite happy to stay for the rest of the weekend.'

'Well ... that's very good of you, our Viv, and ... er ... yes, I'd appreciate you being on hand should I need you. I was thinking it'd be nice to have a family dinner tomorrow. Because of the way things have gone, the last one we had was at least a month ago to welcome Bob home. I know you told me, Kay, that he's finding it hard to be around sick people because it brings back such bad memories of his experiences in the war, but, yer know, he's got to face this kind of thing sometimes. We are all family, after all. I must say, I can't understand it meself. Don't look at me like that, our Viv. I'm *not* saying that it's happened and Bob should just get on with it – or maybe in this case he should? Surely it's better to face up to yer demons and deal with them than avoid them and prolong matters?

'Anyway, try and persuade him to come, lovey, as it won't be a proper family do if he's not here. Oh, best ask Mr Cheadle to join us too. Yer can't very well leave him out. You could ask Frank to come, Viv, it would be a nice way to thank him for all the help he's given while I've been ill.' Mabel paused, looked at her sister for several long moments and added, 'You could make the pudding.'

Viv's eyes widened in astonishment.

'Be my pleasure. I'll make a trifle as I've still got the tins of peaches for the one I offered to make for Bob's dinner in me pantry.' Mischief glinted in her eyes as she added, 'Using your recipe, of course, Mabel. Oh, I shall look forward to doing that. It'll make me feel I'm making a contribution. Right, come on then, Kay, let's leave yer mam to it.'

As the pair of them arrived downstairs Herbie looked up worriedly. 'Is everything all right, Viv? Kay?'

'Yes, why wouldn't it be?' his sister-in-law asked. 'We've some good news for you, haven't we, Kay?'

She nodded.

'Mam's back's better and she's getting up.'

The delight on her father's face was wonderful to see.

Trevor pulled a face. 'I've missed me mam while she's been ill, but that means back to strict rules and regulations. You ain't such a stickler for house rules, are yer, Aunty Viv?'

She looked at him with a smile.

'Yer might just find yer mother a bit more relaxed in the future.'

'What d'yer mean by that?'

'Yes, what *do* yer mean?' asked Herbie.

'Just wait and see,' Viv replied evasively.

Bob was most surprised to find pans bubbling on the stove when he arrived home from his shift that Saturday afternoon.

'Mam's better, I'm glad to say,' Kay said as he walked in. 'She woke up this morning to find all her pain had gone. Of course, she needs to take things gradually for a day or two just to make sure she doesn't have a relapse. I'll be popping in still for at least the next week to see if I can do anything for her.'

'Oh, it's good that she's better,' said Bob, stripping off his coat to hang it up along with his shoulder bag. 'What's for dinner then?' he asked, looking expectantly at the pans on the stove.

'Fried cod, peas and mashed potatoes. I'm just about to dish up. Oh, talking of dinners...' Kay looked across at him tentatively. 'We're all invited to Sunday dinner tomorrow at Mam and Dad's, including Tony. I was hoping you might feel up to coming? Mam's better now and Trevor's more or less on his feet so it's only Dad you'd have to contend with in the invalid way. But he's got a blanket covering his plaster casts so it's not like you're facing the terrible sights you had to do during the war.'

Bob was looking at her pensively.

'I suppose not. Well, yes, I'm sure I'll be fine. I'll look forward to it.'

Kay's face lit up. Dare she hope that this was a sign Bob was finally picking up the pieces of his life and beginning to move forward?

'You'll come? Oh, Bob, that's good news. Mam and Dad and everyone else is really looking forward to seeing you. Hopefully now you're really settling back home, this will be the start of many family visits back and forth.'

'Shall I call Tony through for dinner?' he asked.

Kay flashed a surprised look at him.

'Tony? He's here? I've been in nearly an hour and I hadn't a clue he was home. I thought he'd be flogging his wares down the market today so I haven't cooked him any dinner. I was going to do him some fresh when he came in later. Oh, well, he'd better have mine then and I'll do myself his fish and have that with some bread. Tony's not working then, I take it?'

'I don't know what he's doing workwise. His business is his own.' Her husband shrugged. 'I just happened to notice his shadow crossing the window when I passed by to make my way down the entry, that's how I know he's in.'

'Oh, I see.'

Kay wondered what Tony was finding to do in his bedroom all this time. Whatever it was, he was going about it very quietly as she hadn't heard a sound coming from his room, though she wouldn't have as she'd been in the kitchen since getting home. Come to think of it, though, he had been at home the last few days when she had arrived with the men's dinners from her parents' home at midday, which was good for her because it meant she hadn't the problem of trying to keep his meal hot. Nevertheless it was most unusual for Tony to be in at that time of the day. The fact hadn't registered with her until now as previously she'd had more pressing matters occupying her thoughts. But now she thought about it, she realised he had also been there every afternoon lately when she got back at tea-time from her parents', and had hardly been out in the evenings either. Once tea was over he had announced he'd things to do in his room and, once there, hardly ventured out. It seemed to her that the man who ever since his arrival had been out at all hours of the day and night had suddenly turned into a recluse.

Her thoughts were interrupted by Bob saying, 'I'll get him then, if you're about to dish up.'

'Pardon? Oh, yes. Thanks, Bob.'

CHAPTER NINETEEN

As Kay was dishing up the dinner, a few streets away Eunice was looking very pensive as she cuddled her sleeping daughter on her knee.

'What's up with you, gel?' asked her husband as he walked into their living room, dressed warmly for outdoors. 'You look really bothered about summat. Yer don't mind me going to the match with the lads, do yer?'

'Oh, don't be silly, George, 'course I don't. Gives me a couple of hours' peace and quiet from yer,' she said jocularly. 'I'm just thinking about Kay, that's all.'

'Why, what's up with her?' asked George, perching beside her on the sofa, and gazing fondly at his sleeping daughter.

'Well, nothing's wrong with her health, and when I met her in town today shopping she told me her mam was up and about again, so she ain't got all that toing and froing to cope with anymore. It's her Bob that's bothering me. According to Kay all he does is go to work and come home to sit in his chair, listening to the wireless.'

'Well, what's wrong with that?'

'It ain't much fun for Kay, is it?'

Her husband shrugged.

'Could be worse. Bob could be out boozing every night and come home plastered and give her a good hiding. The bloke's just taking his time to settle, that's all. He's only bin back a matter of weeks, give the chap a chance. I know some blokes who've been back a few months and they still ain't got themselves a job yet. At least Bob has.

'You did tell me he'd had a nasty experience out in the Far East? Maybe he's taking his time getting over that, especially if he only just escaped with his life. Bert Chapman, me mam's neighbour, was a man who hardly said boo to a goose before he went off in '39, and look at him now. His poor wife and kids cower at the sight of him, and I bet she's wishing now he was one of them that never come back. You can hear him bellowing at them through me mam's walls, morning, noon and night. It took me a while to settle too when I got back, didn't it? I tell you summat, it ain't easy picking up from where yer left off after what we went through, but everyone seems to expect yer to.'

'Yeah, I suppose. I told Kay time will tell. I was just wondering though...'

'Oh? Yer've got that look on yer face. What yer up to now?'

'Nothing. Only ... I was just wondering if Bob needs a bit of a helping hand?'

George looked at her warily.

'In what way?'

'Well, I thought he could do with a mate to knock around with. You know, someone to encourage him to get off his arse and do things.'

'He's got that chap he brought back with him. Did some heroic deed and saved his bacon or summat, didn't he?'

Eunice scowled. *'He's* no mate, or not what

yer'd call a real friend. He's just a leech, and the sooner he skedaddles the better. I mean a real mate, George, someone for him to go to the football with, or down the pub now and again. Give him summat to talk to Kay about when they're sitting together in the evening. I just wondered if for some reason Bob was finding it difficult to make friends. He's not from Leicester originally, is he, so he's not like you with all his old pals to look up. You weren't back five minutes before some of them were banging down our door, asking if you were coming out to play, and Bob hasn't had any mates to knock for him.'

George narrowed his eyes at her questioningly.

'And you've someone in mind as a mate for him?'

She smiled engagingly at him.

'Yeah, you.'

He tutted. 'I shoulda seen this coming! Well, I don't mind. He's welcome to come down the football or to the pub with me and me pals anytime.'

'Well, yer could ask him yerself when we pop in tonight.'

'Oh, Kay's asked us round, has she? Yer never told me.'

'Well, no, she ain't exactly. But I'm her best friend, I don't need an appointment to see her. Look, if we wait for Bob to decide when he's ready to face the world again we could wait months, I'm afraid poor old Kay will go doo-lally herself meantime. She's got nothing to look forward to at the moment, George. I mean, it's all well and good being married and yer don't expect to go out every night – well, yer can't afford it for a start – but now and again isn't too much to ask, is it? A night at the pictures; a drink with friends; a night round here with us or us at theirs, sharing a couple of bottles of beer and plate of sandwiches; a walk down by the canal. Bob might be happy sitting listening to his wireless every night but he seems to have forgotten that Kay needs more than her housework to look forward to.'

'All right, yer've made yer point. I still think yer should leave well alone and let the bloke sort himself out in his own time, but I know you won't take no notice of me so I might as well get this over with. Now can I get off or I'll miss the kick off?'

'Yeah, and don't be late home. I'll have yer tea on the table at five-thirty and yer pools coupon ready for yer to check off.'

Kay was most surprised to hear the back door open at seven-thirty that night and Eunice call out a greeting: 'Cooee, it's only us.'

Kay, who had just sat down after finishing off her chores for the day and was about to pick up her knitting, jumped up from her chair to welcome them in. 'It's Eunice and George,' she said to Bob, sounding delighted as she hurried off into the kitchen.

'We were just passing and thought we'd pop in,' said Eunice, taking off her coat and hanging it up with her husband's on the back of the door. She pulled Kay aside and said quietly, 'I know what yer told me about Bob not being up to socialising yet, and I know not to expect too much of him, but sometimes a nudge in the right direction can do wonders. Well, me and George are here to give him that nudge. George is just gonna suggest going for a pint. Hopefully Bob'll accept. Once he's amongst George's crowd and has a laugh and a joke with them, it'll spur him on to do it again. Then Bob's yer uncle, so to speak. It's a good idea, don't yer reckon?'

'Oh, yes, Eunice, it is. Anything's worth a try.'

Her friend grinned, pleased.

'Where's yer lodger tonight then?'

'Oh, he disappeared into his room straight after tea. I'm not sure if he's still in or has gone out.'

'Well, let's hope he don't show his face. Right, you go through, George, and make yerself known to Bob while me and Kay make the tea. Got any biscuits?' she asked.

George went through. Seconds later he returned. 'Bob's not there,' he said to Kay.

'What do you mean, he's not there?'

She made her way into the living room and stared bemused at the empty chair she had left Bob sitting in only a couple of minutes previously. Where had he disappeared off to? she wondered. Then she heard a sound coming from upstairs and realised he was in their bedroom. 'I won't be a moment,' she apologised to Eunice and George.

To her bewilderment, she found the bedroom in darkness and realised Bob was in bed. Feeling her way around, she leaned over and gently shook his arm. 'Bob, what are you doing in bed? Eunice and George have come to see us.'

'I've a blinding headache,' he moaned. 'I've had

it for the last couple of hours and was about to say something to you when your friends arrived. It suddenly got worse, I was seeing flashing lights. I'm sorry, Kay, you'll have to entertain them by yourself.'

'Oh, I see. Can I get you anything?'

'No, I just need to sleep.'

Kay returned to face her visitors, a look of deep regret on her face. 'I'm so sorry but Bob's ill. Got a raging headache and has had to go to bed.'

'Oh!' Eunice exclaimed, disappointed. 'Well, that puts paid to that.'

'Yeah, shame,' said George. 'I was hoping to get acquainted with him. Look, tell Bob I'm really looking forward to getting to know him. And say if he fancies going to the football with me and me pals a week Sat'day when City play Sheffield, he's welcome to come with us. Or for a couple of pints any Friday night down the local. We're usually there between six and eight.'

'Oh, I will, thank you, George. You're not off though, are you?'

'Yeah, best we do, being's Bob's not well. Last thing he wants with a headache bad enough to send him to bed is hearing us all babbling away downstairs.'

Eunice pecked her friend affectionately on her cheek.

'See you soon, gel.'

Kay smiled wanly at her.

'Thanks for coming.'

After she had seen her friends out she returned to the living room where she turned the gas mantles down low and huddled in an armchair, her feet curled under her. It was such a pity Bob had taken ill tonight. Eunice's idea to help him on his way had been a good ploy and one that could possibly have worked once the two men got talking. George was a good sort, the type she'd far sooner see her husband become friendly with than Tony's kind. Her mind drifted back and she remembered how Bob had been before the ravages of war had changed him for the worse. The vision of their joint future she had harboured then was nothing like the life she had now. Worry began to gnaw at her. Her love for Bob had never waned in all the time they had been parted, but she did not know if that love could be sustained if his attitude to life did not improve soon. She'd loved Bob as he was five years ago, not what he had become during their time apart.

Then a thought struck her, one so worrying it made her gasp. She didn't know if she truly loved Bob at all as he was at the moment, or even liked him as a person! She was getting nothing from him to feed her love and keep it alive; nothing in the way he acted was calculated to please her. At the moment all she was doing was living in hope that the character traits he'd possessed formerly would show themselves again. But what if they didn't? What if this was how Bob would remain? She shuddered as she saw her life stretching before her, living with less than a shadow of the man he used to be. Against her parents' advice to wait until she knew him better, she had married Bob for better or for worse, a lifetime commitment. All her family and friends – with the

329

exception of Eunice who she knew would never betray a confidence to anyone – all the people who loved her so dearly, were under the impression she was happy with her marriage and Kay could never under any circumstances dispel that illusion as she knew this knowledge would distress them all greatly. She sighed despondently. Should this be her life now, she had no choice but to endure it and make the best of it. All she could do was carry on doing her best to encourage Bob and hope that one day a miracle happened.

CHAPTER TWENTY

Bob was still sound asleep when Kay rose the next morning and stayed that way the several times she went up to check on him. An hour before they were expected at her mother's Kay went up again and gently shook his arm. 'Bob,' she whispered, 'we're due at my mother's for dinner soon, we'll be late if you don't get up now to get ready.'

To her dismay he opened his eyes and said self-pityingly, 'I still don't feel very well. My head's still pounding and my stomach's churning now. I'm wondering if it could be anything to do with that fried egg you gave me for tea yesterday. I didn't say anything to you but it did taste a bit off to me. I'm really not up to going. I'm sure your mother will understand. You must go, though. I don't want you missing out because of me.'

The egg was fresh, one of three she had bought from her neighbour who kept chickens in his yard. He had told her it had been laid only that morning. It had certainly looked all right to Kay and hadn't wafted any bad smell to her when she had broken it into the pan. Regardless, she felt terribly responsible for Bob's suffering.

'Oh, I couldn't possibly leave you...'

'No, really,' he insisted. 'There's no point in us both missing out. It's not like you can do anything. I just need to stay in bed and sleep it off.'

Despite her feeling of guilt for abandoning her husband, she was looking forward to the family get together. The absence of her husband was met with expressions of regret and good wishes for his speedy recovery. It was her mother's response that surprised Kay the most. She had expected a dressing down for her own possible responsibility for her husband's incapacitation, an instruction that in future she should break all eggs into a cup first and closely inspect them to be as certain as she could that they were free from imperfections.

Instead her mother patted her arm and said, 'Well, dear, these things happen. The cause could be anything, not necessarily something you've done, so stop worrying. If Bob's still got a gippy tummy when you get home, give him a dose of Epsom salts and that should do the trick.'

Her aunt, who had been present at the time, pulled Kay aside to whisper, 'I do believe in miracles after all.'

The meal was delicious, as usual, and Kay marvelled at the way her mother managed to feed them all so well on what little was available. Mabel's praise of her sister's attempts at the pudding seemed heartfelt. Viv was pink with pleasure.

The main topic of conversation around the table because of the family's strong connection with the Royal Mail was of a robbery from a Leicestershire village postman two days previously. He'd been knocked off his bike and a full bag of mail stolen. It had all happened so unexpectedly and swiftly that the only description of the culprit was that he was male and tall. As yet he was still at large. Thankfully the postman escaped with only a few bruises. Herbie in particular was incensed that such an outrage could have been conducted against a service so highly trusted by everyone in the country, and loudly hoped that when he was caught the perpetrator would suffer the severest penalty.

Kay did notice that her aunt was unusually quiet during the meal. The reason for this was made clear when, after they'd all finished eating, a nervous Frank announced to them that he had taken the plunge and asked Vivian the previous evening if she would do him the great honour of becoming his wife. Much to his surprise, she had accepted.

The gathering were jubilant, and none more so than Kay herself. She knew that if she hadn't accepted Frank's explanation of events with Tony and his promise that it was an isolated incident which would never happen again, her aunt would now be nursing a broken heart instead of looking forward to future happiness. In honour of the occasion the rest of the bottle of whisky was produced and a measure given to those who wanted it. The others were provided with lemonade, and several toasts were made to wish the happy couple well as they embarked on their new life together.

All talk then turned to possible dates for the wedding and associated topics. As much as Kay would have loved to stay and participate, they all understood when she announced her early departure as she wanted to check on Bob.

On her return she was relieved to find him sitting in his armchair listening to the wireless as usual. He seemed fully recovered and expressed some keenness to tackle the plate of dinner her mother had put up for him and their lodger. They both did justice to the meal. As soon as he'd eaten the last scrap on his plate, Tony announced he had things to do and disappeared off to his room. Kay was very thoughtful as she busied herself with the clearing up. She just could not understand why he had suddenly taken to spending most of his time closeted there. What could he possibly be finding to keep him so occupied?

Bob as usual was engrossed in listening to a variety show on the wireless by the time she sat down and picked up her knitting.

'Eunice and George were so sorry they never got to have a good chat with you yesterday evening because you weren't well, Bob,' Kay said. She flashed him a tentative look and said casually, 'George said to ask if you'd like to go to the football match a week on Saturday with them? He and his pals are a good crowd, Bob, I'm sure you'd enjoy their company. And he said if you'd like to join them for a drink, they go down the local on a Friday night from six to eight. That was nice of him, wasn't it?'

'Eh ... yes, it was.'

'So you'll go?'

'I'll let him know.'

Well, he hadn't said no so that was something at least.

'Eunice especially was looking forward to seeing you again and catching up on old times. I was thinking, I could ask them to come round one evening for an hour or so, if Eunice's mother will babysit. What about Tuesday night, Bob?'

He was staring across at her.

'This Tuesday? The day after tomorrow?'

She nodded.

'It would be nice for us to have some friends round. We haven't done anything like that since you got back. Don't you think, Bob?'

'Oh ... er ... yes, I suppose it would.'

Kay smiled at him happily.

'I'll arrange it then.'

A warm glow filled her. Oh, to have something to look forward to apart from just her housework! Dare she hope that this was the beginning of better things to come? She'd do her best to make sure the evening was successful.

CHAPTER TWENTY-ONE

The next day Kay was relieved that the weather looked set to be fine and dry and unusually warm for the middle of November. She was particularly pleased because it meant she had a good chance of getting her weekly washing dry and ironed all in one day, instead of labouring over it for at least three when the wintery weather left her no choice but to dry it as best she could in front of the fire or hanging from drying cradles. The condensation caused by this unavoidable practice was no joke to deal with. The spare set of sheets she did possess was being used to accommodate her lodger which meant that the laundering of bed linen in particular had to be dealt with in one day, no matter what the weather, or the alternative was sleeping on a bare mattress covered by coarse woollen blankets. Although she had no fondness for her lodger, her self-respect would not allow that to occur, and in order to do her best to make sure it did not she rotated the bed-changing on a weekly basis so that each bed was changed once a fortnight. This week it was her lodger's turn for clean sheets and pillow case.

As she put his breakfast in front of Tony, she said, 'While you're eating, I'll go and strip your bed.'

No sooner were the words out of her mouth than he jumped up, proclaiming, 'You stay here,

I'll do it.'

She was left staring after him, speechless. He had never once offered to do anything in the house for her in all the weeks he had been living under their roof. He returned moments later to thrust the bundle of used linen into her arms. As he sat down again at the table and picked up his knife and fork, he looked at her and said, 'When it's ready to go back on, give it to me and I'll do it.' He must have noticed the look on her face as he offered, 'Well, won't hurt me to help you out, will it? You needn't worry about cleaning my room either. I'll do it if you give me the stuff.'

She was too taken aback to mutter any more than, 'Er ... thank you. I'm much obliged.'

It was nearly twelve o'clock. The washing was blowing on the line, promising to be dry enough to iron later that afternoon, and Kay was just about to make a start on Bob's dinner when a knock sounded on her back door and Eunice walked in. She smiled at her friend cheekily.

'I know I don't usually see you Monday, it being wash day, but yer don't fancy making yer friend a cuppa, do yer? I've had a hell of a job with grizzly guts all morning. I think she's got a cold coming or summat, I ain't been able to get any of me housework done. In desperation I plonked her in the pushchair and thought I'd take her for a walk, see if I could get her off to sleep. The pushchair sort of made its own way here and I was just walking down your entry when she finally nodded off. I bleddy hope she's in a better mood when she wakes up.'

'Hadn't you better bring Joanie inside, Eunice?'

'No, she'll be fine out there, she's well wrapped up. Besides, getting the pushchair over the doorstep might jolt her awake and that's the last thing I want. Get the kettle on then.'

As Kay busied herself with her task, Eunice asked, 'So how did the dinner go yesterday?'

'Oh, it was lovely, Eunice, thank you. Mam did us proud as usual. How on earth she fed us all is beyond me. Although … well, Bob was still feeling poorly so he couldn't go.'

'Oh, that's a shame. Is he any better now?'

'Yes, he's fine, thank you. Thanks too for what you tried to do on Saturday night. If Bob hadn't been taken ill … well, who knows? Oh, my aunt announced her engagement to Frank Ambleside yesterday. Well, Frank announced it. We're all so chuffed.'

'Oh, that's good news. Will I get an invite?'

Kay promised, 'I'll see what I can do when the time comes.' As she handed Eunice her cup of tea, she said, 'Are you doing anything tomorrow night?'

'Depends. Why?'

'I wondered if you and George would like to come round for a hour or so? I told Bob how disappointed you were that you never got to see him because he was ill and that George had offered to go for a drink and to the match with him. I suggested you both come round Tuesday night if you could manage it. I was so thrilled when he agreed.' Kay's smile lit up her face. 'I'm hoping things are looking up at long last, Eunice. It would be lovely to start having a proper social life again. So will you come?'

'Yes, most definitely. Oh, Kay, there's lots we can do together as couples now Bob's...'

'Eh, let's just take one step at a time. I don't want him to have a setback. If George can persuade him to go out for a drink on Friday night, I'll be delighted with that for starters. I had another shock today.'

'Oh?'

Cradling her cup of tea and leaning back against the sink, Kay told her about it. 'My lodger offered to strip his bed and remake it, and also to clean his room.'

Eunice gawped at her in amazement.

'Bloody hell, gel, a man actually volunteering to do something for a woman without having to be nagged into doing it? Well, wonders will never cease. Yer could send him round to my house. Maybe he might teach my old man a thing or two. On second thoughts, I don't want my George mixing with his type. Talking of your lodger, as I turned the corner of your street a few minutes ago I saw him letting himself in at your front door with what looked like a heavy kit bag slung over his shoulder. He seemed to be in a dreadful hurry to get inside and shut the door.'

Kay frowned at her quizzically.

'Oh, really? I never heard him go out or come back either. Well, I probably wouldn't as I've been in the kitchen most of the morning, doing the washing and hanging it out. My mangle was playing up. Every half-turn it seemed to stick and I had a hell of a job getting the sheets through.' She frowned. 'I wonder what Tony had in his kit bag? It was heavy-looking, you said?'

338

'Seemed to me as his shoulder was all weighted down. He sort of heaved it in front of him as he entered your front door. Maybe it's full of stuff to sell on the market?'

'Well, I don't think he's selling stuff there anymore, or door to door come to that.'

'What makes you think that?'

'You have to be out most of the day to make a living like that, don't you, and as far as I know Tony hasn't been out much. Not since the day we saw him selling that stuff on the market a week last Saturday. I have to say that I've had my mind fully occupied for the last couple of weeks with taking care of my family but it suddenly struck me last Saturday that every time I arrived here last week with the dinner to coincide with Bob getting home from work, Tony was here too *and* when I got home in the evening. I was just too pleased I hadn't got the problem of keeping his dinner hot to think of much else at the time. But he was always out before that Saturday we saw him on the market, and now he's always in. So he can't be selling to earn his living, can he?

'Maybe the thought of that copper catching up with him and him landing in jail put Tony off. He's spent most of his time in his room apart from coming out at mealtimes and seems to have stopped going out in the evening too. I can't for the life of me think what he does in there all that time by himself. By the way, it was hot water bottles he was selling that day we saw him. He offered me one for five bob, which of course I declined, suspecting how he got hold of them.'

Eunice scowled at her, annoyed.

'I wish you'd told me, I could do with a new bottle especially at that price. Mine is so old it's spouting like a watering can.' The look her friend gave her had her muttering, 'Well, all right, maybe I don't need one that desperately. Just what *could* he be finding to do in his room for hours on end?'

'I've already told you, I haven't a clue.' Kay still looked puzzled. 'Eunice, say he was buying stuff to sell on and that's what was in the kit bag you saw him bring in just now? And say he was storing it in his bedroom ... well, apart from the fact I hope to God the police don't come knocking, it still doesn't explain why he hardly comes out of his room. He doesn't seem to be selling it on, which would be the whole point of buying it in the first place, surely? His behaviour is very confusing.'

'So how do yer reckon he's earning his living? I mean, he might not be going out in the evenings down the pub or whatever he does socially but he's still his lodgings to pay for and his personal bits and pieces?'

'Well ... he's not actually paying us board.'

Eunice stared at her, stupefied. 'What!'

'Bob won't hear of charging him anything and as far as I know Tony's never offered. The only thing I've had out of him since he arrived is his ration books.'

Eunice demanded, 'Oh, yer've gotta be joking? He's living here for n'ote?' She shook her head disbelievingly. 'Bob sure does feel he owes that man a debt, doesn't he?' She looked at her friend thoughtfully for several long moments. 'Yer know, it strikes me that yer lodger's offer to strip his bed and remake it and clean his room for you is because for some reason he doesn't want you in there.'

'Oh, Eunice, I never thought of that. Do you think that's really why he offered, just to keep me from going in his room?'

'If he's got something to hide, yes, I do. If I was you, I'd demand a look inside it to see what he's up to.'

'And what excuse would I give him for demanding to inspect his room, Eunice?'

'Yer don't need an excuse, this is your house. Or have you forgotten?'

'Yes, I know, but say I insist on seeing inside his room and find nothing incriminating, I'll look a right fool and Tony will have every right to be furious with me and want to know what I'm playing at. I can't exactly tell him that it's because I know he gets up to criminal activities, can I, not without telling him what I know about the scam with the whisky, then he'd know it was me that put the kibosh on that.

'And there's also the problem of Bob being really angry with me if he finds out I've tackled Tony. He'd only accuse me of trying to catch him out as an excuse to get rid of him. It's caused bad feeling enough between us before, I don't want to risk that again if I can help it, not now things are beginning to get better between me and Bob.' Kay gave a helpless sigh. 'Oh, Eunice, if only we hadn't seen what Tony was doing at the allotments that night, he wouldn't still be living here. He would have been long gone by now and me and Bob well rid of him.'

'Yeah, well, we *did* see him and we *do* know what we know, and we can't change that.' Eunice put her cup down on the table. 'Won't be a minute.'

'Where are you going?'

'You just listen out for Joanie.'

With that she darted through the house and Kay went after her. She peeked around the kitchen door to see her friend with one ear pressed hard against Tony's door.

'Get back here,' Kay whispered urgently, beckoning her back. 'Eunice, what if he comes out and catches you?'

She put her finger to her lips, flapping her hand in a warning for Kay to get back inside the kitchen. Heart thumping in fear should Tony suddenly emerge unexpectedly from his room and catch Eunice spying on him, she took shelter inside the kitchen and paced up and down for several frightening moments until her friend came back, closing the kitchen door behind her.

'Well?' Kay demanded.

'All I could hear was the sound of tearing paper. Well, that's what it sounded like to me.'

'Tearing paper?'

'That's what I said.'

'But what can he be tearing up?'

Eunice shrugged.

'Ain't a clue. Oh, what about old newspapers to make a huge pile of fire tapers for you?'

'Oh, stop being stupid.'

'Well, you make a suggestion then?' she snapped.

Kay pulled a face.

'I can't think of any reason he'd be tearing up paper. It doesn't make sense. It was definitely paper you heard?'

'Positive.' She looked at Kay keenly. 'You want rid of Tony, don't yer?'

'Oh, Eunice, more than anything I do. Apart from the fact his just being here makes me feel uncomfortable, I strongly suspect that he's...' She stopped herself from blurting that she was fully of the opinion the presence of Tony in the room below them was the cause of the chill in bed between Bob and herself '...well, that his presence in our house is not doing me and Bob any favours.'

'Right then, for you to get rid of him once and for all you need proof to show Bob he's up to no good. It's a pity we didn't think of it that night down the allotments. Now it seems to me that since Tony doesn't want you in his room there's more than a possibility that your proof lies on the other side of that door. We need to get in and have a look. If we don't find anything suspect then ... well, yer won't have an excuse to be rid of him. But at least yer can sleep easier in yer bed and just hope he goes of his own accord, sooner rather than later.'

'Yes, you're right. Er ... you keep saying "we", Eunice?'

'Yes, I'm in this with yer too.'

'Oh, but I can't expect you...'

She scoffed, 'You weren't so thoughtful when you made me your accomplice that night down the allotments.'

'No, I wasn't, was I? All right, how do we get

343

this proof we hope to find when Tony never seems to go out these days?'

'Well, he must do sometimes, like today, for instance, for me to see him come in.'

'Oh, yes, how stupid of me. But I don't know if he goes out every day or at what time or for how long.'

Eunice rubbed a hand over her chin.

'Well, it's not like we need him to be gone long. Your front room ain't that big it'd take us long to look over it. A few minutes should do the trick. Even if he's out just long enough to visit the paper shop, it'd take him at least ten minutes to get there, get served then get back. That's providing there ain't a queue. We'll just have to make sure we're here when he next goes out and then one of us can have a nosey around while the other keeps a look out.'

'Oh, I don't know, Eunice. Remember I witnessed Tony that night he was drunk after finding out the whisky had vanished and, believe me, he frightened the wits out of me with what he threatened to do to the culprit.'

'Well, it's up to you. You either pass up this chance to catch him up to no good again or else you put up with the man living here for however long he chooses to – plus the chance that you and Bob could be put in the frame too if the police knock on the door.'

That thought terrified Kay more than Tony's anger should he catch them snooping around his room.

'If he is up to no good, like we suspect he is, we can't just turn a blind eye, can we?'

Eunice patted her arm.

'That's my girl. Oh, this is so exciting! Right, we need a plan. Er...' She screwed up her face as she thought. 'Got it. Tomorrow I'll get me mam to have Joanie for the morning. I dunno, I'll give her some cock and bull that I've heard a rumour the Maypole has had a delivery of tins and I need to get in the queue. Then I can be here with you all morning.'

'Oh, but I don't like the thought of you lying to your mother like that. And what is she going to say when you don't bring home any tins?'

'Oh, Kay, for God's sake, you're too honest for yer own good sometimes. I'll tell her the rumour was wrong, and should Tony not go out tomorrow and we need to do this again the next day, I'll think of another excuse for her to have Joanie, and then again the next day until we *do* get a chance to get inside that bloody room!'

'But what if he goes out in the afternoon?'

'You really are the limit, Kay. Tomorrow afternoon or any other afternoon would be even better 'cos Bob's here himself then, ain't he? All you have to do is listen out for the front door to go and then use some excuse to go into Tony's room. I'm sure you can come up with one. If you do spot anything suspicious, you can alert Bob straight away and he can't make any excuses for Tony when the evidence is staring him in the face, can he?'

'No, he can't. Bob never believed me the last time because we'd got rid of the evidence, but this time we'll have it. I still can't think what on earth Tony could be up to, though.'

345

'Neither can I. For all we know it could be perfectly innocent, but I don't think so somehow.'

'No, neither do I.' Then a thought suddenly struck Kay. 'Oh, no, we've a problem neither of us has thought of.'

'What's that?'

'Well, it's not so bad for you, it's just the mornings you'll be here with me, but if I'm keeping a full vigil here for Tony going out, when am I going to do my shopping and get the old dear living next door her bits and pieces? I still pop in to see if my mother needs help every afternoon as well.'

'Mmm, yes, you have a point. Well, it seems the afternoons are out then. We'll just have to hope that Tony goes out in the morning sometime. Eh, now listen, don't you go all peculiar in front of him and get the wind up him we're on to him. Just be like you normally are with him.'

Kay gulped, 'I'll try. Oh, God, Eunice, this is all your fault, same as it was that night down the allotments. Both times you came here unexpectedly and both times I found myself facing cloak-and-dagger situations.'

She pursed her lips at Kay.

'If you remember, at first I didn't want any part of what we did down the allotments, it was you that made me help yer. I'm offering me services this time, but if you don't want them...'

'Yes, I do, Eunice. Thank you.' A thought suddenly struck Kay then. 'Oh, God, what's the time?'

'Er...' Eunice went to the kitchen door, put her head around it and looked across at the mantel clock. 'Nearly one.'

'Oh, hell, Bob comes in in an hour and I've not made a start on his dinner. He'll wonder what I've been up to all morning.'

'For God's sake, tell him it'll be a bit late today 'cos you've been washing all morning and it took longer than normal for some reason. What time does Tony have his breakfast?'

'About eight-thirty.'

'Oh, right, man of leisure, ain't he? Most men have done half a day's hard work by that time. Right, I'll flash around with my housework and be here as soon as I can manage before ten. Let's just hope he don't go out before then.'

CHAPTER TWENTY-TWO

The next morning at just after nine-thirty an extremely anxious Kay was vigorously sweeping her kitchen floor. Despite her need to find a way to be rid of her lodger she wasn't happy about the methods she and Eunice were employing, but at the same time knew there was no other way to go about this. She just prayed they did not get caught in the act.

How she had faced Tony and Bob the previous evening, doing her best to carry on as normal, while knowing what she and Eunice were going to attempt the next morning, she did not know. Thankfully Tony had gone to his room straight after tea and remained there for the rest of the evening. Bob's behaviour, though, had worried her. He had seemed very preoccupied and when Kay had enquired of him if everything was all right, afraid that he somehow sensed she was up to something behind his back, she had been relieved when he'd explained that he was tired, that was all.

She herself slept fitfully that night, her dreams invaded by visions of herself and Eunice trapped inside Tony's room, clutching each other and cowering, eyes riveted on the closed door as the sound of thudding footsteps steadily approached. They were both aware of the terrible fate that awaited them at the hands of whoever was about to come through it. She had awoken, sweating profusely, just before the alarm clock was about to go off, totally convinced she couldn't go through with what she and Eunice were planning. Then she'd reasoned with herself that if she didn't she would never know what was keeping Tony practically imprisoned in his room. This was Kay's home and she was entitled to know what went on in it.

Since she had seen Bob off to work, she had kept herself busy and managed to appear calm and collected when Tony came through for his jug of hot water then brought the bowl back through to empty it. He'd eaten his breakfast before returning to his room. They had passed no more than the usual stilted conversation and she prayed Eunice did not arrive while he was around and come charging through the back door in her usual manner, blurting something out that would instantly alert him to their scheme.

Her friend was due anytime now and Kay wanted to finish sweeping the kitchen floor now she had started it. She pushed the brush under the table to sweep up the daily debris and, as she pulled it back, the head caught the leg of the table and shot off. She tutted in annoyance as she went over to retrieve the brush head from where it had landed by the back door. She then examined the end of the handle and the brush head. It appeared that the nail holding it on had come out. Searching around she found it, then realised she'd need a hammer to mend it.

Her father had thoughtfully supplied her with a small box containing basic tools she and Bob would need when she had first moved into their house. Up to now she had not needed it and had kept it in the small dark cupboard under the stairs. Propping the brush pole against the table, she put the head and nail on top of it and went over to the cupboard under the stairs which was next to the door leading to the front room. She could hear Tony moving about so knew he was in. The only items Kay kept in this cupboard were things she needed infrequently as it was a musty-smelling cavity inhabited by a variety of spiders and other creepy crawlies which Kay herself had no fondness for. Despite the way these household places were frequently cleaned out the insects had a habit of quickly finding their way back again so she wasn't looking forward to delving inside it.

Down on all fours, she pulled out the tool box, opened it up and took out the hammer. She was just about to push the box back into place when she noticed a bulky-looking object, a canvas bag

349

of some sort, shoved in at the back. Then she realised it must be Bob's kit bag which he must have put in there himself for some reason because she had folded it up and put it on top of the wardrobe after emptying out his belongings when he had first arrived home. The cupboard under the stairs, to her mind, was not the place the bag should be stored because during winter months, as was now the case, the cupboard became damp and the bag would become mildewed and eventually unusable. It was unlikely that Bob would ever have need of the bag again but nevertheless she felt it a shame to let it knowingly rot away.

Thinking she would find a more suitable place to store it, she leaned over, grabbed at the end of it and pulled it out. Standing up, she bent down to pick up the hammer and the kit bag and as she made to shut the cupboard door after her heard the thud of something landing on the floor beside her. She looked down and to her surprise saw a small red book lying open on the lino and scattered beside it what looked to be a substantial amount of paper money. She realised then she was holding the kit bag upside down and the book and its contents had obviously fallen out of it. Automatically she picked up the book and realised it was Bob's Trustees Savings bank book which had fallen open at the page showing the last transaction. She couldn't help but look at it. The date showing that transaction was if she remembered rightly the day he had come home with his motorbike. The balance before that day was shown to have been £65 10s which Bob appeared to have accumulated at the rate of approximately one pound a week over the period up until he'd been shipped out to India. But the balance now showed nil, which meant he'd drawn all of his savings out on the day he'd bought the bike. She wondered why he'd done that.

Kay bent down to gather the money together, meaning to replace it inside the book, when it struck her that despite having no idea what the motorbike had cost him or the model construction kits either, the amount now in her hand far exceeded what had originally been in his bank account before he had drawn it all out. She quickly counted the money, which was mostly in five-pound notes. The total came to £138. Even if the purchase of the motorbike and model kits had come to £10, which she felt was generous on her part, that left over £80 more than he had had. Where had Bob acquired the rest of the money?

She stood for a moment, deeply confused, then it struck her. Of course, he must have received his government gratuity. But why had he not told her it had finally come through? Instead he had hidden it somewhere she was very unlikely to find it. She would not have if she hadn't happened to be in need of the hammer, and might never have done even then if she hadn't felt that the cupboard under the stairs was not a fitting place in which to store his kit bag.

Then a memory stirred. Bob had said originally he had not told her about the gratuity payment because he was going to surprise her with it. Maybe that's why he had hidden it away. He was waiting for the right moment to come along to

351

spring his surprise on her. What a lovely thing for him to do, she thought. Although it still did not explain why he had drawn all his savings out. She was sure, though, that Bob must have good reason for doing what he had and would tell her when the time was right. Not wanting to ruin his surprise, she put the notes back inside the bank book, put that back inside the kit bag then replaced the bag back exactly where she had found it inside the cupboard.

She had repaired the brush and finished sweeping the kitchen floor when Eunice arrived.

'Oh, I don't know how I contained meself last night,' she said, taking off her coat and hanging it up. 'George asked me several times why I was acting like a cat on hot coals.'

'You never said a word to him about what we've planned?' Kay shot at her worriedly.

'Don't be daft! If I'd even hinted that me and you were in league to try and catch a criminal at it, he'd have demanded to know the reason why we suspected your lodger of being up to no good in the first place and then I'd have had no choice but to tell him what happened down the allotments. You're still up for this, ain't yer, Kay?'

She drew a deep breath. 'To be honest, I've switched back and forth a few times, talking myself in and out of it, but I need to know what he's doing, Eunice, one way or the other.'

'Yeah, so do I now. It's really intriguing me what that tearing sound I heard could possibly be. Have yer managed to have a listen at his door since I did yesterday and heard anything else yerself?'

Kay shook her head.

'Well, I was by his door a few minutes ago as I needed to go into the cupboard under the stairs but I was frightened he'd suddenly come out and catch me with my ear pressed to the door. I wouldn't have known what to say to explain myself. I could hear him moving about, though, so I know he's still in.

'Listen, Eunice, Tony does come out now and again to see if I'm mashing a cuppa so we'd better make it look like you've come round for a social visit just in case he does. Was your mam all right about having Joanie?'

'Oh, she loves having her, she was delighted when I asked, and because me and George are coming round here tonight, me mam said she might as well keep her until tomorrow, save me toing and froing with her. That's good for me, ain't it, as it means I have the day all to meself. I've got me shopping to do this afternoon but I'm free all morning to play sleuth with you. Oh, George and me *are* looking forward to tonight, by the way.'

'Yes, so am I, but I can't think about that until we've got this over with,' Kay said, wringing her hands nervously.

Eunice looked at her in annoyance. 'Stop feeling guilty, will yer? Remember, you have every right to see what's going on in yer own front room.'

'So I might have, but it still doesn't make me feel any better about doing this.'

They'd been sitting at the table for nearly two

hours, chatting away like any two normal woman would do, and were on their third pot of tea.

'I'll be awash with this stuff if I drink any more,' Eunice moaned. 'I badly need the lavvy but I daren't go in case I miss anything.' She lowered her voice to a hushed whisper. 'Oh, if Tony's going out, I wish he'd hurry up and get on with it.'

'Maybe he's not going today,' Kay whispered back, looking over at the clock. 'It's gone half-past eleven.'

Just then they both jumped as a noise came from the front of the house.

'That was your front door opening,' Eunice said, her eyes lighting up in excitement.

Kay heard a clatter coming from the yard just then. 'No, it's the dustbin men. I forgot it's their day today.'

'No, I'm sure it was the front door opening,' Eunice insisted, jumping up from her chair to dash off and check for herself from upstairs. Moments later she came running back down. 'You'll never guess what I just watched from your front bedroom window. I was right, it was your front door opening. I peeped round the side of your nets and saw your lodger handing the dust-bin men three full sacks of something which didn't seem that heavy to me, by the way he was carrying them. Then after the dustbin man had slung them on the back of the cart I saw Tony hand summat to the man. It looked like it could have been a couple of shillings for his trouble. Then Tony shut your front door and went off down the road. He had his kit bag over his shoulder but as far as I could tell it was empty.'

Kay's face creased in surprise.

'Yes, I heard the front door shutting just before you came down,' she said. 'What could have been in those sacks, Eunice?'

'Dunno, but now the coast is clear, maybe we can find out. Come on,' she urged as she shot off in the direction of Tony's room.

Kay joined her, looking very apprehensive.

'Oh, I don't know about this, Eunice. Anyway, I thought one of us was supposed to be keeping a look out in case he decides to come back?'

'We could have been in and out and Tony none the wiser while you've stood here dithering.' Eunice made a grab for the door handle, turned it and gave it a push to open it. The door refused to budge more than a fraction. 'What's wrong with this door?' she said, pushing harder against it. 'There seems ter be something at the other side stopping it from opening.' She rattled the door. 'Yeah, seems to me Tony's wedged something under the knob to stop anyone getting in. A chair or something.' She clicked the door shut and looked at Kay meaningfully. 'Now that definitely is suspicious, don't you think?'

Grave-faced, she nodded. 'Yes, I have to say it is. What on earth do we do now?'

Eunice looked at her as though she was stupid. 'What d'yer mean, what do we do now? We get in by the other door, yer daft clot! Forgot yer had a front door, have yer?'

Kay hadn't used it for so long she actually had forgotten she had access to her house that way.

'Oh, how silly of me, of course.'

355

'Got yer key?' Eunice asked her.

'I'm not sure about this...'

'Just give me your front door key,' Eunice cut in. 'Your lodger's hiding something and I mean to find out what, even if you're too chicken. Come on,' she said, flapping one hand at Kay.

She hadn't used her front door key since Tony had taken up residence, even arranging for the postman to deliver their mail around the back of the house to respect his privacy. She wasn't sure where she had put it. With Eunice spurring her on, she eventually found it at the bottom of her handbag. At the street end of the entry splitting Kay's house from the one adjoining, they poked their heads round to look up and down the street for any sign of Tony returning. There was none.

Eunice addressed Kay. 'Right, I'll stay here and keep a look out for him coming back. You let yerself in and have a look around. Come on, get to it before he comes back,' she urged, giving Kay a push out of the entry and into the street.

Heart hammering thunderously, feeling like a criminal herself, she darted across to her front door, hurriedly inserted the Yale key in the lock and let herself inside.

She immediately noticed that against the door leading from this room into their living room a chair had been positioned, its back wedged under the door knob. Obviously done to prevent her or Bob from entering this room during the time he was out, she thought. Obviously, though, it hadn't occurred to Tony that should she want to get into his room badly enough she could let herself in by the front door. But then, after offering to strip his

356

own bed, remake it and clean the room himself, there really wouldn't be any reason for her to come in here and maybe he had banked on that. But what exactly was it he was trying to hide in this room? That was the question.

On her first quick glance around, apart from the chair wedged under the door knob, nothing else seemed amiss to Kay. She hadn't any preconceived idea of what she might expect to find but she had expected to see a pile of something obviously wrapped in paper to account for the ripping sound Eunice had heard. There was no evidence of anything of such a nature. The room was small, the single bed, wardrobe and shabby wash stand holding a cracked jug and bowl almost filling it, leaving not much space for anything else. The bedding looked rumpled, as though it had been pulled quickly together after the occupant had got out of it that morning and had been sat upon afterwards. She hurried over to the wardrobe and pulled open the door to check inside. A couple of shirts, a pair of trousers and a suit were hanging up, a couple of jumpers and a spare pair of underpants and vest were piled on the bottom. Nothing unusual there. She shut the door.

She heard Eunice call out to her in an urgent tone, 'Yer found anything, Kay?'

'No, nothing yet,' she replied in the same hushed tone. 'Any sign of Tony?'

'No, I'd have let yer know if there was.'

There was nothing under the wash stand. Kay lifted the bed covers and bent down to look under the bed. There was just Tony's suitcase.

357

About to pull it out and check inside it, she suddenly caught sight of what looked like a letter that appeared to have got stuck under the castor on the bed leg at the top end. Curious, she got down on all fours to ease it out from under the castor and as she did so saw a pile of empty sacks shoved behind the back of the bed up against the wall. Eunice had told her she had seen Tony handing over at least three bulky bags, although it seemed to her by the way he was handling them that they were not heavy. Was the supply behind the bed kept there in readiness for future filling with rubbish? But rubbish discarded from what?

The letter eased out, Kay stood up, opened it out and read it. Dated a week ago, it was from a Mr Bishop living at an address in the New Walk area of Leicester and was addressed to a large store in London. 'Dear Sirs,' it ran. 'Please find enclosed postal orders to the value of £8 7s 6d to cover the cost of purchasing your catalogue number 23645FC plus postage and packing. I look forward to receiving my order at your earliest convenience.' It was signed by Mr Bishop. Kay frowned quizzically. What was this letter doing in Tony's room?

She almost leaped out of her skin when she heard a voice hiss at her, 'For God's sake, Kay, how long does it take yer to have a nosey around?'

Clutching her chest and spinning around, she uttered, 'Oh, glory be, Eunice, you scared the hell out of me! I thought you were supposed to be keeping a look out for Tony coming back?'

'Well, I called you a couple of times and you

never answered so I came to see what you were up to. It's all right, I had a good look up and down the street first and there's no sign of him returning. Have yer found 'ote incriminating?' she demanded.

Before she answered Kay dashed to the door, poked out her head and flashed a look up and down the street. Satisfied there was no sign of Tony, she returned to Eunice's side. 'Not really, but then...' She quickly told Eunice of the pile of empty sacks behind the bed and showed her the letter she'd found.

As Eunice read it her face screwed up in bewilderment. 'How on earth did this come to be in his room?'

'I can't begin to guess,' Kay answered her.

'Looks just like any normal bedroom,' said Eunice, a mite disappointed. 'The wardrobe's just got clothes in, you said, and nothing behind the bed but a pile of empty sacks?'

'And Tony's suitcase.'

'Sorry?'

'Under the bed. The pile of empty sacks and Tony's suitcase.'

'What's in the suitcase?'

'I don't know. I was just about to look when I spotted the letter. It'll just be full of those hot water bottles we saw him trying to get rid of down the market.'

'Well, maybe so, but let's leave no stone unturned before we get the hell out of here. You pull the case out while I just have a gander up and down the street to make sure the coast is still clear.'

Eunice went back to the door while Kay knelt down and pulled out the case. As she lifted the lid, Eunice dropped down to a squatting position beside her. 'So far, so good. Still no sign of...' Her voice trailed away as the case revealed its contents. 'What on earth...?' she gasped, stunned.

Kay too was staring at its contents, stupefied.

Inside the case was a variety of expensive-looking items including several women's and men's silk scarves, pairs of leather gloves, packets of nylon stockings, boxes of silk handkerchiefs, a selection of good jewellery, at least six wrist-watches that they could see, and there was also a bundle of letters, a roll of pound and five-pound notes, and piles of postal orders in varying denominations.

'Where has he got this lot from?' asked a puzzled Eunice.

Everything inside the case was baffling to Kay but what interested her most was the bundle of letters. She picked them up and flicked through them, then took out the contents of the top envelope, opened the letter out and quickly scanned through it before replacing it inside the envelope. Her face grave, she looked at Eunice.

'That letter was from a woman to her friend telling her of a secret affair she's having. The type of letter, Eunice, that in the wrong hands could be used as blackmail material. But what's even more worrying to me is that none of these letters has been through the sorting office. There are no post-marks on any of the envelopes.'

Her friend was gawking at her, mystified.

'But ... well ... how did Tony get hold of them,'

Kay? And all this other stuff – has he been housebreaking, do you think?'

She shook her head, eyes narrowing angrily.

'No, Tony's not been up to anything so simple, Eunice. Oh, this is so awful! I thought we'd find piles of stuff he'd bought on the black market. Something along the same lines as those bottles of whisky. I never dreamed for a minute we'd discover anything of such ... such...'

Eunice grabbed her arm and shook it frenziedly.

'Oh, fer God's sake, Kay, if you know how Tony came by all this stuff then tell me!'

'He's the post bag robber,' she blurted out. 'He's got to be.'

'The post bag robber?'

'My dad told me last week that a village post-man had been robbed of his mail bag. I assumed my dad meant he was delivering the mail but he must have just collected it from the post boxes and post office to take back to the sorting office. That robber was Tony. This is the evidence. That's why he never left his room unless he could help it, for fear me or Bob should accidentally discover what he was up to. The ripping sound you heard was him opening all the mail to see what was inside that could be of use to him. All this stuff ... the scarves, watches, jewellery, money, postal orders and the rest, are things people put in the post as presents to friends and family or else money and postal orders to pay their bills. The sacks of rubbish he gave the dustbin men contained all the packaging from this lot and whatever else was in the postbag that was no good to him. I suspect he's kept this bundle of letters because of the incriminating contents and is going to blackmail the writers, that's if he hasn't already. Oh, Eunice, I can't bear this, it's so dreadful!'

'Oh, it is, Kay,' she uttered, then asked, 'But where d'yer think he's gone now with his empty kit bag?' Her eyes became knowing. 'To rob another postman? He must be, Kay, and *that's* what he must have been up to when I saw him come back here yesterday with his full kit bag. It was full of the contents of another stolen mailbag.' Eunice jumped up. 'Shut the lid and put the case back under the bed,' she ordered. 'Quick, Kay, in case he comes back. We're off to fetch the police.'

'Oh, but don't you think we should wait for Bob....'

'Like hell we'll wait,' she interjected. 'The sooner your lodger is behind bars the better. We fetch the police now. Bob can't make excuses for Tony this time, Kay, and yer'll have the police to back you if he still refuses to believe his pal's a crook.'

Kay slammed shut the lid of the case and thrust it back under the bed.

'You're right, let's go.'

After a quick check round to make sure the room looked just like it had when Kay first entered, should Tony return before the police arrived, they hurriedly left for the police station.

CHAPTER TWENTY-THREE

Kay was dashing around the kitchen attempting to put a meal together for Bob whose return from work was imminent. She was highly charged, dreading telling her husband what had transpired that morning. She knew he was going to be upset to learn that the man he had thought to be his friend had cold-bloodedly abused their hospitality to cover his own criminal activities, seemingly with no regard for the situation he had put them both in. No one wanted to believe that a friend could treat them so appallingly, as Bob had proved before, but this time there was no disguising the man's misdemeanours. Bob had to believe it, whether he liked it or not.

Tony had arrived back while she and Eunice were down at the police station outlining their discoveries first to Constable Pringle, then again to Detective Finch. Leaving Kay and Eunice in the safety of the police station, Detective Finch and Constable Pringle, accompanied by two other policemen in a Black Maria, paid a call on Kay's house, positioning themselves in such a way that Tony had no means of escape. He was completely oblivious to anything untoward going on when they surprised him in the middle of sorting through a bag full of mail. At their knock on the front door, he had opened it an inch or so, fully expecting it to be a caller for Kay, to be

363

redirected round the back. The shock he had received when the door was forced open against him and two burly policemen stepped inside was most apparent. Despite that, he tried to make a break for it, but was quickly overpowered, handcuffed and frogmarched into the Black Maria which had been strategically parked a few doors down so as not to alert him that the strong arm of the law was about to pay him a call.

All the evidence of his criminal activities was collected up and as soon as Tony Cheadle was securely inside the police station, awaiting questioning, Kay was informed she could now safely return home. Detective Finch had told her he was satisfied that both she and her husband had no idea what their lodger was up to but said that regardless they would be called upon to answer further questions. Kay didn't mind, she had nothing to hide and nor had her husband.

Eunice had gone off to do her shopping and was going to call by on her way home to check Kay was all right and offer to explain to Bob anything that needed further clarification.

At the sound of the back door opening, Kay spun round to face her husband.

'Oh, Bob, you're home,' she declared. 'I'm sorry, your dinner is going to be a little late today. You see...'

'I don't want any dinner,' he shot back at her. 'Look, I've ... er ... something to tell you, Kay, but first I must see Tony.'

She was staring at him, confused. What did he mean, he didn't want any dinner? And what had he to tell her? He was acting very oddly, as if he

364

was highly nervous about something. He hadn't even taken his coat off, as though he wasn't stopping.

'Oh ... er ... what do you want to...'

He had gone into the back room and she went after him just as he was about to knock on Tony's door and enter.

'Tony's not in, Bob. He's gone,' she called.

He turned to her, a look of surprise on his face. 'He's gone? He's really left then?' He looked mortally relieved. 'Oh, thank God, I thought ... oh, never mind.'

She took a deep breath. 'Tony didn't leave of his own free will. He's ... look, I'm so sorry to tell you that Tony's been arrested. You won't believe what he was...'

'Arrested!' Bob erupted, his face filled with alarm. 'No, that can't be true! You're lying, Kay. Please tell me you're lying?' he frantically beseeched her.

The shock of her announcement was most apparent. Kay was stunned to see her husband physically crumple before her eyes, as if his life's blood was draining from him. This news had clearly devastated him far more than she had envisaged. Her heart went out to him.

'Bob, I'm so sorry. I know he was your friend and you trusted him, but he's not the man you think he is, he's really not. He was using our home to cover up his criminal activities. He's down at the police station and they're question-ing him about the mail bag robberies.'

Bob's face was ashen now, parchment white, and he was staring at her as if frozen.

365

'Oh, God, dear God, I'm finished!' he uttered, scraping his hands despairingly through his hair. He began pacing up and down before her like a man demented. 'It's all over for me. Oh, God, I tried to warn him ... told him he should call it a day last week. Be glad for what he'd got already and make a run for it. But he wouldn't listen! This scam was a gold mine, a bottomless pit. Another opportunity like this would never come along in his lifetime and he meant to make the most of it. Another week, he said. Just another week.' Then Bob's face contorted in horror. 'Oh, God, they'll be coming for me any minute once he starts blabbing. I've got to get out of here!'

Kay was staring at him dumbstruck, mouth gaping, eyes bulging as what her husband was saying sank in. She had to be wrong, she had to be! Bob hadn't known what Tony was doing ... he just couldn't have.

Now he was by the cupboard under the stairs, down on all fours, his head inside, reaching into it for his kit bag.

She threw herself down beside him, grabbing his arm to shake it frenziedly.

'Bob, please tell me you knew nothing about this. Please, Bob?' she implored.

Bag in hand, he scrambled out of the cupboard and glared at her.

'You idiot! Where do you think Tony got the mail from each day? The mail bag robbery was nothing to do with him. Even if he doesn't tell the police it won't take them long to work out that he was getting the mail from me, a Royal Mail collector, for Christ's sake.'

She gasped with horror. 'NO! Oh, Bob, please tell me this isn't true! You'd never do such a thing.'

'Tony made me, I had no choice,' he blurted out hysterically. 'It wasn't meant to be like this. I never wanted to come here in the first place ... it was too risky. I tried to make him see that, but he would have it. Said this was the perfect cover for him. No one would suspect him, living under the roof of a seemingly law-abiding couple. All I had to do was keep my head down and play my part. He'd give me a share. I didn't want a share, I told him that, but he gave me no choice. Said if I didn't do this for him he'd tell the authorities my secret.' His eyes blazed at her accusingly. 'If only you hadn't stuck your nose into the whisky business he'd have been happy with his profit from that and we'd both have been long gone by now. Look, don't get in my way, I've got to get out of here before it's too late.'

He pushed her forcibly from him and, kit bag in hand, dashed up the stairs. Sprawled on the floor, she heard his footsteps pounding across the bedroom floor and the sound of the wardrobe doors being flung open.

Kay's heart was racing, head pounding as her thoughts raced. From what he had blurted out to her, Bob had known all along what Tony had been up to and was in league with him. But no, he couldn't be? Not her Bob, he wouldn't do anything like this. She must have misunderstood what he had said. He was upset at finding all this out about Tony, didn't know what he was saying. And what secret had Tony blackmailed him with?

But there was something else going on, something she couldn't fathom. Something about Bob himself. He had said he hadn't wanted to come here in the first place, and now he was leaving her.

She went after him into their bedroom. Bob was stuffing his belongings into his kit bag any way he could. He jumped when she burst into the room, closing the door behind her and standing with her back against it.

'You tell me everything, Bob,' she demanded. 'I want to know what's going on. You're not making any sense. I can't believe you were in on this with Tony. This isn't you. You'd never do anything like this, I know you well enough to know that. How did Tony make you help him? What hold has he got on you? What do you mean when you say you never wanted to come here in the first place? You can't want to leave me. Why, Bob, why? Tell me, I want to know.'

'Leave it, Kay,' he hissed, turning his back on her to continue his packing. 'Let me go, forget I ever existed.'

'What? But you're my husband.'

He spun round to face her and shouted, 'That's just it – I'm not.'

She stared at him, stupefied. 'You don't know what you're saying. Of course you're my husband. Who else can you be?'

Eyes blazing, he jabbed himself in the chest and cried hysterically, 'Norman Drinkwater, *that's* my name, *that's* who I am.' Then his whole body sagged, his legs starting to buckle as he collapsed on the bed to cradle his head in his hands despairingly. 'Norman Drinkwater. I'm Norman Drinkwater.' His face crumpled in defeat. 'You might as well know it all, you're going to find out anyway. I don't know how the police got on to him but Cheadle's bound to think it was me who shopped him to them because no one else but us knew what was going on. If he's going down, he'll do his best to take me with him. He always promised me that, and that's one promise I've no doubt he'll keep.' He took a deep shuddering breath. Seeming to forget Kay's presence, he began to tell her his incredible story.

'The war came like a blessing to me, a way of escaping the awful life I led. A nagging wife, three screaming kids, her scrounging parents, all of us living in a miserable hole, the only money coming in the bit I earned as a labourer in an iron foundry. My life was a living hell. I couldn't get any peace to listen to the wireless, let alone have a few coppers spare each week for a pint or two, and I saw no way out of it. Then like a miracle war broke out and, believe me, I rushed to be first in the queue to join up. Of course I had no idea then that I was swapping one hell for another.

'I met Bob Clifton when I arrived at the training barracks. He'd joined up the same day as me and we were in the same billet. Right from the start chaps remarked on how strongly we resembled each other, and even we couldn't deny it. Bob was larger built than me. I was on the thin side, always had been. We both hailed from Northampton but weren't related as far as we knew though we could easily have been taken for close relatives. We never exactly became what you could call bosom buddies but were friendly enough.

'I remember the night he came back to the billet after meeting you for the first time. He was full of it, told any of the chaps who would listen that he'd met a wonderful woman, the love of his life, and was going to marry her. I think it was then I started to envy him. We looked like each other but that's where the similarities in our lives ended. I couldn't help thinking how unfair my life had been to me. When I married Thelma she seemed a decent woman. She'd make a good wife for me, I thought, never dreaming she'd turn into a nagging banshee and I'd end up with three screaming kids *and* her folks to look after, and no life whatsoever to call my own.

'After a few months of training we got word we were being shipped to India. Bob and me got split up then. I ended up in Poona, Bob in Calcutta. I was there for just over two years. Then in '42 the British were being sent into Burma and my unit was dispatched to the Arakan coast. That was when I met up with Bob again. He'd been shipped out to Burma at the same time and we landed up in the same unit. He was a corporal by then, my superior as I was a private. We looked even more like each other as Bob had lost a lot of weight, and the other chaps started to mix us up. We could have been twin brothers, it was uncanny. It got to be quite a joke amongst the lads and now and again Bob and I would play tricks on them for a laugh. Boy, we needed a laugh out there.

'That's when I first came into contact with Tony Cheadle. He'd joined Bob's outfit in Calcutta with the wave of soldiers that came out after us. He wasn't what you'd call popular among the others, I wasn't that struck by him myself for that matter. He was the type you stayed in with, though, as if there was anything to be got that you wanted, he was the man to see. His sort's always handy to know.

'I'd thought that India was bad enough, but Burma was terrible. If you weren't soaking wet in monsoon downpours, you were stifling hot in steaming heat, bitten to death by mosquitoes, and thought yourself lucky to get a half-decent meal. The likes of sugar was bought and sold by the troops like precious metal. Getting tobacco was even worse. If you smoked, that's where half your pay went.

'I was no different from any of the other men. I was desperate for the war to end, most times terrified I'd never live to see British shores again, but I couldn't face going back to the life I'd had before. The thought of it made me feel physically sick, but should a Nip bullet not have my name on it, sooner or later, I knew I'd have to.

'The end of the war in Europe meant little to us out in the Far East. We were glad, of course, but we still had an enemy to fight and the Nips didn't look like they were going to give up so life barely changed for us out there. In September '45 news had come through to our senior officers of an enemy platoon about fifteen miles to the south of our camp. Twenty of us, including Bob, meself and Tony, were sent out to track down and deal

371

with them.

'Ten days we spent trailing them through the jungle. We'd come up against other small bands of Japs and managed to dispose of them although we lost a couple of our own men in the battles and our wireless took a hit so we were out of contact with our base, but didn't find anything of the little bastards we'd been sent after. Rations were getting seriously low and we were hungry, tired, just about on our knees in fact by this time, but we couldn't go back until we'd accomplished the mission we'd been sent out to do. The advance scouts came back with news of a village up ahead. If nothing else, we thought the locals would treat us to a bit of hospitality. As soon as we got into that village it was apparent something wasn't right. The place seemed deserted. Then all hell broke loose. We were being attacked. It was an ambush. The Japs we'd been tracking had been tracking us, and were waiting for us there.

'We split up, diving for cover anywhere we could find it. I belted around the back of a row of huts and jumped head first through one of the windows. After checking to make sure I was alone in the house, I started to make my way towards the front to get a vantage point by the window, see if I could make out where the Nips were attacking from. I was in the middle of the house by this time. It was then I heard a noise behind me. I panicked, thinking it was a Jap, and the next thing I knew I'd spun round and fired.

'He dropped like a stone, blood pouring from a wound at the side of his head. It was then it hit me what I'd done. I couldn't believe it, I'd killed one of my own men. When I went over I saw it was Bob Clifton.'

The thud of Kay dropping to her knees on the floor by the door sent Norman Drinkwater's head jerking up to look across at her. He seemed suddenly to realise she was there, having temporarily forgotten her presence as he relived his story.

Her face a frozen mask, she uttered, 'You killed my husband?'

He jumped up from the bed and began pacing the room. 'It was an accident! I never meant to do it, it was war, for Christ's sake. These things happen.' As he paced he scraped his hands over his head repeatedly. 'As I stood there staring down at him a crazy idea came to me. It was like a prayer from heaven, the miracle I'd been hoping for, a way to rid myself of the life I detested, that I dreaded going back to, and change it for a completely new one. I could swap places with Clifton. My family would be told Norman Drinkwater was dead, so no fear of them trying to track me down, and with my new identity I could do what I pleased, with no ties whatsoever to my past life at all. Bob was dead, he'd no use for his identity anymore, but I could certainly use it. We'd been mistaken for each other often enough. All I'd got to do was pass myself off as him for the rest of the war, and once that was over I could make a home for myself in a new town where no one knew me.

'It seemed so simple. Too good an opportunity for me to pass up. I had no time to think about it, I knew someone could come in at any minute and then my chance would be gone. It was now or never. All I had to do was swap my shirt for Bob's with his corporal's stripes and exchange our back packs. I had to remember to wear my cap at the angle he did, and not to smoke as he never did, but then I could always take it up afterwards as people do. I knew enough about his life to get by, he'd talked about it often enough on the lonely nights we were all closeted together in our billets or in the jungle camps out on manoeuvres. The only one worry I had was that I was starting to lose my hair and Bob wasn't. I just had to hope no one noticed.

'I'd finished swapping our stuff over when I heard someone come in behind me. It was Cheadle. The fear of God came on me then as I fully expected him to twig straight away what I'd done. I can't explain my relief when he came over, looked down at Bob and said, "Norman Drinkwater's bought it, I see. Come on, Bob, he's dead, there's nothing you can do. Grimble, Simmons and Meadows got it too. We've pushed the bastards to the other end of the village and those of us left are grouping in a hut further down to decide what to do next, so come on."

'We'd just made our way out of the hut when to our amazement we saw two British trucks rolling into the village along with a dozen or so infantry. Where the hell they'd come from we had no idea, but to us the cavalry had arrived and, God, were we relieved. One of the men shouted that the Japs had surrendered three days ago which of course we hadn't had news of because our radio had been out of action. The next I knew the last of the platoon of Japs we'd been sent after were killed or captured, and those of us left alive from our original sortie were bundled on the back of one of the trucks and driven back to camp. We were exhausted and slept all the way back.

'Arriving back at camp, I was terrified someone would spot the swap but to my relief no one did. I'd been with Bob enough to blag my way through his duties and as a safeguard I kept my beard for a while and as low a profile as I could.

'The task of getting us all back home to England was a massive operation, it took months, and during that time I became Bob Clifton. Convinced myself I was him. Finally news came through that our lot were going home at last. I'd plans already made. As Bob Clifton, as soon as I was officially demobbed I was going to begin my new life back in Blighty in a town somewhere as far away from Northamptonshire as I could get. Little did I know that Tony Cheadle had other plans for me.

'After arriving back in England we were sent to a camp to await news of our demob. A couple of months went by until it came through and we were given a date two weeks ahead. That's when Tony made his move. After thinking I'd got away with switching places with Bob, I was frantic to hear that I hadn't after all. Tony had witnessed what I'd done. Through the back window of the hut, he'd seen me kill Bob accidentally and then change places with him. I'd got myself a new life now and he wanted me to help him get himself a new one too. If I didn't do what he asked, he said he'd tell the authorities he'd seen me murder Bob in cold blood and change places with him. I'd been masquerading as him for months so it'd be hard for me to deny anything. He said I might have fooled everyone into believing I was Bob Clifton so far but it wouldn't take the authorities long to find out I wasn't once they started probing. Even if the charge of murder wasn't proved, I'd still be jailed for taking over Clifton's identity. A long military jail sentence seemed worse to me even than the life I'd been desperate to get away from. I didn't see as I had a choice but to do what Tony wanted.

'It was too dangerous for him to go back to his own home town. All he needed was somewhere kosher to hole up in for a couple of weeks, a month at the most, while he found himself a way to make a quick killing so he could get started on the sort of life he wanted for himself. Landladies are nosey types, always keeping an eye on their paying guests, and someone spying on his movements was the last thing he needed. Bob Clifton was an upright citizen, a respectable sort of bloke, and if I took Tony home with me, passed him off as my friend, covered his back if anyone did ask awkward questions about his activities, he was more likely to get away with it.

'I told him it wouldn't work. Pleaded with him to leave me alone. It was one thing fooling my Army comrades, quite another the woman Bob had married and her family and friends. Tony said it *could* work and it was going to, it was up to me to make sure it did or else I knew the consequences. He said Clifton's wife hadn't set eyes on her husband for five years, they had only just got married when he was shipped out to the Far East. If I'd managed to fool people both Bob and I had been living closely with, then I'd certainly fool her and her family and friends. It wasn't like we were planning to stay around long enough for suspicion to set in. All I had to do, he said, was play the dutiful husband and avoid any situation where my identity might be compromised. Just keep myself to myself as far as possible. He made it sound easy.

'Tony made a deal with me, though. He said should Clifton's wife show the slightest doubt as to my identity at the station when we first met then we'd make a run for it together and forget the whole thing.

'I couldn't believe it when you accepted me without question when we came face to face that first time. To Tony it meant we were home and dry. To me, though, every minute I spent here has been like walking a tightrope, terrified that somehow you would guess I wasn't your real husband, or else one of your family or friends would, despite the way I avoided them as far as I could.

'The welcome home dinner your mother laid on nearly had me running, I was so relieved when Tony made it clear he meant to be there in case I needed him. I couldn't believe it all went so smoothly but I was determined not to get into a situation like that again if I could help it. I wasn't keen to have marital relations with you. I didn't know you, did I, you were a stranger to me, but Tony said I should make an effort at least once, just to keep you happy.

'I was frantic when you told me Bob's friend

had come to visit. I didn't know how I was going to get out of that as I'd no doubt he'd spot I wasn't the real Bob Clifton once he started reminiscing over the past, expecting me to chip in. Thank God I found Tony and he concocted that story about the old woman that saved my bacon. I did make a couple of blunders which Tony soon put me right on. He said I was mad to have bought the model kits as I was supposed to be a skilled carpenter. If I made a botch up of putting them together questions would soon be asked so that's why I abandoned them. And he said I was stupid to have bought the bike as I'd not be around long enough to rebuild it, let alone have a ride on it, so I lost interest.

'I had to take that job at the Mail or it'd have looked suspicious. In a way it did me good as it was a job where I was mostly on me own and could relax and more or less be myself for a few hours during work time. On the social front, I only felt safe when I went out with Tony those couple of times to the pub because he was good at talking his way out of sticky situations should one crop up.

'I'd already made up my mind I was leaving today – well, really, you gave me no choice. You'd invited your friends around tonight and I couldn't see how I could get out of that situation again so soon after them calling round unexpectedly and me pretending I was ill. I couldn't use that excuse again to avoid them and I couldn't think of another one that was plausible enough. Eunice had met the real Bob. I couldn't risk her spotting something amiss. Be just my luck after getting away with it so far. Yesterday I told Tony it was getting too dangerous for me and that it was only a matter of time before I was sussed out. Whether he liked it or not I was leaving today straight after work.

'I was going to tell you it wasn't working out for me and that it was best that I went and left you to start a new life. I told Tony that if he'd any sense he'd leave too. He wasn't happy, tried to persuade me to change my mind, but I stuck to my guns. I told him I'd give him one more bag full of mail and he'd have to content himself with what he'd got.

'You gave him the idea for the mail scam yourself when you told him about the valuable items that people posted. So you could say you were responsible for it in a way. For the last couple of weeks Tony's been meeting me in a prearranged spot just off my round and I've filled his kit bag with mail from my collections. People are just starting to report the non-arrival of mail so our days were numbered anyway.'

He stopped his pacing, dropped his hands and stared across at Kay, slumped on the floor against the door, her face like death.

'Look, if it means anything, I'm sorry. I never meant to kill your husband, it was an accident. And as for your father's attacker, that was nothing to do with me. That was Tony's way of getting hold of your father's shed to store his contraband. I'd no intention of ever coming here but I had no choice. I made no money from this myself. All I have is a bit saved from my Royal Mail pay, my gratuity payment – oh, and I've helped myself to Bob's savings. I counted that as a little unexpected windfall as he's not here to need it, is he?'

Then a look of panic filled his face as the sudden realisation of his need to escape filled him. He grabbed his kit bag, moved her roughly away from the door and ran downstairs.

As she heard the back door slam and the pounding of boots down the entry and out into the street, Kay clutched her stomach and put her head back and let out a wail of such a pitch and intensity it could be heard several houses away.

CHAPTER TWENTY-FOUR

Eunice plonked a heavy shopping basket on Kay's kitchen floor and, walking into the back room, asked: 'So how'd it go then, ducky? How did Bob take what yer had to tell him? Has Constable Pringle been around with any news on what's happening to...' Her voice trailed off as the state of her friend registered. Kay was sitting in the middle of the sofa, head bowed, hands clasped tightly in her lap. She looked to Eunice like doom itself had paid her a visit. 'Good God, Kay, what on earth... Oh, that's someone coming through yer back door.' She stepped back far enough to look through the open door into the kitchen to see who had come in. 'Oh, it's yer Aunt Viv. Oh, and yer mother. Oh, and Constable Pringle too.' Eunice then noticed the grave expressions on their faces and immediately knew something bad had happened. She sucked in her breath as she silently watched Vivian and Mabel sit down to either side of Kay, and Constable Pringle removing his helmet and standing stiffly by the dining table.

Viv looking on in concern as Mabel placed one hand gently on top of Kay's clasped ones.

'It's Bob, lovey,' she said, her voice choked with emotion. 'There's no easy way ter tell yer but, well.' She drew breath. Her eyes watering, she said, 'Bob ... well, he's been arrested. Seems him and your lodger have been up to no good. I can't believe it, I really can't. Constable Pringle came to fetch us to break the news to you as it would come across as a terrible shock!'

Kay lifted her head and looked blankly at her.

'That man's been arrested. Good. But it's not Bob.'

Mabel and Viv exchanged worried looks.

'It *is* Bob, me darlin',' said Viv softly, placing a comforting arm around her shoulders. 'We don't know all the ins and outs yet of what they've been up to as Bob and Tony Cheadle are still being interrogated, but Bob had identification on him, so there's no mistaking who he is.'

Kay slowly turned her head. Looking at her aunt she said quite calmly, 'It wasn't my Bob who was arrested, Aunty Viv.'

Viv and Mabel looked at each other again.

'I know this is hard for you to accept, Kay,' said Mabel. 'His bank book and birth certificate and other things proved who he was.' Her face screwed, bewildered. 'Why did Bob have all his

381

belongings and all that money...'

'Mabel, that can wait,' her sister warned her.

She looked ashamed. 'Yes, of course.' She looked across at a stricken-faced Eunice now standing next to Constable Pringle. 'Will you go and put the kettle on, dear?' Then Mabel tenderly smoothed Kay's hands, her own face etched with deep sadness. 'Be best you come home with me for a bit where we can look after yer, help yer through this. Yer dad's distraught he can't be here 'cos of his broken legs, and so is yer brother. They can't believe this of Bob. We all thought him such a decent sort.'

Kay looked at her mother then at her aunt.

'Will you both please listen to me? The man down the police station is not my Bob. My Bob was killed out in Burma by a man called Norman Drinkwater, and it's *him* who's been posing as my husband for the last seven weeks and who you're now telling me has been arrested.' She lowered her head, wringing her hands together so tightly her knuckles stood up like stepping stones. 'Norman Drinkwater told me it was an accident. These things happen in war, he said. But he still killed my husband, accidentally or not, then he swapped places with him. They looked so like each other, you see. People used to make mistakes all the time. Well, he proved it, didn't he? They resembled each other enough to fool me ... fool all of us. After he'd killed him, Norman Drinkwater saw changing places with my Bob as a chance for him to be rid of the awful life he said he had with his own wife and family. With my Bob's identity he could start afresh. He said Bob was dead and wouldn't have any need of his name anymore so why shouldn't Drinkwater have it?'

The other four people in the room were looking at her, dumbstruck.

Her mother shook her head, bemused.

'But ... but...'

'I know you must think I'm mad, Mam, I would if I was listening to such an absurd story, but I'm not. Norman Drinkwater told me it all before he left. Since he went I've been sitting here, trying to make sense of it. I can't, though. I just can't. I can't take it all in. That man told me he never intended coming here after swapping places with Bob. I suppose I was just going to be left to think that my husband had deserted me and never know why. But unbeknown to Norman Drinkwater, Tony Cheadle had witnessed what he'd done. He blackmailed him into coming to live here for a few weeks, to provide Tony with a safe place from which to carry out his dishonest activities. When he was satisfied he'd got enough to finance the kind of life he wanted for himself, both of them would go their own separate ways.'

Kay's face crumpled and she wrung her hands even tighter.

'Oh, I can't believe I've been so blind, so stupid, as not to see what was staring me in the face! When we met at the station that man *told* me he was my Bob. He *looked* like my Bob. I had no reason to doubt for a minute he was who he said he was. Aunty Viv warned me before I went to meet him to expect Bob to be changed, so in a way I was prepared for him to be different. I didn't expect him to be *that* different but I put it

383

down to what he'd suffered in the war, and everyone said that settling back home again wasn't easy for a man. Not once did it enter my head that the differences I was seeing were because he wasn't my Bob, wasn't anything like him in fact when it came to personality. That's why he avoided coming into contact with you all or anyone who knew the real Bob as best as he could, in case he said or did something that would arouse suspicion.

'And no wonder I didn't feel anything for him in that way when ... when ... well, I couldn't, could I, because he was a stranger to me. Oh, how could he? How could anyone be so cruel as to do what he did to me for his own selfish ends? How could someone stand over the body of someone they'd just killed, accidentally or not, and cold-bloodedly plan to steal their identity?' A swell of fat tears filled her eyes, to tumble down her face as a great wave of physical pain engulfed her. 'My Bob's dead. Oh, I can't bear it! What am I going to do?'

Both Viv and Mabel slid their arms protectively around her, looking at each other helplessly.

This story was so shocking they all were having trouble taking it in.

A grave-faced Constable Pringle cleared his throat. 'Well, I've been hearing so many wicked stories about what men have got up to on coming back after the war but this beats the lot, I have ter say. It most certainly does. Mr Cheadle is still in the process of being questioned now over the mail thefts and it was him that told us about Mr Clif– well now I realise it's Norman Drinkwater we're dealing with, but I'm sure we won't have any trouble getting confirmation of the new information.'

'Tony Cheadle. What?' erupted Mabel. 'Kay, what on earth has been going on here?'

She choked back a sob. 'I couldn't speak to you about any of this, Mam, nor you, Aunty Viv. I didn't know what was going on properly myself, either with Tony or ... with the man posing as my Bob. I didn't want to let you know I was so unhappy when you thought I was all right. Besides, I'd married Bob for better or worse, and because I didn't know any better I thought it was his experiences in the war that had changed him, and that wasn't his fault. As his wife, I had to stand by him and get on with it.'

'I feel so terrible,' said Eunice who while waiting for the kettle to boil had been listening just inside the doorway. 'Kay told me how she was trying to understand and cope with B– that man's behaviour, which was totally the opposite to what we both remembered of Bob's. I'd had experience meself of my George acting out of character when he came back so I told her she needed to have patience. Give him time to settle and it'd be all right in time, like it was with George.'

Viv sighed, mortified. 'Same as I would have told her if Kay had come to me.'

'And me,' muttered Mabel.

'Mrs Drinkwater will need to be told of all this,' said Constable Pringle.

Kay's head jerked up.

'I need to be there when she is.'

'Oh, but, Kay...' her mother began.

385

'No, I do,' she insisted, wiping her wet face with the back of her cardigan sleeve. 'From what that man told me, I can't imagine they led a good life together, but he was still that poor woman's husband and she thinks he died out in Burma. It's all going to come as a terrible shock finding out that not only is he still alive but he came back and has been living here as my husband all this time. He'd planned to live out the rest of his life as Bob and she'd never have known it. She might think I had something to do with it. I have to explain to her I knew nothing of any of this.

'And Mrs Drinkwater will know where my Bob's been buried. She'll have been given that information by the Army, won't she? It'll take a while for us to get it from the authorities but I need to know where my Bob's been laid to rest, and I need to know now. I want to go and see his grave as soon as I can. If it takes me years to save for the journey, I don't care. I have to say my goodbyes to Bob. I need to see Mrs Drinkwater,' she beseeched.

Scratching his square jaw, Constable Pringle looked uncertainly at Kay.

'Well ... it's not the done thing, but in the circumstances I'll see what I can arrange, Mrs Clifton.'

She flashed him a grateful smile then her eyes narrowed darkly.

'Constable Pringle, my husband has been buried under the name of Norman Drinkwater and I can't allow that. I need to set the record straight. I don't want *that man*'s name tarnishing my husband's memory in any way whatsoever.'

'That'll be done, Mrs Clifton, rest assured it will. I'd er ... best get back to the station and try and explain all this to my superiors.'

'I can't begin to imagine what yer going through,' said Mabel, hugging her daughter protectively.

'No, nor can I,' uttered Viv.

Mabel looked at her sister meaningfully.

'Kay's going to need both of us by her to help her through this, and I know we'll both be there for her in our own way.' She looked tenderly at her daughter. 'Now I'm taking you home where yer belong.'

CHAPTER TWENTY-FIVE

Two days later Constable Pringle stood poised to knock on a door. It showed the years of neglect it had suffered as did the small two-up, two-down terraced house it led into. The crumbling street was situated in a rundown area in the poorest district of Northampton, the people residing in these houses amongst the most needy in the country. The policeman had thought Leicester had grim areas of its own, but they seemed afflu- ent now compared to the poverty that reigned here.

He turned to look at the woman standing stiffly by his side, knowing the brave face she was showing hid a turmoil of grief after learning of the death of her husband and trying to come to terms with the cruel deception of the man who had passed himself off as Bob Clifton, who was now facing a lengthy term in jail.

'Are yer still sure you want to face this, Mrs Clifton? I mean, yer bereaved and coping with a lot as it is without heaping more...'

'I do,' Kay cut in resolutely. 'I've already explained why I need to do this, Constable Pringle. I can't rest until I have. I appreciate the strings you've pulled to arrange for me to do this, and your accompanying me.'

He sighed, 'All right, let's get on with it then,' and rapped purposefully on the door.

Nothing happened, so he knocked again.

They heard a voice from within shout, 'You all sit there on yer arses, then – I'll get it. As if I hadn't enough to do...'

The door was opened to reveal a scrawny, lank-haired, shabbily dressed woman who couldn't have been more than thirty but looked at least ten years older. 'Yeah, what d'yer...' She pulled a knowing face. 'Oh, I wasn't expecting yer for another week. When I brought him home I was told they'd be sending someone to check how it was going after a couple of months, and that ain't up 'til next week.' She scanned Constable Pringle up and down, then scowled at Kay. 'He might not be right in the head at the moment but he ain't dangerous, there was no need to bring protection with yer. Yer'd better come in,' she said, heading off down a dingy paint-peeling passageway.

Kay and Constable Pringle looked at each other, bemused, before they followed her through.

The room she led them into was sparsely

388

furnished with an odd assortment of shabby old furniture. The whole house, but this room in particular, stank of stale food, bodily odours and cat pee. A sickly-looking elderly man and woman sat opposite each side by the fireplace and eyed the two visitors blankly as they entered. Two skinny, pale-faced children, a girl and boy of about eight and nine, were lolling on the threadbare sofa reading tatty comics; another girl, a little older, was sitting at the cluttered table peeling potatoes into newspaper.

Thelma Drinkwater addressed the children. 'You lot scarper while we adults talk. Go on, get going.'

They went, slamming the back door behind them, and could be heard squabbling together as they made their way down the yard and out of the back gate into the jetty that split the rows of houses.

Sweeping her hand across the sofa to clear it of three mangy-looking cats that howled their displeasure at being disturbed, Thelma ordered her visitors, 'Sit yerselves down.' Grabbing a rickety-looking dining chair, she pulled it over and sat down herself, crossing stick-like legs encased in holed woollen stockings. She looked at Kay closely.

'Ain't seen you before. New, are yer?' Before she could open her mouth, Thelma launched into a verbal torrent. 'The doctor at the hospital said bringing him home could do the trick. Familiarity was what was needed as they couldn't do no more for him medically. Well, you can tell that bleddy doctor from me it ain't worked! He's bin back here seven weeks now and still ain't got a clue who he is or who we are. In fact, there's bin no improvement in that way since yer gave me no choice but to have him home. The last memory he's got is of waking up in the hospital. He can't remember none of his past at all before that.' She gave a sniff. 'I didn't want him home, I made that clear enough. I'll tell you like I told them, I was glad he'd gone to war and I didn't care a damn whether he came back or not. In fact, I hoped he never.

'He was no husband to me. Lazy git never lifted a finger in the house and did nothing but moan at me and the kids, and he was a misery to live with. As fer me mam and dad coming ter live here ... well, he never let up about that, calling 'em scroungers and all sorts. Well, what could I do? Couldn't leave them on the street when they got evicted from their house, could I, but that's what he expected me to do.

'He never even bothered to tell me he was joining up until he was packing to leave. I never heard a word from him while he was away, not one sodding letter, even a scribbled note. I was convinced he was dead but the authorities hadn't got round to informing me. Let's put it this way – I was *praying* he was dead. I'd got meself someone else. Happy with a man for the first time in me life. Harry's a good chap. He gets on with the kids and Mam and Dad. Likes the booze but yer can't have it all, can yer? He's still waiting for me, hoping that things don't work out with me old man.'

Both Kay and Constable Pringle were looking

at her in bewilderment.

'Mrs Drinkwater, please forgive me, but who are you talking about?' Kay asked her.

Thelma looked at her as though she was stupid.

'Eh? Who the hell d'yer think? My husband, Norman Drinkwater.' She looked at Kay in confusion. 'You being medical, maybe you can explain it. Norman might not know who he is or recognise his family from Adam, but the injury to his head seems to have knocked some sense into him. Since he's bin back he's a changed man. He's ... well ... nice. He helps around the house. Plays with the kids. He *never* played with the kids before. He does what he can for Mam and Dad too. He's bin fixing things up, suddenly found a way with tools that he certainly didn't have before his injury. The window in the kitchen was falling out and he put a new frame in and some new hinges on the front door. He doesn't know how he learned what he did, ain't a clue.

'If yer want the truth, I'm quite enjoying having him around like he is now, might even fall in love with him. Trouble is, though, I'm worried about when his memory does come back. Maybe he'll go back to being how he was before. Well, I don't want that,' she said with conviction. 'Oh, and another thing that's bothering me. He's told me he keeps having these dreams about a woman. She's wearing a shiny grey costume sort of outfit with this matching hat with a grey feather sticking out of it. He's no idea what her name is but he knows she's important to him somehow. I wanna know who this woman is.'

Kay gasped. Thelma had just described what

she herself was wearing on her wedding day.

The front door opened and closed then and footsteps sounded along the hall.

'Oh, I didn't realise it was that time. Norman's home for his dinner from the foundry and it ain't cooked yet. Norman!' Thelma shouted at the top of her voice. 'The people from the hospital are here to check on yer progress. I thought it was next week they was due but I must have got the date wrong.'

As he entered the room Kay's eyes fixed on him and her hands flew to her mouth in stupefaction. Then, in a dreamlike state, she slowly rose and walked across to stand before him.

He looked at her strangely. 'I recognise you,' he said with a puzzled frown. 'You're ... why, you're the woman in my dreams! I ... I know you, don't I.' It wasn't a question but a statement.

Kay's heart was hammering away. It felt as if a million fireworks were going off simultaneously in her head while the rest of her was floating on air. She nodded.

'Yes, you know me.'

'Oi!' shouted Thelma, leaping up from her chair. 'What's going on?'

Constable Pringle jumped up to take her arm. 'Come with me, Mrs Drinkwater,' he said, guiding her off into the kitchen. 'There's a story you need to hear.'

CHAPTER TWENTY-SIX

Bob encircled Kay in his arms and pulled her close. He kissed the top of her head lovingly. 'Your idea for me to return to my roots and spend some time here until my memory fully returns was just the job, my darling. The doctor at the hospital advised me to stay in familiar surroundings and be with loved ones, and you most certainly are the one person I love more than life itself. So he was right, wasn't he?' He breathed in deeply and glanced up and down the Northampton street he'd grown up in. 'It was so strange when we first arrived four weeks ago. It felt as though I knew this place but I didn't recognise it at all, if that makes sense. Memory loss is an awful thing to experience, Kay.'

She pulled away to gaze up at him with the deepest affection, and with the tips of her fingers gently traced the length of the deep disfiguring scar that ran from the top of his forehead, pulling down his left eye, to end in the middle of his cheek.

'It must have been dreadful for you living with the Drinkwaters, being told you were the man of the house but at the same time feeling you didn't belong there.'

'It was,' he sighed.

Bob's mind drifted back to when he had first woken in the Army hospital, with no memory at all of how he'd come to land there. The Army medics explained to him that he'd been found in a hut after a battle with the Japs and assumed to be dead from the terrible injury to his head. Very luckily a diligent soldier, helping to take what he had thought to be a body for burial, had noticed this one was breathing. The doctor at base camp had done what he could for him but during the four weeks he had remained unconscious none of the medical staff thought he would pull through. Miraculously he had, only to have no memory of his life whatsoever before then.

The name Norman Drinkwater, when they told him who he was according to his ID, had meant nothing to him and neither had it felt right, but he'd had no choice but to accept what he'd been told. On being shipped back to England he'd spent several weeks in a mental hospital. When it became apparent to the doctors that what medical help they were giving him and the reluctant visits from the woman thought to be his wife were doing nothing to his memory, it was decided that the only option was to send him home and hope that familiar sights and sounds back in the bosom of his family would do the trick.

He had tried his best to integrate himself into the hovel that the Drinkwaters called home, to accept that Thelma was his wife, the three children his and to be a father to them, to treat her mother and father with respect as his in-laws, despite feeling no emotional attachment to them or recognition whatsoever. Of course no memory had been triggered there because the home and

family he had been sent back to had no connection with him, nothing about them set off any
memories. Nothing did until his eyes had settled
so unexpectedly on the one person he had
dreamed about and, slowly and patiently, that
wonderful lady had helped restore him to his old
familiar self, Robert Clifton.

As if what he himself had suffered at Norman
Drinkwater's hands was not bad enough, when he
learned what his beloved Kay had been through,
Bob was appalled. But, thank God, that was all in
the past now and it was best they put it behind
them. Drinkwater and Cheadle were behind bars
where they belonged. It was ironic, though, that
in a way Kay and Bob both had something to
thank Tony Cheadle for. If he hadn't blackmailed
the real Norman Drinkwater into helping him
line his pockets, Kay would have had no reason to
pay a visit to the Drinkwaters, and Bob might
possibly have spent the rest of his days as Norman
Drinkwater. It didn't bear thinking about.

He looked down at his wife, a bright smile
lighting up his blemished but still handsome face.
'I'm ready to go home to Leicester with you,
darling, to start our married life together properly
– can't wait, in fact. I'm so looking forward to
living in our own home, not these lodgings we've
been in since we've been here in Northampton.
I'm looking forward to doing all the things that
happily married couples do, the things we talked
about doing together once the war was over. I'm
so looking forward to meeting up with your ... no,
my ... family again, and those that I haven't met
yet. Your brother and his girlfriend, Aunty Viv's

fiancé, Eunice's George. I'm looking forward to getting my carpentry business off the ground too, with your help of course, and I can't wait until your father and I are working side by side on our allotments together.'

As Kay gazed up at him, she shuddered at the memory of the two dreadful days she'd spent, cocooned in the bosom of her family, trying unsuccessfully to come to terms with what Norman Drinkwater had done to her while also suffering the terrible physical and emotional pain of learning of her true husband's death. She could never begin to explain to anyone the shock then the utter elation when at the Drinkwaters' she had discovered her beloved Bob was still alive. Now she thanked the Almighty Himself every day that she had insisted on going to explain her side of events to Drinkwater's real wife. Had she not, the consequences didn't bear thinking about.

Kay laughed, an infectious chuckle that betrayed to anyone who heard it how totally happy she was.

'Baiting each other to see who can grow the biggest marrows! I can foresee plenty of friendly rivalry in store between the Stafford and Clifton households. Time will tell who the best man is. My mother will bet on my dad but I'd place all my money on you. My ... our family are all desperate for me to bring you back home.' She looked at him in concern. 'You don't mind that we'll be staying with Aunty Viv until we find a new place of our own, do you? You understand I couldn't step foot in that house ever again after...'

'Shush,' Bob said, pressing his fingers gently to

her lips. 'No more talk or even thinking about that time again. Although it was terrible for both of us in different ways, it has brought us closer together, if that's possible. We must look to the future now, Kay.' Bob took her hand and held it firmly in his own. 'I'm desperate to get on with it.'

She smiled up at him adoringly. 'Yes, let's do that.'

The publishers hope that this book has given you enjoyable reading. Large Print Books are especially designed to be as easy to see and hold as possible. If you wish a complete list of our books please ask at your local library or write directly to:

Magna Large Print Books
Magna House, Long Preston,
Skipton, North Yorkshire.
BD23 4ND

This Large Print Book for the partially sighted, who cannot read normal print, is published under the auspices of

THE ULVERSCROFT FOUNDATION

THE ULVERSCROFT FOUNDATION

... we hope that you have enjoyed this Large Print Book. Please think for a moment about those people who have worse eyesight problems than you ... and are unable to even read or enjoy Large Print, without great difficulty.

You can help them by sending a donation, large or small to:

**The Ulverscroft Foundation,
1, The Green, Bradgate Road,
Anstey, Leicestershire, LE7 7FU,
England.**
or request a copy of our brochure for more details.

The Foundation will use all your help to assist those people who are handicapped by various sight problems and need special attention.

Thank you very much for your help.